Sumer Lovin'

by Nicole Chardenet

Deux Voiliers Publishing

Deux Voiliers Publishing
First Edition 2013

Library and Archives Canada Cataloguing in Publication

Chardenet, Nicole, 1963-
Sumer lovin' / Nicole Chardenet.

ISBN 978-0-9881048-4-6

I. Title. II. Title: Sumer loving.

PS8605.H3669S94 2013 C813'.6 C2013-900418-1

Cover Art and Design by Ian Thomas Shaw

Cover Photo by Heinrich von Schimmer, Berlin (licensed from Photographer)

Author's Photo by Sonya Young, Toronto

Red Tuque Books distributes *Sumer Lovin'* in Canada. Please place your Canadian independent bookstore and library orders with RTB at www.redtuquebooks.ca

To Sharon Landis,
my favourite Jewish matchmaker,
and Kat Spiwak,
who's trying to save Toronto
from chronic celibacy

ACKNOWLEDGMENTS

Thanks to Enoch Tse for his input and advice on Chinese culture and sayings.

Thanks to Reem Shahin for providing some of the more colourful omens and divinations from the Middle East.

Thanks to Ron Hutchison in the heart of Red Country for encouraging me every step of the way.

Also to Lynn Holtz, Scott Berry and Lisa Marion for providing proofreading and making various suggestions and edits.

Thanks to Sonya Young for providing the author picture.

And many thanks to the Canadian government for not being very picky about immigrants! (Good grief, they're letting in Americans! There goes the country!) I appreciate the many opportunities and good fortune I've had since I moved here. And many thanks to Toronto for being a vibrant, alive city where my writing can flourish and where I am surrounded by so many circles of wildly different creative people.

CAVEAT EMPTOR

Be aware that the story that you are about to read is a little wacky —and with Sumerians! After all, what sick ancient mind came up with a demigoddess like Lamashtu? Seriously? Some rabid, man-hating, cuneiform-scribing feminist? Well, it wasn't me. I swear to Goddess.

Lamashtu is from ancient mythology, and seriously, I don't know how those wacky Sumerians came up with her.

When I started writing Sumer Lovin', I thought, "I want the villain to be a woman. Maybe more than one, I don't know. Women never get to be villains. And Goddess knows we can be just as evil as men, and we look totally better with our shirts off. So I hit Google and...ho--lee--Schlitz--I found Lamashtu and her nasty little surprise. Later I hit Google again for another horrifying demon-thingy and geez, I found Lamashtu's arch-enemy and his really disgusting--oh my Goddess. Only a man could have come up with that. Ewwwwww.

Look, you'll just have to read it and find out for yourself.

All I can say is, the Sumerians had way dirtier minds than I did. And with a very, uh, David Cronenberg twist.

CHAPTER ONE

"I tell you, Mahliqa, Canadians and Americans should be more like us," Amita said as she adjusted the sari around her shoulder. "Our cultures have the right idea. Marry first, and wait for love."

Mahliqa, still handsome at forty-eight with huge dark eyes behind stylish glasses under an attractive green *hijab* shot through with gold thread, hmmphed as she dug into her mango ice cream. "Westerners aren't ready for arranged marriage."

"Don't be silly! They only stopped doing it a hundred years ago," her friend retorted. She sipped her chai tea and enjoyed what little of the warm June sun penetrated the hazy smog smothering Toronto. At least today's miasma wasn't deceptively overcast-looking like last week.

"I read Casanova's *Memoirs* years ago. He mentioned many marriages that had been arranged for his various mistresses by their parents. The Europeans did it as much as we did. They married cousins too--"

Mahliqa snorted. "Try mentioning that to a Canadian today! They act like it's unholy."

"They're just silly. Who better than a member of the family? They have this ridiculous idea that cousins marrying is like incest. I'm married to *my* cousin and we have five beautiful children together, and your sister married your cousin Omar and her children are perfect."

"Except for being little hellions!"

"That's their father's fault. He lets them do anything they want. They're boys. The point is, they don't have the deformities or the inbred stupidity Canadians fear."

"Westerners are too obsessed with love," observed Mahliqa. "The children don't listen to their parents. *I* wouldn't have listened to my parents if I'd had a choice. I wanted to marry Mahdi, the boy who sold grapes in the plaza. A boy with no future! My father quite rightly made me marry Jabir. Try telling that to some flighty Canadian child—"

"So you agree with me."

"That arranged marriages are better? Not always, Amita. It depends on your family, and the man himself, and his family. I'm happy with Jabir because he's an enlightened man. Not like Tawfiq, my other sister's husband. What a conservative nut! Insists she wear that ridiculous *abbaya,* won't let her drive - and they live in Germany, not Saudi Arabia! I couldn't be married to that man."

"You know what gets me?" asked Amita. "The divorce rate! Canadians and Americans, they're always divorcing. And over what? *Love!* 'I thought I loved her.' 'I thought he loved me.' I didn't love Manjeet when I first met him. I liked him well enough—"

"But he wasn't your *soul mate!"*

Amita threw back her head and laughed, her tawny face tilting toward the sky. "What is a *soul mate?"* she cried. "Who invented this thing? I don't even know what that *means."*

"Neither do Westerners," Mahliqa snorted, "but that's all they talk about. If you look at the personal ads online, they're always going on about *soul mates."*

"They get that from the Americans."

"They come up with *all* the foolishness."

Amita sipped her tea and sat back. She stared across the street from beneath the umbrella of the small Mississauga café. The warm June day beat down on her shoulders. Once again, she was thankful for her light sari and uncovered head, unlike Mahliqa's uncomfortable-looking *hijab.*

"Have you ever seen the computer sites for single people?" she asked. Mahliqa shrugged and polished off the rest of her ice cream. "They're sad. So many young people with fuzzy pictures, vague descriptions of what they think they want in a mate. The girls show off their—everything. The boys clearly want their—everything. Nothing about values or morals or family, the *important* things. The only thing sadder are the older ones, the ones who are long past a decent marriage age, the ones in their thirties and forties and more. Some of them divorced, some more than once. No one will want them. They're ruined, finished."

"That's a little harsh," Mahliqa said gently. "People do find themselves single again at later stages. Think of your widow communities, Amita."

"Yes," she sighed. They still existed in India, although modern enlightened Indians preferred not to think of them. "But the world still is as it is."

"If only the children could be saved. I see these beautiful young Canadian youths, barely out of school, and I think, ah, wouldn't you be happier with someone to come home to every night, a woman who will cook for you and take care of your children, or a man who will buy you nice things?"

A fly buzzed by lazily and landed on Amita's arm. Disgusted, she brushed it away.

"Well isn't *that* interesting," said Mahliqa, grinning broadly. "In my culture, when a fly passes you by, it means a visit from someone far away!"

☆ ☆ ☆

Rachel Brinkerhoff regarded the intense young woman on the other side of the table in the Second Cup booth. *Oy,* she just knew she'd be a nightmare to work with.

"So what matches have you got for me?" Alexis asked, leaning forward. Her glossy straight brown hair brushed her shoulders as she watched Rachel from behind her severe rectangular glasses. The brown eyes behind them were striking, but also hard and relentless. What must it be like for some poor young man, squirming beneath that penetrating gaze?

"I moved to Toronto a few months ago, so I'm just getting my service up and running," Rachel explained. She deliberately spoke with an unhurried tone, hoping to buy time to think of a good way to handle this. "I'm trying to select a pool of candidates so it'll probably be a few more months before I can start suggesting matches—" Oh, this was good. It would take at least a few months of working with Alexis just to make her presentable for a date.

It's not that the 31-year-old wasn't attractive. Alexis was quite lovely, actually. Medium height and fit, with a pretty heart-shaped face. The severe glasses weren't so bad when she smiled - then her penetrating eyes turned friendly and her rich full pink lips invited passionate kisses. The problem was she had a very bad attitude—cynical, jaded, and Rachel just knew she was being treated for depression. Or should be, anyway.

Alexis glanced at Rachel's left hand. "So why aren't *you* married?" she asked. The question was straightforward, like Alexis herself - but the tone less judgemental than when she talked about the men in her past.

Rachel sighed and smiled. She hoped her crow's feet didn't show too much. "That's a good question," she said. "I'll admit, I just got divorced. I made a bad choice and the marriage wasn't going anywhere so I got out." Technically true. Austin was never going to change, although one might argue the marriage was going somewhere - in a very ominous direction. "I've learned from my mistakes. I'll choose more wisely next time." Rachel hoped this wouldn't be a deal-killer for Alexis. She felt she could help her, if she was open enough to change.

"I know how it is," Alexis nodded. "My friends always come to me for advice on how to handle the men in their lives. And I've helped out several of them. It's just not so easy to take your own advice, you know?"

Rachel smiled and slid out of the booth. "I'll be in touch," she replied. "I have another appointment in forty-five minutes. Would you know how to get to Yonj and Bloo-er from here?" She dug a wrinkled sticky note from her pocket and squinted.

"It's Yonge and Bloor," Alexis smiled, pronouncing it *Young and Blore.* "Are you driving or taking the subway?"

"I'm driving."

Alexis gave her some quick directions and stood up, her glossy hair swinging. "Good luck trying to find men for your database," she said as she headed toward the exit. "You might want to focus on immigrant men. I think you'll find Toronto guys are uninterested in women."

Rachel had yet to find Yonge and had lost Bloor a good ten minutes ago. She tried rolling down her window and asking people on the street but the first person didn't speak English, the second said she was just visiting from Hamilton, and the middle-aged couple turned out to be American tourists. And Toronto's downtown was just as impossible to park in as New York's.

She spotted a convenience store up the street, so she parked there and headed toward the entrance, only to notice that it sported a big CLOSED sign. What, on a Wednesday? Underneath was a hand-written explanation in a language only mildly resembling English indicating something about renovations.

Glancing at her watch, Rachel ducked into an office with a painted sign that said, 'Love Comes Later.' She opened it, stepped inside, and froze.

A middle-aged woman looked up from behind the desk. "Oh, hello, do come in!" she greeted. She was wearing one of those *hijab* things and that conservative long-sleeved dress. It was a very pretty *hijab,* bright purple with little blue flowers, quite fancy compared to the drab colors favored by most Toronto Muslimas. Rachel gulped and remembered that her own religion wasn't nearly as obvious. These Muslims, they made her so nervous. There were so many more of them in Toronto, whereas Jews outnumbered them nearly three to one in New York.

"Hi there, I'm really lost, can you tell me where Yonge and Bloor is?" Rachel asked. She pushed the wrinkled sticky note at the woman. "I'm looking for this restaurant, Just Desserts—"

"I know where that is, they have wonderful sweets," the woman replied. "You're not that far from there, just a few blocks, really. Where are you parked?"

Rachel told her and the woman gave her some fairly simple directions.

"Are you visiting from New York?" the woman asked with a big smile. She was quite handsome, Rachel thought.

"I'm from New York City. I moved here a few months ago," Rachel explained. She was mesmerized by the woman's smile. Muslims seemed such a humorless bunch, especially the traditionally-dressed women. They walked down the street or in the shops and malls in Mississauga, uniformly sullen. A smiling Muslim in a *hijab* was about as common to her experience as—a smiling New Yorker at rush hour.

"That's wonderful. How do you like Toronto so far?"

"Nice, very nice—the people here are friendly. Much friendlier than they are in New York," she felt compelled to add, as always, before someone else did. "And I think I've fallen in love with Smarties candies."

"Why did you move to Toronto?" the woman asked.

"Oh—uh—well, I'm—" Oh, she might as well tell the truth. "I've just gotten divorced and my ex-husband's a little bit crazy and I knew he'd never follow me to Canada."

Austin hated Canadians. *A pathetic bunch of limp-wristed dope-peddling pot-smoking faggots and hedonists,* he'd called them. *Socialist Commie terrorist-coddling liberals,* he'd added. Austin, a Homeland Security guard at JFK Airport, blamed Canada for having a 'porous border' that any old goddamn raghead could pass through without so much as a whatcha-got-in-the-trunk-there-Achmed. *You should go there, Rachel,* he'd told her. *They hate America just as much as you do. You can shoot heroin with your dyke lover and forget you ever had a real man between your legs!*

"I've been to New York. I quite liked it. I went to the top of the World Trade Center with my husband just a few weeks before—" The woman's voice broke. "What those evil idiots did." She glanced down.

Rachel felt a little embarrassed for her. "It's okay," she said.

The woman glanced up again and managed a brave smile. "I'm sorry, I feel compelled to say something. I want to make sure everyone knows we're not *all* like that. I was sick when it happened. Absolutely sick. I hope you didn't lose anyone."

Rachel shook her head. Not just to reassure the woman, but to shake the memories away. She'd been uptown when it happened. Austin, a cop at the time, certainly hadn't helped, the big dumb macho doofus. Not answering his cell phone when she called sixteen times, frantic to find out whether he was one of the rescue workers crushed by the falling towers.

"What sort of business is this?" Rachel asked, glancing around. The windows were draped with chiffon and silk rather than curtains, and various Indian and Middle Eastern paintings dotted the walls. The Indian paintings depicted couples in romantic poses, and the Middle Eastern decorations were more abstract, flowers and geometric designs.

"We're new, we just opened up," the woman replied. "Please pardon the decor, the *feng shui* expert hasn't come yet. My partner and I have formed a consulting service for Canadian parents who want to arrange marriages for their children."

Rachel's eyes opened wide. "You're kidding me," she exclaimed. "Arranged marriages? For *Canadians?"*

The woman smiled widely and opened her arms. "Love Comes Later," she said. "We believe there are many Canadians who could benefit from choosing marriage partners from a traditional Eastern perspective. We want to counsel parents on how to persuade their children to go along with it. We believe that older married people are more experienced and knowledgeable about what makes marriage work than headstrong young people whose heads are full of silly Hollywood movies. We're hoping to find someone who can help us arrange marriages too. You know, we could probably help you, my friend—if you don't mind me saying so, you are a very beautiful woman! You look like that American movie star—what's-her-name—Elizabeth Taylor!"

Rachel smiled shyly and hoped once again her crow's feet didn't show too much. She'd heard the comparison many times.

"You even have violet eyes like she does! If I didn't know better I'd swear you're sisters."

Her face was so friendly Rachel started laughing. *"Oy Gevalt,* if only you knew—" she began, and then she froze.

The woman's eyes, already huge, grew wider behind her large glasses. "Oh, are you JEWISH?" she cried.

✯ ✯ ✯

In another part of the city, a guy desperately in need of a date sat back from the computer, removed his glasses, and wiped his wrist across his eyes. Dave Gillpatrick had been entering medical codes for the last two hours and his brains felt fried. This job sucked. He hated the work he did for a large American healthcare company, but at least it paid better than fixing peoples' old computers and he could work from home. Since he'd never gone to university, his career choices were fairly limited. If he could earn enough money he'd go to college and earn a computer trade degree. What he wanted to do more than that, though, was move out.

It was after three. He still had fifteen more pages of codes. He thought of what he would do after dinner and decided he'd design an OS-tan for Mandriva Linux. Maybe something kind of witchy, with a revealing black bodice, and a fleur-de-lis at the end of her wand.

The knife twisted a bit in Dave's heart. He tried not to think of how he was once again designing the woman he'd never have, a computer operating system icon of the cute little lovely-eyed girl with the round bosom and the wasp waist of his dreams.

Because when Dave was around women his hands went cold, his tongue tied up, and he had to fight the urge to run and hide. At thirty-five years old, he was still just as much of a yutz with women as he'd always been, and he had a secret that was now just too embarrassing to contemplate revealing to anybody. A woman would laugh her head off if she found out. He cruised the singles profiles on Lavalife and Plenty of Fish sometimes, late at night after his parents had gone to bed, but no one ever emailed him, probably because his profile wasn't that impressive and he had no picture. Women wanted to see what you looked like, and Dave didn't want to show them what a fat little shrimp he was.

So instead he poked through the womens' profiles, looking at this ad and that ad, wondering what the girl was really like, whether she always smiled like she did in her picture, and imagined what it might be like to go sailing on Lake Ontario with her or maybe walk around the park. Maybe if he lost a little weight and got contacts and wore sunglasses to cover his bland hazel eyes, just maybe, a woman might want to meet him and take him out on her sailboat. Or maybe she'd walk beside him when they went hiking through a nature preserve, quietly impressed as he pointed out all the native Ontario plants and the different types of scat they found.

His hand drifted to the little ad he'd clipped from a local entertainment newspaper last week. 'Love Comes Later,' read the copy, and it seemed to offer some kind of matchmaking service. He wasn't sure why love came later but he thought it was worth a try.

"Honey? Would you like some samosas?" his mother called up the stairs.

Dave rubbed his eyes and put his glasses back on. "No thanks, Ma," he called down. He got up and searched for his wallet. Before he left, he fed his forty-eight gerbils in a Habitrail the size of the downtown Skywalk and set BitTorrent to begin downloading the first three episodes of the last season of *Dr. Who.*

He was going down to Love Comes Later, now. Maybe they could find him a fellow virgin.

✯ ✯ ✯

"Yes," Rachel replied stiffly, and she tried to smile. *Relax,* she told herself. *There are Jews in the world, lady. Get over it.*

"Oh, terrific!" the woman cried, clapping her hands together in front of her chest. She sounded as excited as if Rachel had told her she'd just won the lottery.

A bit surprised, Rachel waited. Her smartly-tailored pantsuit tightened around her like some corset from Hell.

"It's okay, I'm not going to bite you. Or blow you up," the woman smiled. "I'm sorry, I shouldn't have said that. It was rude."

Unsure how to respond, Rachel simply held her hand out. "Allow me to introduce myself," she said. "My name is Rachel Brinkerhoff. I'm a matchmaker, by the way."

"A matchmaker!" The woman's eyes had begun to resemble some comic book anime character. "Oh my, we have to talk! You and myself and Amita! You're just the sort of person we're looking for!"

Rachel swallowed her surprise. A Jew, working with a Muslim? What would her mother say?

"My name is Mahliqa. Mahliqa Fakhoury." She shook Rachel's hand. "It's so good to meet you, Rachel. I mean what I say about how we should sit down together. You must be trying to establish yourself in Toronto, and we have a consulting service where we will meet eligible young people. Do you have a few minutes? I will call Amita and if she's near here maybe she can swing by and we'll run down to the corner for some tea—"

"Actually, I have to leave—I have an appointment with a young lady who's interested in my services. But I could come back later," Rachel added. "This shouldn't take more than an hour. I just have to find Yonge and Bloor."

"Why don't you come back around 4:30?" Mahliqa asked. She pulled her cell phone from some hidden pocket in her dress. "I'll call Amita and tell her to be here. Would that be okay?"

Rachel glanced at her watch. She had exactly fifteen minutes to find Yonge and Bloor, then a parking spot, and then Just Desserts. "That's fine," she said. She reached up and scratched her eyebrow.

"Oh, that was a good omen! What you just did, in my culture, that means money is coming your way! See, God is sending you a sign that this will be a good partnership!"

"Uh, okay," said Rachel, who had no idea what she was talking about.

"Good-bye! I look forward to speaking with you again!" Mahliqa called after her. As Rachel opened the door, she found a fairly nice-looking man outside. With her professional eye she scanned him quickly, assessing him. In his thirties, light brown hair, wire-rim glasses, medium build, a little short, kind of cute in a quiet nerdy way. Just the sort of person she'd like to add to her database if only there was time to talk. "Oh, excuse me," she said as she graced him with what she hoped was a sparkling smile. She held the door open for him. He walked in, slowly, his eyes on her face. She tried not to turn away with embarrassment. *Yes, I'm middle-aged and losing my looks, and I know all about the wrinkles around my eyes,* she thought to herself. She pushed past him.

At the last minute she turned around quickly and faced his back. Standing on tiptoe, she looked at Mahliqa and mouthed the words, *I want him!* as she pointed. Mahliqa nodded once, subtly, and motioned for the young man to come in and have a seat. Rachel departed.

Dave stepped up to Mahliqua's desk as though in a daze. "Who was that woman?" he asked. "She's the most beautiful woman I've ever seen!"

"That's Rachel, hopefully our new partner, and she wants you," Mahliqa smiled beatifically, looking for all the world like a radiant Madonna, if the Madonna had been from Pakistan, wore Revlon Burnished Mahogany nail polish, and was horrifically nearsighted.

Dave just stared at her, gaping.

Speaking of dateless Daves, in downtown Toronto, a systems adminstrator for a famous large enterprise middleware software company close to the Manulife Centre was thinking about the speed dating event his friend Dave (a network engineer for a travel agency) had talked him into trying that night.

A strange little factoid about Toronto: a disproportionate number of I.T. professionals there are named Dave. You'd think a male-dominated industry like I.T. would have a fair number of Mikes, Marks, Johns and Scotts. But in the GTA - as the locals call the Greater Toronto Area - I.T. Daves rule. Needless to say, the middleware guy's name was Dave too. Now pay attention, and don't confuse either of these guys with Dave the Virgin, as we shall call him since no man alive wants to be known as The Gerbil Guy, since, as a certain nasty urban legend about a certain movie star would attest, people would automatically assume you're regularly turning yourself into a human Habitrail. Dave the

Tarantula Guy (he has a pet tarantula he keeps in a terrarium on top of a rack of servers that keeps Pookums warm) is multiply-divorced, and the other Dave (Dave The T.G.'s buddy), who knows more about configuring and maintaining Beowulf clusters than anyone else in Canada and is far too into it for his own good, was also divorced and usually managed to drive women away with his incessant computer talk.

(What are Beowulf clusters, you ask? Ask Dave. Make sure you have at least three hours.)

Dave the Tarantula Guy wasn't at all convinced speed dating was a good idea, but Dave the Beowulf Freak wanted to try it and had bribed him with a pitcher of Labatt's Blue. It seemed a bit false to spend eight minutes talking to someone and trying to make a snap decision on whether you wanted to date her or not. On the other hand, as Dave the Beowulf Freak pointed out, you got to see what they looked like in person, as opposed to some ancient or Photoshopped picture on Lavalife, and if they weren't hot you only had to talk to them for eight minutes.

Without question, neither of these two nerds had the foggiest clue what they really wanted in a woman. Dave the Tarantula Guy was from Alberta, where men were men and so were the women, and Dave the Beowulf Freak was from Newfoundland, where men were men and the sheep were nervous.

The tarantula was from Brazil.

It's also a little-known fact that Toronto lies on something called a *ley line* - a straight mystical path of energy connecting several other sites of Really Awesome Mystical Energy. Ley lines are believed by many Witches, Eco-Pagans, Aquarians, Crunchy-Granola Earth Mothers, Extreme Shamans, Astrologers, Dowsing Plumbers, Pseudo-Gurus, Early Morning Talk-Show Hosts and Movie Stars to be scattered all over the world. What ley lines are capable of doing depends on who you ask in the Really Weird Shit community, but it's generally agreed they're responsible for a whole lot of totally cool awesome mystical stuff.

Or not, in some cases. More in a minute.

Toronto's ley line passes through Detroit (a giant Uniroyal Tire on the side of I-94 marks where Jimmy Hoffa, a secret ninth-level Ancient Hibernian Knight of the Cabbalistic Templars Arch-Mage is buried), Chicago (home of a Devil Monkey), Kansas City, Missouri, where you will find the Pythian Castle, which is where a lot of weird ghosty things happen all the time, Kansas (Satan owns a timeshare there; you don't *really* think all those tornadoes are due to complex climatological conditions, do you?), Albuquerque (not so far, really, from Roswell), and ends in Sedona, Arizona (you've probably heard of their sacred energy vortexes). Or it might end in San Diego, no one can be entirely certain. However, if there's anything mystical about San Diego it's news to everybody.

See, all this mystical energy ley line stuff happens underground, because ley lines are *chthonic,* or Earth-based. And what happened is that all that repressed male sexual energy up above in Toronto collided with Hoffa's ghost who was getting it on with Cleopatra's ghost. This released a massive jolt of Sacred Vortex Stuff from Sedona which is like a frickin' chthonic nuclear bomb of sexual weirdness, which ejaculated a gigundous load of the most awesome assemblage of erotic energy the world had ever known and it was headed straight for Our Canadian Heroes. And poor Toronto, which had never done anything mystical to anybody, was jarred by a fairly scary although not exactly massive earthquake in the middle of the night.

It woke up a whole bunch of people, several of whom crapped their Toronto Maple Leafs pajamas with fright, but then it ended fairly quickly and things went back to normal and everyone looked around and decided the damage didn't look too bad, eh, so maybe they'd just dreamed the whole thing and they went back to sleep.

Little did they realize, that Toronto was about to get *completely* fucked up.

And horny.

CHAPTER TWO

A woman recently relocated to Toronto from pretty much anywhere else will soon realize there is something weird about Toronto men. It's true that the latter act like they have no interest in the former. Some wonder if a Toronto man would even notice if a woman walked down the street stark naked. The cops might notice, because it's illegal for anyone to display their naughty bits unless a) They're at Hanlan's Point, the nude beach on Toronto Island or b) They're in the annual Gay Pride Parade. (Foreign men will be thrilled to hear it's legal for a Canadian woman to swing her flying Canucks in public if she so chooses; a court case in 1998 ruled it was discrimination to allow men to go topless and not women. It was either let the women wave their Canucks in the breeze or prevent men from displaying their heavily tattooed hairy-chested beer guts during the summer, and no one wanted *that.)*

Although Amita and Mahliqa denied it, Rachel discovered that Toronto men did in fact avoid attractive single women. She'd noticed that only men with foreign accents ever approached her with the Universal Pickup Script, which she suspected horny guys were either downloading off the Internet, or maybe were ordering it via some spam message. Or maybe they got the U.P.S. for free if they ordered two bottles of useless pills designed to turn their weak lovemaker into a powerful and impressive love gun *(She will slave to your glorious pecker of desire!).* At any rate, the conversation usually went something like this:

"Hi there."

"Hi."

"You know I've seen you around here before."

"Uh-huh."

"You know you are a very beautiful woman."

"Unh."

"No, really, you've got beautiful eyes/hair/lips/legs (here the guy would fill in a random set of body parts, hopefully none of which were *boobs*). Are you married?"

"No."

"You're so pretty. You've got beautiful [different set of body parts]. I can't believe a beautiful woman like you isn't married. Do you have a boyfriend?" And blah-blah-blah-more-you're-so-pretty crap until he asked for her phone number, which she never gave him.

Rachel had been out on a few dates since the move, but she'd found the immigrant men as annoying and shallow on this side of the border as on the other side. They were only interested in service for their love gun, and the Toronto guys, well, let's just say she was beginning to wonder if they were subjected to a particularly severe *bris* at birth.

Okay, Rachel admitted to herself, it's not like I look like I did when I was 25.

She wasn't a conceited woman, but there was no denying she'd been a major babe magnet before she got old (she was 41, but had felt old since 37). The comparisons to Elizabeth Taylor weren't unreasonable. She did in fact have violet eyes and dark hair, although she was plucking more and more gray ones now and suspected she'd soon have to start coloring it. Now all she could see were spider webs around her eyes and faint laugh lines around her mouth. And if anyone was in doubt about how old she was, it was quickly dispelled the moment she pulled out her reading glasses.

Despite ten questionable years married to Austin Eustache, Rachel was ready to tie the knot again, and soon. Most of the immigrants who approached her were young men, ten, fifteen, even twenty or more years younger. Wasn't there anyone in this town old enough to remember 8-track players who might still find interesting a woman who wasn't too bad-looking for her age, hadn't gained a lot of weight and had managed to live a rich, full life?

"But without any children!" A grating voice bumped down her vertebrae. "You're not getting any younger, Rachel! It's now or never!"

"I know, Ma," Rachel growled through gritted teeth as she pulled into her apartment complex.

Dave the Virgin had to deliver most of his forty-eight gerbils to a large pet superstore across town. Breeding gerbils was something Dave did for extra money because the damn things multiply faster than V!@gra-crazed rabbits on Ecstasy, and it was always easy to sell them to various pet stores. Why he turned into a massive gerbil factory is thanks to the idiot who sold him his first two gerbils when Dave was sixteen. He was supposed to get two males, but one of them turned out to be somewhat less male than advertised. The only down side was sometimes the parents ate the inventory.

Forty-eight gerbils were a lot even for Dave but he hadn't had time to make a delivery lately, and he needed to get rid of them before the Habitrail went all *Night of the Living Gerbil Dead* or maybe *Lord of the Gerbils*. So he sat on the subway with forty of them in a big box on his lap, surrounded by zombie Torontonians who clearly felt they had better things to do with their time than ride the subway. He glanced only with the mildest interest around him, noting briefly the attractive dark-haired girl that sat a few seats from him. At any other time Dave would have spent the rest of his trip furtively watching her, but now his thoughts were preoccupied with Love Comes Later. He'd been disappointed to find out it was a service to help arrange marriages, not that he'd be adverse to someone arranging a marriage for him since it seemed the only way he was likely ever to get a woman. But he could tell by

Mahliqa's face, after their brief interview, that she found the placement of an underemployed non-university-educated chubby computer geek with the beginnings of male pattern baldness to be more than a little daunting.

Still, she'd suggested he talk to Rachel Brinkerhoff, their matchmaker. The gorgeous woman. Rachel wanted him, she'd said.

Dave knew in his heart of hearts that Rachel most likely just wanted him to become a paying customer, which was about as likely as the gerbils turning into a harem of beautiful women all dying to relieve him of his maidenhead, but he decided he'd live with a pleasant delusion for the time being.

"Whatcha got in the box?" a little kid asked Dave, attracted by the scratching and scurrying and occasional squeaking.

"Gerbils," Dave replied.

"Wow. Can I see?"

"No."

"Why not?"

"Because if I open the box the gerbils will escape."

"That would be so cool!"

"No it wouldn't!" snapped his mother.

✯ ✯ ✯

Amita stared at the elderly couple sitting across from her desk. They seemed awfully old to have children of marriageable age. They looked more like grandparents.

And then she understood. Ah yes, that must be it. She'd read that many Western seniors had begun raising their own grandchildren when the parents couldn't for one reason or another - bad divorce, substance abuse, prison terms, or abuse and neglect. So tragic! This is what came of the silly Western idea that two people in love should get married. If people didn't make such bad decisions when they were younger, their lives would turn out so much better.

"Is your son - Dave, I believe you said - still in university?" she asked.

The old gent shook his head. "No, he's finished."

"Wonderful. We recommend that children finish their education before they think about settling down."

"That's hardly a problem," sighed the mother. "If only I could get him out of the house!"

Amita smiled. She was more excited than she let on for Love's first potential clients. "That's a problem many Toronto couples have," she informed them. "A lot of kids moving back in, and not just young people either. With real estate and the cost of living so high, even children in their forties and fifties are moving back home. It's a problem in the States too."

The couple looked at each other with woeful expressions.

"Has your son had many relationships?" Amita asked. She hoped he was good-looking. He sounded like he had a good job. What she needed to do now was smoke out any potential problems - existing children from a teenage fling, a lack of seriousness, an unwillingness to settle down.

Dave's mom shook her head. "He dated more when he was younger. He doesn't appear to have had many dates since his divorce."

"Divorce?" Amita looked shocked. "Dave has been married before?"

"Oh yes, three times," Dave's dad replied. "No one knows better how to pick a psychotic loser than our Dave. That's why we're here. We know we can make a better choice for him next time."

“That awful spider doesn't help,” Dave's mom commented.

"Er—how old is your son?" Amita asked, resisting the urge to swallow heavily.

"Forty-seven."

People were still talking about the earthquake that had rocked Toronto even though, as earthquakes go, this one barely warranted a 3.5

on the Hysterical Media Reaction scale. A few buildings were slightly damaged, some ex-heirloom bone china had sadly made the long last trek to a giant landfill in Michigan, some CDs and DVDs reportedly fell behind the couch, and some Toronto City Hall executive assistants, enjoying a smoking break (one was enjoying a toking break) by the fountain in Nathan Philips Square, noticed a large crack had opened up at the bottom of the shallow pool surrounding the fountain. It bubbled occasionally and issued a few lazy puffs of steam which might have been regarded as a tad unusual had they been paying attention, but they were too busy debating what was going to happen next on the reality TV show *Who Wants To Murder Their Boss,* and the one with the jay-jay was so fried she didn't notice her skirt was all caught up in the back from her last trip to the washroom.

The earthquake was also the hot topic of conversation down the street at the Eaton Centre shopping mall, where weary shoppers rested with their shoe store and Bay Company bags on the benches curving around what one might call the Stealth Sexual Fountain.

The S.S.F. is weirdly mesmerizing, although few visitors ever figure out exactly what is so gratifying about watching it. Mostly they hang around for the grand explosion, but few grasp the symbolism. The S.S.F. is a large bowl with an impressively phallic-shaped fountain in the middle, which for several minutes gently cascades water into the bowl, which slowly and casually builds up to the brim until suddenly the water drains down through an opening at the bottom of the bowl. And if you wait—just wait—oh yes, just wait, it's coming, it's coming!—suddenly with a mighty rumble the fountain jets forth a powerful column of water that almost reachcs the skylight above (and we're talking a three-story complex here, people!) And then it does it AGAIN. And then AGAIN. Observers often squeal from the excitement.

On this lazy afternoon people watched as the water slowly built up into the symbolically vaginal bowl and waited with anticipation for the grand climax. Except this time the water didn't drain down after reaching the halfway mark. This time, the white fountain rumbled and shook and several shoppers gasped audibly, grabbing their bags and wondering whether they should hang on to their benches or run for dear life in case this was an earthquake aftershock. And then their attention was drawn to the fountain and they realized something was happening in the very center.

Something dark and brown began to rise up. Like it was on some unseen lift. It rose up through the apparatus of the fountain and looked like it might be sort of human, and then the fountain stopped and the water began to drain down and in the center of the metal frame stood an extremely beautiful (if awfully thin, even in these supermodel-obsessed times) and thoroughly soaked young woman.

She was tall and gorgeous, if awfully lean, with full breasts and dark brown nipples. Her skin was a burnished bronze, perfect and flawless. Her belly was flat and her waist so cinched you could count her ribs. Her hips jutted out. Her bottom was comprised of two heartrendingly rounded bowls that glistened invitingly. Drops of crystal-clear water slid sensuously down her long slim thighs which melted into her thin calves which ended in impossibly tiny ankles and delicate brown feet as smooth as a newborn baby's. If anyone had had the courage to pull out a ruler and measure the downy and inviting cleft between her hips, they'd have found a perfect isosceles triangle (although it's unknown if anyone would have survived the attempt, which no one did).

Her face possessed an unearthly beauty - high cheekbones supporting a pair of huge dark elongated eyes lined with lush eyelashes. Two delicate curved eyebrows hovered like angels above. Her dark wet melted chocolate hair fell halfway down her back.

In any other time and place she would have been considered unnaturally thin, but in the 21st century she could have easily signed a contract to model for Abercrombie & Fitch.

The mysterious woman stepped forward, balancing on the edge of the fountain mechanism. No easy feat (ar ar) considering their sharp edges, but she posed as though standing on cushy green grass. She looked around a bit haughtily, surveying the semi-circle of shocked faces and dropped jaws.

"Holy shit, who the hell is that?" asked one chubby middle-aged man who hadn't yet noticed that his chubby middle-aged wife looked like she'd just swallowed a live grenade.

"Shukr Allah!" one young Muslim man breathed as he gazed up at the awesome creature. *"Allahu Akbar!"*

"Brandon! Don't look!" cried a mother as she tried to cover her thirteen-year-old son's eyes, but he wrenched away and looked anyway, his eyes the size of Hummer off-road tires.

"I love Canada!" cried an Indonesian man who was only in Toronto for his sister's wedding, but decided right there to apply for immigration.

The unearthly woman nimbly leaped forward and landed on the lip of the bowl. It was smooth and exquisitely choreographed with no loss of balance - the most fluid, graceful motion anyone had ever seen, although her breasts bounced momentarily and shook free some drops of water which landed on the Indonesian man's head, who promptly fainted from the excitement.

"Damn, I'm starving to death," she said, looking around as though this was the Mandarin Buffet.

And the Stealth Sexual Fountain ejaculated toward the ceiling, its impressive explosion hanging for one brief moment in space, then splitting up into tiny foamy ejaculates and falling dramatically back into the bowl.

And again.

And once more. Except now, for the first time in anyone's memory, it actually splattered forcefully against the skylight.

☆ ☆ ☆

"Mike, don't touch that!"

Dave the Virgin turned just in time to see the little brat lift the lid of the box to peer inside. The kid wasn't expecting an *explosion* of gerbils, and he cried out and fell backwards, tripping on his own feet and falling against the pretty dark-haired girl. She caught him but screamed as several gerbils varying in size from small-enough-to-fit-in-a-dessert-spoon to looks-to-be-the-size-of-a-Humvee-to-my-hysterical-eyes jumped at her. And if there's one thing gerbils can do, it's *jump*. Friggin' greased lightning they are if they escape. And forty gerbils had just made a mass diaspora on the Bloor-Danforth line.

Passengers screamed and fought off the horde of marauding rodents. At least three-quarters of them had seen *Willard* and very few knew that gerbils were herbivorous. Absolutely no one besides Dave considered that the gerbils were probably even more panicked than the passengers, and the only person who was laughing his ass off was the little brat Mike, who had not yet been told by his hysterical mother that she was no longer going to buy him the latest *Harry Potter* video game, as punishment.

The little brown terrorists erupted against a background of screaming shrieking passengers until the subway pulled into Yonge & Bloor and the doors opened. A few tiny cannonballs led the chaotic exodus from the car and commuters waiting to get on the train fell back to avoid being trampled. Many ran back several steps, assuming there'd been a violent altercation. The train conductor came running, only to be inundated by several furry rockets. Dave emerged with his empty box dangling from his fingertips and a forlorn look as $100 worth of inventory began slipping down to the train tracks and disappearing under the subway car. When the train finally pulled away there were no disgusting remains of ex-gerbils so one must assume they all found safety somewhere in the bowels of Yonge & Bloor.

"It was depressing, Amita," Rachel told her new friend over tea. She'd gone to a Welcome2Toronto evening drinks and chat gathering she'd found on the Internet, hoping to find potential clients for her database, as social functions were her primary source for new matchmaking blood.

"His name was Jason, and he was really good-looking," she said. "Tall and muscular and bald with big blue eyes, about forty. He said he'd been a wrestler in college and liked to play soccer on the weekends. He was so charming, and so funny, and he wasn't wearing a wedding ring, and he hadn't said anything about a girlfriend. And I hadn't yet told him what I did for a living because I don't like to seem pushy. But the more I talked to him, the more I liked him myself. So I smiled and tried to be funny too, and we really seemed to hit it off. I hoped he'd ask for my phone number."

"I can see where this is going," said Amita. Her big brown eyes scanned Rachel. She couldn't understand why a beautiful woman like her didn't have an ocean of men vying for her hand. She hardly looked her age and despite that awful accent, she wasn't loud and annoying like a lot of Americans, and particularly New Yorkers.

Rachel propped her elbow on the table and slumped against her hand. "Yeah, I'm so beautiful, I look just like Elizabeth Taylor. Jason asked me what I do for a living and I told him, and his eyes lit up and he asked if I could fix him up with someone."

"What did you tell him?"

"My heart sank. I knew he wasn't going to ask for my phone number. Before I could say anything he said, 'Can you match *me* up? I like really slim gorgeous girls with great hair who know how to dress really well. You know, like those *Sex In The City* gals. I'm one of the few guys who actually watched that show. Someone like Charlotte! Have you got anyone like her? Oh, and she should be young, around thirty.'"

"Oh Rachel, I'm sorry."

"Yeah, me too. Story of my friggin' life. I *adore* guys like him. Big and strong and manly and outdoorsy. And of course he didn't think of *me,* Ms. Elizabeth Taylor Look-Alike. Let's face it, Amita, I'm too old. Always a matchmaker, never a bride."

"That's not true," Amita told her. She stroked Rachel's hand and her eyes filled with sympathy. "He's a very foolish man not to see how beautiful and perfect you are. You see, this is why Toronto needs a service like ours. People have such silly ideas of what they want in a mate. They watch too many TV shows and movies and think they want someone who doesn't even exist. You know what I'm talking about, Rachel. What would a man have to talk about with a young girl like that Charlotte character? I remember her. She was the foolish romantic. High maintenance, as you Americans say."

Rachel sighed and sat back in her chair. "Yeah, but you know what, Amita? Maybe it was for the best. Maybe you're right, maybe I should just shut up and let you arrange a marriage for me. I don't know what the hell I'm doing. Jason was a lot like Austin when I first met him. Austin made me so—*hot* when I was around him. He was a cop for the NYPD and when he wore his uniform he could get me to do *anything* for him. Then we got married and after a couple of years he changed. He got more macho, really into-the-stratosphere overly-masculine. Then September 11th happened and that just sort of—radicalized him, and a couple of years later he got a job with Homeland Security. After that, he turned into a total—well, pardon my French here but he became a real dickhead."

Amita nodded slowly.

"He became emotionally and verbally abusive. He never hit me or nothing but the main reason why I left is I thought it was coming. When he got security detail at JFK he just became impossible to live with. I saw him a couple of times when I had to bring him something at the airport. It was like he was totally in his element, bossing people around, barking orders and strutting around like a bantam cock on steroids. He loved that shit. If you didn't move fast enough he'd yell at you. If he didn't like you he'd find a reason to make you go stand at the end of the line again. And no one could do anything because he was Homeland Security and he had a gun and a Taser and you just knew he was dying to use one or the other on you."

"I'm sorry, Rachel," Amita whispered.

"Yeah. I'm sorry too. Sorry I ever laid eyes on the bastard." Amita noticed her accent became more pronounced when she felt depressed or upset. *Sorry I evah laid eyes on the bastuhd.* "And it's kind of my fault too, y'know? I mean, *I'm* the one that's got a thing for big dumb and stupid, yuhknowwhutImean?"

"Then maybe it's a good thing this idiot didn't like you," Amita replied. She drained the rest of her cup. "You can change, Rachel. You can find a better man for you than this Jason." She took the two cups to the sink in the nearby kitchen. "I refuse to think you had any sort of bad fortune at this event. I am glad you didn't get a date with such a shallow man. I tell you, *meri jaan,* I would arrange a marriage to a nice man for you if I could. Except I don't know any good Jewish men!"

She smiled sweetly and Rachel smiled back. At least she finally had friends here.

The beautiful wet naked woman walked outside the Eaton Centre. The sun was high in the sky. It had been awhile since she'd been around people and she noticed they were mostly dressed. A pity, because she knew how beautiful she was and adored showing it off. Still, do as the Romans do as Caligula was fond of saying. Despite her fondness for him, though, not to mention his amazing sexual powers, she'd never joined him and the rest of the Romans when their lewd festivities involved a horse.

"Heh-heh-hey pretty mama!" "Yeah baby!" "Hey chickie-baby, over here, over here!" The woman walked past a gauntlet of catcalls and whistles, her head held erect and her ripe breasts held high. She felt pride. The women regarded her with fury - nothing much changes over the millennia! - and several called out to her to cover up, that she was about to get arrested. She had no idea what getting arrested meant but if it involved a few minutes alone with a virgin she'd push to the head of the line.

She paused at a street corner. It sort of looked like something the Sumerians might have constructed except the buildings here were much higher, and decorated with all kinds of flashing colors. Even more amazing were the moving pictures. She stared at them as she crossed the street, oblivious to the cars that screeched to a halt or the angry curses flung in her direction. She reached the other side and faced a square filled with merchants offering all kinds of pretty baubles and shiny things.

She walked up to a merchant whose stall offered beautifully coloured fabrics fluttering in the breeze.

The man, a Lebanese who had some vague knowledge of who she was - or what - regarded her with a mixture of horror and unbridled lust - as though he wasn't sure whether to grab her and shag her silly, or to run screaming through the streets until he jumped into Lake Ontario and started swimming for Centre Island.

The woman, ignoring the Tent City that had gathered around her (all male), calmly fingered the various fabrics and took a few off the racks, holding them up to the light or against her hips. She turned to a young man and said, "What do you think? Now be honest. Is this my color or does it make me look sallow?"

No more than twenty or so, he gulped and struggled with his words. "It's—you—the dress—is beautiful—but—you aren't going to put it on, are you?"

She gave him one of those well-DUUUUHHH-are-you-like-the-world's-biggest-dumbfuck-or-what looks, her large brown eyes narrowing at the corners and giving her face a leonine look. "Well *gawd,"* she replied, "who did you *think* it was for, my dad?"

Twenty male faces looked like they'd just learned they were losing the Toronto Blue Jays to Duluth or something. Unhurried, the woman continued flipping through the various fabrics, which weren't dresses, really, but long wraparound skirts that could be worn as dresses many different ways.

She finally picked out a gorgeous two-layered dark green and maroon and purple number with a wide gold filigreed border and turned to the merchant, who had also joined Tent City and looked, actually, like he might explode with all the fervour of the S.S.F.

"I want this one," she said with such a beautiful smile he merely stared at her, dumbstruck, lost in her fathomless eyes with the delicately arched eyebrows, if not occasionally distracted by her exceedingly slim frame and those gorgeous, ripe, crying-out-to-be-squeezed luscious breasts...

He nodded. It was all he was capable of doing.

She looked at him, tilted her head sideways, and raised her eyebrows, questioning.

"So I can have it?" she asked, and the merchant nodded again, and, against his will, his eyes dropped from her face.

"Wonderful!" she gushed, and right there she began wrapping it around herself, a bit inexpertly, which is only to be expected if you're not familiar with those million-in-one dresses they sell in Dundas Square. She managed to tie it over one shoulder, leaving the other bronzed work of art bare. Wordlessly, the heavily-breathing merchant handed her a wide gold belt which she attached around her waist. She turned to face the crowd. Even dressed, she was as breathtakingly beautiful as ever.

A policeman pushed through, followed by a couple of angry-looking young women. "All right, what's going on here?" he asked, because he looked around and saw no nude woman after all.

The woman turned to him and looked up into his face. Her hair had begun to dry in the summer breeze and it fell over her shining shoulders in damp waves. Her brown eyes, huge and innocent, bathed him. She must be the one these girls had seen, he thought—and then his thoughts evaporated as he lost himself in the contours of her face.

"I'm looking—for a naked woman," he said to her, dreamily, as though it were merely a formality. "Was that—was that you?"

"It was her, all right!" cried one of the angry young women.

"Is that true?" he asked the lissome undine standing before him.

Slowly, she nodded, her eyes never leaving his.

"You—you can't—it's not done—it's illegal—er, don't do it again," he breathed, and he leaned closer, his lips parting slightly.

The beautiful young woman looked convincingly contrite, and her lush lips parted and she shook her head slightly.

"I'd—I'll—uh, have to arrest you if it happens again," he breathed.

She nodded, then stood on bare tiptoes to reach up and kiss him lightly, once, but lingeringly, on the mouth.

There was a collective explosion from the crowd. It was probably just their exhaled breath, but one never knows.

The woman turned and walked away.

It did prove, in fact, that Toronto men *would* notice a woman who walked down the street stark naked, after all.

CHAPTER THREE

Dave the Virgin sat, morose, on a bench near the Freedom Arches of the Nathan Philips Square fountain which, despite the suspiciously American-sounding name, had not actually been built or named by Americans. Not only was he gerbil-less, but now he had to appear in court for creating a public disturbance. And it wasn't even his fault. It was that snot-nosed kid. The policeman hadn't listened to his explanation. He said it was Dave's responsibility to make sure animals won't pose a hazard or an inconvenience to other passengers when one brings them on the subway. Ontario is a very pet-friendly province, you'll see dogs in Zeller's and rabbits on the subway and little puppies peeking out of some old lady's elaborately embroidered purse on streetcars, but even animal-loving Torontonians draw the line at forty panicked gerbils on the loose. Especially on the subway.

A voice over his shoulder said, "Hey, aren't you the gerbil guy?"

He jerked around and found the pretty young woman from the subway. "I'm not a gerbil guy!" he declared hotly. "I just raise them for money. I don't do anything else with them!"

She came around the bench and sat beside him. "Well of *course* not. Why would I think that? I'm sorry about your gerbils. I wasn't scared by them, just startled when they leaped out. That kid should be grounded until he's thirty-five for what he did."

"Yeah," Dave replied. She really was very pretty. Long dark hair and beautiful brown eyes, although her glasses were a bit severe. She was slim, too. Okay, she was no Rachel Brinkerhoff but Dave was unaccustomed to attractive women sitting down and willingly talking to him. Without a dare being a motive.

"Still, it was kind of funny, don't you think? I was trying not to laugh. Everyone was completely freaked out, like you'd let loose a bunch of rats. I mean, they were *gerbils,* for cryin' out loud. Did these people not have childhoods? Have they never been to a pet store?"

"I don't know." Dave punctuated his expression of ignorance with a lackadaisical shrug. Now he felt even more depressed, not just because he was out $100 which had been destined for the Fan Expo Convention in August. It was because this really good-looking woman, who did not apparently have to be dared, threatened, or dragged and hog-tied to sit next to him—in public—where she might be seen by someone she knew—was probably just making small talk and he'd never have a chance with her in a million years anyway.

Despite being from Toronto, Dave the Virgin was, in fact, into girls. Well okay, maybe not in the strict technical sense—ever—but he would if he ever had the chance. At least he thought he would. At thirty-five, he wasn't sure he'd ever let a girl get close enough to find out—he thought about Rachel Brinkerhoff again—maybe he would.

Then again, since Rachel was even more beautiful, he probably had a better chance with this girl. In the sense that, perhaps, all of humanity might disappear tomorrow and they'd be the last man and woman left. And they'd have to repopulate the planet together...

Dave shifted uncomfortably. It wouldn't be manly to cross his legs, but against his own will, he imagined her naked. *Oh shit...*

Masculinity be damned. Dave crossed his legs.

"My name is Alexis," she said, extending one hand, unaware that she was buck naked. He shook it, and answered, "I'm Dave. It's nice to meet you, Alexis."

Just as he was about to have another unbidden thought involving what it might be like to massage her pert pink nipples - and Dave was completely certain she had them - Alexis stood up.

"I have to go," she told him. Completely clueless as to the rise in his Levis.

Shit. "Okay," he said, "it was nice talking to you."

He looked up into her face, squinting against the bright sunlight. A cooler guy would have asked for her phone number. A cooler guy, actually, would have told her she was really beautiful and that she had lovely hair or eyes or breasts or something—no, wait, not breasts, that would be perverted and fucked up—but he'd pick out something about her—not difficult with this one—and then he'd see if she had a boyfriend and then he'd ask for her number. Yes, that's what a cooler guy would do.

But Dave the Virgin was about as cool as a bunch of middle-aged ex-hippies wearing bell bottoms and coordinated pantsuits at a *Partridge Family* concert reunion.

"It was nice talking to you too," Alexis replied, and bizarrely, she actually sounded like she meant it. "I hope your court case goes okay. You should totally beat this rap, it's complete crap."

"Yeah, it is," Dave nodded. "I'll see you around sometime, Alexis?"

"Hey, I'm around Toronto," she replied, having no idea he'd just asked her out. She smiled and her whole face lit up, then she gave a little wave and turned and walked away.

Dave was disappointed, but not exactly surprised. Even he knew that was a totally lame ask-out line that no normal woman would ever actually catch.

He leaned back against the bench and watched a gaggle of attractive college girls dangling their feet in the water. On the other side of the pool, three middle-aged guys with pot bellies and hairlines that had receded into the next province dangled their bare feet in the water as well. It was what people did at Nathan Philips Square on a hot summer day.

Near the center of the pool, just a little beyond the fountain, the water bubbled mysteriously.

✯ ✯ ✯

Rachel prepared for another New2Toronto function. Just as she'd put on a pretty pink dress, one that accentuated the color of her eyes, the phone rang.

Her heart sank when she saw the caller ID. There was no escaping the inevitable.

"Hi Ma."

"Hello, Rachel dear. I just wanted to call you and see if everything's all right."

Oh sure.

"Everything's fine, Ma. What made you think something was wrong?"

"I haven't heard from you in at least a week. Have you forgotten me? Does Canada not have mothers?"

"I haven't forgotten you, Ma. I've been busy getting my business together. And it hasn't been a week, I talked to you on Tuesday."

"That was last week."

"That was *this* week."

“I didn't call to argue with you. A mother has a right to worry about her only child. How is your new life? Do you ever miss me?"

"Of course I do, Ma."

"Then why don't you come home? Why you ever moved to that godforsaken land of *goyim* and snow is beyond me. Are you meeting some nice men?"

Yes, and they're not interested in me. Alexis had called it correctly. The men here appeared uninterested in anybody. Truth was, even an attractive woman could forget she was pretty in female-averse Toronto.

"Yes, Ma.”

"Any husband material?" That was Ma, always cut to the chase. At least it kept the phone calls short.

"I don't know, I've only been here a few months."

"I'll bet you're meeting lots of men and putting them into that stupid computer. Why do you do this, Rachel? Why do you spend your life fixing up others when you can't even find a husband yourself? Who takes a divorced matchmaker seriously?"

"Ma, I've got to go to a party tonight," Rachel said through gritted teeth. She fished through her closet for her black heels. Had she unpacked them yet? There were still many unopened boxes in the living room.

"I'm just reminding you, time is running out, *Rachella.* You're forty-one years old. You're not getting any younger, and God knows neither am I. I'd like to be a grandmother before I'm old and dead, which won't be much longer now."

"You're the healthiest sixty-three-year-old in New York, Ma. You're going to bury that new rabbi at the synagogue—"

"Rabbi Belzer! Such a good-looking man he is. And you had to move to *Goynada!"*

"I'll find someone. Just not now, I don't have time."

"Time is all you have, Rachel. And not much of it left. Just make sure he's Jewish!"

* * *

Alexis waited at the street corner for the light to change. The hot June sun beat down upon her and the short bearded guy with a backpack next to her.

The man turned to her and looked her up and down, once. "You know, you're a very beautiful woman," he said with what he hoped was a winning smile.

She snapped out of her reverie and barely glanced at him as she replied, "Sorry, but I'm too busy with work for a boyfriend." The light changed and she strode past him.

Alexis never had time for The Universal Pickup Script.

The beautiful brown woman, drawing stares now not because she was naked but because she was so jaw-droppingly lovely in her new wraparound sari-fabric dress, walked down the street in her bare feet, looking around and sniffing the air. It was good to be back in Toronto again. She didn't much remember her last trip here a few years ago, when she snuck in from the Underworld via a mirror and inhabited the body of a pretty young teenage girl, and she'd almost forgotten what a motherlode of food was right here.

Others, walking the opposite direction, passed her and she took a sniff at each man. This one - European. No. That one - Indian. No. A Jamaican - oh no, not only wouldn't he do but eating a Jamaican only made her fuzzy-headed and contemplating her navel, and they gave her the munchies.

Then a man walked by and when she sniffed - it was 'a slice of heaven', as her mother *(the bitch!)* would have said. The woman's body twitched, and her pulse throbbed at the nearness of his vitality. He smelled like a pot roast dinner, a baked Cornish hen, and clam linguine all rolled into one. Not literally, of course - but every bit as delightful as if he'd been a real meal.

Not here. Not in front of everyone. There were so many of them, so many virgins in Toronto begging to be taken, begging her to feed off their life force, that she knew she could take her time.

Not too much. Her body twitched again, and her heart fluttered in her chest.

✯ ✯ ✯

"Why are we getting so many old people and their old children, Mahliqa?"

Amita and her friend grunted as they moved a large old desk into place. In a box near the door was Mahliqa's nephew's old computer, without a monitor.

"I guess we never counted on desperate parents, my friend."

"What happened to the young people? Don't Canadians want their children to marry well?"

"You *know* how they are. They want to do it all themselves. It will take awhile before Canadians will walk through here with pictures of children younger than thirty." Mahliqa tugged at the edge of her yellow sequined *hijab*, which had become snagged on one corner of the desk.

"How can we advise the parents of that man Dave?"

"Which one, the one who keeps a pet spider or the—" Mahliqa's voice dropped to a whisper, even though the women were alone —*"virgin?"*

"The one with the spider."

"Ugh." Mahliqa grimaced.

"You know, the gray-haired one with the high hairline in his picture. Who's been divorced more often than that—that—actress Rachel looks like! What's-her-name, Elizabeth Taylor!"

"I don't know, Amita, who are we going to find who'll put up with that awful pet?"

"We don't have to, my friend. That's Rachel's job."

"This is hardly arranging marriages, Amita. We're just recruiting for Rachel. She's a lovely woman, but what does she need us for? All we're doing is providing people for her matchmaking."

"It was your idea, remember. You and I provide consulting services for young peoples' families. Remember what the spider guy's parents told us? That he prefers younger women? What does a young woman have in common with someone like that? He's thinking with his *lavde*."

"It's part of both our cultures, Amita, for men to marry much younger women."

"That's because the men of our cultures think with their *lavde!"*

"I think the problem is our office. It's arranged poorly, with no thought to coordinating its energies. When is the *feng shui* expert coming?"

"Next week," Amita grunted. With a mighty heave she pulled the old desk into place and sat back, wiping her brow with her *palloo,* the edge of her sari. "I found him in Chinatown. His name is Mr. Chaoxiang Wan. He comes highly recommended. My friend Pritika says he worked wonders with her husband's office!"

"I hope so," Mahliqa replied as she hefted the heavy computer box onto the desk. "I also hope Rachel appreciates the effort we've put into setting her up in our office!"

Dave the Virgin morosely stared into the pool around the Nathan Philips Square fountain. He wondered vaguely when the city had added the bubbling thing and whether it was supposed to smell vaguely sulfurous. It wasn't pungent, but every now and then he got a whiff of eggs 'of a certain age.'

A shadow loomed from behind. Someone sat beside him. Dave glanced up reluctantly from his dark abyss and did a double-take.

She was the most beautiful woman he'd ever seen.

Better-looking than Rachel, even. Light-years beyond Alexis. And —she had one ripe, beautiful, bronze breast with a mesmerizing brown nipple hanging out of her dress.

Dave gulped, paralyzed. The dress was a dizzying pattern of dark green, maroon and purple, one of those wrap-around things you could buy around town, tied over one shoulder. Loosely. One breast had fallen out, the one closest to Dave. The woman didn't seem to notice. He couldn't think about how it was rude to stare. He couldn't take his eyes off that luscious golden apple. Slowly, langorously, she raised her burnished arms above her head, arching her back so that that gloriously large chocolate-brown nipple pointed toward the curved buildings of City Hall as though to say, "Right over there! That's where you may go to dispute your parking ticket!" Her arms came to rest on the back of the bench, one provocatively behind Dave. As she leaned back, looking like a glorious lion with a mane of tangled brown hair, her uncovered breast sat there, hanging there, *floating there,* for all the world to see, crying out to be touched and kneaded and squeezed and kissed and licked and —

Dave crossed his legs.

Rachel hung up the phone with a silent prayer of gratitude for goodbyes. She turned on the radio to keep her company while she tried on different dresses. Despite her mother's pressure, she did in fact want to meet an eligible man, preferably one who didn't mind a woman with a little mileage on her and who might be considered 'damaged goods' because of her divorce.

"—Yeah, I don't know *what* they're smoking over at the Eaton Centre there," came the afternoon-drive host, a young-sounding guy named Angus.

"They're saying she came *right out of the fountain?"* asked The Dillweed, his sidekick.

"Yup. Which is totally impossible, of course. So I don't know where she really came from but it seems pretty clear that a naked woman walked out of the Eaton Centre and went into Dundas Square and bought a dress."

"You are kidding me, right? I mean this is *Toronto,* that sort of thing just doesn't happen here."

"Apparently several witnesses have called this station to report exactly that. She's very beautiful, almost anorexic according to one report, and described as about five-foot-four with brown skin, long dark hair, and a really great pair of bazongas."

"Damn, WHY do I always miss these things?"

"Because you lead a cursed life, my man. A representative from a modeling agency for Abercombie & Fitch has called too, wanting to know where he can find her. We'll have more in a minute, guys. Don't go away. We'll be back with the Dipstick Report right after this break."

A commercial for a domestic beer followed. Rachel discarded the pink dress as being too tight across her midsection (which would have been okay if she hadn't gained a few pounds) and tried on a green one that showed off her cleavage, although in a demure way.

"It tastes great, isn't too filling and was brewed right here in Ontario," the ad announcer gushed.

Rachel didn't really like the green dress. Her mother had picked it out for her birthday. It was more suitable for a cocktail party.

"It's summer time! What are you going to do about all that back hair, you big Sasquatch?" came a different voice. *Oh, you've seen my ex-husband,* Rachel thought. The back hair was an unpleasant reality she'd discovered too late, after, unfortunately, falling in love with Austin. She slipped out of the green dress, throwing it on the bed, and pulled out a black summery number she'd always liked. Was it appropriate for a social mixer? Oh, why the hell not?

"This week on *Corner Gas—"* began yet another voice.

Rachel slipped into the black dress and shimmied as she tried to zip it up, so hard to do when one is alone.

"Welcome back, fellow Hogtowners! The Dillweed's got the Dipstick Report, not that anything can top a naked chick rising out of the Eaton Centre fountain and buying a dress across the street—"

"Well this first story is pretty funny, Angus. Speaking of beautiful women, it seems the town of Alliance, Ohio has just discovered that last year's Carnation Queen used to be a man! Alliance calls itself the Carnation City and every year they hold a Festival, including a beauty contest for their Queen. And last year, apparently, this really hot-looking chick won, and—"

Yes, this black dress would do. It was cotton with a V-neckline and a wide belt that would hide the most recent sins accumulated since the last *they-tried-to-kill-us-we-won-let's-eat* Jewish holiday. She dug around in the closet for her black pumps.

"And in Moose Jaw, Saskatchewan, a guy named Billy Grier is suing his mother-in-law for taking his children to a Scientology recruitment center where they were hooked up to one of those lie detector things and asked a bunch of questions about Grier's sexual preference—"

Rachel dug the electric curling brush out of a bathroom drawer and plugged it in. She began scrubbing facial cleanser onto her cheeks and wondered if she'd have time for a quick bite.

"And get this, Angus. At JFK Airport in New York some Homeland Security sparky has been suspended pending an investigation into his arrest of an eight-year-old boy who was bringing home some rocks he'd picked up on the beach on Long Island."

"Rocks? An eight-year-old? What's wrong with rocks?"

Rachel stopped in mid-scrub, staring into the mirror but seeing nothing.

"That's what his dad asked. And this sparky, named Austin Eustache, apparently gave the guy and his kid a really hard time, claiming you were supposed to put weapons in your checked baggage."

"How big were these rocks?"

"Not very big, according to the father. They're smooth and good for painting pictures on them, which is why his son wanted them."

"Sounds pretty reasonable for a kid."

"So apparently Eustache created this huge scene, asked the father if he was planning on attacking anyone on the plane with these, and said it was disgusting of him to use his own son to plan a terrorist attack."

"He said that? He called it a terrorist attack?"

"Yeah, and witnesses say he picked up one of the rocks and brandished it in the kid's face, the kid was totally terrified and near tears, and the sparky was yelling that his father was going to go to jail for being an American-hating terrorist-lover and a dirty muslin."

"Don't you mean Muslim?"

"No, the guy said *muslin.* Several times, in fact."

"He accused the guy and his son of being an unwashed textile?"

"At least until other Homeland Security guys came up and hauled him away. They apologized to the father and let him and the kid through with the rocks—"

"That's even better than the beauty queen who used to be a dude."

"Yeah, man, who needs TV when we've got Americans?"

Dave the Virgin wasn't the only one paralyzed with excitement.

He couldn't know the bare-breasted woman thought he smelled like baked lobster with basil stuffing and bow tie pasta with goat cheese, and a 2002 Verget Grand Elevage Bourgogne finished with a passion fruit souffle lightly topped with warm caramel sauce.

It was all she could do to keep from leaning over, seizing him in her arms, ripping off his pants and locking her legs around his hips. She was so hungry she didn't even have the strength to kill all the babies she'd passed in her walk to the Square. Still, she knew it was important not to draw too much attention to herself. Hey, it was hard enough being the most beautiful creature Toronto had ever seen, it just wouldn't do to create a disturbance by killing their babies and virgins in broad daylight.

She wasn't sure why there were so many male virgins in Toronto in this day and age, but not only did it encourage her to stay in such a cornucopia of life-giving energies, but it was far away from her bitch of a mother and her petty jealousies.

☆ ☆ ☆

Two of the pot-bellied middle-aged men had removed their shoes and were dangling their feet in the pool. So had the young college lovelies, who didn't notice the men as much as they noticed the ladies.

One of the men turned to one of the others and said, "Hey Gordon, have you been getting hair implants? You look a little younger, eh?"

Gordon turned to him and said, "No, John, I haven't, but you look like you're losing a little weight. What do you think, Bruce?"

Bruce, who hadn't removed his shoes for a hot-afternoon foot dangle, looked at the other two and said, "I never noticed it before, but actually, you two *are* looking a little younger. What about me? Do I look younger and hotter?"

Gordon and John looked at him, looked at each other, looked back at him, and shook their heads.

"No."

☆ ☆ ☆

"Hi there," the beautiful woman said, turning to Dave so that now the nipple that reminded him so much of a Hershey's kiss *(no no mustn't think of it as a kiss, or kissing it)* pointed at him impudently. Like a third eye. Watching him. Daring him to uncross his legs, so she'd see what she was doing to him.

Dave sat, terrified, for several seconds before gulping and turning just enough to look her straight in the nipple—*no, the eye!*—and replied, "Hi." It sounded like a squeaky gear.

"What's your name?" she asked, propping her elbow on the back of the bench and resting her hand on her head under her hair, so that she looked like someone about to wrap up a shampoo commercial. The exquisite breast bounced a bit when she moved, and the nipple pointed at him accusingly.

Something else was pointing accusingly too, and Dave was petrified someone would notice.

This wasn't happening. This just wasn't happening. It was illogical enough that a woman who looked like Alexis would talk to him, but two women in one day? And the last so impossibly beautiful that he must surely look like a mound of pigeon crap next to her? He glanced around nervously, looking for the hidden cameras.

"Dave," he managed to squeak. A trickle of sweat ran down his forehead, but he didn't dare wipe it away because it was on the same side as the nipple with the courtroom attorney stare. If he brushed it, even by mistake—

"What's yours?" he asked.

"Lamashtu," she smiled, and suddenly he was lost in her huge beautiful leonine nipple.

No, her eyes. Her long leonine eyes.

☆ ☆ ☆

"You want to WHAT?"

Dave the Tarantula Guy half-rose from the table as he turned accusingly on his parents.

Amita jumped back in her seat. Mahliqa adjusted her bejewelled *hijab* nervously.

"Did I just hear her right? Mom? Dad? Did she just say she wants to *arrange a marriage* for me?"

"No, not Mahliqa. We would," his mother said. "Try to keep an open mind."

"Oh yeah. I can see where this is going. You want to foist me off on someone *you* think is acceptable. Never mind what *I* think."

"Please—Mr.—Urquhart, is it? It's not like that," Mahliqa explained. "No one is forced. It's more like a dating service, really. It's just that your parents will play an active role in finding you a suitable wife."

"And what if I don't want to get married again?" Dave bellowed. His face had begun to turn red and his eyes fairly popped out from behind his glasses. "Or what if I don't like who they choose for me? You know what kind of women my parents would favour, Miss—Ms.—"

"You can call us Amita and Mahliqa," Amita replied gently. Mahliqa sat mute in her chair. She was never good with angry feelings.

"Amita," he said. "You know who my parents favoured when I was a teenager? They liked the boring girls. The good church girls, the studious ones, the ones with curfews who never challenged them or snuck out at night."

"You should have listened to us," replied his father. "Son, we're not trying to hurt you. It's just that—your judgement regarding women hasn't always been the best."

"You never liked anyone I brought home."

"That's not true," said his mother. "I liked Melissa."

Dave snorted. It was still a sore spot after all these years. It wasn't his fault Melissa didn't stick around.

"We tried to warn you about Diana, you know," his mother reminded him.

"Diana was a fine woman," Dave sniffed. "I might still be married to her if *you* hadn't chased her off with all your stupid accusations."

"Dave, she ran off with the eighteen-year-old pool boy from the Four Seasons!"

Dave sniffed, crossed his arms and looked away. "Those were only rumours."

"And Jamie, the Nova Scotian girl. She was a lesbian."

"She said she wasn't really sure."

"She'd been a member of the Lesbian Avengers for ten years and once spent three days in jail for pelting a statue of Mother Theresa with goddess-shaped dildoes and yelling, 'Come out, come out, whatever you are!'"

"And what about Marian?" asked his mother with a cocked eyebrow.

Dave, arms still crossed, looked away.

"What was wrong with Marian?" asked Mahliqa, too curious to keep quiet.

"She was from *Arkansas,"* Dave's mother replied.

"Are you from around here, Dave?"

Lamashtu bathed him in a bewitching smile. She'd moved to face him, with one leg tucked under her and the other extended so he could see her thin calf and delicate brown foot with the perfectly-shaped toenails.

He nodded, and licked his lips. With nervousness, not lust.

"I just moved here," she said.

"How do you like it?" Dave asked, still in shock with how his life was going today. But at least he'd found his tongue and vocal cords again.

She shrugged, causing that enticing breast to bounce once. A lock of dark hair fell over her shoulder and curled around the nipple. *Don't you wish you were me?* it seemed to say.

"I don't know. I mean I really just got here. Maybe you could show me around, Dave. I don't know anyone here."

This had to be a joke. There was no way a woman this beautiful, not to mention brazen, didn't already know every man in Toronto.

Dave turned away and wondered how she'd react to *You know, you're a very beautiful woman.* Someone once told him chicks dug being told how beautiful they were. Not that it had ever worked for him before. Mostly it made them depart the city at warpspeed. Best not to chance it. There was no way he was ever getting a real date with this woman, and if staring at her perfect brown breast was the best he could get out of this, he was more than willing to oblige her.

"How come you moved to Toronto?" he asked, turning back to her. He found he could look into her eyes yet watch the boob out of his peripheral vision.

She turned and leaned back against the bench, casually untying the loose knot at her shoulder so that the fabric of the dress fell and exposed her other equally-perfect brown breast, with its dark Hershey's kiss. Oh dear God, he thought, two for the price of one!

She arched her back seductively, letting the sunlight caress her skin. Her graceful neck extended over the back of the bench, and her long dark hair cascaded down. Her coppery arms stretched over the edge again. She looked gloriously decadent, but strangely, the middle-aged men with their feet in the water and their still-shod friend didn't seem to notice. Nor did the young college girls. No, they were waving and blowing kisses to the men now.

"I wanted to get away from my mother," she replied. "I couldn't stand her, she's evil, and she didn't like my boyfriend."

"Oh, I can understand that," Dave lied. "My mother can be difficult too. Although I wouldn't describe her as evil."

"My mother hates me," Lamashtu continued. "My boyfriend Adam - well really, my *old* boyfriend now, because the bitch totally split us up - said she'd always been difficult, from the very beginning. He said she thinks too much of herself and doesn't listen to anybody. And he's so right about that."

"She split up you and Adam?" asked Dave, his voice dripping with sympathy. Despite his non-existent self-esteem, he was exultant to hear she was single. Hey, maybe she was completely crazy and really would let him escort her around town. And if she wanted to do it looking like that—

He shifted his legs painfully.

"Yeah, she was totally jealous that I was with him," Lamashtu replied. "She kept hunting us down and dragging us into fights. She accused me of all kinds of terrible things until he finally believed her."

"That's just awful," Dave said. He hoped he sounded properly indignant.

"She never left me alone. Even when I wasn't with Adam, she

followed me everywhere, accusing me of all kinds of stuff and saying she was watching me to make sure I didn't do them again. And it was completely unfair, all I wanted to do was be with Adam but she was mad because he wanted *me* and not *her."*

"Your mom was after your boyfriend?" Dave asked.

"Oh yes. Not that he wanted anything to do with an old dried-up pod like her. But she was relentless, and eventually he believed her lies, and he broke up with me and said he never wanted to see me again."

Dave looked across the pool, unsure what to say. He wondered what her mother had accused her of but didn't think it was his business to ask. The college girls picked up their sandals and began to march across the fountain toward the middle-aged men. John and Bruce waited with wicked smiles on their faces and prominent tents in their drawers. Gordon just looked confused and perhaps a bit alarmed.

When Dave turned back to Lamashtu the lost little girl was gone and the desperately seductive woman had returned. She threw her hair back, her breasts jiggling, and reached up a perfect finger, touching Dave's cheek, then drawing it slowly down his neck, pausing at his chest above his first shirt button.

"Would you like to go somewhere more private, Dave?" she asked him with a blinding smile. She cocked her head and gazed up at him through her thick lashes.

He stood up quickly, unconcerned about the tent in his own pants. "I'm sorry, I have to go," he said abruptly, and he backed away, as though she was a rabid dog. "My mother will be serving dinner soon."

Dave knew that metaphorically spraying her with the ultimate Female Repellant was something he was really going to regret. Later.

CHAPTER FOUR

Rachel worked the crowd at the social mixer, collecting business cards and talking to people to find out who was single. It had gone exceptionally well; she had four new prospects for her database, all nice, normal people who genuinely seemed interested in meeting someone, including a gay man. Rachel had never worked with gays or lesbians before but told him she'd keep her eyes peeled for him.

As she stood at the bar with a Long Island Iced Tea, a tall, handsome black man approached her.

"Hello there," he said. "My name is Freddy. I wanted to meet you when I heard others talking about you. You're a matchmaker, right?"

Rachel's eyes swept him quickly, easier to do surreptitiously in a dim bar like this one. He wouldn't be a hard one to match, that's for sure. Large brown eyes, full mouth, close-cropped hair, nice suit. Deep, earthy, sexy voice. Already her mind was flipping through her mental Rolodex.

"Yes, I am," she said, extending her hand. "My name's Rachel Brinkerhoff. I just moved here a few months ago."

"From New York," he smiled, displaying a row of even white teeth.

Momentarily, Rachel felt a little embarrassed to be appraising him like a horse for sale. Still, he was good-looking, clearly had a decent job, and would be easy to place. Alexis, maybe? She wasn't concerned about race and wanted a man who was well-off.

"Brooklyn," she replied with a self-conscious smile.

"What brought you to Toronto?" Freddy asked.

"You could say my ex-husband," she replied. "I got divorced and I needed to get away from him. He's a little crazy. Not in a dangerous way," she added quickly, even though she knew he probably was, and just hadn't gotten around to it yet. "He was just—he became impossible to live with, so we went our separate ways."

"I can understand that," Freddy replied. His handsome eyes swept up and down. "You look like that movie star from the Fifties—what was her name? The really pretty one with the dark hair."

Rachel waited silently, not wanting to prompt him. It would sound a little conceited to blurt out the name of the woman regarded as one of the most beautiful film stars ever.

"What was her name?" Freddy said, snapping his fingers next to his head. "Arched eyebrows, striking eyes, famous for her beauty—"

"That could be anyone," Rachel said vaguely.

"Hedy Lamarr!"

"Hedy Lamarr?" She'd never gotten *that* one before.

"Yeah, you know, she was in *Boom Town,* and *Ziegfeld Girl,* and *Samson and Delilah.* You familiar with her? Not everyone likes old movies the way I do."

"Oh, I know who she is! She was in *Let's Live A Little,* that was my favorite!"

"Wow, you like old movies too? If you pardon my saying so, you look a little too young to have been exposed to them much."

Rachel colored a bit with embarassment, but knew it was too dark for him to tell. "My late father kept an amazing collection of old classic movies."

"That's just wonderful. So tell me, who's your favorite actor?"

"Errol Flynn. I was going to marry him when I was a kid until my mother told me he was dead."

"Errol Flynn! *Captain Blood!*"

"And don't forget *The Sea Hawk!* You know that scene where he swings Brenda Marshall from one ship to the other? I thought that was the most romantic thing ever! I had dreams about that for years after."

"Yes, I remember that! And Basil Rathbone! Wasn't his French accent just awful? My family's from Jamaica and I grew up around French speakers and that was just the worst!"

Rachel laughed, and they sat at the bar and spent the next half hour talking about old movies, the differences between New York and Toronto, and whether the Toronto Maple Leafs would ever win the Stanley Cup. Finally Rachel glanced at her watch and said, "As much as I hate to do this I have to say good-bye. It's late."

Freddy put a friendly hand on her arm and said, "I had such a great time talking with you tonight, Rachel. I wonder if maybe we could continue this conversation over drinks some time?"

And as bad an idea as she knew it would be, Rachel, dazzled by his beautiful brown non-Jewish eyes and his remarkable movie trivia knowledge, said yes.

☆ ☆ ☆

Alexis listened to CROT, Canada Rocks Out Totally, a modern-rock radio station, while she got ready for work. The morning drive show host and his sidekick were the typical arrested-adolescent lame-asses that most morning drive show teams were, with a predilection for bathroom humor, homophobia, women's breasts, and insulting each other's penis size. They were only slightly less offensive than the bozos who handled the afternoon drive slot. She mostly listened for the news and traffic reports which included problems on the bus and subway routes.

"Is there any more news about that naked woman from the Eaton Centre?" asked The Dillweed, Angus's sidekick.

"Yeah, someone this weekend called the station and said they'd seen her at Nathan Philips Square talking to some guy and she had a tit hanging out. This would have been shortly after she allegedly bought a dress at Dundas Square," answered Angus, the host.

"She was flaunting a boob and only one person saw it?"

"Supposedly others were there, but I've only heard that through the grapevine."

"You'd think something like that would draw a crowd."

"Yeah well, it appears the crowd at Nathan Philips had something on their mind other than some skank's naked tit. Did you hear about what happened?"

Alexis smeared on a little brown eye shadow and thought about the report she'd have to work on.

"Did the chick do something else?"

"No, it seems there was this group of older guys, and these hot young things from one of the colleges, and they started getting it on at the fountain!"

"Oh, you're kidding me. You mean like clothes off and everything?"

Alexis paused and looked at the radio. Was this when she was there talking to that Dave guy? She thought she remembered the people they might be talking about, sitting on opposite sides of the pool. Three middle-aged guys who had 'boring married soccer daddies' written all over them, and some attractive younger women.

"Yeah, and they started doing the nasty right there! There were like three guys, although only two took part, and there were these two girls. Supposedly, the girls walked across the pool to the guys—"

"You're not supposed to do that. They don't like people walking in the pool."

"Yeah, well, they frown on public shagging, too, but it was just an all-around chaotic afternoon of lawbreaking, I guess. The witness says everyone started pulling off their clothes and then they started, well, you know!"

"And what about the chick with the tit hanging out?"

"It seems the guy she was talking to left, and by then she had *both* tits hanging out!"

"You *can't* be serious. Both? And the dude just *walked away?"*

He must be a Torontonian, Alexis thought as she applied mascara, then stopped in mid-swipe.

Was it that Dave guy she'd been talking to? He'd seemed really shy and kind of tongue-tied. Of course, he was still upset about his gerbils. Was he the guy this ho was talking to after Alexis herself had left?

"Ran away is more like it," said Angus.

"And he didn't even try to cop a feel? Oh I would have *so* been all over that—"

"Probably a fag-ola," Angus replied. "Can you imagine it? This guy's talking to a half-naked chick, I mean she's got one, then *two* chumbawumbas waving in the breeze, and not only does he not cop a feel, not only does he *not* join in on the action clearly going on in front of him, but he *runs away*. The person who saw this said he looked to be in his thirties with brown hair."

That sounds like Dave, Alexis thought as she finished her mascara and pulled out her powdered blusher. That woman must have shown up right after I left.

And that Dave? He clearly was from Toronto.

✯ ✯ ✯

Lamashtu walked through Yorkville, turning heads wherever she went. She was dressed, but barely. She wore white cotton draw-string pants loosely tied around her hips, perpetually threatening to slip down around her ankles. Her top, if you could call it that, was a thin gauzy white veil that wrapped around her ample breasts, also loosely. In bright light you could see through the fabric and just make out her Hershey's kisses nipples, and it was another cloudless day over Toronto.

The blinding white fabric called attention to her coppery skin, her long sensuous bare midriff with its perfect oval navel. She'd gained some weight in the last few days, and not in a bad way. She no longer sported that just-liberated-from-Dachau look, and her ribs no longer showed. Her calves, if the gawking men on the street could have seen them, had become quite shapely. Her glossy dark hair fell dishevelled over her shoulders and her eyes were covered with an expensive pair of large Ray-Bans. Her full sensuous mouth was smeared with Harlot Scarlet lipstick that would have made anyone other than someone with her skin coloring look like a big skanky whore.

It was amazing what you could do with absolutely no money when you were a stunningly beautiful woman in the rich section of town.

"And you know what else is going on?" asked Angus. "There's a weird hum going on somewhere downtown."

"A weird hum?" echoed The Dillweed. "What kind?"

"No one's sure yet. But lots of people are talking about it. I went down York Street last night and I could hear it. It's weird, kind of low and quiet, and if there's a lot of traffic you can't hear it at all."

Alexis half-listened as she combed her smooth shiny hair. She tried not to be too angry about all the losers from Lavalife who'd blown her off in the last week. What did these dickless idiots want, anyway? She was attractive, she was smart, and she was a lot of fun. There were lots of attractive, smart, fun-looking guys who sometimes dropped her emails, but they invariably stopped emailing her after a couple of times and if she emailed someone first, she almost never heard back from him.

"Where's it coming from?"

"We don't know," said Angus. "I walked around trying to find the source and then I asked a few people, but no one was sure."

"That's really strange. Isn't there supposed to be some kind of weird hum somewhere in the US, like Arizona or Nevada?"

"Yeah, or New Mexico. I think it might be New Mexico because that's where the Roswell flying saucer thing supposedly happened. There's a weird hum in some town there and no one knows where it comes from. Well now we've got the Toronto Hum."

"Is it the hockey song they play at the Maple Leafs games?"

"No, and it's not *O Canada* either."

"Is it *Blame Canada?"*

Rachel dragged herself and her box of silly desk decorations to Love Comes Later, completely unmotivated to do any work. But she knew she'd have to force herself, as she'd been here for more than three months and her savings wouldn't hold out forever. She put on her game face because she didn't want any pushy questions from the owners.

"Good morning!" Amita greeted her. She looked up from a takeout order of *puri bhaji,* a fried flatbread and spiced mashed potatoes dish. At her elbow was *chai* in a recyclable cup.

"G'mawnin, Amita," Rachel smiled back. "Didja have a good weekend?"

Amita's smile fell only slightly, probably not enough for Rachel to notice. That didn't sound good. Rachel's accent was more pronounced. She'd known her long enough now to recognize she sounded more New Yawk when she was upset about something. Amita decided not to ask any questions.

"I had a nice weekend with the family," Amita replied. "We went to visit my husband's brother and his family in Brampton. We had a barbecue in the back yard. How was your weekend?"

"Freakin' ducky," Rachel said, and Amita pretended she believed her.

"We set up your desk over there, and the computer should be working too. My son got you set up on the Internet. Your new email address is on a sticky note."

"Got it," Rachel said, picking it up. "And my phone numbah and extension too, I see."

"Yes. Would you like a *puri?"* Amita held out the plate of flatbread. Maybe some food would cheer her up.

"Oh, no thanks, I ate somethin' awready," Rachel remarked. She sat down and put her hands out as though testing it to see if it was real.

"Is that okay?" asked Amita anxiously. "We can move it if you like. We might have to anyway, depending on what the *feng shui* man says."

"The what?"

"The *feng shui* expert. His name is Chaoxiang Wan. He's coming this morning to make sure our business energies are in alignment."

"Your—your what?" Rachel stared at her.

"*Feng shui.* You mean you've never heard of it? You, who are from New York?"

Rachel shook her head.

"Oh! I thought New Yorkers had *everything,"* Amita smiled. She was dying to know what bothered Rachel, but didn't know her well enough to ask. She also wanted to cheer her up, as both she and Mahliqa had grown fond of her. Especially Mahliqa, who was privately excited by the fact that she now had a Real Live Jewish Friend.

"We may have *feng shui,* but I've nevah heard of it," Rachel said.

"Oh, you'll find out this morning! It's an ancient Chinese science. Mr. Wan is coming down from Newmarket to see our office and tell us how we can arrange it to enhance our business energies, so that Love Comes Later will prosper and succeed. With your help of course, and you'll prosper and succeed with us!" she added.

"Is this like sacred furniture-arranging?"

"Er—well, yes, sort of, I guess. Mr. Wan says if your *feng shui* is in order it can help you achieve your goals."

"Oh. Well. That's—interesting," Rachel commented, and she began removing things from the little box she'd brought. Her desktop decorations from her last office. A few framed pictures, a plaque that read, *If at first you don't succeed, redefine success.* And lastly, her little Yente the Matchmaker doll from *Fiddler on the Roof,* which she placed next to the computer monitor.

"Rachel, would you mind terribly waiting here for Mr. Wan? He'll be here at ten. It's just that Mahliqa is off today, one of her sons is sick, and I have to run out and pick up a few things for a dinner party next weekend. I'm so sorry to ask this—"

"Oh, it's awll right," Rachel remarked with a dismissive wave of her hand. "I have to get my database set up here, and email my clients to let them know where they can reach me, and maybe come up with some flyuhs I can stick undah peoples' windshields—"

She's certainly upset about *something,* Amita thought, bursting with a desire to know. She's becoming more New York than Rosie O'Donnell!

But instead Amita pulled her keys from her purse and stood up. "Thank you so much for helping me out, Rachel. I should be back just before lunch. I was thinking of picking up some *samosas* and a curry, would you like me to bring you some too?"

Rachel thanked her but shook her head. She was too depressed to eat.

Amita left and Rachel was surrounded by blessed quiet. She tried to concentrate on entering her data but all she could think about was Freddy, and how attracted she was to him, and how she had a gut feeling that he was going to call, and soon.

And she heard her mother's voice, over the years, warning her.

"I'm not a prejudiced woman, as you know," she said. *"But don't you dare bring home a* schvartzer!"

I'm forty-one years old, Rachel thought to herself. My first husband was an asshole (but Jewish), and most guys my own age want younger women like Alexis, and I've moved to a city where the men really do seem oblivious to women. And a *mensch* like Freddy comes along, and I'm so lonely I could hang myself with my own Prada belt, and I'm worried about what my *mother* thinks.

"You bring home a schvartzer, *and your father will* plotz *in his grave! And I will join him!"* Ma shrieked in her head. It wasn't like Rachel had ever threatened to bring home a *schvartzer* before. Still, it was clearly something her mother worried about.

"I got it, Ma," Rachel said aloud. "No *schvartzers."*

Lamashtu turned a corner and walked up a different street. She wasn't going anywhere in particular; she was simply exploring her new home and smelling all the lovely food. She loved Toronto; it was her second visit but the first time she'd possessed another and so didn't remember it so well. But there were so many virgins, and that Dave fellow she'd met had been the purest of them all. He had never known the touch of a woman who wasn't his mother or some other relative. As surprising as it was to find someone like that in this day and age, Dave had, she knew, never even been kissed. She had to find him again. She must. He would restore her to full power far more quickly than the others would.

Lamashtu's sustenance was male virgins. Fortunately, they were so easy to score, usually. Men were drawn to her like helpless flies to the honeypot. Except what they found wasn't so sweet.

And she loved, absolutely *adored,* walking down the street and turning the head of every man she passed. They watched her, she could feel it, their eyes on her hips, wondering if the drawstring was going to give way and slide down her thighs. Occasionally, only very occasionally, she turned and looked at one of the men, or stopped to speak to him. More often than not, they backed away, stammering.

She was so beautiful she scared the living snot out of them.

She turned another corner and just managed to stop herself from snarling.

Babies!

Two of them, twins, being pushed in a double stroller by their proud mother. They were pretty little things with shoulder-length honey-brown hair.

As Mama passed with her two prizes, Lamashtu slowly turned to watch, lowering her Ray-Bans and keeping her eyes fixed on the infants.

She narrowed them slightly, and suddenly, both began choking.

The mother screamed and tried to pull them both out of their seats at once, but in her panic, forgot they were both strapped in. A young man stopped to help her as an older man pulled out a cell phone and dialed 911.

Lamashtu turned away and continued walking casually, pretending not to notice. Inside, she was fuming. She hadn't killed either little brat.

Shit, she thought, *I'm still nowhere near my full power. Too bad I couldn't just eat them.*

CHAPTER FIVE

At 10:00 am sharp, a short Chinese man came through the door with a large attention-hungry golden retriever.

"Good morning, I am looking for Amita Lanka," he said. His eyes glanced around the office and rested on Rachel, lingering for a moment before he smiled.

"You must be the *feng shui* guy," Rachel said as she rose from her chair and extended a hand. "I'm Rachel, Amita's and Mahliqa's partner." She smiled and tried not to look too depressed.

"I'm happy to meet you, Rachel. I am Chaoxiang Wan, Chao for short."

And he was short, a good half-head under Rachel. Balding, fortyish, but with a big sincere smile.

"I hope it's okay that I brought Dim Sum here. Perhaps I should have asked."

"Oh, it's all right, I'm not allergic and I'm big-dog friendly." Dim Sum licked her hand with the enthusiasm normally reserved for a human who's just prepared pork chops.

"Amita had to run out this morning," Rachel explained. "Do you want any coffee or tea?"

"No thank you, I'm fine. I took a look around outside and made some notes, now I have to see the inside. Do you need to see my ID? Just so you know I'm not casing the place for a robbery." He smiled, showing his straight teeth, and Rachel laughed. His mild Chinese accent signalled he'd been in Canada for a good many years.

"Naw, it's okay, I trust you," she said. "Do you need me to do anything? I've never dealt with a *feng shui* expert before."

"No, no, I'll only be a few minutes. I'll call Amita later with my recommendations. You sound American, am I correct?"

"Yeah, I can't put anything over on anyone with this accent," Rachel replied with another smile. Chao was certainly lifting her spirits. She needed a few good laughs.

"How long have you been in Toronto?"

"Only a few months. My divorce finally came through, and I'm making a clean break." Might as well just throw that in there, since everyone asked anyway. In the US, people were far more interested in whether she was planning to give up her American citizenship.

"I see. Have you had your home checked out for proper *feng shui*?"

"I can't afford a *feng shui* expert right now," Rachel said. Not to mention the fact that she wasn't at all certain she believed in this Eastern mumbo-jumbo, but it was clear her partners did, and she surely wasn't going to insult this nice man.

"You can't afford *not* to have good *feng shui,"* Chao told her. "If the *qi* energy doesn't flow properly, all your good luck can flow right out the door, and all the bad luck can flow right in."

"I'm still trying to get my business going here," Rachel said. "Maybe in a few months."

"What do you do?"

"I'm a matchmaker. I'll be helping Amita and Mahliqa set people up once they get their heads around an arranged marriage."

"You arrange marriages?" Chao asked, head cocked and looking a little confused. He clearly didn't think Rachel looked the type.

"I don't, I'm a traditional matchmaker. Like Yente here," she said, and she picked up the little doll to show him. "I know, I know, I'm a living cliché. Jewish matchmaker and all that. Amita and Mahliqa counsel the families to get them to accept the idea, and then I work on marrying off the kids." Who weren't always kids, in fact so far *none* of them had been actual kids. Overgrown kids, maybe...

"I see," Chao said, wrinkling his nose in an endearing way. He radiated happiness and warmth. Probably his *feng shui* was perfectly aligned with the planets or something. "Good luck with your new life, Rachel." He watched as she put Yente back by the computer monitor. "I'd better get to work."

☆ ☆ ☆

Dave the Tarantula Guy pulled his eyes away from the computer to watch Pookums. She was acting up again, scrabbling at the side of the aquarium as though desperate to get out. Had she been a wild spider at one time, it might have been understandable, but she'd been born in captivity. She'd always been a placid creature, even when slowly ambling up Dave's arm. Now she was agitated, and she had been since this morning. She'd done this a week ago, too.

"Hey Pookums, what's the matter?" asked Dave, and he lifted the protective screen. He reached in and held his hand palm up. Pookums stopped what she was doing, seemed to consider the offer of human contact, and finally crawled on. Dave slowly lifted her out and held her up to his face, stroking her furry back with his free hand. "I've never seen you act like this. Are you okay? Are you sick?"

Pookums gave him eight hairy eyeballs. She waved her pedipalps - front appendages - as if to say, "What the fuck are you waiting for? Let's get the hell out of here!" But Dave, not being fluent in Arachnidese, just thought his buddy needed a little more attention. It had been several days since he'd let her out, and the last time he'd let Pookums walk around on his desk because it was late at night and no one was likely to come in and freak out. He always had to make sure she was in her aquarium when Dave the Beowulf Freak came by, who was arachnophobic as hell.

"Aw, little fuzzball, have I been neglecting you? I'm sorry, I've been so busy I haven't thought of you at all. See, we're getting in a new set of servers next week and I have to upgrade the Exchange server and you have no idea what a hassle that is. But it's not fair to you, is it? You've gotta be getting bored in there. Hey, I know, why don't I bring you a nice juicy cricket from the pet store tomorrow? I'll stop by and pick one up before I hit the Tim Horton's." He held Pookums up and kissed her, lightly, on the back.

There's a reason why Dave was single at forty-seven.

Meanwhile, at the Gillpatrick residence, Dave the Virgin's remaining gerbils were flaking out too, trying to make a mad desperate break from their Habitrail prison. He looked up from his computer to find all eight of them jumping at the plastic sides and running down the tunnels like they thought they just might find an exit ramp if they looked closely enough.

Dave got up from the computer, walked to the Habitrail and peered inside. The gerbils began squeaking and leaping like mad.

They'd acted like this just before the earthquake, too. Although at that time there'd been forty-eight miniature furry weather prognosticators.

Lamashtu turned down Cumberland Street, her bronze hips swinging and swaying like the Girl from Ipanema, except she was a lot less innocent-looking. The loose pants dangled around her hips and men turned to stare, and women to glare, but she pretended not to notice. She also pretended not to notice the newspaper dispenser with the headline in the *Globe & Mail* that read, "Second Dessicated Body Found Near Leslie Spit."

A beautiful woman passed by and Lamashtu's head snapped around. It wasn't often she felt anger at another woman because most couldn't hold a candle to herself. But this one was striking. Beautiful dark hair and brilliant violet eyes. Perfect skin. A cupid's-bow mouth. Men's eyes watched her as she walked down the street, but like

Lamashtu, she appeared not to notice. Was that her game too?

Bitch. Still, Lamashtu could afford to ignore her. What was one other beautiful woman in a city of four million?

Lamashtu was looking for *him,* the Pure One. But she could afford to be patient. She was surrounded by food. Just—less powerful food than *he.*

Across the street, a mother held her toddler's hand as they headed for the street corner. Lamashtu burned with the old familiar anger and hatred and lowered her Ray-Bans. Narrowing her eyes, she stared hard at the child.

The toddler cried out and her heart exulted. He began to choke and his mother swept him up in her arms, pounding him on the back and screaming.

Damn. It was all she could do for now. But one day, eventually. Things would change. When she found the Pure One she'd mount him and get her full strength back and she would kill every last little snot-nosed brat in this entire city. She had destroyed whole villages, once. Cast the fruit of a woman's womb upon the ground. Back when the world was a little bit younger and Adam still loved her, before her meddling mother split them up.

Lamashtu burned with hatred, as equally for her mother as for the children of the world who still lived.

"I'm finished, Rachel."

Chao stood in front of her desk, a notebook in one hand and a pen in the other. Dim Sum, who'd settled down comfortably near Rachel, having decided she was his second-favorite human in the whole wide world (no one would ever replace his master as his favorite, but any human who showed interest in him was always his current Close Second Favorite) jumped up to greet Chao as though they'd been separated since the Han Dynasty.

She looked up from her documents and peered at him through her reading glasses. "Uh, okay," she replied. "What do you want me to tell the ladies?"

"Just tell Amita I'll call her in a few days with my recommendations. She's okay for now but she'll need to make a few changes. She has poison arrows outside the building and her *qi* is all bollixed up near the entrance. That's not good, but I can fix it. The Southwest corner needs work, and they'll need some running water in the north corner."

"Of course," said Rachel, as though she had the slightest clue what he was talking about. "Water in the north, got it."

"Now tell her, and this is important, that her *kua* number is four and Mrs. Fakhoury's is 1. I'll get into the colors and appropriate directions when I call her. Can you remember that?"

4 = Amita 1 = Mahliqa Rachel wrote on a sticky note. Then she added, *kooa #.*

"I think that's all for now," Chao finished. "I know Amita's anxious to make sure everything is in order. She told me yesterday she'd consulted her astrologer to plan the next few months. If she needs me to cast the *I Ching* I can do that for an extra fee."

E Ching extra, Rachel dutifully added under the *kua* numbers.

"It was so good to meet you, Rachel, I hope we'll meet again," said Chao, and he extended his hand. Rachel took it, and he covered hers with his other hand, pumping it warmly. "You're an extraordinary woman, I could tell as much when I first saw you."

"Thank you, Chao, it was good to meet you too," she said.

"Does Amita have an email address?"

"I think she does, but she doesn't know how to use email, if you can believe that today! I may have to show her how to use it. You want to email me for now and I'll pass it along?"

"That would be wonderful." Chao handed his notebook and pen to Rachel, and she scrawled her address for him. "Thank you. You'll hear from me in a few days. I'll attach my report." He turned to leave.

"Oh, and one other thing, Rachel," he said as an afterthought. She looked up and took off her glasses. "The little doll on your desk is all alone, that is not good *feng shui.* Not for a woman who I think wants to find her proper match once again. You should have a male figure too. Single women should always group things in twos, especially statues, and always male and female."

Rachel managed a half-smile. "Thanks, Chao, I'll remember that." She turned back to her documents.

She waited until he and his canine dumpling left before she rolled her eyes and shook her head.

☆ ☆ ☆

It had been a long day. Rachel had fielded a phone call from a client who was, shall we say, a tad put off by the grilling he'd gotten from Alexis on their first date.

"It was more like an interrogation," he said.

"I'm sorry it didn't go so well," Rachel replied with a sinking heart. Not an auspicious first attempt in her new city. "Maybe I could talk to her."

"I don't want to talk to *her* again. She was more interested in how much I make and what my career ambitions were than in myself. I know that's important to women but she didn't have to be so blatant about it."

"I'm really sorry. Okay, I'll keep you in mind. I'm still building my client list, as soon as I find someone else for you I'll let you know."

Then she drove to a meeting with a client at a restaurant only to find, when she came out again, the trees covered in toilet paper, and her car as well. Not only had the miscreants performed this childish act of vandalism in broad daylight, but according to one of the shopkeepers who saw them, none of the suspects were under forty.

"What the hell is getting into everyone these days?" the woman fumed. "We've got people shagging on the benches at the Square, others are hallucinating naked women emerging from fountains, and now so-called grownups are acting like teenagers! I tell you, ma'am, this whole city is going to hell."

And just to keep things irritating, Rachel fielded a call from her mother.

"Hello Rachel dear. This is your mother. Just to refresh your memory, I'm the woman who gave birth to you forty-one years ago."

"Ma, it's only been three days since we last spoke."

"It's all right, I understand, you've got your happy new life in Toronto far away from your gray-haired old mother who's more of a pain in the *tuchis* to you than a chronic hemorrhoid, but it's all right, I don't mind being alone, I've had to get used to it since your father died —"

"So how's New York?" Rachel asked, since this usually veered off into when she was going to get remarried and give her *mamelah* some grandchildren.

"*Oy,* it's been horrible. So hot I think my clothes will melt off my body. And the air conditioning is on the fritz again."

"Have you called the repairman?"

"I did, but the useless *schmendrick* says he can't come out here for two weeks. Two weeks! I'm an old lady *schvitzing* up a storm who could die before then, like those old people in France a few years ago—"

"You're sixty-three, Ma. When Nana was your age she was dating a concert pianist."

"*Oy,* don't remind me about that bum! Such shame my mother brought to the family. And he was a *goyim* too."

Rachel thought bitterly of having to turn down Freddy when he'd called. Heaven forbid she should bring home a *goyim,* or worse yet a *schvartzer.* Six million Jews died in Germany, young lady, and it's our duty to replenish the tribe!

"And *Oy Gevalt,* things are even worse here. You won't believe who moved in next door."

"Who?"

Ma's voice dropped to a whisper. *"Muslims!"*

"Muslims?"

"Shhhhh!"

"Ma, I'm in *Toronto."*

"I know, I know, but those people, they hear *everything.* They're watching me. They know I'm Jewish."

"How do they know that?"

"Their spies are everywhere."

"Ma—when did they move in?"

"This morning."

"They moved in this morning, and they've already discovered you're Jewish? Ma, you don't even *look* Jewish. Unless you were dancing the *Havah Nagilah* on the front porch with your prayer shawl and your *teffilin* attached to your forehead, they're not gonna know."

"Oh, they're awful. You should see them. The father was wearing that long white robe with that little matching hat, and the mother is in one of those *burqa* things, and the little boy looks like he just got out of terrorist school—"

"Ma! Now cut it out. They're not all terrorists. And Muslims have had a tough time in New York since 9/11."

"Now you know I'm not a prejudiced woman, Rachel—"

Rachel rolled her eyes.

"—But these people are *awful.* They're dirty, they're loud, and I tell you, that kid is going to a *madrassa!"*

"Is it in Brooklyn or Jersey?" Rachel asked.

"Now don't you be smart with me, young lady! Right here in New York. There's that temple of theirs down the street—"

"Muslims don't have temples, Ma. That's us, remember? We're Jews."

"I should just hang up on you, you ungrateful wretch of a daughter."

I wish, Rachel thought.

☆ ☆ ☆

"Dude, there's something weird going on at Nathan Philips Square."

"Yeah, the fountain seems to have been damaged a little by the earthquake. People are saying there's something bubbling up from underground."

Alexis only half-listened to the radio while nibbling a whole wheat bagel smeared with fat-free cream cheese and reading the newspaper.

"Think it's poison? Or chemicals?" asked The Dillweed.

"I don't know, but the City is investigating," said Angus. "I talked to a government official there yesterday and he said they're going to explore it today. They've put a fence around the pool and signs warning people not to touch the water."

"I don't think people are supposed to do that anyway."

"Yah, like that ever stopped them. It's weird, though. There's a rumour that it makes you horny."

"Horny? That's not what I heard. Some lady I met there yesterday said it makes you look and feel younger."

"Looking at the fountain?"

"No, putting your feet in it. She said she brought her husband down because he's like 77 and hasn't been able to do it to her in like fifteen years, and the two of them put their feet in the water and hung out for awhile, and she swears they both got younger. Then he dragged her home and, well, I guess he did her. She said it was awesome."

"She said it made them both look younger?"

"Yeah, she said she threw away her anti-aging creams."

"So it makes you horny *and* look younger—"

The phone rang, and Alexis dragged her eyes away from a story about a weird hum near the lake to answer it.

"Hello, Alexis? This is Rachel. I'm not catching you at a bad time, am I?"

"No, I was just having a snack. What's up? Did you talk to Gene? Does he like me?"

"Well—er—he, uh—didn't think you two were right for each other."

Alexis dropped her bagel and wheeled around. "What does he mean by that?" she cried. "He's *perfect* for me. He makes a good living, he's got a clear career path at the law firm, and he likes Canadian art movies, just like I do. He says he wants a smart and ambitious woman. I mean, how is that not me?"

"He—says he felt a little—I think the word he used was *interrogated* by you. He says he felt like he was at a job interview."

"That's so not true! I laughed and smiled at his jokes and stuff."

"I think—maybe in the future—you might want to not try to find out everything all at once."

"But how else am I going to know if I'm wasting my time or not? I don't want to be with some loser who still lives with his parents and doesn't know what he wants to do with his life. I've been through enough of *those.* And I don't want someone who doesn't earn at least as much money as I do. A marriage is a partnership. Now, I don't expect a man to support *me,* so I expect the same of him."

"Maybe you need to give the man a little more time to get to know you."

"Rachel, I haven't *got* time. I'm 31 years old and I want to have a baby before it's too late—"

"You're still plenty young enough to have a child."

"Egg quality starts decreasing after thirty. I've done the research. By the time I'm 35 my egg quality will have dropped by more than ten percent. By forty it'll have dropped by a third. I need a husband, and fast."

"Alexis—I sympathize with you, I really do. But there are some things that can't be rushed. Men can sense desperation."

"He's got to have a good job, Rachel. Too many of the bozos in this town can't even support themselves. Gene was perfect."

Gene was adequate, Rachel thought. She knew he was what Alexis was looking for, although she hadn't been at all certain about the reverse. She'd hoped maybe Alexis would open up, act a bit warmer with him.

"He liked *Canadian movies,"* Alexis added, almost sullenly. "Just like I do. Do you know how many men would prefer to see some lame comic book movie or stupid action hero flick from the States? How many men actually understand the subtle humour of *C.R.A.Z.Y.* or cried during *Séraphin?"*

"A good match has less to do with common interests than you might think," Rachel replied. "What about qualities like loyalty, trustworthiness and reliability? How about shared values, a similar background? Gene was from a working-class family, Alexis. He's from Oshawa. He went to university on a scholarship. How would you have felt the first time you met his family?"

"I'm not a snob. I would have accepted them."

Somehow, Rachel didn't think the always put-together Alexis with her expensive suits and severe eyeglasses would handle a prospective father-in-law who'd worked the factory line at the GM plant.

"There are other men I know who I think would be a good match for you except they don't earn as much money as you."

"Then I'm not interested in meeting them, Rachel. It costs a lot of money to raise a baby."

"All right, I'll see what I can do."

Alexis hung up and gritted her teeth. Her face grew warm and she trembled. Another great guy who just couldn't handle being with a strong and confident woman. Wusses, every last one of them.

"—So the weird hum seems to be coming from the Bank of America building on Front Street," Angus was telling The Dillweed.

Her heart hardened a little. This reminded her of Dave, the guy from the speed dating event who'd said he'd call her after the first date and then didn't.

"It's hard to hear, but if you stand right in front of it you can hear it loud and clear."

What she had never told Rachel was that her eggs weren't just getting older, but she had also been diagnosed a few years earlier with mild endometriosis. While Alexis probably wasn't infertile, she couldn't know how difficult it might be to get pregnant. She didn't want anyone to know, least of all a prospective husband, who might not marry her if he thought she wasn't perfect.

"How about inside the building?"

"I tried going in. It totally disappears in the reception area."

Did I really dig him or does it just seem like I've been kicked back to the starting line yet again? she thought to herself, and she slammed her hand down on the table, rattling the dishes and knocking the remnants of the bagel onto the floor. Gene was, after all, ten years older and slightly paunchy.

"Did you talk to anyone in the building?"

"Yeah, I asked the security guard and he says he can't hear a thing."

"What is he, retarded or something?"

My baby might be retarded if I have to wait much longer.

"I don't know. Maybe."

I hate dating. I can't even remember what it's supposed to be like anymore. I used to have fun. When am I going to meet my soulmate? When am I going to have a baby? I'D MAKE A WONDERFUL MOTHER!

Alexis sat down and looked at the paper. A small story at the bottom said more than ten babies had been admitted to local hospitals, all of them having suffered sudden choking attacks. Three of them almost died. Health officials were beginning to fear another mysterious SARS-style crisis.

"So basically, the Bank of America is giving Toronto a hummer?"

"SHUT THE FUCK UP!" she yelled at the radio, and she threw it across the room.

CHAPTER SIX

"Look at this, Rachel." A newspaper dropped in front of her on the desk. "Something terrible is happening in Toronto."

She looked up. Amita's smooth face was knit with concern. She adjusted her *palloo* and tapped a long brown finger in the center of the paper. Her gold bangle bracelets jangled to emphasize the point.

"Babies are dying here. A bank building is humming. People who touch the water at City Hall are acting crazy, making love, vandalizing, clubbing in the Entertainment District with the kids. There's a rumor that a dog was splashing around in the pool for awhile and came out a puppy!"

"I haven't followed the news much since I got here," Rachel explained. Especially not last week when she opened up the *Toronto Star* and saw an article about Austin's foolishness at the airport. She was glad she'd gone back to her maiden name after the divorce.

Dirty muslin. What the hell had ever possessed her to marry such a semi-sentient ape? Why was she such a slave to hard muscles and an attitude that made the Terminator look like a mincing pouf?

"It started after the earthquake. I think it's responsible."

Rachel scrutinized her. "You think the earthquake is making people act weird?"

"Yes. It all started after that. You can't deny it."

"Well—I dunno, Amita, maybe there's another explanation."

"Like what?"

"Well—uh, why do you think all these things are related, anyway?"

"Because it's craziness! These things don't happen, a building humming and no one knows why, or people acting like children!"

"You've obviously never met my ex-husband," Rachel mumbled.

"And what about these babies? This is horrible! This is tragic! All of a sudden, all over the city, little babies are suddenly choking and nearly dying! And now pregnant women are miscarrying or giving birth prematurely. No one knows why. I think an evil spirit was released with that earthquake."

"I dunno, Amita. That could be anything, y'know. MRSA, the new superbug, or that *c. difficile* bacteria in the Quebec hospitals."

"Those are infections. That's not what's nearly killing babies and causing women to abort."

Rachel wasn't sure what to say. She had never had much of an interest in mysticism or supernaturalism. She was a good Jew from western Long Island who used to go to temple regularly and celebrate the holidays, at least until her divorce when she became too depressed to do anything for awhile. Austin had never gone with her, he was Jewish by maternal blood only. He was otherwise a big dumb French Texan who seemed like he'd always make her feel safe when they got married, at least until he got a job with the newly-established Transportation Security Administration. Then, there came a day when Rachel knew she'd have to get the hell out of there before his newfound Nazi persona turned violent.

Mahliqa arrived, looking grim. "Good morning, Amita, Rachel. Do we have any tea left?"

Amita nodded, pointing at the cabinet above the sink. "In there. Mahliqa, my friend, what's wrong?" Mahliqa drank tea to relieve stress the way Canadians reached for alcohol.

"There's a crime scene set up down on Jiminez Road," she replied. "I just walked by it. There's yellow tape surrounding it, and—and—" Her hand shook as she reached for the tea canister. She knocked it over, and it fell with a bang on the sink.

She turned to Amita and Rachel. "They've found another body, just like the other ones."

Amita raised a hand to her mouth. "Dried up?"

Mahliqa nodded. Tears pooled in her huge brown eyes. "They had a body bag, Amita! I didn't see the—the—victim, they had a sheet covering him but—I heard the police talking, he wasn't very old, and they say he was like the others. His trousers were down around his legs and—between his legs—" She looked away.

Both Amita and Rachel waited, mutely. Knowing what was coming.

"Red, swollen and bumpy."

"On the—" Amita didn't finish.

Mahliqa nodded.

✯ ✯ ✯

"Mom, I don't even know if I *want* to get married again."

Mrs. Urquhart studied her son's face. "Sweetheart, are you happy with the way things are?"

Dave the Tarantula Guy fell silent. He thought of the lame speed-dating event he and Dave the Beowulf Freak had gone to. Lots of beautiful women, and few of them were interested in a balding middle-aged guy. He made a decent living, but he wasn't rich. These young, lithe girls wanted money.

His father twirled spaghetti around his fork. He hadn't expected his wife to bring this up on the boy's birthday. This was a nice restaurant, and he'd hoped to loosen him up with a few more drinks and perhaps a nice *crême brulée* (Dave's favorite) before they brought up this sticky subject.

"We don't want to force you into anything, sweetheart. This wouldn't be an arranged marriage, you know. This is more like—a family dating service. The Love Comes Later owners have a partner now, a matchmaker. She's got years of experience finding good matches for couples and she will help you after you speak to the owners again."

"She's not going to set me up with a dog, is she?" Dave asked.

His mother opened her mouth, shut it, gulped and then glanced at her husband. He touched her arm as though to calm her.

"Maybe you should think about factors other than what she looks like."

"She's gonna set me up with a dog, isn't she," he replied, like a petulant child.

"No one says she'll be unattractive. But who knows, maybe the love of your life isn't really beautiful. Diana was lovely but she wasn't very faithful, was she?"

Mrs. Urquhart thought privately that Dave probably couldn't attract anyone like that anymore anyway. As much as she loved her son, she could see he was getting grayer, wasn't as fit as he used to be, and sported a mustache that made him look older than he was.

"Son, we just want you to be happy," his father said gently. Dave looked at him, bald and wrinkled and hands covered with brown age spots. His dark eyes, though, were kind and radiated his love for his only child. "If you don't want to remarry you just say so and your mother and I will leave you alone. But if you do, we want to help you this time."

"If you'll let us," his mother said, and Dave, at forty-seven, began to cry.

☆ ☆ ☆

Lamashtu paused on the street corner. She wore a colorful skirt she'd picked up in the fashion district that clung tightly to her hips and broke at mid-knee. She sported expensive Mahnolo Blahnik stillettos that further showed off her long curvy legs. For a top, she'd improvised again with a long pink and purple silk scarf. She'd placed the center of it on the back of her neck and had crossed the lengths over each breast, then tied it in the back. It was too small for her large breasts, which strained mightily against the thin fabric.

It had gotten her another virgin, and she'd left his lifeless corpse on a side street near Yonge & Bloor. This one had had some money in his wallet.

When she'd finished, his eyes were glassy and dead but his face was frozen in horror and pain. She threw him behind a dumpster in an alley and pulled her skirt on, tall and strong and feeling his life-giving energy pulsing through her. She felt so good, so powerful, and she zapped a five-year-old down the street but, to her chagrin, he fell down choking like the others and didn't snuff it on the spot. Damn, the rush felt strong but her powers were still weak.

Dave. She had to find that delightful virgin she'd spoken to by the fountain a few weeks ago. So fresh and untainted. So desirous of curvy young women in the pictures she sensed he drew. He was too frightened of her that afternoon but she knew if she met him again she could gain his trust.

She sniffed the air, turning around slowly, her eyes closed, her mind and spirit opening to the city. Dave was here somewhere, and she would find him.

Her nipples stiffened against the silk and drew stares from every man she passed. She could sense they were on tenterhooks, waiting to see if the scarf would shift and expose one of her bountiful charms.

She smiled slowly as she sashayed down the street. She smelled Dave.

To: rbrinkerhoff@lovecomeslater.ca
From: chao-wan@yahoo.ca
Subject: Feng shui report

Dear Rachel,

I have attached my report on the feng shui for Love Comes Later. Please forward it to Ms. Amita and her lovely friend. I included a few suggestions for you even though I can tell you don't believe in feng shui. But that's okay, maybe Ms. Amita can make you see reason. I promise if you pay more attention to the qi flow around you, you will be a happier person who will achieve everything she wants in life.

I enjoyed talking with you the other day. I hope to see you again soon. As we say on the Chinese New Year, "May whatever your heart desires become true."

Your friend,

Chao Wan

Feng Shui Expert & Certified Acupuncturist

Me...a skeptic? I trust you can prove that.

>>>Download Tagline Express 4.1a here at......

To: chao-wan@yahoo.ca
From: rbrink@lovecomeslater.ca
Subject: Feng shui report

Hi Chao,

I printed out your report for both ladies. They thank you very much and Amita will call you later to settle the bill. She seemed very excited overall and she wants to come to Chinatown soon to find a few of the decorations you suggested to fix the flow.

By the way I liked your tagline. I used to have a tagline generator for my business e-mails when I was still in New York but I just haven't gotten around to setting it up yet for my new e-mail account. I used to have a tagline that said, "Do dyslexic insomniac atheists ever lie awake at night and wonder if there is a Dog?"

Have a great day,

Rachel Brinkerhoff

To: rbrinkerhoff@lovecomeslater.ca
From: chao-wan@yahoo.ca
Subject: There are no atheists in dog pound

Dear Rachel,

Some say there is no Dog but I say the proof is there if you look around you. If there are no atheists in foxholes, there are surely no dog deniers in dog pounds, when they stumble upon the evidence and must scrape it off their shoe.

Your friend,

Chao Wan

Feng Shui Expert & Certified Acupuncturist

Dead Atheist: All dressed up and no place to go

>>>Download Tagline Express 4.1a here at......

To: chao-wan@yahoo.ca
From: rbrinkerhoff@lovecomeslater.ca
Subject: There are no atheists in dog pounds

Hi Chao,

Ah, The Blind Dogcatcher's Hypothesis as described by the famous scientist Richard Dawgkins. However he claimed to have destroyed it with the argument that the presence of dog poop does not necessarily imply creation by a gluttonous Dog - that in the random, chaotic universe, sometimes Poop Happens.

Via the Big Fang, of course.

Have a rational, poop-free weekend yourself. Me, I'm going to go chase a car. ;)

Sincerely,

Rachel

Dave the Virgin's heart skipped a beat as he boarded the streetcar. He'd avoided the subway since the embarrassing Gerbil Incident. Rachel, the beautiful matchmaker who apparently now worked at Love Comes Later, had contacted him to see if he was interested in becoming one of her potential matches. He was about to warn her he lived with his parents and didn't have a real job in case the Arab lady hadn't, but decided he wanted to see her again even if he knew he didn't have a doughnut's chance in Homer Simpson's office with her. As beautiful women went, she made him a lot less nervous than that crazy boob chick at the Square.

"Hi, Alexis?"

"Speaking."

"This is Rachel Brinkerhoff. Have you got a moment? I wanted to bounce an idea off you."

"Sure, Rachel. What's up? Have you found me another match? Hopefully this one will have more brains than the last one."

"Not yet, but I had an idea. Something that might help you. I've been looking over the reports of the two guys I've set you up with, and the relationship history you gave me when we first met for coffee. I think I see a pattern here."

"What sort of pattern?"

Rachel paused. This was the extremely delicate point. Alexis was so tightly-wound, especially about men, that she was afraid of setting off an explosion if this wasn't handled just right. However, Rachel didn't see any chance of success if the girl refused any help.

"You've got a pretty good idea of what you're looking for in a man. However I wonder if you're perhaps limiting yourself too much. You want someone who's reasonably nice-looking, makes at least as much money as you, and shares your interest in wine-tasting and bike-riding. You also stated in your essay that you wanted someone who was your 'soul mate.' I already told you I think that's vague and perhaps a little unrealistic. No one really knows what a 'soul mate' is and personally, I think it was invented by women for women, to fake ourselves into thinking there's 'one perfect man' for us."

Rachel held her breath.

"Well—" Alexis paused. For only a few seconds, but Rachel felt as though they were hours. "I told you I read *Your Soul Mate Seeks You Too*. It says when you find 'the one' your whole body tingles and your soul just resonates for this person."

Rachel managed not to heave an initial sigh of relief. So far, so good. Too many women bought into the whole soul mate bullshit and reacted strongly to anything that challenged that view. Alexis had bought it too but she seemed open to gentle challenge.

"I know," Rachel said, "and I read it too. I read a lot of the popular literature as part of my job. I've just seen so many people get together who didn't initially fall madly in love with each other, who didn't know the moment they laid eyes on the other that this was 'the one', and who discovered a certain chemistry that was based in something other than looks. And honestly, men never mention 'soul mate' to me when I'm interviewing them."

Rachel held her breath again.

"Well—-" Alexis paused. "You know how important it is to have 'chemistry' with someone. Unattractive men simply aren't going to interest me. He doesn't have to look like George Clooney. I think I'm probably less motivated by looks than a lot of women."

Yeah, thought Rachel, *every woman thinks that.*

"But he does have to share my interests. I hate going to wine-tastings alone. I did it to meet men but too many of them at these events are married or in relationships. And I do like learning about new wines."

"I know how you feel, Alexis," Rachel said, and she thought of how hot Austin looked to her the first time she saw him - large, powerful, bulging muscles, and enough hair that he wasn't yet combing it over. And that big, confident grin of his - she just melted in her Louboutins. She wanted to tear his clothes off right there, and when she found out he was Jewish she knew she would marry him. It didn't matter that he never went to temple and didn't observe any of the holidays and even ate pork and bacon. She fell in love with him and so did her mother, although her father's reaction had been slightly more subdued. Looking back, Rachel thought he was probably more clued in about Austin.

Good call, Dad, she thought. She wondered if she would have listened if he'd raised any objections.

"I just think that chemistry sometimes comes later. See, I've been talking to Amita and Mahliqa and we've been exchanging ideas on relationships and marriage and what makes for a good match. They advise parents on how to handle helping their children find the right person for them—"

"You can't *possibly* suggest I let my parents arrange a marriage for me?" Alexis asked, horrified. She knew all about Love Comes Later, she'd read the recent article in the *Globe & Mail* on them, which included their partnership with Rachel.

"No no no, of course not. We're Americans—er, North Americans—and we don't come from a culture of arranged marriage. What they're trying to do is bring the principles behind arranged marriages to Canadian relationships."

"Yeah, like marrying off women my age to guys twenty or thirty years older?" Alexis snorted.

Oh shit, Rachel thought, she's getting mad.

"That's not an arranged marriage. That's a forced marriage."

"My parents would pick someone totally inappropriate for me. Someone who's boring and conservative who looks and acts like Wally Cleaver."

"I don't want to involve your parents. I just think it might help if you booked an appointment with one of these ladies - or maybe both, if they're in the office that day - and get some of their opinions on what to look for in a man. I have to admit, I'm learning a few things from them myself about what people should focus on. I've always known that family is important, because an awful lot of problems and divorces have come from difficult family members and in-laws. But they talk about the importance of getting to know the family much more thoroughly than most people do. And to consider whether someone with a quirky personality is going to be a real problem for you."

Rachel held her breath again. Was Alexis going to explode at the subtle suggestion that she really didn't know what the hell she wanted, of which she accused most of the men she went out with? Rachel privately thought it would be a *wonderful* idea if Alexis let her parents help her out, like that spider fellow's family Mahliqa and Amita were working with now, but she knew the girl would never go for it.

"You know, one thing I can't stand - and I never thought of it until now - is men who let their mothers rule their lives," Alexis finally replied. "There are so many guys who will never stand up to their mothers, even when they're married and should be sticking by their wives. Like Charlotte's first husband in *Sex In The City*."

"Yeah. You see? That's something I never would have thought of either," Rachel said, quite relieved that Alexis hadn't blown up at her. "Here's another thing: Amita and Mahliqa said sharing interests and hobbies weren't as important as many people think. So, like, if your guy didn't like wine-tasting, couldn't you just accept that and go with a friend?"

"I'd prefer to go with my husband," Alexis said. She thought of all the times she felt like an aging idiot, surrounded by couples when she, the pathetic single girl who could never hold on to a man, was standing there waiting for the next moron to approach her with the Universal Pickup Script.

"What do you really want though, Lex? A man who'll go to a wine-tasting with you, or a man who will be there when you get home and snuggle with you in bed? Who has a mother who's easy to get along with and who thinks you're the most special girl he's ever met?"

Alexis thought about it.

"It's not like everyone at the wine-tasting's not gonna know you're married," Rachel continued. "Because you're gonna have a giant rock on your hand!"

But when Rachel hung up the phone she felt a little of Alexis' anger. Because the truth was, she was getting a bit impatient herself. After finally settling in in Toronto, when was she going to meet *her* soul mate?

Not that, like, you know, Rachel bought into any of that soul mate stuff.

Alexis was right, Rachel thought as she drove to Love Comes Later. Toronto guys really did show very little interest in women.

The only Canadian-born male clients she had were from Quebec.

The rest were from other countries. Lots of her female clients were Canadian, but the men here—she shook her head. Not only did they send out no signals - they didn't respond to them either.

At least no one else was into pet spiders like her latest acquisition from Amita and Mahliqa. Where did they find these guys?

The night before Rachel stood in a long line at Tim Horton's to get a coffee and chocolate danish to go. She started chatting with the man behind her who seemed very nice and friendly who said he was from Oakville. Rachel liked him - he was large and masculine but didn't possess Austin's cocky arrogance - and she tried flirting with him a little, although it was kind of hard as she found the energy in Toronto seemed to discourage it. But she smiled and stroked her hair oh-so-casually a few times and looked him in the eyes a lot because she knew that, despite the crow's feet, her unusual violet eyes commanded the most attention. He smiled back and seemed friendly enough but he didn't ask for her phone number or suggest they get a table together. So she bought her coffee and danish and lingered at the napkin counter, hoping he might catch up with her, but he walked out the door with his own purchases.

Julia Roberts couldn't get laid in this town, Rachel thought to herself.

If it hadn't been for the earthquake, which had opened up a whole chthonic can o' worms for sedate, polite, conservative Toronto, the newly-unveiled Royal Ontario Museum Michael Lee Chin Crystal would never have activated. Or 'Cristal Michael Lee Chin Crystal' as it says on the sort of *2001: A Space Odyssey* monolith-shaped sign out front. This conforms to the bilingual needs of a neighboring province that still isn't completely cool with being part of a country that has the audacity to ask for *snails* rather than *les escargots* and who don't sort of sing when they answer a business phone (*"Booooon-jooooür! Comment mai-je vous aideeeer? 'Allooooo! 'Ow may I 'elp yoooouu?"*)

See, the ROM Crystal was lauded as a brilliant piece of unique and original architecture destined to pull in the tourists by the buttloads, and derided as a truly godawful monstrosity which was going to make the whole damn city the architectural laughingstock of the rest of the world, particularly with those damn Americans who were so goddamn superior and thought everything Canadians did was cute and quaint and totally irrelevant.

What neither Mr. Chin nor the architect realized, the whole time they were designing this brilliant and gawdawful monument to exceptional aesthetics and consummate disaster, was that it just happened to conform to the exact dimensions and shape of a huge crystal-shaped central government building and temple that had once formed the hub of the legendary lost continent of Atlantis (technically it was more of an average-sized island than a continent, but ancient writers were as prone to gross exaggeration as they are today). It had been originally designed with the aid of super-enlightened beings from the farthest reaches of the Pleiades who'd once drunkenly crashed their flying saucer between two ancient cities in the Middle East after a particularly alcohol-drenched keg party on Mars. (Yeah, everyone knows there's no intelligent life on Mars and never has been. That's why they went there. Also, their parents didn't know about it. Never mind that there isn't enough oxygen to support most carbon-based life forms and that it would be too cold. Don't assume everyone is built and designed just like you, you small-minded petty carbon-based-biased bass-ackwards rube. Geez, like don't be so friggin' provincial. Get out of your bloody backwater and go visit another planet once in awhile, why don'cha!)

Anyway, there was this huge gigantic explosion and this really impressive fireball which totally hosed everyone living in the two cities except for this one family who'd left town in a big hurry and who didn't see it except the wife who watched the whole thing. The biology of the intergalactic drunk drivers was such that temperatures approximating a nuclear explosion caused nothing more than the sort of ouchie a human being would experience when spilling a cup of coffee on herself (although the aliens were too sophisticated—and hammered—to sue anyone over it). The bottom line was they were kind of stuck here on this crappy little planet located in the part of a galaxy which they jokingly referred to as The Sticks back home, and so they eventually wandered around and finally found some life-forms here, although they weren't too intelligent and hadn't gotten too far in their evolution and hadn't even invented quantum teleportation or anal exploration yet.

These dolts, glorified apes, really, I mean they were *barely* down from the trees, were clearly too stupid to invent or build anything decent on their own so the aliens stuck around and showed them how to invent and build everything decent. The dolts lived on this cool island with lots of fruit trees and environment-friendly vegetable gardens and crystal-clear springs and fairies and unicorns and everyone was really good-looking and white and had smooth shiny wavy hair and were totally into personal hygiene, so the aliens gave the babelicious dolts the blueprints for this really neat crystal building thingy. This would like enlighten everyone and give them amazing psychic powers and levitate and move objects with their minds and stuff, which became immensely useful when they began building the Atlantean Superconducting Supercollider. Except that someone fucked up something somewhere and when they switched on the Supercollider to try to identify the Twelve Olympian particles, it created a perfect synergy of mystical chthonic energy combustion, and the whole damn Crystal exploded, destroying the entire island and everyone on it.

Fortunately for Toronto, there was nothing resembling a Superconducting Supercollider anywhere nearby, not even in Texas where they tried to build one once but which was killed by Congress due to its massive cost overruns. So while the New Atlantean Crystal, now disguised as the Michael Lee Chin Crystal, posed no level of utter destructive danger to the city, its mystical chthonic design had however unleashed yet another portal from the underworld (what, you thought this ROM thing was the only one? Like the weird shit happening in Nathan Philips Square and the shopping mall fountain weren't your first clues?) mostly thanks to the copious quantities of ley line energy it just sucked out of the ground like a giant metaphysical Hoover.

It was going to make the good people of Toronto very sorry, but not nearly as sorry as the ex-inhabitants of Atlantis or of Sodom and Gomorrah.

CHAPTER SEVEN

It was getting harder and harder to get up every morning.

Rachel was tired all the time. Every night she wished she could just go home, heat up a quick TV dinner and go to bed but there was always something to do. Grocery shopping, laundry, new client interviews, social functions at which she hoped to meet new clients for interviews - even when she got to bed by nine or ten she still woke up beastly tired in the morning. She'd begun to think this whole bloody exercise was pointless - this life thing she'd gotten stuck in the middle of at forty-one. Moving to Toronto hadn't been as much fun as she'd thought it would be and she wondered if she could have somehow identified before she moved here that the men weren't much interested in women. But who would have ever thought *that?*

She dragged herself to Love Comes Later and forced herself to sit at her desk and work. The bills weren't going to pay themselves. Amita was already there and she frowned slightly when Rachel said, "Good mawwwwnin', Amita." If Rachel hadn't been so oblivious to everything around her she would have noticed Amita watching her with slightly knit eyebrows.

What Amita knew - and Mahliqa, by extension, who wasn't nearly as observant but was just as good at listening to gossip as anyone - was that Rachel had slipped into depression.

Rachel didn't know it because she could be remarkably un-self-aware. She'd tried to keep a stiff upper lip as the British say after her divorce, and in truth, once Austin Eustache and his bordering-on-sadistic emotional abuse was out of her life, it had looked a little brighter. She wanted to get out of New York, where the men were all soulless money-grubbing Wall Street machines and the women were high maintenance neurotic *Sex In The City* Barbie dolls.

Rachel was so busy keeping up with all the new trends in dating and man-hunting, she had no time to read *I'm Okay, You're Okay.* Especially when a new book called *He's Just Not That Into You* has debuted and suddenly single women everywhere were talking about it. She tried to cut corners by reading the *Sex In The City* book rather than watching all six seasons of shows, but potential clients referenced them so much she knew she had to watch them all because clearly the storylines resonated with these women and colored their approach to dating. So she schlepped on down to the video store and rented one season after another, until she thought she was going to toss her cookies if she had to endure another scene involving stilettos or anal sex or impotence.

She'd still been in school when Phil Donahue's daytime talk show was popular, she didn't read women's magazines and she had only rudimentary knowledge about treatments like Prozac or Zoloft. She wouldn't have thought they applied to her anyway. Rachel had spent so much time paying attention to what other people wanted in a mate that she'd spent no time considering what *she* wanted.

She just knew he had to be tall, because she was, and sexy, and not as crazy as Austin.

And she had no idea what the hell she was doing wrong, so she slumped at her desk while Amita watched her and frowned that she hadn't listened to any of Chao's *feng shui* suggestions. If the woman was serious about wanting to meet someone, she needed to pay more attention to her *qi* flow rather than those nimrods she met at parties. Was she learning nothing from herself and Mahliqa?

"Rachel, we're going into Chinatown this morning to pick up a few things Mr. Wan suggested for the office. Why don't you come along with us and get some fresh air."

Mahliqa smiled a little. "Yes, Rachel, have you seen Chinatown yet?"

Rachel looked up from her computer. "No, but I doubt it's much different from the one in New York. I don't really feel like going out but thanks anyway."

"Oh come on. It's a nice morning. It's not too hot yet. You look like you could use a break."

"Who's going to mind the office? What if a client comes here?"

"No one's scheduled for this morning. We'll just put up a sign on the door saying that we'll be open this afternoon. We don't get much walk-in business anyway."

"She's right, Rachel. It'll be ladies' time out. We'll stop for lunch there. One of Mr. Wan's brothers owns a very nice restaurant on Spadina Avenue."

"I don't know nuthin' 'bout *feng shui* stuff. I'd be useless," she mumbled, sounding rather a lot like Robert DeNiro.

"We'll teach you," said Mahliqa.

"Thanks, but I don't think it's my kind of thing," Rachel said with a sigh. "Look, don't take this the wrong way, but we—uh—New Yawkuhs just aren't into the whole *feng shui* thing or cosmology or acupuncture or anything like that. I don't even know what my astrology sign is."

"Oh, don't be such a - how did you put it the other day? - a *schlemiel,"* Amita replied, and Rachel couldn't help but smile at the Indian woman using a Yiddish term. "It'll be fun. It's too nice a day to waste indoors. For once, Ms. Brinkerhoff, put your work aside and do something social for a reason other than finding new clients."

Amita smiled so nicely, and Mahliqa nodded like a fashionably-*hijab*ed bobble-head doll, that Rachel finally relented.

"Awll right," she said as she stood up. "But don't blame me if I say somethin' stoopid." She winced.

"What's the matter?" asked Amita.

"Ow. I bit my tongue."

"Oh, that's good!" Mahliqa exclaimed, her eyes alight. "In my culture, when you bite your tongue, it means someone's going to give you a gift!"

"I hope it's Vin Diesel, with a bright red ribbon tied around his, uh, chest!"

Lamashtu was starving.

Not in the physical sense. She was fit and healthy and curvy in all the right places, but she no longer could score an Abercombie & Fitch modeling contract. Her belly - which was almost always bare - was still smooth and shapely, but you could no longer see her ribs, and you couldn't hang the entire Milan fall collections on her hips. Her arms were still slim and by most peoples' definition a work of art, but rainwater didn't collect in her collarbones and she didn't look like she was in desperate need of her next fix. No, she was too fat to pose on a billboard at Yonge & Dundas advertising the latest in trust fund heroin chic.

No, she just needed another virgin. There were so many in this town but her powers were at their lowest ebb. It was annoying, but she'd been lost in the underworld for so long after her mother banished her that her powers had shrivelled and almost died. She didn't remember much of the first time she'd been here because her memories had mixed with those of the young girl she'd possessed. Now, having been released once again, Lamashtu was able to seek her power sources but it was taking a long time for the energy to build up again. She was able to cause women to miscarry, now, because fetuses were far weaker than born children. It gave her great pleasure to wipe the smirks off those bitches' faces when she gave them The Stare and their water broke. The papers had run stories about the mysterious wave of miscarriages and wondered if they were linked to the choking children that now filled the hospitals and clinics.

She had to find her prey. There was something slightly different about his scent now, the faintest aroma of danger. Not to himself, but to Lamashtu. He had done something to bring himself closer to finding a woman, and she wasn't sure what. But she detected the slimmest hope now and while she felt there was no immediate chance of him ruining himself for her, she wanted to corner him before he was able to begin ruining himself with some other woman's touch.

She walked quickly and purposefully toward the lake, her brown hips sashaying in the breeze. This time they were loosely fitted with another colorful skirt from Dundas Square, one that broke at the knees but cut with an uneven line so that it showed less leg here, more leg there. And since Lamashtu never bothered with underwear or slips, the slightest breeze threatened to lift the curtain upon the most glorious portal the world had ever seen (some might say second-most, but never mind about that for now). And that's what every male eye was doing as she looked straight ahead, her eyes covered by the expensive and opaque Ray-Bans. Because the day was so bright you could see through the skirt that she probably was going commando, but not quite enough to get a glimpse of the Holy Grail. Which was quite unusual in a town as windy as Toronto, but even when the breeze kicked up those filmy panels stayed stubbornly around her thighs.

Those who weren't watching her legs noticed the cutoff top she wore that threatened to expose the bottoms of her round untethered breasts.

She reached the lakefront, paused, sniffed the air, and cruelly smiled. She made an almost robotic quarter-turn to the west. She walked across a bridge over a marina and down near the water, staying off the boardwalk while she searched the milling people enjoying the day. Careful to approach from behind, and her nipples erect at the excitement that lay ahead, she silently sat beside someone on the bench and stretched one langorous arm across the back of it.

As he turned to look at her she smiled sweetly and said, "Hello, Dave."

☆ ☆ ☆

Alexis bought some street meat and a can of soda from a corner vendor and strode down to Nathan Philips Square to sit down and eat her lunch. She had to get out of the office, she couldn't concentrate, she was just so filled with rage. She looked quite attractive in the summer sun with her long shiny brown hair flying behind her and her smart summer suit hugging her curves in all the right places, but her face looked so fierce even the immigrant guys didn't have the nerve to approach her with the U.P.S.

It was all over something minor, she knew, but it was the straw that broke the camel's back. She went out with someone she'd met on Plenty of Fish for whom she'd had to lower the bar a bit. He was a civil servant, for starters, hardly the up-and-coming young professional she'd always imagined for herself, and he had a bit of a bald spot on the crown of his head. Still, he was European and had a penis so presumably he wouldn't be afraid to let her near it some day.

It went better than she thought but she never heard from him again, and when she finally broke down and called him his *mother* answered the phone and *she blew Alexis off!* By the tone of her voice, Alexis knew the son had instructed Mommy to screen all his calls and always say *he's not here right now* if she called. She knew the tone because her own mother had used it to screen out boys she didn't want to talk to in high school.

Blown off by *his mother!*

He hadn't mentioned THAT in his profile. And how dare he blow her off, he should be *grateful* someone with a *real job* consented to meet him at all. Did he think he was going to do better, Mr. Few-Short-Years-From-A-Combover? Perhaps she could have inspired him to strive for better than the low-level administrative position he held.

Blown off by *his mother.*

Well, served her right for lowering her standards, she guessed.

But she was no closer to settling down than she'd been a week ago, a month ago, a year ago, or six years ago when she first learned about her fertility issues.

And she would have a baby. Her own. No one was going to stop her. Not even the pathetic losers in this town.

Amita and Mahliqa combed the crowded Chinese gift shop for *feng shui* energy channelizer thingies, or whatever, while Rachel browsed the boxes and shelves with disinterest. She didn't really want to be here, but she didn't want to be in the office either. She wasn't sure where she wanted to be. Maybe nowhere. She didn't much care.

She paused near the front of the store, leaning against a dusty glass display case and picked at her fingernail polish while she waited for the ladies to finish their shopping. Maybe a good Chinese lunch would cheer her up, she thought, although she wasn't hungry. However, a glass of wine interested her.

"Well hello, Rachel," came a friendly and deep voice, and she looked up.

"Hi there Chao," she replied. "Fancy meeting you here."

"This is my brother's store," he said, and he smiled, but it wasn't quite the same big smile he'd had when he'd visited Love Comes Later. It seemed a little more strained. There were stress lines around his eyes.

"I know," she said. "How've ya been, Chao?"

"All right, I guess," he said with a little shrug. His dark eyes glanced at her, then looked away. "Things are a little—uh, strange, I guess."

"Strange? How?" she asked, reminded for the first time in days that life had gotten progressively weirder in Toronto, where, according to the adolescents she listened to on CROT, the hum at the Bank of America building had grown louder, people who visited some fountain grew younger, and a very bizarre sort of serial killer was hunting men in the city.

But before Chao could answer, a small yellow dog ran into the store and turned around excitedly at Chao's feet. He was just a puppy, really, all big eyes and panting tongue and utterly adorable.

"Oh, how sweet!" Rachel cried, and she bent down to pet the dog, who greeted her as though she was a long-lost friend. "You got a new puppy! He's just scrumptious. How is Dim Sum handling it?"

"Rachel," Chao said so gravely that she looked up, "that *is* Dim Sum!"

Oh dear God *no!*

With an involuntary yelp, Dave leaped to his feet and backed away a few paces. Not *her!*

"I'm sorry, did I frighten you?" she asked with a sly smile. He was so *innocent.* Like a very young boy on the brink of manhood, but it was clear by his receding hairline that he was long past his teen years.

Dave stared at her, mouth half-open. Was he trembling?

"I apologize if I scared you. I have that effect on people sometimes," she added, privately smiling to herself to think of all the men she'd scared since she'd arrived in Toronto. The local men were the skitteriest. More frightened than your average virgin anywhere else. Lamashtu had been everywhere, all over the world, in other times and places, and virgins were virgins, dying to lose it as soon as possible, and preferably to a beautiful woman. Here in Toronto they seemed to cling to their maidenhead like a life preserver. Lamashtu found she had to wait for them outside bars, to catch them while their defenses were down, spirit them to a quiet area and work her—er, magic.

Even a Toronto man would succumb to a beautiful woman eventually if he had enough liquor in him.

"Come on, sit down. I won't bite," she said.

Dave sat down again. As far away from her outstretched arm as he could without falling off the end of the bench. At least she had her kawangas covered this time. If she started stripping, though, he was *outta there.*

"So what have you been up to since I last saw you?" she asked.

"Working and helping my mother paint my bedroom," he replied, since she'd clearly forgotten he lived with his parents. He wanted to get as far away from her as possible, but without being impolite.

But instead of turning away like most women would have done, Lamashtu reached over and tweaked his shoulder playfully. "Such a nice thoughtful man, you are," she said. "I'll bet you've got a wonderful mother. I wish mine were the sort who'd help me paint my bedroom."

"Oh. Uh. Still not talking to your mother?"

"Of COURSE not. The woman's evil. I haven't talked to her in *ages."* Not since the beginning of the Renaissance, anyway. The last time her mother visited her.

"You can't just work it out with her?" Dave couldn't imagine not speaking to his mother at all. She got on his nerves sometimes, and only rarely they had actual fights, but even after their very worst he couldn't imagine never speaking to her again.

Lamashtu rolled her eyes and sat back. The movement stretched her short top up, exposing the bottoms of her breasts. Dave braced himself and prepared to bolt. So concentrated was his effort that he didn't even think to cross his legs.

Seemingly without thought, she reached up and jerked down on her blouse a little as she stared across the lake. Dave relaxed slightly. As mesmerized as he was by her breasts he knew there was something desperately wrong with a woman like her who wanted to spend time with a guy like him. The only thing he wanted more than to squeeze those ripe melons was to get the hell away from her. Manitoba wouldn't have been overkill.

"You don't understand what my mother is like. She is beyond bee-yotch." That was a new word Lamashtu had learned today, in a coffee shop where two teenage girls complained about their rivals at school. "She's an ancient old bag who hates me because Adam wanted me and not her." Now she turned to Dave and bathed him in her liquid gaze. "But enough about my mom," she said. "I want to know something, Dave."

"What's that?" he asked cautiously.

She dipped her head closer to his and tilted it sweetly to one side. "Would you like to go somewhere with me?"

"A *scorpion?"*

"I'm not kidding, dude. That's what the autopsy reports on all three victims of the suspected serial killer say."

"Wait. Back up a minute. Now refresh my memory. 'Coz if I'm not mistaken, these guys were all stung on the *yinyang!"*

"Yeah. That's right. These guys died from scorpion stings on the ol' pie-packer."

"Okay, no. That's just insane. That's impossible."

Angus and The Dillweed, the CROT morning-drive team, were having a world-class freakout on the air.

"It's not impossible, dude."

"But wait. Scorpion stings on their dongs. How? Why? Who gets stung by a scorpion in *Ontario?* Did someone bring them up from Mexico or something?"

"Some people keep them as pets."

"And what, try to have sex with them?"

"Er, well—remember that news story we did about that guy who died from cobra bites and they found snake scales in the guy's mouth *and* his anus?"

"Yeah but—okay, as screwed up and stupid as it is I can see *how* a guy might try to have sex with a snake—and a cobra is large enough if you're going to do it, you know, the Team Rainbow way. But how do you even try to have sex with a scorpion?"

"I don't know. Maybe it's some S&M thing. Or like those Christians in the southern U.S. who dance with rattlesnakes in their mouths, to see if they can do it without getting bitten. Maybe they got off on having a scorpion on them and not getting stung. I mean, I've heard of people putting leeches—uh, down there."

"Yeah, but leeches don't kill you," said Angus.

"No, but neither do scorpions, at least most of the time. I looked it up, most people don't die from scorpion stings unless they're allergic."

"But *damn,* man, I mean on the yinyang?" Angus audibly shivered for his audience. "I can't even begin to imagine how much that must have hurt. I think that would kill *me.* A guy could go into shock or something."

"That's true."

"Have the police found any scorpions?"

"No, but they're still looking around. They've searched the areas where all three bodies were found but haven't found any yet. People are asked to report any scorpions immediately if they find them."

"This is messed up. This is SO messed up. Dude, this city is getting crazier and crazier. So, like, if you're right, and this is some weird sexual practice, is this like a new thing? Is this something that came out of California, or did the gay community invent this like they did gerbilling?"

"Dude, don't say that. We're going to get all kinds of hate mail. No one has ever been shown to have stuck a gerbil up his ass."

"What about that movie star?"

"Not even the movie star! Now don't say it again unless you want to answer your own damn e-mail."

"Okay, gay people, I take it back! Don't write me nasty e-mails because The Dillweed will just delete them. Geez. So Dillweed, did you look on Google to see if this is a new, like, *thing* going on? Some weird scorpion sex cult?"

"I did look, and no, I didn't find anything. Maybe these guys have invented it all on their own. Maybe this is a new Toronto thing."

"Now that would be the weirdest thing that's happened yet. Toronto inventing a new sexual perversion."

"That's the *same dog?"* Rachel cried.

The little golden puppy licked her ankles and peed on the floor with the excitement of seeing her again. His second-favorite human in the whole wide world.

Chao nodded slowly.

"You can't be serious." Rachel searched his face, looking for signs of delusional fantasy or just flat-out batshit insanity.

"It's the same dog. He still had his collar and tag on." Chao stooped down and picked up the puppy, who squirmed delightedly in his arms.

"But Chao, how could this happen?" Rachel asked, and she was actually more interested in how he could arrive at this zany conclusion than with the notion that it was possible for a full-grown dog to regress into a puppy. Literally.

"It happened just before Canada Day. I was walking him downtown and tied him up outside a grocery store while I stepped in to pick up a few things and when I came out he was gone. I panicked, I thought he'd been abducted but someone said they'd seen him running down the street. I followed in that direction but it was awhile before I found him, and that was purely by accident. I had been looking for a couple of hours and I was despairing of ever finding him, so I sat down by the pool at Nathan Philips Square, and the next thing I knew, this tiny little puppy bounded out of the water and jumped in my lap."

"With the collar and tag on."

Chao nodded, eyes closed.

"Chao, that's—that's—" Rachel struggled with the words.

"Crazy, I know."

"Well—yeah."

"But I tell you, that's what happened. Rachel, I'm not the only one. Others in this town are saying it's a Fountain of Youth."

One side of Rachel's mouth curled up in the classic Brooklyn sneer. "Yeah, I'm shoo-ah," she replied. "If that were the case, the whole damn world would descend upon Toronto and crush each other in the stampede to get into it."

"Obviously you haven't been watching the news," Chao said.

✯ ✯ ✯

"No. Thank you." Dave stood up. "I have to get home. My mother's waiting for me."

"Such a sweet boy," Lamashtu said. She reached up and stroked his arm. Her touch excited him. "Call her and tell her you'll be a bit late."

"No. I can't. I have to go. Now." Dave backed away a few paces. Oh God, he was being rude. A cardinal sin for a Canadian.

"It'll just be a few minutes. I want to show you something." She looked at him through her long lashes. He tried not to gasp at the suggestion. *No, she can't be serious, she's got to be up to something.*

He couldn't even get ugly women to look his way. They looked right through him, as though he was invisible.

"Oh c'mon. It'll just take a couple of minutes."

He started and was about to say, 'Hey!" defensively, then realized it wouldn't do to concede he knew what she was suggesting. He sensed danger, and wanted to get out of there fast.

"I'm sorry, uh—what's your name again?" Oh no, forgetting her name was even ruder!

"Lamashtu," she purred, and she didn't seem the slightest bit offended. She stood up. It was the first time she'd ever stood near him. She was a good two inches taller than he. Oh just great. Something else to make him feel even less of a man.

She took him lightly by the shoulders.

"I—I—have to feed my gerbils," he squeaked.

But it was too late. Her full red luscious lips were descending upon his in horrible yet delightfully fearful slow-motion.

✯ ✯ ✯

Alexis approached Nathan Philips Square and slowed down when she saw the crowd. The square was thick with bodies, all of them attempting to converge on the same spot. Police cars lined the perimeter and several cops were attempting to break up the mob scene.

Her dating anger forgotten for the moment, she approached slowly and with a growing look of disbelief on her face. People were shoving and heaving at each other, trying to break through the crowd to something. There was swearing and threats and policemen threatening to break out the pepper spray if everyone didn't disperse in an orderly manner. Not wanting to be arrested, Alexis hung back, watching. Somewhere in the distance, she was aware of a faraway hum.

A man appeared from the rear of the crowd and walked in her direction. When he came close she said, "Hey, do you know what's going on here?"

He was middle-aged and with a receding gray hairline, and he looked a little irritated. "It's the Fountain of Youth," he said. "Not that you can get anywhere near it."

"This is the Fountain of Youth?" Alexis asked. In Nathan Phillips

Square?

"That's what they say," the man replied. "Everyone wants to wade or bathe in it. But they also want autographs."

"Autographs?"

"Yes, it seems a whole planeload of movie actors and actresses arrived from Hollywood this morning. They're in the center of it."

"You're kidding me. A bunch of people from Hollywood?"

"Well, they didn't all come from there. A few of them were in Scarborough already, shooting a new Mike Myers movie."

☆ ☆ ☆

"Wait, Rachel, I have something for you."

Rachel turned to face Chao. Amita and Mahliqa waited outside, loaded with bags of Chinese coin strands, candles, crystals, golden carp, ribbons, statues and mirrors. And a Buddha fountain, for the north.

Chao looked a little uncomfortable, like he thought she'd find him crazier than she already did. As much as she wanted to believe him, Rachel kept looking at the puppy alleged to be Dim Sum and wondering if the *feng shui* expert simply wasn't the victim of some clever switcheroo.

"Look, this may be a bad time to bring this up because I know you think I must be soft in the head," Chao began, and he forced himself to look at her.

"No, I don't," Rachel said, but even she knew what a terrible liar she sounded like.

"Yes you do," Chao said, "and I for one don't blame you. I think myself sometimes that I've gone soft in the head. All I can tell you, my dear matchmaking friend, is that there are a lot of crazy things happening in Toronto right now."

"Like guys dying from scorpion stings," Rachel added quickly. She honestly liked Chao and didn't want to offend him. "Stung on the—" she stopped, embarrassed.

"Little birdy," Chao finished for her.

She raised her eyebrows.

"Chinese euphemism," he explained with a half-smile. She smiled back, relieved to be off the semantic hook.

"I don't know when I'll see you again so I want to give this to you now," Chao continued. He dug into his pocket and pulled out a small statue. He held it up for Rachel to see.

It was about three inches tall, a little Chinese man in a long red robe. He was half-bald and with a decorative band around his forehead. He carried what looked like a guitar in one hand and a bejewelled loaf of French bread in the other. He had a pleasant smile on his face and his tiny black eyes gazed at Rachel appealingly.

"Now don't laugh, and don't think ill of me, because this was the only statue my brother had," Chao half-smiled, and he extended it to Rachel. "This is Fuk," he said, pronouncing it Fook, "who represents wealth and prosperity to the Chinese. He is part of three deities every Chinese household has. His brothers are Luk, the god of power and influence, and Sau, the god of longevity. I don't want you to think I chose the one with the funny name because I'm an old pervert!"

Rachel gave a self-conscious laugh and took it.

"It's not the name that's important. You need to put him with the doll on your computer. It is not good for a matchmaker to be single herself, so he will help you balance the *feng shui qi*. Placed with the lady doll, together they will help bring the proper energies to your work space so that you will find a good man who will take care of you and love you the way you deserve."

Rachel choked back a bit of a sob. She was touched by the sweet gesture. It didn't matter now that she privately thought *feng shui* was just a bunch of crap and that dogs just didn't turn into puppies by bathing in a public fountain that a lot of dogs frolicked in every day. She clutched the gift tightly and thanked Chao, trying not to choke or let her voice waver.

"Thank you, Chao, that's very sweet of you," she said, and her violet eyes softened. "It's a lovely gesture, and I hardly know you."

"You are a good woman, Rachel," he told her, and his dark eyes were solemn. "I wish you only the best in life."

* * *

Time slowed to a crawl for Dave the Virgin.

Her lips loomed and ballooned and filled his entire field of vision. The sounds of the lake—the cries of the seagulls, the conversations around them, the hum of the traffic—faded away as those luscious pillows relentlessly descended. Then they were upon him and they pressed down, soft, velvet, smooth, electric—and Dave was paralyzed, helpless, knowing he couldn't stop her no matter what she did to him now.

He had no idea what to do. At thirty-five, Dave Gillpatrick had just received his first kiss.

What would she do? What was he supposed to do? Should he open his mouth? Should he slip her some tongue? Should he tilt his head? Should he close his eyes? Should he open them?

"Hello, Dave? Are you in there?"

He shook himself awake. Her lips were gone. Had it all been a dream?

Lamashtu stood before him, a faint smile on her lips, which were now parted playfully.

"Are you going to answer me?"

"Er, what?"

"I said, *Would you like to slip behind the marina over there?"* she said, and pointed.

What had happened to her lips? They were here a minute ago. He was sure of it. He could still feel them, warm upon his own. Oh my God, it had been the greatest thing he'd ever experienced. She had kissed him. *Dave Gillpatrick.* Toronto's biggest virgin. And total loser.

He stared at her. Dumbstruck. His larynx wouldn't work. What he wanted to say most was, *Oh please, do it again!*

She stepped forward and reached around him. She ran her fingers down his spine, over his thin cotton shirt. He felt the delicious tingly trail of her fingertips.

She shifted her shoulders a bit, and the cutoff hiked up. Just enough to show him Paradise again.

Involuntarily, Dave stepped back. Even though he didn't want to. Maybe in some deep part of his brain he remembered his vow in case she started flashing her flying Canucks again.

She stepped forward to meet him. She leaned in and touched his neck gently with one perfect hand as she whispered in his ear, "I know what your secret is. And I swear to you I will never tell a soul."

Oh, so that was it. She was *that* sort of woman. The kind who liked to deflower virgins.

What kind of idiot would turn *that* down?

"It's okay," she said with a smile. She took his hand and led him, dumbstruck, to the marina.

Dave didn't even think about how embarrassing it was to walk around with a tent in his pants.

Deep inside Lamashtu, something poisonous and deadly stirred.

CHAPTER EIGHT

Pookums was freaking out again.

Dave the Tarantula Guy watched as his pet raced around the terrarium, scrabbling to get out. She was more agitated than ever. Dave wanted to pull her out to soothe her, but was almost afraid Pookums might bite him in her excitement. While tarantula bites weren't deadly, they were painful.

"What's the matter, girl?" Dave said. He hated to see his baby so worked up. He hoped this didn't herald another earthquake.

Pookums vainly tried to climb the smooth glass walls. Dave considered maybe opening the terrarium and tilting it for her to climb out onto his desk. Maybe being near daddy would calm her, and at least he'd be less likely to be bitten.

Just then, a rumbling shook the building.

"Oh shit," Dave said.

It stopped a few seconds later. If that was an earthquake, it felt more like a large truck lumbering by, not that he could have felt it this high up in the Manulife Centre.

Dave rushed to the window and looked down. It was hard to tell whether anyone else had felt it or not because traffic had stopped. But that was typical for downtown Toronto.

When he returned to his desk, Pookums had retired to a corner for a snooze.

"What the hell was that?"

Rachel gripped the door handle in Amita's car.

"I hope it's not another earthquake," Mahliqa said. She turned to look at Rachel in the back seat. "Are you all right?"

"Yeah, just rattled," Rachel replied. She clutched Fuk in her jacket pocket, like it was a life preserver. The reassuring little Chinese man seemed to tell her that everything was going to be all right. Not just with the sudden jolt, like, *everything.*

"That didn't feel like an earthquake," Amita said. "It felt more like —like, a reverberation."

"Of what?" Mahliqa asked, but her friend shrugged.

"Chao is right, this city is getting weirdah an' weirdah," Rachel remarked. Her fingers still clenched the door handle even though she had no intention of leaving the car. They were stopped in the middle of the street along with everyone else, despite the green traffic light. They'd felt a rumble and then a loud noise and pedestrians stopped, covered their ears, and bent over. A moment later, they staggered back, as though pushed by an invisible wave.

"What was that noise?" asked Rachel, but no one had an answer. The pedestrians were staring in the general direction of the Bank of America building.

"What the hell are they doing?" Rachel breathed, but again, no one knew.

"Amita, try to get out of this traffic. Maybe we can escape down the lakefront," said Mahliqa.

Amita began to inch forward.

Dave the Virgin lay still, abjectly terrified. He was in the galley of a small pleasure craft bobbling in the marina, in a strange bed with his pants down around his legs. The most beautiful woman in existence had taken off her clothes and stood before him in all her naked bronzed glory. He couldn't take his eyes off her exquisite breasts, her deliciously flat belly and curvy waistline, and legs that seemed to go on forever. He couldn't even look at what was between them. He was thirty-five years old and he was still a—

Lamashtu slid onto the bed beside him, leopard-like, and began to unbutton his shirt with her teeth. The torture was the most erotic thing he'd ever felt, which was saying something for Toronto's most experienced self-toucher. The buttons popped open between her talented lips and she spread it slowly open. Then she sat up in a fluid motion and slid her fingers around the top of his Fruit of the Looms. Slowly she slid them down his hips. His erect member popped up and she smiled as though greeting an old friend. She slid the underwear down his legs and over his feet, throwing them aside.

She was almost quivering with desire. Not for Dave, for whom she held no lust at all - Lamashtu could only feel lust for her only true love, Adam. She desired, however, with every fiber of her being, the potent energy she was about to draw. She was starving. With Dave's perfectly pure energy - well, what was left after her two leg-wobbling kisses, massaging his tent pole with her crotch the second time - she would regain all her power. The energy she'd lost during all those long years in the subterranean world, looking for a way to escape.

First, she would celebrate by killing all the damn babies in Toronto. Including the ones still in their mothers' wombs.

Then, she would find her mother and destroy the bitch once and for all.

She gazed lovingly at Dave's rock-hard member.

Oh, the poor boy, he looked so terrified. She struggled hard not to laugh. If only he knew.

She sat up and moved over him, straddling his legs, her perfect isosceles triangle hovering near his erect member.

"Touch me," she whispered, and with trembling hands, Dave reached up and touched those perfect breasts which had taunted and teased him so at Nathan Philips Square.

And the moment he felt those perky chocolate kiss nipples, he exploded onto his chin.

"Hey guy, did you feel that?"

Dave the Beowulf Freak burst into Dave the Tarantula Guy's office.

"Yeah, what, that rumble? What was that? Pookums was all freaked out," Dave the T.G. replied.

"I don't know, but turn on the radio."

Dave the T.G. reached over and switched on the small boom box he kept on the other side of his desk. Away from Pookums, who didn't share his passion for Steppenwolf or Christina Aguilera. Dave the T.G. tended to listen to CROT, because they had the funniest morning show in the Western hemisphere.

"We're still waiting for word on what caused the explosion on Front Street," came the lunchtime deejay. "All we know for certain is that the mysterious hum at the Bank of America building suddenly increased, then built to a crescendo and there was a loud noise. We don't know if anyone was hurt or if there were any casualties. Please don't call the station, people, one of our reporters is heading for the scene right now. Stay tuned as we learn more."

"So, no one knows," said Dave the T.G.

"I don't think it was another earthquake," replied Dave the B.F. "I wonder if a building exploded?"

"Maybe it's a terrorist attack?"

Dave the B.F. shrugged. "You think maybe this is our 9/11?"

"I don't know. Did you hear any planes?"

"I don't think so. I'm not sure. Where would a terrorist hijack a plane in Toronto, Pearson or the Island?"

Toronto had two airports, the main international one and a smaller one on Toronto Centre Island.

Dave the T.G. looked at Pookums, sleeping peacefully under part of an old thick tree branch, and then out the window. "There's no smoke in the sky."

"Oh no, we'll never get out of this!" Amita moaned. The traffic inched along, but only at a grudging pace. It was the mainstay of living in Toronto, sitting in traffic. Those who didn't ride the TTC or walk were doomed always to reach the party last, unless it was in the suburbs.

"I think it's gonna rain," Rachel commented as she glanced at the sky. The formerly bright sunny day had begun to look a bit foreboding. Gray clouds began to wipe out blue sky like some cosmic Etch-A-Sketch.

"I don't want to think about how much gas we're wasting," groaned Mahliqa, and she laid her head against the window. "Although I suppose we can write it off with Revenue Canada."

"Nothing to do about it," Amita remarked. "We're stuck here, ladies. I tried to get to the lakefront but I failed. It looks like we'll have to drive down Front Street."

"What's the holdup?" demanded Mahliqa.

"I guess we'll find out soon enough," Amita replied. She hit the left turn signal.

* * *

"You IDIOT!"

Lamashtu leaped off the bed and glared at Dave the Virgin with liquid malice.

A red-faced Dave cowered on the bed, horrified and embarrassed.

He reached a shaky hand for the corner of a bed sheet to wipe off his face. He was glad it hadn't hit his eyes. He'd read in *Portnoy's Complaint* that it really burns.

"Couldn't you have waited ONE MORE MOMENT?"

She was no longer beautiful. Her brown eyes blazed and her dark features, with her arched eyebrows, now knit in the center, looked positively satanic.

"I'm really sorry," he squeaked, wiping his face clean. "Look, I—uh —haven't done this much before. It's, uh, been awhile—"

"Yeah, like FOREVER!" she screamed. "You've NEVER had sex before, and now you just RUINED it!" Lamashtu was so angry she felt like blasting him, just like she did the babies and toddlers. But that would really burn an all-important bridge. He was so pure, so critical to her success. Although Toronto was far more populated with gentle male virgins than she ever expected to find in a modern city, he was still among the purest. He had never known the touch of a woman, never been kissed (until today), never been pleasured orally, never gotten near a woman's delta of Venus (until today, of course). He was too perfect. Just thirty more seconds and it would have been all over—by now she'd be blasting babies wasting space in the city hospitals.

"Could you please keep your voice down," Dave asked in a quavery voice, now turning ten more shades of red. He really didn't need the entire city knowing his shameful reaction. Her angry eyes raked him over.

"Just a few more minutes—*just a few more minutes!"* she shrieked, in a voice so high it couldn't carry outside the pleasure craft, for which he was supremely grateful. "I could have had it all, I could have—"

She turned to him, her eyes sweeping over his semi-naked form. He'd pulled the sheet over himself and was now reaching for his pants, unmindful of his underwear tossed in a corner.

"I think I'd better leave," he mumbled, having turned a few more shades of purple just for good measure. His heart was going to explode. This was not normal, she was not normal. He felt like he'd just dodged a bullet but he wasn't sure why.

He hastily pulled on his pants, keeping one wary eye on the angry naked beautiful woman before him.

"No, wait, sweetie—" her voice turned liquid and teasing again, her eyes softened and her sensuous lips parted as she held out her shapely arms. She knelt and walked across the bed on her knees, reaching for him. "Look, I'm sorry too, it's all my fault, I should have known it would be like this, you're so—uh, new at this. I shouldn't have yelled at you. I'm so sorry, Dave, come here and join me and we will wait a few minutes and try again."

A few more minutes. Why hadn't she remembered that? This was not the end of the world, it was merely a minor setback. She'd known other virgins who burst their seed before they'd united, and all it meant was a little more of that tedious stroking and the silly words of encouragement until he could get hard again, and then she was ridding the world of infant scum.

What an idiot she'd been! Man, it *had* been a long time underground if she couldn't remember how men's things worked.

But Dave grabbed his shirt, pushed past her and dashed up the steps to the bow of the boat. He leaped the short distance to the pier and ran as fast as he could, barefoot, naked from the waist up, his shirt flying from his clenched fist.

"What the hell was *that?"*

Alexis looked away from an aging ex-supermodel slap fight in Toronto's new Fountain of Youth, and she and the stranger looked around.

The throng of people stopped thronging, and they stood in the water, which had been up to their ankles before all the shoving and fighting had pushed half of it onto the pavement surrounding the pool.

"Turn on the damn water!" that old guy from that silly TV series about a car yelled, because City Hall had cut the fountain in an effort to discourage the crowd.

"That sounded sort of like a nuclear explosion," replied the stranger, although he didn't look too concerned.

"You think it was a *nuclear explosion?"* cried a horrified Alexis.

"No, I said it just *sounded* like that. Did you see any planes? Nothing dropped on us. There's no mushroom cloud. It just made that sort of muted *poof* sound you hear in the old military movies of atomic bomb testing."

"I hope it's not a dirty bomb," Alexis commented, since she watched more Fox News than was good for a Canadian.

"I doubt it's a terrorist bomb," remarked the man, rolling his eyes. "Geez, we're not America. No one hates us."

"Hey, listen. There's no hum," Alexis replied, and she cocked her ear.

The man cocked his ear too. "You know, you're right."

Amita made the slow turn onto Front Street. The Bank of America building appeared to be the reason for the massive traffic jam. People milled about it and police cars parked with their lights flashing. It was glaringly clear that no one was going anywhere fast, because the people closest to the building had begun to exit their cars which they left right in the road.

"I guess we're not getting back to the office today," commented Rachel as she sat back dejectedly on the seat. She fingered the little Fuk statue and took comfort in it. She wasn't sure he'd bring her a nice new husband at all, but if he could calm her frazzled nerves perhaps there was something to Chao's Chinese hocus-pocus, after all.

"Let me get out and see what's going on," said Mahliqa, and she opened the car door and pulled herself and her long dark robe after her. Rachel and Amita watched as she strode down the street to the mob in front of the bank building, and then strained to see over others' heads, then weaved her way through the crowd.

Several minutes later her tall dark form weaved its way back. Mahliqa hurried back to the car and opened the passenger door. She leaned down, her arm against the edge of the roof, and looked in at the two women.

"What's going on, my friend?" asked Amita.

"You will never believe it," Mahliqa grimaced. "It's another cursed Native *land claim blockade!"*

* * *

"Okay people, it's official. Toronto is now completely <bleep>ed up."

"Angus! You can't say <bleep> on the air." Jay the lunchtime deejay was annoyed. He never said <bleep> on the air. He didn't want Angus and his idiot sidekick on his show, which was meant for grownups, but the station manager had called them both in to help cover the Astoundingly Tremendous Story breaking downtown.

"<Bleep>! I forgot, I'm sorry."

"And you can't say <bleep> either."

"Oops, sorry about that too."

"So what's going on?"

"The Dillweed is down at the Bank of America building, which you'll remember has been in the news in recent weeks because of a mysterious hum that no one could identify. Well, the building is no longer humming."

"Okay. How come?"

"Well there was a sort of explosion, except it wasn't really an explosion—"

"How can there be an explosion without an explosion?"

"Well, there was an explosive sound, and the glass doors blew open and shattered, but there wasn't any other debris or anything. This isn't like a bomb."

"Then what's it like?"

"Well that's just the thing, man. It's not like *anything.* There was this weird blast noise that was described as what happens when a giant amplifier at a rock concert suddenly blows. It was a sort of electric sound, and then it was silence."

"And then what?"

"Now that's the really <bleep>ed up part—"

"Angus!"

"I'm sorry, I'm sorry! I keep forgetting. This whole thing is just so weird and exciting. Dude, Toronto is totally f—er, I mean, screwed up. I mean, we've got movie stars rioting in Nathan Philips Square, guys are getting stung on the tubesteak by a tropical insect - hey, a scorpion's an insect, right?"

"Actually, I think it's a member of the spider family."

"Okay, well, anyway, it's not supposed to be in Ontario but it is. And now we've got the Native land blockade to end all blockades down on Front Street—"

"Which tribe is it?"

"Dude, that's the weirdest part of all!"

Dave the Still-Virgin had actually missed the big sort-of-explosion at the Bank of America building, despite being less than a kilometer away, because, quite coincidentally, he'd shot his load at the exact moment. Since his hands were on Lamashtu's Hershey's Kiss nipples and he was, he thought, about to get laid for the first time in his more than thirty-five-year existence, you'll have to pardon him if his brain wasn't really attuned to what was going on around him.

Now he ran as fast as he could from the marina, looking over his shoulder to make sure the psychotic bitch wasn't following him on a broom or something. Despite being in the usual bad shape a dedicated mouse potato, fanboy, OS-tan-designer, and world-class computer porn wanker like him usually is, he actually made pretty good time, because he was running on pure adrenaline.

Later, he would curl up in his bed with the door locked, refusing his mother's offer of dinner, turn twenty shades of red, and maybe cry a little at the afternoon's grand humiliation. But for right now, all he could think about was how shit-fire scared he was, and not how much his feet were going to hurt as soon as he stopped running barefoot through the city.

Somewhere up ahead was a crowd, gathered around the Bank of America building. Dave felt there'd be safety in numbers, so he glanced over his shoulder, determined that Lamashtu was not following him on foot, broom, roller blades, or Segway, and he slowed to a canter.

Meanwhile, Toronto was now officially On Edge.

This shit was just *not normal.*

This weird crap was the sort of thing that happened in other countries, especially the United States. You know, countries where people are already stupid and gullible and deserve their retarded UFO sightings, Sasquatches, born-again Presidents with delusions of monarchy, and Virgin Mary sightings in ice-cream stains. Or Scotland, with their crappy weather and bad attitudes and ridiculous lake monsters.

Canada, on the other hand, was nice, diplomatic, multicultural, cosmopolitan, adult, and above all, resoundingly *normal.*

And the worst thing of all, the very creepiest thing that had happened so far, is that damned Fountain of Youth had made everyone horny again, like they were silly teenagers.

Even *Toronto guys!*

CHAPTER NINE

Native land claims are the bane of Canadians everywhere, but you can never admit it because you are required by law to suffer the Canadian White Man's Burden.

Broken government promises are most commonly disputed by virtue of the *blockade,* which means wherever you're trying to go, you're not getting there. Because Natives are blocking the highway, bridge, neighborhood entrance or railroad, and no one's gonna stop them because *they have suffered greatly at the hands of the white man.*

Okay, granted, the white people were pretty awful to them. They did what white folks do best when they show up on one's shores, which is to kill their men, steal their women, enslave their children, take their land, destroy their language and culture and stick them on a crappy little piece of infertile earth that no one can live on (called a *reserve* in Canada).

After awhile, the Canadian Natives (often called *First Nations*) got pretty fed up with this crap and were even more pissed off about the fact that the Canadian government, much like the American one, only ever honors a treaty purely by mistake.

The result, of course, is that sooner or later, First Nations folks are going to show up somewhere inconvenient and claim the land belongs to them. Canadians - to their credit - feel far guiltier about their past treatment of the aboriginals than the Americans do. Not enough to actually *do* anything about it, mind you, except write righteously indignant letters to the op-ed section of the paper about how we *owe* these people, dammit, because they were abused and their cultures were destroyed and they live on shitty reserves on flood plains with lousy water and scabies and no food for miles around, drinking themselves into oblivion and huffing gasoline and killing themselves in appalling numbers. And politicians regularly get editorially flagellated for not having done enough to end the poverty on reserves, and the government is regularly pushed to apologize for this or that, and no one questions anything the First Nations say or do because the Natives know that they can shut up even the hardest-core white critics with just two words: *residential schools.*

Americans, on the other hand, stick their Natives on reservations that make Canadian reserves look like the Ritz Carlton and mutter, "Only good Injun is a dead Injun! Pass me the hollow point bullets, Bubba."

So when Mahliqa twisted around and asked Rachel if she wanted to see a real blockade for herself, Rachel, having nothing better to do at the moment, said sure. Amita went too, since she had nothing better to do either. The three of them walked toward the blockade while Mahliqa explained all about them and why Rachel, a New York Jew who'd never oppressed anyone in her life, should feel guilty too. After all, she and Amita, a Sunni Muslim and a Gujarati Hindu, felt guilty, and hell, they hadn't even been *born* here. Feeling guilty about past Native abuses was just part and parcel to being a happy, healthy, guilt-ridden Canadian. Even if you weren't white.

As Rachel got out of the car, something rained down on her arm. "Oh God, a bird just plopped on me," she groaned.

Amita fumbled in her purse for a tissue and handed it to Rachel.

"In my culture, when a bird craps on you it means you're going to receive good luck!" Mahliqa noted. She looked up at the sky and held out her arm. "Here little birdy, come plop on me too! Amita and I need some customers under thirty!"

As they approached the men behind the blockade Rachel commented, "Gee, they don't *look* like Native Canadians."

And it was true, they weren't sporting the traditional Native Canadian Blockade Uniform of bandannas and jeans jackets and T-shirts and backpacks. They wore no army caps nor carried banners displaying the Mohawk flag with slogans like, "This land is our land, it isn't your land." They didn't even wear any token signs of Native affiliation like brightly colored jackets or shawls or bear-claw necklaces. Although they did stand united against a makeshift barrier and look all proud and strong and defiant and righteous.

There were about twelve men. Their eyes were heavily lined in black and several had beards cut to a point in the middle of their chins. Some of them wore long brightly-colored robes with striped patterns. A couple were shirtless and barefoot and clad only in a knee-length skirt wrapped around their hips. Most wore rude sandals. All of them sported lots of jewelry and small sheathed knives. The scents of balsam, sandalwood, myrrh, and other perfumes swirled about them.

One particularly striking and handsome tall man wore a robe that wound around one shoulder and left the other bare; his arm bore a wide gold circlet. A large knife in a crudely-jewelled scabbard hung at his hip.

"They're, uh, darker than I expected, too," said Rachel, who'd seen enough westerns to know.

And the Natives' skin did show a strong bronze tint, not even close to Tonto tone.

Several stood with arms crossed. Their proud copper faces stared out at the sea of Canadian faces - some curious, some equally defiant, some confused, and some just wanting to get the hell back to the office before the boss thinks they're whiling away the afternoon in a pub, thankyouverymuch. Rachel noticed an Orthodox Jew standing to the side in his long black coat and a white *yarmulke*. Not too far from and pointedly ignoring him were a cluster of three young bearded Palestinian men.

"So—what band are you with?" asked Mahliqa, who was well-versed enough to know that you never use the word *tribe* anymore.

The tall handsome one turned to her. "We have come to reclaim our land for Kana'n."

"You guys aren't real Indians!" came a voice from the crowd. "You came from inside the bank building!"

"Don't call them Indians!" came a female voice. "They're *First Nations!* Or *Native Canadians!"*

"She's got a point," said Amita. "I should know, I *am* an Indian."

"Kana'an?" asked Mahliqa. "I've never heard of that band before."

"We were here since the beginning of time. Then the Others came and destroyed our people."

Rachel, being white, looked away.

"They called us godless. They said we were heathen, barbarian savages. They said their god wanted them to kill us all. They called our religion evil. They insulted our gods and slaughtered many and enslaved the rest. They destroyed our temples, made us speak their languages and killed our infants."

"Did they give you smallpox-infected blankets?" asked one of the Palestinian men.

The large Kana'n band member squinted at him and asked, "What's smallpox?"

"White people suck," said another Palestinian. "They hate us, too, because we're Muslim."

The large man squinted at the Palestinian. "What's a Muslim?"

The Palestinian looked at him, agape. "What do you mean, 'What's a Muslim'? How can you not know what a Muslim is?"

"Yeah, don't you even read the newspaper?" asked a defiant-looking white guy behind him. "They blow people up and stuff."

"Hey! Watch your mouth, Christian! Not all Muslims are terrorists!"

The Kana'n man just squinted at the white guy like he was a complete idiot.

"I don't know who all you people are. But we want you off our land. It is ours. We are reclaiming it, after far too many passages of time."

"What treaty do you claim is violated?" asked the politically-correct white woman. She stepped forward. She was tall and thin with somewhat frizzy hair and no makeup.

A Kana'n band member with tight curls and an equally curly pointed beard said, "I don't know what you're talking about. We know nothing of a treaty. Or blowing people up. How do you even do that, anyway? Inflate them like a goat's bladder? Our children played with such things, before the Others took them away."

"You have to claim some treaty is violated before you can reclaim land," the white woman explained patiently.

"Why do we need this thing called a treaty? It is our land, and the evil *Habiri* stole it from us! Now we want it back. And we will fight for it! There are many of us, do not be fooled by the few you see now. There are many more where we come from."

"From the bank building?" someone asked, and the large man, who appeared to be the leader, nodded. "No problem then, the police can just go in and arrest them."

The large leader fell silent, as though he didn't care what the police did, and stared out over the crowd.

"We want all of you off our land by sundown," he proclaimed in an imperious voice.

A titter wavered through the crowd. "It doesn't work like that," the young white woman explained. "First the media has to show up, then the city council gets involved, and your supporters will bring you food and water and blankets—"

"Don't forget to treat them with smallpox first," said the defiant-looking white man, and the young woman glared at him.

"We don't have smallpox here," said a man behind Rachel. "They'll have to settle for SARS."

"That is SO not funny!" screamed the white woman, wheeling on him.

"On what basis do you claim this land?" asked Mahliqa. As a Pakistani of Palestinian-born parents, she was sympathetic to the plight of people who were pushed off their land and oppressed. "This lady is correct, you need to reference a broken treaty or produce an ancient agreement to get anyone to take it seriously."

"We MUST take it seriously anyway," the woman scolded her. "These Natives have suffered a lot at our hands."

"My hands have never oppressed a Native," said one of the Palestinians. "Just some Jews, but of course they deserved it."

"Hey!" cried Rachel angrily. "Jewish here!"

"You people should get off *our* land," snapped the Orthodox man at the Palestinian. "We were there before you!"

"Our people have been there since before time!"

"No one can be anywhere before time, you idiot. And Islam is only 1,400 years old. You invaded us."

The Palestinian man opened his mouth to respond, but the tall Kana'n leader interjected. "You people settle your own differences," he said. "We want to remove the evil *Habiri* from our land."

"Hey!" cried the Orthodox Jew. "Who the hell do you think you are, anyway? What right do you have to demand such a thing?"

"What's a *Habiri?"* asked Rachel, confused.

The Orthodox Jew threw her a disgusted look. "And you call yourself a Jew?" he spat. "Do you truly not know the ancient name of your people, the *Hebrews?"*

"Habiri are Hebrews?" she asked.

"You must be Reformed," he remarked.

"You are both *Habiri?"* asked the tall Kana'n leader.

"We're Jews," explained Rachel. "In Biblical times our people were called Hebrews."

"Then you are the enemy! You are the ones who massacred our people and raped our women because your god commanded it!"

"Jews totally suck," said one of the young Palestinians.

"Hey, they bulldozed my grandfather's house in Jenin," said another.

"Shut up!" commanded the young white woman. "This isn't about your claims in Israel, this is about *their* land claims *here."*

"You shut up!" the Palestinian shot back. "My family is here in Canada because Jews pushed us off our land!"

The Kana'n people suddenly huddled together and whispered among themselves in some strange language.

Finally the leader's head popped up. "What is Canada?" he asked.

"What do you *mean,* 'What is Canada'?" spat the young Palestinian, exasperated. "Are you people *complete* idiots? This is Canada. We are all Canadians. Including you."

"They're not Canadians!" cried the young white woman. "They don't recognize our sovereignty, and the Canadian government accepts that. First Nations call North America *Turtle Island."*

"Canada?" remarked one of the pointy-bearded men. "There must be some mistake. We have never heard of this place. We are looking for *Canaan!"*

* * *

Dave slowed to a walk. He glanced back for the millionth time but still didn't see Lamashtu. Maybe she wasn't following him. Maybe she'd given up because of the way he'd failed and then bailed on her. He guessed he probably wasn't the only virgin in Toronto; if she had a thing for them she could probably find someone else.

Now that adrenaline wasn't powering him like an F-16, Dave suddenly realized just how tired he was. His breath came in desperate gasps. His muscles screamed. And his feet were burning.

He looked at them, lifting up one and then the other. The soles were bloody. Bits of gravel and dirt stuck to them. He wished he hadn't left his shoes back in the boat, but there'd been no time. He was lucky to have his shirt. He pulled it on and buttoned it up.

Up ahead, he saw a huge crowd of people. Ignoring the pain in his feet he approached them. In numbers there'd be safety.

"Canaan?" cried the Orthodox Jew.

"Yes. We are Kana'nites! Refugees from Kana'n, where our people lived since the beginning of time until we were chased out, enslaved, and murdered by the evil *Habiri!* Who, apparently, are going by the name of Jews these days, so shamed are they by their evil deeds."

"Oh boy, do you people not know Jews," a Palestinian wisecracked.

"My name is Ammishtamru," the tall, handsome leader said as he looked out over the crowd. "We want all you Jews off our land by sunset!" The look on his face indicated he brooked no nonsense from anyone.

"Yeah, you tell them!" one of the Palestinian men shouted. "You heard them, get off their land!" He looked pointedly at Rachel and the Orthodox man.

Ammishtamru turned to the Palestinian. "Who the hell are you guys?" he asked.

"We are Palestinians! We are Muslims! We want them off our land too!" one of the Palestinian's friends replied.

"Where do you come from?" asked the Canaanite leader.

"Israel," one of them answered. "What was once called Canaan."

Ammishtamru glared at them. "Then you get the fuck off our land too!"

* * *

"Dillweed. Are you trying to tell me that these Natives are some *ancient tribe from the Bible?"*

"Angus, that's what I'm getting from Jay. He got there a few minutes ago and he says some guy calling himself Ammishtamru is calling for all the Jews to leave Toronto."

"Just the Jews?"

"Um, not sure if he means *just* the Jews. Jay says it looks like he thinks all Torontonians are Jews."

"Why does he think that?"

"Not sure," replied The Dillweed. "But maybe we should all drop trou to settle the matter."

Dave limped toward the crowd looking somewhat less naked than he had running maniacally away from the Harbourfront.

Above him, gray storm clouds began to gather. Hardly a notable event in Toronto, where the weather could turn on a dime.

A blockade. Oh, probably the First Nations.

But as he approached he saw that the Natives didn't look like First Nations people. For one thing, they were a lot darker. For another, they were a lot less dressed than the Nations, who tended toward Assimilated Working Class Canadian garb. Except on pow-wow days, when they wore outfits so outrageously decorated, in such head-splitting fluorescent colors, with such modern-day textiles that hadn't been known before the Age of Plastics, that their ancestors would have shaken their heads, reached for the herbal equivalent of Excedrin, and upchucked their pemmican beef strips.

He was just within earshot when he heard one of the tall bronze men cry out, "Whaddaya MEAN we're not in Canaan?"

"Where's Aqhat? He had the damn map!" cried one of the bronze men.

Dave shook his head and turned away. They looked too much like Lamashtu. He'd had enough foreign weirdness for one day.

✯ ✯ ✯

"Shit, Pookums is acting up again," said Dave the Tarantula Guy, pointing.

Dave the Beowulf Freak suppressed a shudder. "Great. He's probably going to bust out of there and eat us."

"She, not he," Dave the T.G. corrected. "And don't be an idiot."

"How do you know it's a she?"

"I've sexed her."

Dave the B.F.'s eyes widened with abject horror.

"No, you tool, I've had her sex determined from her *exuviae!"*

"Her *what?"*

"Exuviae. Shed skin. It's almost impossible to tell a tarantula's sex without it."

"I don't suppose you can just look between its legs—"

"Dave, it's a *spider!"*

"I know, I know. Spiders are disgusting, Dave. Why can't you get yourself a nice normal pet, like a Rottweiler?"

"Dogs eat too much and have to be walked. You know I can't take care of a dog with my schedule."

Pookums was scrambling around like she needed to get out of Dodge before Black Bart showed up.

Dave the T.G. sighed. "There's something coming, my man."

Dave the B.F. looked out the window. "Yeah, looks like a thunder storm."

"No, I mean something else. Pookums was acting crazy before the earthquake, too. Then again just before this explosion. She doesn't act like that every time we have a storm. Now, well, I don't know what the hell's wrong with her, but she seems to be pretty sensitive to—uh, weird stuff."

"Toronto's gotten pretty weird in the last few weeks. Did you hear about the riot at the City Hall fountain?"

"Yeah, the movie stars? They're saying it's a Fountain of Youth or something."

"People are saying it works, though."

"Does it really?"

Dave the B.F. watched Pookums nervously. "I heard peoples' dogs bathe in it and come out puppies."

Dave the T.G. searched his friend's face carefully. "Do you believe that?"

"I think I do. I've heard it from enough people, and they're not all flakes."

Dave the T.G. sat back in his chair and watched the darkening sky. After a few minutes he said, "I think more hot women would be attracted to me if I got my hair back."

His friend replied, "I wish I wasn't so gray. My mom says I look distinguished but I think I just look old. And these wrinkles around my mouth don't help."

Dave the T.G. swung around in the chair to face him. "Um, you want to go down there and see for ourselves?"

"It looks like it's gonna rain."

"Dave, we're going to get wet anyway!"

Things were not going well for the Canaanite Liberation Front.

"AQHAT!" Yassib the Canaanite screamed in the direction of the Bank of America building. "Get your ass out here right now, and bring the damn map!"

"Why did you let *him* be the navigator?" Ammishtamru demanded angrily. "You know what a fuckup he is, even if he *is* our best scribe. Remember that time we got lost trying to find Ugarit because Barley-For-Brains had bought a map he couldn't read written in Cypro-Minoan Linear B?"

"Yeah, he bought it from that wanker Mhr-Anat. That guy was so pretentious. He couldn't just sell Aqhat a map in nice normal Akkadian, noooo, he had to go and show just how learned he was by giving him Cypro-Minoan Linear B—"

"AQHAT!" Yassib screamed again, and another Canaanite emerged from what had been the Bank of America's front door. He was short and heavyset with chubby brown cheeks and long black hair that fell to his shoulders. Like several of the others, he wore a simple cotton wrap around his hips. He also had a gold anklet and some tattoos on one wrist. He gripped something in his hand.

He hurried up to his compatriots and wiped the sweat from his brow. "What's the matter?"

"Is that the map?" demanded Ammishtamru.

"Yes, yes. I heard Yassib yelling something about it. Is there a problem?"

"Yes, there's a problem! These people, who are not *Habiri,* well, except for those two over there, tell us we are in a kingdom called

Canada, and not Canaan."

"Canada? Where the hell is that?"

"That's what *we'd* like to know," sputtered Ammishtamru. His handsome face screwed up and he looked more like an angry baby than an important chieftain. "Show us your map!"

Aqhat held up a scroll. He unrolled it and three or four of the other Canaanites crowded around. So did a few of the largely non-Jewish Canadians, straining to see over their broad copper shoulders.

"It's an English-language map," one of them breathed.

"I can't read this," said Ammishtamru.

"I couldn't use one of our old maps," explained Aqhat. "Remember, these are modern times and we came from the Underworld."

"Is Lebanon still around?" asked Yassib, heavy black eyebrows raised. "They had the best cedars. My brother, a carpenter, made this great chest for our sister's dowry—"

"That's not the point!" bellowed Ammishtamru. "I can't read these words, but I can see by this map that we're nowhere near Canaan."

"Did you stop and ask for directions?" asked Rachel, and Amita tittered near her.

Ammishtamru ignored her. In his culture, women knew their place, and the only good *Habiri* was a dead *Habiri.* Even if she was the hottest-looking *Habiri* he'd ever seen, and Ammishtamru was in a position to know, having had far too many concubines for his own good and having visited a good many brothels in his day. Now Donatiya the Shulamite, *there* was a really good piece of Astarte!

"This map is damaged!" cried Yassib, pointing to a piece at the top that had ripped off.

"Yeah, I think that happened while we were passing through the Gates of Mot. Remember how the void kind of sucked us through quickly? I didn't have time to roll it up and I think it caught on something."

What it said at the top was, "MAP of CANA."

"You stupid Avite!" screamed Ammishtamru, and he whacked Aqhat on the back of the head. "Did you not notice when you bought this map that it said CANADA, and not CANAAN?"

"I didn't have a chance to look at it!" Aqhat replied, raising his hands defensively. "Look, we had to leave the Underworld fairly quickly after the passage opened. I don't even know where Mhr-Anat got this thing. I just made sure it was in English, which I learned from Thomas Jefferson when he joined the Underworld, and not Cypro-Minoan Linear B."

"Yeah, we wouldn't want another fuckup like that Ugarit thing," snarled one of the Canaanites.

"Hey, eat my loincloth, Niqmaddu," Aqhat snarled back. "It's not like *you* can read any maps, in any languages. You just fell off the ox-cart at Elam, you big dumb sheep-packing oaf!"

Niqmaddu started toward Aqhat but Ammishtamru held up a hand and pushed him back. "We don't have time for this, you idiots," he growled. "Aqhat, did you look at this thing at all? Did you not look for anything familiar, like, for instance, the Dead Sea?"

"Yeah, it's there!" replied Aqhat. He poked a chubby finger. "See, it's right there!"

Ammishtamru squinted at the map and shoved it at him. "I can't read this. It doesn't look like the Dead Sea to me. This lake runs east to west, not north to south!"

Aqhat held it up and slowly read out the name.

"Laaaaake Onnnnnta-ree-oh," he droned.

"Lake Onta-Rio? What the hell is that?"

"Maybe it's some Jebusite name for the Dead Sea. You know those guys, they always came up with dumb names for everything. Like calling Shiloh Shit-Low."

"That always killed me," said Niqmaddu, snickering.

"It's *Lake Ontario,"* said Mahliqa, stepping forward. She pointed to Aqhat. "You led your friends to the wrong place. You're not in Canaan, you're in Canada. The land you call Canaan is now several other countries. It's about a seventeen-hour trip from here if you fly."

"I can't fly," said Aqhat with a confused look. "How far is it by camel?"

"Uh, depends on how well the camel can swim."

Aqhat shook his head slightly. "Why do you wear that thing on your head?" he asked, pointing to her *hijab*. "Are you a Perrizite?"

She shook her head. "I'm a Muslim."

"One of those guys?" He gestured toward the young Palestinians.

"Yes."

"Then get the fuck off our land."

Ammishtamru hit him upside the head again.

"You stupid Avite, we're not ON our land!" he shouted. "We're on THEIR land! You got us lost again! This is worse than your Ugarit screwup!"

"Whaddaya expect from a dumb Avite?" Yassib snorted.

"What's an Avite?" asked Amita.

"A bunch of dumbfucks who got their asses kicked by the Philistines," Yassib explained. "They lost their land and became our beggars. They were always driving us crazy, asking for handouts, pretending they had a bunch of children to feed when in fact what they wanted was the wine of Amon-Ra."

"Yeah, they couldn't settle for the cheap Greek crap, they wanted the really good stuff," sniffed Niqmaddu. He turned to the defiant-looking white man, who'd been largely silent for the last few minutes.

"Do you have a people you make fun of because they're the stupidest people you've ever seen?"

"Yeah, we do," the white man nodded. "We call them Newfies."

"So what do we do now?" asked Yassib.

"I don't know, but I think it's going to rain," remarked Niqmaddu. He tightened his skirt which was about to slide off his hips. He hoped the evil *Habiri* was watching because he had a really nice ass and she had an even nicer one. Like most men, Niqmaddu was willing to put aside ancient enmities and long-simmering resentments if it meant getting a really good piece of Astaroth.

Rachel stepped forward and stood before Ammishtamru, their chief or king or general or whatever he was. The tall handsome Canaanite looked upon her and was not unmoved by those brilliant violet eyes and her thick wavy dark hair.

"Hi there," she said, and she smiled.

Behind her, Amita and Mahliqa looked at each other uneasily.

"My name is Rachel Brinkerhoff," she said, and she extended a friendly hand. Amishtammru, who had no experience with handshakes, merely stared at it.

"Er, well," Rachel stammered as she withdrew it, embarrassed. She didn't notice Niqmaddu scowling behind him.

"I am Amishtammru," he replied, and his large dark eyes swept her. She tried not to shiver from the pleasure of it. "I was named after a great king. I am the general of this army."

"I—I just wanted to tell you—" she said, stammering again, because he was so handsome, "that you could—maybe—stay at a motel I know of in Etobicoke."

Amita and Mahliqa turned to each other as they rolled their eyes again. Where Rachel lived. How convenient. *What the hell is she doing?* their silent glances asked. *Is she trying to nail her ancient enemy? Has she learned nothing from that nutty ex-husband of hers?*

"Where is this—this—how do you say it?" Ammishtamru said, his eyes watching her intently. He found himself quite distracted by her beautiful lips. No concubine he'd ever known had lips like those except maybe his sister Nisaba who became his favorite wife when he discovered just what she could do with those lips. *This woman's a Habiri!* he told himself, but, like Niqmaddu, was willing to put aside their differences for a few hours alone with this lovely creature.

"Ee-toe-bi-coe," Rachel said slowly, enunciating each syllable. "It's only a few kilometres from here."

"Kilometers?" The large warrior looked confused.

"Uh, cubits, I meant a few cubits," she said. "A motel is—uh, a place where you can sleep for the night. Like an inn."

"Will you be there?" Ammishtamru asked, and his lips parted to reveal amazingly good teeth for an ancient soldier who'd lived in The Time Before Pepsodent.

"Oh, uh, er," Rachel said, looking down. She hadn't expected that.

Ammishtamru took her hand. His own was remarkably warm, if a bit rough. To be expected of a soldier, she thought. Damn, but he was hot.

He leaned in and his voice was deep as he growled under his breath, "I wish to take you into my bed tonight."

Rachel looked up, jaw agape. Even New Yorkers usually weren't that direct.

But before she could answer, Ammishtamru's attention moved to something just beyond her shoulder. His jawline tightened, he stood erect, he dropped Rachel's hand, and he reached for the knife at his hip.

"Lamashtu," he growled, and the other Canaanites braced themselves.

CHAPTER TEN

"Oh, it's you," came a voice behind Rachel. She turned around to find the most exquisite woman she'd ever seen. The woman for whom they invented the word 'breathtaking.' For a moment, Rachel forgot to breathe.

"Our ancient enemy," Ammishtamru growled. He looked so fierce Rachel stepped back a few paces. He reminded her just a little too much of Austin at the moment.

"Shall we kill her?" asked Yassib, although he couldn't seem to take his eyes off Lamashtu's too-tight cutoff top. As before, the bottoms of her breasts showed. The Ray-Bans, which she no longer needed with the threatening clouds, swung from the top of her blouse.

"As if you could," she drawled in her strange accent, and she put her hands on her slung-out hips. It accentuated the lovely curve of her body. The three Palestinian men stood, paralyzed. Even the Orthodox Jew appeared unable to move.

Her gaze fell upon Rachel. Her eyes narrowed and her lip curled slightly. Rachel just looked back with a mystified expression. She was unaccustomed to people taking an immediate dislike to her.

"What are you doing here?" Ammishtamru demanded. He alone seemed unaffected by the bronze leonine vision before him. For which Rachel was grateful. She felt like a bow-wow near this woman. *Maybe I should just crawl into my kennel and eat my Alpo!*

"I'm looking for a friend," she smiled, and her lips parted and every man in the crowd gasped. She shifted and so did the cutoff. It slid slightly up to a chorus of expelled air.

"Put your clothes on, you Jezebel," the Orthodox Jew growled. Lamashtu giggled, cocking her head. Slowly she raised her hands, gripped the cutoff, and pulled down. Untold pairs of angry male eyes turned upon the spoiler.

"Jezebel was a friend of mine," she said. "We had a lot in common. Too bad they killed her."

"Go back where you came from, woman," Ammishtamru commanded. He turned to Rachel. "Has she killed your babies?"

"Has she what? Killed our babies?" Rachel asked, confused.

Someone poked her in the back. She turned around. "I wonder if he means all the babies who have that choking disease!" Amita said.

"Babies are choking?" Ammishtamru turned and looked at the crowd. "Are your babies dying?" he bellowed.

"Shut up, you stupid old man!" Lamashtu hissed, and her teeth pulled back into an ugly snarl. For a moment, Rachel thought she saw the twisted face of a demon. She stepped forward and raised a perfectly-sculpted hand. "I will kill you for that—"

Two of the Canaanite warriors stepped forward with spears pointed.

"You can't kill me, you idiots," she told them.

"Perhaps not, but we can make you feel much pain," one of them replied.

Ammishtamru grabbed Rachel by the arms. "Has she hurt anyone's children?" he demanded.

"Babies are choking. Not dying, but almost," Amita answered. He turned to her. "It's been very recent."

“Women are miscarrying,” Rachel added.

"And men are dying too!" Mahliqa said as she too stepped forward.

Ammishtamru squinted at her large eyeglasses curiously. "Three so far."

"How?"

"Stung to death," she replied. Her eyelids fluttered nervously. "By a scorpion."

"Where?" he growled.

Mahliqa glanced at Rachel for help. Rachel turned to him. "Uh, on the—uh, little birdy," she replied.

"The little birdy?" Ammishtamru looked more confused.

"On the—uh—down there," Rachel explained. She might have been more frank with fewer people around.

"On the *lingam?"* he asked, his dark brown eyes fixed upon her.

Rachel glanced at her friends, with no idea how to respond.

"Yes, on the *lingam,"* replied Amita. Her brown eyes flicked away as she said the last word, but then they rested on Ammishtamru's. "And the victims are shriveled like a prune. It's a terrible death."

He turned and pointed an accusing finger at Lamashtu. "It is she who does these terrible things," he said.

Rachel looked back and forth between them, horrified. Lamashtu looked really irritated. "She—uh—kills guys by—uh—putting a scorpion on their—uh, *schmuck?"*

Amita looked at her. *"Schmuck?"* she asked.

"The *lingam,"* Rachel explained.

"She doesn't put it on them," Ammishtamru said, and he gave Lamashtu a murderous look. "She has it *inside her."*

Alexis returned to the office to find everyone crowded around a large TV set in the lobby. "What's going on?" she asked. The last time she'd seen the world stop during a workday to watch the CBC was on September 11th. She didn't think a riot of youth-obsessed movie stars in the City Hall fountain would warrant on-the-spot live news coverage.

"You'll never believe this," said Dennis, a young auditing assistant. "A bunch of ancient warriors has come out of the Bank of America building and shut down traffic!"

"Oh. Wow! You know what, I was in the Square when we heard this weird electronic-sounding boom, and then the hum stopped."

"Some psychic was on earlier who said a portal had opened up in Toronto and that weird beings were coming into the city. She said the earthquake had something to do with it."

"Oh. Well, I don't know," said Alexis, who didn't believe much in psychics.

"She also said aliens might have something to do with it."

"Of course." She rolled her eyes.

"Where are these men from? They were initially thought to be First Nations Natives making a land claim, and in fact, that's what they thought they were doing," said ace reporter Dirk Bly, who stood next to an Orthodox Jew. "But it soon came out that they are not First Nations, but men who claim to be from the ancient—uh, kingdom, not sure what you'd call it—"

"Region," said the Jew helpfully.

"Thank you. They claim to be from the ancient region of Canaan, which is mentioned in the Old Testament. I'm speaking with Rabbi Barrak Chofetz from the Jewish Studies department at the University of Toronto who says the many tribes of Canaan existed from—" He turned to the scholar.

"The third millennium before the Common Era," replied Rabbi Chofetz, carefully avoiding its more common name, B.C.

"And these Canaanites, these were the ancient enemies of the Jews, right?" asked Bly, holding the microphone for the rabbi.

He nodded sagely. "The Pentateuch - that is the first five books, Genesis, et cetera - make it clear that God instructed the Hebrews to stay away from them."

"And why was that?"

Rabbi Chofetz looked a bit uncomfortable but he managed to smile when he said, "They engaged in immoral acts and worshiped pagan gods."

"And what do these fellows want today?"

Rabbi Chofetz shifted slightly and glanced over his shoulder. "They say they want their land back."

"They want their land back," Bly repeated. "Why would they say that?"

"I thought we were going to talk about the history of the Canaanites?" Rabbi Chofetz asked.

"Well yes, we are, but we need to know why they're blocking Front Street. This is a busy avenue. It's creating quite a traffic jam, as you can see behind me. So where was Canaan located?"

"Uh—today we'd call it Israel."

"Israel?"

Rabbi Chofetz nodded, gulped, and said, "Yes."

"And who do they think took their land?"

"An ancient people called—uh, the *Habiri."*

"Habiri? Is that Hebrew?"

Rabbi Chofetz shifted nervously and tugged at his collar. "Yes."

"So today's Jews in Israel are on *their* ancient land?"

"The Palestinians too," he replied, a bit defensively.

"But they named the Jews specifically."

"Yes. The Muslims didn't invade until the seventh century. The Canaanites had been assimilated by then and no longer existed as a separate tribe."

"So how did the Jews—or, the Hebrews—get the land?"

Rabbi Chofetz adjusted his collar again and looked around. "God gave it to us!"

☆ ☆ ☆

"Where is everyone?" asked Dave the Beowulf Freak. He and Dave the Tarantula Guy looked around at a largely deserted fountain at Nathan Philips Square.

"They all went to check out the explosion," said one young man standing in the fountain. He was sticking his hands in the water and splashing it onto himself. His clothes were already pretty soaked.

"So, uh, does this really work?" asked Dave the T.G., who felt more than a little foolish.

"Does it work?" The young man grinned. "I'm eighty-six years old!"

☆ ☆ ☆

"Shit!" Angus cursed as he watched WSIB-TV. "Those sonsabitches got to them first!" He pulled out his cell phone and punched a few buttons.

"Dillweed? What the fuck's going on down there? Why am I looking at some guy named Niqmaddu being interviewed on TV? Why don't I have a Canaanite dude here yet?"

"I'm sorry," came The Dillweed's voice. "But keep in mind that WSIB is in the bank building and the CBC is right next door. There's no way I could have beaten them here."

"Shit," Angus cursed again. "Well never mind, just get one of them and bring him back here."

"I can't," replied The Dillweed. "The police are here. And someone from Immigration Canada is coming. Obviously, these guys are illegal aliens."

“Just bring me back a Canaanite guy. I need that story!”

“I'll do my best. Does that mean I should blow off investigating the gerbil population explosion in the subway system?”

☆ ☆ ☆

Mahliqa's wide brown eyes looked like they were going to explode. "She has it—*inside her?"* she gasped, then shuddered.

Rachel's face registered utter disbelief, but so many weird things had happened in the last several days that impossible had become the new norm.

A stiff wind kicked up. Above, the clouds grew dark and threatening.

Ammishtamru turned his angry eyes upon Lamashtu. "The legends say the space between her legs is like a scorpion," he growled.

Mahliqa looked like she was either going to scream or pass out. She raised a hand to her mouth and stepped back.

Lamashtu's eyes flowed with sheer malice. "I don't know what you're talking about," she snarled.

"You've got to be kidding, Ammishtamru," said Rachel, who looked like she was going to lose her lunch. She reached into her pocket and gripped the little Fuk statue tightly. It gave her solace somehow. Her protector.

He shook his head. "Lamashtu is very old, older than the Canaanites, and she is known throughout the world for her evil. She's right when she says we can't kill her. She is a demi-goddess."

"Not a full goddess?" asked Amita hopefully.

Ammishtamru shook his head. "It doesn't matter. Divine blood runs through her veins. Her father was Anu, God of the Sky. She kills babies because she is unable to have any of her own. If she is not killing babies now, it is only because her power is low."

"That would, uh, explain a lot," Rachel murmured.

Lamashtu's eyes picked her over again. This gorgeous woman had the faint whiff of Dave about her. She hadn't ruined him, but she knew him. Would she know where to find him?

"If her power isn't there, how can she do this?" asked Amita.

"It's easier to cause a miscarriage than it is to kill a child," Yassib said. "The unborn child is much weaker. It doesn't take as much energy."

Rachel, Amita and Mahliqa turned accusing eyes to Lamashtu, full of loathing.

One of the young Palestinians grabbed his friends. "I know who she is," he whispered excitedly, not realizing how far his voice carried. "I remember my mother telling my brothers and sisters and I stories about her. Her mother was an evil witch. Lamashtu makes young children die and women to miscarry."

Ammishtamru turned to them. "And she feeds off the life force of men who have never known a woman."

All eyes turned to Lamashtu, who looked murderous and like she'd given up any thoughts of denial.

"Where does she find virgins?" asked the young white woman.

Lamashtu smiled easily. "Toronto is full of them," she answered. "There are many men here who have never known the touch of a woman." She thought hungrily of Dave, whom she would find if she had to track him down to the ends of the earth. Not that anyone believed the earth had any ends anymore, she thought. She'd spent most of the last several centuries underground, but she'd still managed to pick up a few factoids here and there, including Copernican heliocentrism and that round-earth stuff from that Italian Renaissance guy.

Rachel's memory flashed on something Alexis had said during their interview. Y*ou might want to focus on immigrant men. I think you'll find Toronto guys are uninterested in women.*

"So those men she—uh, killed—" began Mahliqa, "they were all *virgins?"*

“There have been three!” cried Mahliqa.

“There have been more,” replied Lamashtu casually. “You just haven't found the bodies yet.”

“That's how she gets her power,” said Niqmaddu. "She seduces them, paralyzes them—" he gulped—"and then feeds upon their life force."

"Life force? You mean soul?" asked Rachel. The conversation fell outside her knowledge of Jewish cosmology and spirituality.

"I don't know what a soul is," said Niqmaddu, "but the thing that gives you life, the essence, what is in your eyes when you are alive and then makes them go glassy when you die, that is what she takes. Without it, you cannot live."

"What Chao calls the *qi,"* Rachel breathed.

"What we Indians call the *prana,"* Amita said.

"And you say there is no stopping her?" asked Mahliqa, looking from one Canaanite to the next.

Thunder sounded in the distance. The light around them seemed to noticeably darken. Most of the crowd glanced at the sky nervously and tried to remember if they'd left their umbrella in the car.

Yassib slowly grinned and touched Niqmaddu's arm. Wordlessly, he pointed to the sky, then to Lamashtu.

Niqmaddu did the same to Ammishtamru, who looked up and smiled for the first time.

A great rumbling shook their feet. Dozens of crowd members cried out or screamed, but the tremor passed.

"Aftershock," Rachel said to Amita and Mahliqa, who looked rattled.

Niqmaddu shook his head. "Feel that, you vicious bitch?" he crowed as he looked at Lamashtu. "Your mom is coming and she's going to be *really* pissed!"

Lamashtu looked nervous for the first time since she'd arrived in Toronto and stared at her feet. Then she looked up. Lightning split the sky over Front Street. A heavy roll of thunder followed. The first large raindrops splattered on the ground and on several people.

She turned on her heel and fled, her long dark hair banner-like.

One of the Palestinians looked after her longingly, as though he wondered if there was a way to shag her by getting around the whole nasty scorpion thing. "Even if she is an evil temptress," he said to his friends, "she is still the most gorgeous woman I've ever seen."

"If you think she's hot," said Niqmaddu, "wait 'til you see her mom!"

CHAPTER ELEVEN

The erstwhile land claim of the Canaanite Liberation Front broke up and the wannabe rebels retired to the lakefront, where they set up makeshift tents near the beach, since there was no room for them at the inn (*any* inn, which only took credit cards). Immigration Canada, being too slow to show up, wasn't there to stop them, and they built illegal fires and feasted on such fabulous other-worldly delicacies (to them, anyway) like Tim Horton's club sandwiches, brown crispy chicken in a bucket, dead cow with weird green and red garnishes between bread chunks, and stolen food from the gods called *iced lattes.* All cheerfully provided by the locals, who thought it was just too cool that a bunch of ancient warriors had landed in Toronto, and because they still felt kind of guilty (even though Canadians hadn't been invented yet) about the fact that the ancient Hebrews had once kicked them off their land and killed their sheep and wouldn't let them eat pork and stuff.

That was the night of the big storm. Which was no problem for them, they being mighty warriors and all.

Not that a big storm was atypical for Toronto, which occasionally suffered monsoon-like weather, especially during the summer, which the ancient *Habiri* would have regarded as pretty hellacious wrath-of-

God punishment for committing sins like Sabbath labour and statuary. However, in modern-day Canada, it was just regarded as typical wrath-of-God punishment for having committed the sins of fossil fuels and politics. The wind kicked up like a sonofabitch, the trees swayed and bucked like those hurricane videos of Florida you see on the news, the thunder cracked, the lightning rent the sky, the rain fell in sheets and pillowcases and duvets, and a lot of trash blew all over the place, which made the whole city look like a damn dump.

Along about two o'clock in the morning (WHY oh why does everything really *weird* happen at two o'clock in the morning?) the storm let up and people poured onto the streets again (because Toronto never let anything like a pseudo-monsoon get in the way of their late-night partying) and were still partially drunk when another earthquake shook the city and the Royal Ontario Museum Crystal began to shine with an unearthly light.

"What's goin' on, eh?" everyone said to everyone else, and they gathered near the Crystal which now hummed like the Bank of America building before it gave birth to the C.L.F.

"Oh no, it's more weirdness," someone else said, and they saw a shadow darkening the center of the unearthly light.

"I didn't know the ROM was open this late," someone else said, and his girlfriend told him to shut up.

The hum increased, the light flickered and brightened the night and the shadow moved closer to the doors. Then, as if by magic, or maybe by a security guard still working inside the museum, the doors swung open, the hum popped like another really expensive sub-woofer shot all to hell, and a tall, statuesque figure walked out into the night, standing before the crowd in all her naked, breathtaking glory.

She was perfectly formed; Pygmalion's statue come to life. Her body was lean and lithe, her legs long and statuesque, one bent slightly before the other to accentuate her exquisite hips. Her belly was smooth and her navel a long and lissome cleft, a mysterious abyss begging a man to lose himself within. Her full breasts carried delicate dark rose nipples. Her neck was long and graceful, her cheekbones high and proud, her lips full and pink and parted just enough to make several of the men fall to their knees as though to worship her (and it wasn't just because they were drunk). Her dark brown hair with gentle red tints fell in great bounding curls down her back and to her smooth alabaster buttocks. Her dark, perfectly-shaped eyebrows curved wickedly and her long, lined, fully lashed blue-gray eyes regarded the circle of men around her with a lustful air.

"Oh God, not another one," groaned a woman in the crowd.

The otherworldly creature looked around, sighing once, and sending a shiver throughout as her breasts heaved perceptibly, she said, "Hi everyone. I'm looking for my evil daughter. Does anyone know where she went?"

To: rbrinkerhoff@lovecomeslater.ca
From: chao-wan@yahoo.ca
Subject: Coffee

Good morning, Rachel. I hope life is treating you well. Dim Sum is fine, all things considered, although, as a puppy again, he occasionally loses control on the carpet. Ah well. He will outgrow it. Again.

I wondered if you would be available for coffee this week. Perhaps we could discuss the strange things happening in town and try to make sense of them. Please let me know if there is a day and time that would be convenient for you.

Your friend,

Chao

I'm not crazy. I'm just a sane person trapped in the body of a lunatic!

>>>Download Tagline Express 4.1a here at......

A few days later, Alexis showed up at Love Comes Later in tears. She wanted to speak to Rachel.

"I have to get married. I have to. I can't wait any longer," she sobbed. "I had a doctor's appointment on Friday. I've had endometriosis for years, which may or may not have made me infertile. And now I have *chlamydia.* Or I may have had it for years and just didn't know. It's hard to spot by a gynecologist. The more infections you have, the higher your chances of infertility! I have to get pregnant as soon as possible, Rachel!"

Fortunately, they were alone. Mahliqa hadn't come in yet and Amita found an excuse to leave. Rachel handed the young girl a box of Kleenex and tried to figure out what to tell her.

"You don't want to rush into anything," she began, but Alexis cut her off.

"Yes I do. Okay, I don't want to marry the first numbnuts who'll have me but I'm willing to lower my standards. He doesn't have to make as much money as me and I don't care if he likes Canadian art movies. He doesn't have to have a fabulous career. Please, Rachel, you've got to help me!" A fresh storm of tears began.

Rachel had seen this too many times before. Women who had put off childbearing until it was a lot less likely. They came to her, desperate, wanting to meet anyone with a dick who'd impregnate them. These things almost never worked out. They ended up as single parents, and that wasn't what most women really wanted for themselves or their children.

Alexis, poor girl, couldn't be called a career woman who'd put off childbearing for too long, she'd known she had fertility problems when she was twenty-three and had lost an early-term baby she didn't even know she'd had. From that point on she made it her purpose in life to find a man.

"Alexis—look, I know how unhappy you are. I feel it myself because I'm forty-one and I don't know if I can have children either. But —you don't want to choose a husband lightly. I assume you don't want to be divorced in a few years, right?"

"No. I want Mr. Right. Where the hell is he?"

"These things take time. You can't hurry love, like the old song says."

"I spent Friday night registering for *four* different online dating sites. I went out to a singles social and met a bunch of geezers old enough to be my *grandfather.* Can you imagine, an 80-year-old man thinking he should go out with someone my age? There were no decent eligible men there, and Rachel, I went with *lowered standards.* I hoped something would come through the online sites over the weekend but there was *fuck all—"*

Rachel winced a bit to hear her swear. It was uncharacteristic of the otherwise always-dressed-for-the-boardroom young lady.

"—It was just the same old crap, people farting around and playing games and no one was interested in meeting someone like me. I didn't overdo it with the marriage and kids stuff, I just said I wanted to get married and start a family. Look, maybe the other ladies here know someone—? Don't they arrange marriages for people?"

Clearly her meeting with Mahliqa earlier in the week had not helped to straighten her out as much as Rachel had hoped. They'd talked about how common values were more important than shared interests, and how the addiction to 'chemistry' led too many people to think with their crotches and their hormones rather than their heads, and letting the man get to know you. ("You don't like men who try to push you into intimate relations too quickly, do you?" asked Mahliqa. "Then imagine how they feel when you push them on the marriage issue before they even have your cell phone number!")

"That's not what they do, they help families arrange marriages themselves. I'm the matchmaker." Rachel racked her brain mentally for her newest arrivals. There were a few men she wouldn't have otherwise considered for Alexis, but she was reluctant to introduce them. Before this, Alexis wouldn't have liked them, and she didn't want to set her clients up with someone who admitted she was now willing to 'settle.'

"Keep doing what you're doing," Rachel advised, "and I'll see what I can do. I think you need to take a break, though, and think about what you're doing. I can't set you up with anyone as long as you're not thinking clearly. Call me in three days and we'll talk again."

Over a shared lunch with Amita and Mahliqa, Rachel couldn't hide the fact that she had a big crush on an ancient dead guy.

"I went down to the park by the lake last night," she told them. "I found Ammishtamru. He is *so* hot, you should see him, he's all bronze muscles and power, and he always smiles real big when he sees me. Y'know, he's really got good teeth for a Biblical warrior. Did they have oral hygiene in ancient Canaan or do they have a good dental plan in the Underworld?"

Amita and Mahliqa both shrugged, and when Rachel wasn't looking, exchanged concerned and perhaps somewhat fatalistic looks.

"He wouldn't tell me what happens, uh, down below. But it's not like it's Hell or nothin'," she added quickly, as though to reassure them, even though neither woman had reacted to her revelation. "He says it's sort of like heaven, except he didn't call it that, I don't think they knew what heaven was back then. He said it's like this great fertile field and valley with a beautiful crystal stream that runs through it and the dead all live there. But he only described people like himself so I don't think everyone who dies goes there. What did they believe back then? About the afterlife?"

Amita shrugged again and said, "This is not my religion or history. Hindus believe in reincarnation, so I imagine there aren't very many Indians where he came from."

"So I dunno, maybe everyone goes where they think they're goin', y'know? Maybe there's a Christian heaven and a Jewish heaven and a Muslim heaven, but anyway, he says they still have some contact with the world of the living. He says sometimes they can come here when something opens up a portal. He says the earthquake here we had last month did the trick. He says they can study our ways and—"

"Rachel, what are you doing with this man?" asked Amita gently. She pushed her salad away and sat back in her chair.

"I'm not—uh, I'm just talking to him, y'know, I mean we haven't—we're not—uh, involved or anything—I mean, he's an ancient warrior, Amita, how often do you get to meet someone like that? Why aren't *you* down there talking to him? They've got news crews from all over North America there, and the BBC, and anthropologists and scientists, and they all want to talk to these guys, although the Canaanites aren't much interested in talking to *them*—"

"Rachel, my friend," she said with a sweet smile, "I think you're infatuated with this silly man."

"Infatuated? Me? Uh, no," Rachel stammered. "Well—maybe a little. I mean, he's totally *hot,* Amita, you should see him—"

"I did see him," she reminded her. "I wasn't very impressed."

Rachel's face fell. "Why not?"

"You mean apart from the fact that he shouldn't even be here? He came from inside a building that is supposed to be full of offices, and right now no one can enter it because there is some portal to another world at its entrance? Plus, you have told us both how you want a good man with a right heart because your ex-husband was such a bad man, and now you are falling in love with someone just like him?"

"You can do better, Rachel," said Mahliqa. "There are men who would love to be with a woman like you if only you would notice them. You don't need to chase after—what do you Canadians call someone like him? A piece of *cheesecake!"*

"I think you mean *beefcake,"* Rachel smiled, a little forced. "And I'm not falling in love with him, I just think he's great eye candy and he's really interesting, a lot more interesting than most of the men in this town who are oblivious to women. I've had a hard time finding enough men for my database, you know. I have only a few Toronto guys. Most of the men who've signed on are from some place else. So you'll have to pardon me if I find myself fancying a guy who knows how to treat a lady."

She smiled the silly half-smile of the completely infatuated woman hopelessly in denial.

Amita stole a quick glance at Mahliqa who adjusted her *hijab* nervously and took a big bite of the falafel wrap.

"Rachel, this is just the sort of thing we hope to prevent with *Love Comes Later.* You are thinking with your *yoni* right now—"

"My what?"

"Your—well, where you don't have a *lingam."*

Rachel regarded her for a moment with furrowed brows, trying to parse her words. “Oh, the vagina!” she said, as though she'd just answered a particularly difficult question.

Several heads turned to look at her.

“Rachel, sweetheart – please keep your voice down,” Mahliqa whispered as she hunched over her falafel wrap.

“Oh, sorry. But I do not! Think with my, you know—”

“Yoni.”

“Yes.”

“You want a man with a good career, don't you?” asked Amita, all big brown eyes and pouty red mouth. “What does this man do? Herd goats?”

“He's a great general,” said Rachel sullenly.

“Canada already has a military system. And who will he defend us against, the Hittites?”

“He could learn how to, you know, fire a gun—”

Amita shook her head. It was amazing how people could so easily rationalize away the wrong qualities in a mate when they thought with their *lingam* or *yoni*. She had seen it so many times, good candidates for a husband or wife forgotten or left in the dust when someone younger, prettier, or handsomer came along. Business had dropped off once that silly Fountain of Youth was discovered. Oh yes, that was going to solve *everyone's* romantic troubles.

"Perhaps you aren't looking hard enough for the ones with a right heart who might love you," she said kindly. "You know as well as we do how distracted by romantic love and hors d'oeuvres Canadians can get."

"Hors d'oeuvres?" Rachel asked, wondering what canapes and sushi wraps had to do with anything.

"What is it you say when you aren't thinking straight because something inside you is making you do crazy things?"

"Hormones?" she asked, and Amita laughed at herself and nodded.

"Yes, hormones, that's what I meant. I wonder if perhaps you shouldn't let Mahliqa and I help you out. You know, a woman in love will do a much better job of matching up others if she's happy herself."

"I think I got it covered, Amita," Rachel said with a huge dopey grin.

☆ ☆ ☆

That night, Rachel's blood boiled and throbbed. It was like something was calling her from a distance.

She stepped out onto the modest balcony of her apartment and listened to the sounds of the city. The night was warm and a gentle breeze caressed her face. She knew she couldn't sleep.

She went to her car, got in and drove to the lakefront.

The fires were blazing. The sounds of people drumming and feasting filled her ears. It looked like a campground, and she noticed many of the locals were sitting and feasting and talking with the Canaanite warriors. Her eyes scanned the area and she wandered carefully through the crowd.

There he was, speaking with some Canadians. He looked magnificent in the firelight. His coppery skin blazed with its own heat.

Rachel stepped forward and politely waited for him to notice her. When he looked up his eyes scanned her thin summer top and her hip-hugging shorts. Quickly he rose to his feet and his mouth broke into a wide grin.

"Rachel, it is good we meet again," Ammishtamru said, and he took her hand. His touch felt like fire. Rachel tried not to shiver. Her eyes filled with his big brown wide-set eyes, his dark curly hair, his firm jaw and his naked torso, glistening in the firelight like some ancient Egyptian painting stepped off the wall and come to life—

"I was just in the area, so I thought I'd stop by and say hello," Rachel breathed. He was entranced with her smile, and her unusual violet eyes. Amishtammru had never seen such a thing when he was alive, and he had known the charms of women from all over the world, at least as he knew it.

"I am glad you did," he said. "Would you like to join me inside?"

Once again, she was taken aback by his directness, but there was nothing else she wanted more in the world, so she said, with what she hoped was her most beguiling smile, "Yes."

He led her into his tent, from Canadian Tire donated by a nearby family.

✯ ✯ ✯

"Rachel, you've got to help me." Dave the Virgin rose from his chair, the one that passed as the 'waiting room'.

"Uh, what's going on, Dave?" She stared at the nervous man before her. Mahliqa watched from her desk. He'd been waiting for Rachel more than an hour. Dave wore a shirt with the collar turned up, a baseball cap, and sunglasses. Even though the day was overcast.

"I'm in a lot of trouble. I think you can help."

"Me? What kind of trouble?"

"Can we go some place more private?"

"In downtown Toronto?"

"Well—uh—there's a pub around the corner. It won't be too busy this time of day."

"It's ten-thirty, Dave, will they even be open?"

"Yeah, the lunch crowd will start coming in soon."

They went down to the Aardvark & Firkin and picked a booth in the back.

"I've gotta get married, Rachel. Now."

"Oh. Well. There's a lot of that going around this week."

"What?"

"Uh, nothing. So why do you have to get married so quickly, Dave?" She wanted to say *Have I got a girl for you!* but knew it would be a bad idea. Alexis and Dave weren't right for each other. Even if he did have a penis capable of sowing her womb.

"I'm a marked man, Rachel. Someone's after me. This—uh—well actually, this is going to sound pretty crazy unless you've been watching the news."

"You mean all the strange stuff going on in the city?"

"Yeah. Have you heard or read about this chick named Lamashtu?"

"Heard of her? Hell, Dave, I've *seen* her."

Dave's mouth dropped open and he began to shake. His hands gripped the table. "Where?"

"At the bank building the other day where the Canaanite guys were." Rachel tried not to smile. She was actually sore from all the, uh, hellos she'd bestowed upon Ammishtamru for the last few days.

"Oh my God!" he said again, although it came out as more of a squeak. "She was there? When? Where?"

"I don't know, Dave. Amita and Mahliqa and I got stuck in the traffic when the warriors blocked the street. We went up to check it out, and shortly after she showed up."

"She was in the newspaper."

Rachel nodded. "Yeah, I saw that. She was on the news too. I was there when the CBC caught the exchange between her and Ammishtamru. You know she's supposed to be the one responsible for all those guys who died by—uh, getting stung on the—uh—*putz?"*

"Yeah. I think she did it, too."

"I'm not so sure about that part. She didn't deny it or nothin', but I can't see how she could do that—I mean, the autopsies found these guys were initially paralyzed by a scorpion sting on the—uh—"

"Putz."

"Yeah. But I mean, where's she gonna put it? The scorpion, I mean? How does she—oh, no, it's just stupid. She must carry it with her—"

"I think it's true, Rachel. And she's after me."

Rachel looked at him like he'd announced he'd just won eighteen gold medals in the Sexual Olympics.

"She wants me, Rachel. She's determined to seduce me."

Rachel sat motionless in the booth. It's possible for a moment her mind was blown.

"Okay, I know how stupid it sounds. You've seen her, you know what she looks like. What would a beautiful woman like *her* want with a complete tool like *me?* But I'm telling you, that day, not an hour before you saw her, she was with me down at the marina and we were about to—uh—"

"Schtup?" Rachel looked away as she said it. She just wasn't used to discussing such intimate subjects with her clients.

"Uh, well, does that mean to have sex?"

Rachel nodded.

"Then yeah, we were about to *schtup.* You have no idea how close I got to the—uh—scorpion." Now it was Dave's turn to look away.

"What happened?"

Dave shut his mouth and gulped. He sank back into the booth.

"I totally muffed it. Let's not discuss how." He reached up to wipe away a tear from under his sunglasses. As glad as he was that things had turned out as they had, it was still grossly humiliating to remember.

"So why does she want you so badly?" Rachel asked, and she touched his arm. She couldn't see him watching her behind his glasses. He'd forgotten how beautiful she was.

In fact, she looked even *more* beautiful than he remembered. How? Why? She seemed to be glowing. There was an unmistakable softness around her face he didn't remember from before. He recalled passing her on the way out when he first visited Love Comes Later, and she looked away from him. Her face was down, there wasn't much joy in her eyes. Now they sparkled, like polished amethysts.

"It's embarrassing," he began, and he sniffled a little. "I'm sorry, I don't mean to cry, but I didn't tell you this before. I was too ashamed. I was afraid you might not take me on if I told you the truth."

"What's the truth?" asked Rachel, but she already knew.

Dave the Virgin wasn't the only one travelling incognito anymore.

Lately, a quite nondescript figure had begun slinking around Toronto. She looked Indian, in a long ankle-length loose-fitting cotton robe, the kind favored by many Indian women. Her head was wrapped in a white *pashmina* slung over one shoulder. And she wore large, face-eating sunglasses. She no longer walked with the swaying, serpentine movements with which she'd enchanted half of Toronto. Now she hurried through the city, dead hot in so many clothes, unused to travelling with more than the barest of covering.

She always hurried, seemingly late for some important appointment, but in fact she had nowhere to go. She paused on many street corners, sniffing the air discreetly. Occasionally she bought a newspaper, looking for stories about the strange things happening in the city. But then she'd toss it aside and hurry away.

The truth was, she was starving to death.

Lately, the air was bereft of telltale scents - the scent that she alone could detect. The levels of Toronto's male virgins had dropped precipitously, like the Jordan River during a long drought. She caught a few whiffs here and there, but they disappeared like smoke on the wind - there but momentarily, then gone. The words she'd had with the Canaanites had made the TV news, and been reported in the paper. Now everyone knew what she looked like, and those that had seen her before her identity had been revealed all spoke to the media. They were all too eager to talk about the unspeakably beautiful woman they'd seen having a latte at a street corner cafe, or sashaying down to the lakefront the day those weird guys came out of the bank building, or how she hadn't seemed to react when a small child near her started choking.

And, they'd begun to find the other bodies. Which she'd foolishly boasted about.

Now, if she was recognized, the men backed away, and the women didn't - particularly the mothers. Those had been the worst. She'd nearly been killed the other day in Parkdale. They'd chased her down the street, screaming, and if it hadn't been for a police car who picked her up, the mob might well have rent her to pieces.

Not unlike what they did to my friend Jezebel, she thought nastily. *Except they threw Jez to the dogs, rather than do the deed themselves. Cowards.*

Shit and double shit! She'd thought she was going to be very happy in Toronto forever and after, surrounded by food and almost, oh, so close to gaining her powers back so she could finally start wasting those damn babies once and for all.

Because there was nothing in the world that Lamashtu hated worse than babies.

Except maybe her mother.

Alexis was an expert at multitasking. She always kept one ear on the office doorway while she perused the singles sites. Of course, she knew she should be doing actual work but this was an emergency, and as soon as she found an appropriate candidate she would work twice as hard in the future to make up for the time she was sort of, uh, stealing from her employer.

Gerard looked promising but he already had two kids. Still, he hadn't ruled out more children and she couldn't be picky anymore. And Vasilios, he was hot-looking and lived around the Danforth which was only a few subway stops from her apartment.

Dave, now there was a guy. He said he ran his own software company and was only a year older than her. And another Dave who wrote proprietary software code for one of the big banks in town.

Alexis hit Send A Message and began with the Daves.

"Dave, I can't find anyone for you that quickly."

Dave the Virgin's face fell, then turned into one of horror. "Rachel, she'll find me. She's looking for me. I don't know why, you'd think in a city with four million people she could find other guys to chase after - I mean, I can't be the *only one* here—" He turned away again, ashamed. Thirty-five years old and still as untouched as a medieval nun.

"Believe it or not, I just had this conversation with another client a few days ago. Well, not exactly the same conversation—" Rachel added when Dave looked up, surprised. She wished he'd take those sunglasses off.

"I have another client who's—uh, pretty desperate to get married," she said, then immediately regretted it.

"Who is it? Is it a woman?" he asked excitedly.

"Yes, but—you two are definitely not right for each other," Rachel stammered. "She's—uh—looking for someone a little more—uh, stable right now."

"Not some geek who lives with his parents and doesn't have a real job," Dave said sadly, slumping back in the booth.

"It's—uh—a long story. I can't divulge the details."

Dave sat up again. "Do you think she'd shag me?"

Three people came through the door of Love Comes Later. Mahliqa looked up from the phone and motioned for them to have a seat. She covered the receiver and said in a stage whisper, "Just make yourselves comfortable, I'll be finished in a minute!"

They were an attractive trio. One was a handsome young man with thick brown hair and a neatly-trimmed moustache. The other two might have been his parents, or they might not—it was hard to tell, they looked older than the young man, but she wasn't sure if they were old enough to be his parents. Mahliqa hoped they were, though. Now *this* was what she and Amita had envisioned for Love Comes Later. A good-looking young person with a happy face and a willing heart and two open-minded parents.

She came from around her desk when she got off the phone, adjusting her bright pink *hijab* and pasting on her biggest smile. "Good morning, welcome to Love Comes Later," she said as she extended a hand.

"Hello there, Mahliqa, why so formal?" asked the young man as he tentatively shook her hand, as though it was a silly gesture he had to follow through. "I haven't seen you in awhile so I guess we'll shock you a little."

"Erm, do I know any of you?" asked Mahliqa, looking from face to face. They all looked vaguely familiar, but she couldn't quite place them. Had she begun forgetting faces? Was she turning into her beloved grandmother already?

"Yeah, Mahliqa, it's me, Dave Urquhart! And these are my parents, you've met them before."

Mahliqa's eyes grew to the size of CBC satellite dishes. "Aren't you the guy with the spider?"

“Yeah, Pookums. She's doing great, by the way. Have you been down to Nathan Philips Square lately?"

CHAPTER TWELVE

"Can you believe this?" Angus exulted on-air. "We're getting reports that those Egyptian guys—or Canaanites—whatever the hell they are—who have been living down by the lake are having *orgies!* The *Globe & Mail* today says they were engaging in Baal worship! If you don't know what Baal worship is it's in the Bible, I looked it up - it's this total pagan thing, it involves feasting and getting drunk and gettin' *doooown!"*

"Uh, I don't think she'd shag you," said Rachel. She sat back, a bit shocked.

"Are you sure?" he pressed. "Would she maybe do it as a favor?"

"I, uh, wouldn't want to ask her," Rachel said. "Uh, don't you know anyone who could—you

know—"

Dave pulled off the sunglasses and leaned forward, looking into her violet eyes. "Would I still be a v—" he stopped and glanced around quickly, then lowered his voice, "a *virgin* at my age if I could identify one woman on this heliocentric rock who would actually come near me?"

"I, uh, guess you've got a point," Rachel said.

"Then if this woman won't shag me," Dave said, "would *you* shag me?"

Rachel froze, dumbfounded.

"Look, I know it's a very personal thing to ask. But look, I'm *desperate!"* he said, his voice rising in tone if not necessarily in volume. "Er, I don't mean that you're the last person I'd choose—uh, you're, very, uh, beautiful and—" He looked away before he made a complete idiot of himself. *Before? Buddy, you just went above and beyond complete and soared into the stratosphere exploring whole new levels of idiocy never before attained by mortal man—*

Rachel could only stare at him, paralyzed. This had never, in all her years of matchmaking, happened to her.

"Okay, I can't sound any stupider than I already have so I might as well just go for broke." Dave threw the sunglasses on the table and leaned forward, gripping her arm. "Rachel, I'm a 35-year-old virgin. I'm so ugly and fat no sane woman would want me. Hell, even blind women don't want me, and believe me, I've actually looked for women who can't see what I look like. Right now there's a crazy-ass woman out there, the most incredible creature I've ever known, with a scorpion in her vajayjay seeking out Toronto's biggest virgins! Look, if you'll do this thing I'll never bother you again, I'll leave the city if you like, I promise to keep my eyes closed, just please do it, take this damn cherry from me, and I swear to you I won't enjoy it! I mean, I would if the circumstances were different, because you're a very beautiful woman and I'm such a big tool—wait, no, I'm not saying I have one, that isn't a pickup line, it's maybe a little small but it's definitely not micro or anything, I'm saying *I'm* a big tool, and really, if you let me do most of the work in a room by myself all you'll need to do is come in and finish the job and we can turn the lights out and if I touch anything I shouldn't I'll cut my own hands off—"

"Dave!" Rachel shouted. "Get a grip on yourself!"

She winced the moment the words came out of her mouth.

"I didn't mean it that way—uh, you know—"

"Yeah yeah yeah, I know how you meant it. Oh dear God, Rachel, if you can't—uh, fix me, please, please help me find someone who will, I really gotta do this, look, this is a matter of life and death, do you know what she *does* to guys? I mean first she stings them with her—uh—you know, her scorpion thing, and then she drains them somehow! I don't even know what she drains or how but when she's done they look like those shrunken apple dolls they sell in the States! The forensic guys say the sting isn't what kills them, it only paralyzes them, and I don't know if they feel it when she's sucking their whatever-it-is but I don't wanna find out—"

"Dave!" Rachel gripped both his shoulders. "Shut up!"

Which he did, abruptly.

"Now get a—I mean, get control of yourself," she ordered. "I'll get you laid. I'm not gonna do the job myself, but I'll find someone. How do you feel about paying a hooker?"

☆ ☆ ☆

Alexis' ears, highly attuned to catch when someone was approaching, quickly minimized her web browser and pulled up a spreadsheet. When her boss stopped behind her she appeared to be hard at work, squinting at the numbers before her and typing in a particularly complex formula.

"How's the progress on that audit report?" asked Carmen. Alexis turned around and gave her a big smile. "Coming along pretty well," she replied. "I think I'll be done with it by the end of the day."

"Can I see you in my office, please?" Carmen said with a tight smile.

Alexis felt a nervous flutter in her stomach.

☆ ☆ ☆

"—And no one knows where the second naked woman is," the deejay added. "Dozens of people saw her emerge from the ROM Crystal a few nights ago, but no one knows where she went. However, due to the similarities between the way she came to Toronto and this Lamashtu chick, guys, you'd better keep your John Thomas locked up in your pants because it's believed she might have a scorpion in the ol' cha-cha too—"

✯ ✯ ✯

"Amita's not back yet?" Rachel went to her desk and began shutting down her computer. Mahliqa was sitting with three clients at her desk. Rachel didn't recognize them. Must be new. Her heart fluttered a little in anticipation of the evening.

"She'll be back shortly," Mahliqa replied, but she sounded a little distant. However, Rachel didn't notice. Already the inside of her pants were jumping, thinking of hot bronze warrior love between her legs.

"Are you gone for the day?" Mahliqa asked.

"Yeah, I gotta—uh, take care of some business," Rachel replied evasively. "That fellow that was here before, Dave, I need to—uh, introduce him to someone."

"You mean the v—" She stopped herself just in time and clapped her hand to her mouth. "I mean, the sweet young man who thinks he's too fat? Oh good, you're matching him? That's wonderful! I hope it's a good match. I hope it lasts forever."

"Yeah, me too," Rachel said, and then added under her breath, "or at least thirty seconds, which is all I think he's gonna need."

"Where is he? Dave, I mean?"

"He's waiting outside. Tell Amita when you see her that I think I can work something for that fellow who came in last week. You know, the friend of that guy who likes *Beowulf.*"

"The one who likes spiders?" asked the handsome young man.

"Yes, uh—have we met before?"

"Rachel, you don't recognize me? Dave Urquhart! And these are my parents!"

Rachel stared at them. One after the other.

"You—you're Dave—and his parents—"

“Yes.” Dave's grin reached from one end of the room to the other.

“But you—you're—you're all—”

“Young,” Dave smiled. “It's that Fountain of Youth! You've got to try it, Rachel! It's amazing!”

“Uh—” Rachel was dumbfounded. This couldn't be—it was impossible—it was—

—Chao's puppy all over again.

The door opened, and all heads turned. It was Amita, with Chao in tow.

His eyes lit up. "Rachel!" he cried. "It's good to see you again. I was hoping we could go out for another coffee soon."

Rachel responded with an uncharacteristic bear hug.

"I, ah, guess you're glad to see me too," he added.

"I have to thank you, Chao! You were right, I didn't believe in that stuff, but it worked! The *feng shui!* I found a great guy!"

Chao pulled back, confusion in his dark eyes. "What do you mean by that?" he asked cautiously.

Amita and Mahliqa looked at each other, then back at the couple, with disappointment.

"Your little man. The statue you gave me. See? It's right there on my desk!" Rachel pointed to Fuk, standing beside Yente the Matchmaker. "You told me I needed a male statue there to balance the energies so I'd find a wonderful man and you're right, I did!"

"Oh." Chao looked away. He stared at the floor for a few moments, then gulped and said, "I'm very happy for you, Rachel. Who is the extremely fortunate man?"

Rachel babbled away about Ammishtamru, completely oblivious to how crazy it sounded, or to Amita's and Mahliqa's faces, or to Chao's, for that matter, either.

★ ★ ★

"I'm being fired?" Alexis breathed in a quavery voice. Her heart thumped against her chest.

Carmen nodded slowly and played with a paperweight on her desk. "You've been warned several times about the quality of your work," she said. "We've even issued you a written reprimand."

"But that was before Christmas!" Alexis protested. "And you said I'd improved a lot a few months later."

"That's right, you did. But then your work began slipping again. Mostly in the last month, and we soon figured out why. You're using the Internet for non-business purposes and you're making too many personal phone calls."

"I've had to talk to my doctor!" Alexis said, and she struggled to hold back the tears. It wouldn't be professional to cry, and high-powered career women never let their emotions show. "I've been having more medical problems, and they've been running tests—"

"Yes, we know about that, and we're not holding that against you. But you've been overheard having several non-medical, non-professional calls as well, and on top of that, you're using the company computer to surf singles sites and research your health problems. You have to do that on your own time. On your own computer."

"But—but—" Alexis struggled. If she said anything more she would surely burst into tears.

"I will help you get another job, Alexis," Carmen continued. She leaned forward and looked her in the eye. "You were one of the finest analysts we had until your personal problems took over. Believe me, Alexis, other managers as well as myself have the highest regard for your skills. But we can't tolerate sub-par performance anymore. Now I will tell you something I'm not supposed to say. If you use me as a reference I will say the reason you left the company is because of layoffs. I won't tell them about your inconsistent performance. But you will have to do your part and take your next job with a more focused approach than you have this one. If I find out you lost another one for the same reasons, I won't, uh, fudge for you again."

"Babies and small children have disappeared from the streets of Toronto," announced Dirk Bly, crack CBC-TV reporter. "Word has spread the woman called Lamashtu is trying to kill them with the power of her eyes alone."

Dave the Tarantula Guy and Pookums watched the news together. Pookums was perched on his shoulder for a better view.

Bly turned first to a woman on his left. "This is Mrs. Marcia Spieffenbacher who lives in Parkdale. She says she saw the mysterious woman try to kill an infant in a stroller."

"It's true," said Mrs. Spieffenbacher. "It was fairly recent. She was wearing expensive sunglasses, and I noticed her because she was parading down the street like she was the Queen or something, except if the Queen was wearing as little as this woman was, there'd be a major scandal on both sides of the Atlantic! Anyway, I watched the woman lower her sunglasses and stare at the child, and the next thing you know, the poor little thing starts choking!"

"That's a pile of malarkey," said a man to Bly's right, who was tall, middle-aged, and had the look of a stodgy college professor. Bly turned the microphone to him.

"This is Dr. Erwin Pewsinger who teaches biology and life science at York University. You don't think this woman is responsible for the child chokings around Toronto, Doctor?" he asked. "How about the increase in miscarriages?"

"There's no denying that both these things are occurring, but I'm sure you'd agree that it's impossible to cause death just by looking at someone. This isn't the movies, you know."

"Dr. Pewsinger is a member of the Ontario Society of Skeptics," Bly explained to his audience. "The Society takes a dim view of the unexplainable and the supernatural, don't they?"

"We certainly do," Dr. Pewsinger smiled, and he folded his hands in front of him. He hoped it made him look more authoritative. It was the first time he'd ever been on TV. He was glad he'd decided to grow a beard this spring. "I don't have to explain the impossible logistics of this, do I? When has anyone ever been shown to have such powers? This sounds, Dirk, quite similar to the stories told about witches in the Middle Ages. Or what some cultures would call the Evil Eye. Where you look at a person and cause illness or disease, or you look at a cow and cause its milk to curdle, or a cat to give birth to a snake. It was rubbish back then and it's rubbish now. I hope this young lady, wherever she is, is safe from anyone who might believe in this mindless superstition."

"So, what's the Society's take on all these ancient guys that came out of the bank building, and the fact that no one can go in?" asked Bly.

"Uh, that's still under investigation," replied Dr. Pewsinger, looking not unlike Rabbi Chofetz a few days earlier.

✯ ✯ ✯

A factoid Crack Reporter Dirk Bly had failed to uncover - mostly because no one else had taken notice of it either - was that the American border was experiencing an uptick in men from Toronto who had suddenly taken it into their heads to spend a few days in Rochester or Buffalo.

"Yeah, we just came down to do some shopping, eh?" said a fellow named Nigel to a U.S. Customs agent at the Peace Bridge. "Me and my buddy here are looking for, uh, sports equipment and, uh, maybe a computer or something."

"What's your name and where were you born?" asked the customs agent, leaning a bit to catch a glimpse of the buddy.

"Dave Squash," he said. "Born in Sudbury, but I live in Toronto now."

"Yeah, Dave's a senior network tech for the Hudson Bay Company. His Apple just died, so he's looking for another one."

"How long will you boys be here?" asked the agent. She squinted at them, looking for signs of drug use, alcohol, or incipient terrorism tendencies. They were both white, but you just couldn't be too careful anymore.

"A week," said Nigel, at the same time as Dave said, "Two weeks."

"Which is it?" asked the agent. "A week, or two weeks?"

"Two weeks," Dave replied abruptly, before Nigel could say anything. "We might visit a friend in Syracuse."

"Okay, you can go," she said, waving them off. She'd had half a mind to pull them over and look in the trunk, but they were both such geeks she couldn't imagine what they might try to smuggle, and frankly they looked too stupid to be terrorists.

"Hey, thanks! Beauty way to go, eh? You have a nice day, eh!" called Dave as they pulled away, so relieved was he that they weren't going to get turned away. Americans loved that Bob and Doug McKenzie crap.

"I think she bought it, eh?" Nigel said after he rolled up the window.

"You really think we had to cross the border to be safe?" asked Dave. "We could have driven to Winnipeg, or maybe out to the Maritimes. It's really nice out there this time of year. St. John's is a really pretty little town."

"She could still come for us if we'd stayed in Canada," Nigel answered. "But I think she'd have a hard time crossing the border. If she really is that chick that came out of the mall fountain like everyone said, then she won't have a passport."

"Yeah, good thinking, eh?"

Lamashtu stood close to a tall building, trying to look casual as she cautiously sniffed the air. Nothing. No food, anyway. It was like Toronto's virgins had disappeared. She detected several female virgins, who were often from conservative cultures and wore distinctive clothes that tipped her off visually before she smelled them. If worst came to worst she'd have to grab a woman or two, and that would tide her over until she could find some men again. The problem was that a virgin woman's essence wasn't nearly as powerful as a man's. She'd have to feed on several dozen women in order to get her full powers back, and not only would that result in an extremely problematic body count, but she couldn't attract them with her sensual appeal and they'd probably fight a lot more, since she'd have to feed off them like a vampire. She'd have no way to neutralize them. She'd waste more energy fighting than feeding.

She sniffed the air again. Her body tightened. There it was again, that horrible familiar odor - the scent of a storm, the smell of damp earth, and the unmistakeable tinge of musk. She was somewhere in the city, and it was just a matter of time before she found Lamashtu. She'd read the stories in the paper of the beautiful naked woman who'd walked out of the ROM Crystal at two in the morning.

Mother!

There was another scent on the air. Lamashtu sniffed carefully. Not a virgin but—pain. Female anger. She looked around. A pretty young woman shuffled her way down the sidewalk, her head held low, staring at the concrete. She carried a large brown box in her arms. She sniffled and as she drew closer, Lamashtu could smell her emotional pain. *She is like me,* she thought, *but she doesn't quite know it yet.*

Someone yanked the pashmina scarf off her head. Whipping around, Lamashtu found a gang of five children - older ones. Young teenagers, two girls and three boys.

"I know you," said the biggest one. He was almost as tall as she was, and he was stocky and muscled. "You're Lamashtu. The one who's been in the news. You're the one who's been attacking babies and hurting kids."

"And making women abort their babies," snarled one of the teenage girls. Lamashtu noted a gold cross at her throat.

"I don't know what you're talking about," replied Lamashtu, and she tried to back away but met the building wall instead. *Why hadn't she smelled them?* The scent of virgin was overwhelming now. They'd come up from behind, downwind. Her stomach growled to see the three she most wanted to consume.

The other girl reached up and whipped off her Ray-Bans, so fast Lamashtu couldn't react. "You're the one that was on the news," she said. "The Canaanite guy said you're the one who hurts babies and children. He said you hate them because you can't have any yourself. Is that true?"

"You have mistaken me for someone else," Lamashtu mumbled, but there was a tremble in her voice.

"There's no mistake," said the leader, and he stepped forward menacingly. "So, bitch, you think you can choke *me?"*

At one time, she could have, but the older a child was, the harder they were to kill, even when she was at full strength. By the time they reached their teens, they were almost impossible - they required far too much energy, and way too many virgins, for the trouble. And Lamashtu generally lost interest in older children anyway because they weren't cute and innocent-looking like the babies who made her want to throw them to the dogs, like the *Habiri* did to Jezebel.

"How about *me?"* a shorter, skinnier teenage boy with a pimply face and long dark hair poked her in the chest. "Or do you want to sting me with your killer cooch?"

"Kenny! I thought you weren't a virgin!" one of the girls exclaimed.

"I'm not," he said, looking annoyed, "but that's what she does."

"Oh, you're a virgin," Lamashtu said nastily. "You're all virgins."

"Go ahead then, bitch," said the leader. "Sting us. Or try to drain us dry. Just try." He smacked her in the head.

The abuse jarred something deep within Lamashtu. "I used to feed your kind to the wrathful fires of Moloch," she snarled, and she lunged at the boy.

"Back off, bitch!" the third boy cried, and she hung back. "As soon as people recognize you, you'll be lynched. If I were you I'd start runnin'!"

"Listen to him," said the leader, and he raised a fist to Lamashtu's face. His clenched fingers were encased in brass knuckles. With nasty little spikes over each bump.

"The first thing I'm gonna do is give you a couple of black eyes," he snarled, and he pulled back his arm.

Lamashtu turned and ran. The chase was on.

CHAPTER THIRTEEN

"Have you found anyone yet?"

"Dave, this isn't as easy as you think," Rachel said. This was the third time today he'd telephoned her. "I've never tried to score a hooker before. And people are suspicious when they hear a woman trying to find one. And not surprisingly, the hooker biz has suddenly improved here the last few days now that it's known some chick with a killer crotch and a jones for, uh, the untried is prowling the streets."

She tried not to let the exasperation creep into her voice. She was a *matchmaker,* not a pimp! "Are you sure you don't have any friends who could, uh, do you this favor?"

"If I could find someone who didn't mind shagging a fat, ugly, pathetic, balding virgin before this, don't you think I would have?" he asked, and he did indeed sound so pathetic Rachel's anger melted away.

"You're not fat and ugly, Dave," she told him. "You've got lousy self-esteem, but you're not unattractive. I wouldn't have taken you on if I'd thought I couldn't match you."

"You just felt sorry for me," he said, without accusation. "You didn't want to tell me the truth, that I'm unmatchable. What woman would want a loser like me? I never went to university, I live with my parents, and I have a stupid boring crappy job I do at home."

"I won't deny you'll be harder to place," Rachel said in a gentler tone, "but you're not impossible. You're a good guy, Dave, and you're very smart. I'm thinkin' maybe a gal a little like you - you know, a little shy, very bright, maybe someone who's not too materialistic. I know guys like to think that all women want is money but it's not true. The smart ones know that rich powerful guys aren't always very faithful."

"My mother's always asking me when I'll get married," Dave said, and he began to sob. "It's so humiliating. She doesn't mean to do it but that's how I feel. She keeps telling me how wonderful I am and how any girl should consider herself lucky to get a guy like me, but I think even she knows what a total loser I am."

"I know how you feel," Rachel replied. "My mom does the same to me, too. Because she wants grandchildren. Never mind that I needed some time to get over my ex-husband, she started nagging me before the ink was dry on the divorce papers. Hey, at least you can have kids whenever you want," she said with a nervous chuckle.

"I don't know what woman will come near me," Dave sniffled. "Rachel, I've struck out with every girl or woman I've ever approached. *Every single one.* There was one woman a few years ago on Plenty of Fish who agreed to meet me, but when we met for coffee her face fell and as it turned out, she'd gotten my picture mixed up with some other guy she'd been talking to. Some *better-looking* guy, obviously!"

“Listen, Dave, we'll deal with this in a few more days. I'm a little unclear as to why you're so afraid of this Lamashtu, frankly. It's not like she can—force you. I mean, it's not like when you—you know, force a woman. A man has to be ready."

"A man who's not ready for *her* is a man who's been dead at least six weeks," Dave replied. "You wouldn't understand, Rachel, because you're not a man. The woman is incredible. Do you know what she did the first time I met her? She sat there talking to me with one breast hanging out of her dress. She has—the most *incredible* nipples I've ever seen. And yes, I've seen a lot of nipples even though hers were the first I'd met personally. I watch a lot of porn, I admit it. Anyway, she's stalking me. I've seen her. Three times in the last few days. Always sniffing, looking around. I know it's her, even though she's covered up and wears big sunglasses. I know those sunglasses, they're expensive. I pray she hasn't figured out where I live."

"Look, Dave, there's another option we haven't discussed yet. Is there any chance you can leave Toronto for awhile? Like go to another province or New York or something. I'm hearing stories that some guys are headed for the border because this gal doesn't have the paperwork to cross."

"Yeah, I think I could do that," said Dave, and he brightened up a little. But it was only momentary. "See? You can't even *pay* someone to shag me!"

✯ ✯ ✯

Alexis sat curled up on her couch in front of the TV. Her face was red and streaked with tears, and her lank, unwashed hair spilled over both shoulders. She still wore a bathrobe even though it was mid-afternoon. A box of Kleenex stood at her elbow and a pile of them had collected under the table. Some lame soap opera was on but she was only half-watching it. She couldn't see it anyway without her glasses, which were on the cocktail table.

She hadn't eaten in a day and a half and periodically, she pondered the possibility of stepping out onto the balcony and just climbing over. The only thing that stopped her was the knowledge of just how long it would take to fall twenty-three stories, and how much rank terror she'd experience on the way down.

Plus, what if she changed her mind mid-way?

She tried to focus on the TV characters but her mind raced, panicking. She'd been with the company for more than five years. She'd only worked for one other firm before that. At thirty-one, she had little experience and coping skills to deal with job terminations. The last time it had happened she had sort of known it was coming. It was shortly after 9/11, and the economy had tanked. Not as bad as in the U.S., but when the U.S. sneezes, everyone catches the cold. She'd seen the signs, and she updated her resume and put it on Monster and Workopolis. She'd quietly networked and already had a few irons in the fire when the hatchet fell.

But she had no prospects now. None. She hadn't seen this coming. No one had said anything to her in months. She didn't think she'd been using the Internet that much. Now she had condo fees and bills to pay, and no income. This on top of the recent knowledge that she had to step up her husband-finding mission, and *tout de suite.* How would she find the time to do both? Each was equally mission-critical...

The thought trailed off as a sudden pain seized her midsection. Gasping, Alexis leaned forward, one forearm clutching it tight. It grew, and it made her nauseous. Something was wrong, desperately wrong—

She fumbled for her cell phone on the cocktail table next to her glasses and dialed 911.

✯ ✯ ✯

A beautiful young woman parked her car in an underground garage near the lakefront. Her heart fluttered in anticipation and for the first time in years she felt dead-sexy. She turned heads as she walked down the sidewalk. She looked hot in her tight-fitting though tasteful white shorts and her sheer white blouse. She carried herself with a new-found pride and confidence. Men glanced furtively at the delicious curve of her blouse, the cleavage that pointed the way. She wore sparkly gold sandals and her makeup was bold and enticing. And she wasn't just having a good hair day, she was having an Unspeakably Awesome Hair Day.

The radiant vision no longer possessed faint crow's feet.

Rachel couldn't believe her fortune. She believed in *feng shui.* She believed in mysticism and New Age-ness and Fountains of Youth and magic. She wasn't sure why the Jewish religion had missed all this but she didn't care. She was endlessly fascinated with her new man, his stories and philosophies, his eyewitness accounts of battles in the Hebrew Bible he'd said were totally wrong because the *Habiri* writers didn't want to admit when they lost a battle to the pagans. "They outmanned us, and they fought harder, and I will admit perhaps their god wanted them to win more than ours did, but I tell you, Rachel, I personally kicked Joshua's ass on the top of a hill that *your history* claims was won by the *Habiri* because some clown held up his hands until they were about to fall off, and then he got his friends to hold them up for him. Oh, and that duel between one of your god's priests and one of ours, and your god set the fire and ours didn't, and that supposedly proved whose god was real and whose wasn't? Look, that was a draw. Nothing happened. No fire. Everyone got embarrassed and left."

He was fascinating and handsome and brave and he was just amazing in bed. She heard the drumming even from several blocks away and her heart sped up to think of another breathtaking night with the most incredible man she'd ever met.

You're going to get a grandchild sooner than you think, Ma! she thought with a smile.

"Uh, Miss?" came a voice from the dark. Rachel turned around. It was the Orthodox Jew.

He stepped forward and extended his hand. "I'm Rabbi Chofetz from the Beth Hamidrash Synagogue near Bathurst. I also teach at the University. You and I spoke briefly the day the Canaanites arrived."

"I remember." *You accused me of not being Jewish enough,* she thought. "Rachel Brinkerhoff."

"I'm pleased to meet you, Miss Brinkerhoff."

"Rachel is fine."

"Very good, then, Rachel. Are you going down there now?"

She nodded. She hoped he wouldn't ask why. No doubt he wouldn't be impressed. He regarded the Canaanites as the enemy.

"You look a little different," the rabbi commented.

"Do I?" Rachel broke out in eight different grins. "Younger, huh?"

"Well, I don't know—I only met you once. Oh no—you went to that Fountain of Youth, didn't you!"

Of course she had! And it had so been worth it. Ammishtamru was smitten with her, and men followed her down the street like they had when she was younger. She felt lighter, wilder, brimming with confidence. If she'd been in New York and saw Austin she'd totally blow him off.

Rabbi Chofetz said something in Hebrew that sounded like a swear, but Rachel wasn't sure. She'd never learned the language.

"Do you know where I can find this Lamashtu?" he asked. Rachel's eyes widened. Was he *serious?*

"I don't know. She sounds kind of dangerous, though. What do you want her for?" She was immediately sorry she'd asked. It was none of her business, and so far he hadn't asked why she was going down to meet the Canaanites.

"We have to find her. Immediately. She must be vanquished." The rabbi's eyes were solemn behind his simple wire-rim glasses.

"We?"

"Yes. Myself and some others. We can't find her. We have to—she has to be—eliminated somehow."

Rachel's eyes grew wide.

"Not killed," he answered hastily. "Not that we could, anyway. She's —she's as the big general said. She's a demi-goddess. I've been doing some research. I've found some quite—sobering things about her."

"Like what?" Rachel asked.

"How well do you know your Jewish history?"

"I've read the sacred texts. I had my *bat mitzvah.* I read some books." She looked away, embarrassed. If he wanted to call her a crappy Jew she probably deserved it. She hadn't been to Shabbot services in years. She'd always promised herself she'd start going again when she got pregnant, but of course that had never happened.

"The history I know is not the one taught in our schools. It's more —ancient. Obscure. And quite troubling."

"What did you find?"

"Lamashtu was a demon and a demi-goddess. According to myth, her father was Anu, the Sumerian sky god. Her mother isn't recorded, but since her divine parentage is accounted for we can be certain her mother wasn't a goddess."

"One of those Palestinian guys at the bank building said she was a witch."

Rabbi Chofetz shrugged. "I haven't found her mother yet."

"Doesn't this sort of mess up our whole story about how God is the only god?"

The rabbi shrugged. "It's not unknown to our scholars that there may be others. If you'll recall the Pentateuch, our Lord never says the other gods were false; some of His prophets made that claim. Our Lord says himself that He is a 'jealous god.' One cannot be jealous of what doesn't exist."

"I never thought of it that way," Rachel admitted. "I just figured He was jealous of anything that distracted the Israelites' attention."

"He was," conceded the rabbi, "but He makes it clear that He was not alone. Of course, His prophets denied them because the Israelites, as you know, suffered many occasions of backsliding."

Rachel nodded.

"What I found about our enemy Lamashtu is that she hates children because she was unable to have any. The legends say that the combination of divine and mortal blood made her infertile. They also state that she was not born evil, or instructed by anyone; she chose it herself."

"That's what Ammishtamru said," murmured Rachel.

"Ammishtamru. He's the big guy, the general, right?" Rabbi Chofetz asked. She nodded. "He seems to know her well. I was going down there myself to speak to him."

"Oh, you were?" asked Rachel, distressed. She didn't want him seeing her going into Ammishtamru's tent.

"Yes. I can tell you we believe that it is Lamashtu that has caused the rash of miscarriages and attacks on children. And furthermore, she gets her power from the blood of virgins. Male virgins. She seduces them, and, as we all know now, stings them when they're—" He looked away.

"Inside her," Rachel finished, except now she wasn't embarrassed. She felt bolder, wondering why she wanted to keep the rabbi from finding out who would soon be inside *her*. Yes, he would probably make a fuss because she was sleeping with an ancient enemy. But Rachel found she had grown tired of pleasing everyone else. No *schvartzers,* no *goyim,* and God-forbid no Muslims. Since the Israelites were thought by Biblical scholars, archaeologists, and anthropologists to be likely a branch of the Canaanites, Ammishtamru was, technically, Semitic. If an evil pagan, according to the prophets.

"Yes, inside her," the rabbi echoed. "I have discovered a few other things, too. Lamashtu is often present when babies and children die in large numbers. When King Herod ordered the Slaughter of the Innocents, it was at the urging of Lamashtu."

"Isn't that, sort of, not our history?" asked Rachel.

"We do not deny the birth of the teacher Jesus, merely his alleged divinity. Lamashtu was there, in the Palace, and it was she who fed the seed of paranoia in Herod that one of the Jewish children was the foretold 'King of the Jews.'"

Rachel fell silent.

"When thousands of children marched to Italy with the intention of launching their own Crusade to the Holy Land, it was Lamashtu who inspired the young boy whose vision they followed. The legends tell us the children never got close to the Holy Land, they died in large numbers or were sold into slavery. You want an example from *our* history? Remember when Yahweh took the firstborn sons of the Egyptians, because Pharaoh wouldn't free our people? Who do you think carried out the slaughter?"

"Uh, doesn't the Hebrew Bible say it was, uh, Yahweh?"

"It doesn't mention Lamashtu. It doesn't mention her *anywhere*. But the legends and the writings tell us a different story."

"Oh. Uh. She was the one doing it?"

"Yahweh allowed her to carry out the order for Moses' people. Why is that, do you think?"

Rachel shrugged. "I think it would be a little strange for a jealous God to entrust number one, a woman, and number two, a rival deity, to carry out His dirty work."

"Not if she was Jewish," he replied softly.

"You think Lamashtu is *Jewish?"*

He nodded slowly.

"I thought you said her father was Sumerian."

"He was. But Jewish lineage is matrilineal."

"But we don't know who her mother was."

He opened up his hands and raised his eyebrows. "So she *could* be Jewish!"

"Or anything else," Rachel pointed out.

"Except that God wouldn't entrust anyone but a Jew to carry out His order. And, guess who put the idea into His head in the first place?"

"So what are ya gonna do if you find her? Stone her to death?"

Rabbi Chofetz shrugged slightly. "If she's half-divine it wouldn't kill her, it would just make her really, really mad, and maybe give her a grudge against the Jews. Which as you know we don't exactly need."

"So what are you going to do to her, then?" asked Rachel.

"I don't know. *We* don't know. But we must find and neutralize her until we figure out how to deal with her. No baby, pregnant woman, or virgin will be safe until she's gone."

He turned and walked down the street toward the drumming. Rachel hung back.

☆ ☆ ☆

Alexis lay in a hospital bed, moaning, not with physical pain anymore but from deep, psychic pain. Her lower abdomen rolled only a little with cramps, which, in the ambulance, were worse than the worst menstrual cramps, worse than the time she miscarried. She'd cried and begged for them to make the pain stop but they couldn't. She had to see a doctor first.

In two different parts of the city, two different creatures raised their heads. One listened intently, the other sniffed the air.

Lamashtu curled up under a tree deep in the heart of High Park. It was open 24x7 so no one questioned anyone walking through late at night. She pulled a new scarf around her and tried to sleep. It's just that she was *sooo* hungry...

It had been a narrow escape from the children. They were

relentless, and she felt their anger and hatred, and she knew if they caught up with her they would likely kill her. Even though they weren't the sort of children who usually committed heinous acts, they truly understood and believed that she was, in fact, guilty of all they accused her.

Tomorrow, she would find a virgin. She *must* find a virgin. Three of the teens who chased her were boys. Plus Dave. There might be others, too.

✯ ✯ ✯

Rachel approached the sound of the drums. Her heart pounded, and she pushed her fears out of her mind. It was none of the rabbi's business who she slept with. She and Ammishtamru were in love.

If he had made enthusiastic love to her when she looked forty-one, he made wild mad violent love to her now. The first time he'd seen her, looking all of thirtyish, he'd picked her up, his eyes devouring hers, flung her on the air mattress, and began pulling off her clothes.

The Fountain of Youth, it had been a gift from G-d Himself.

The fires were still burning, the locals sat with the warriors and passed bottles of Labbatt's and Molson's and every other modern-day liquor. No doubt it was much finer than the barley crap they drank thousands of years ago beneath a Bronze Age desert sun.

She approached a cluster of the ones she knew. Niqmaddu and Yassib passed a bottle of Stolichnaya. Yassib had been introduced to 'stupid Newfie' jokes earlier in the day by a couple of mischievous Albertans, and had discovered they were remarkably versatile.

"Hey, how does a stupid Avite practice safe sex? He marks the sheep that bite!" Yassib cried, then roared at his own joke.

"What's safe sex?" asked Niqmaddu, but Yassib ignored him.

"Hey, what happens if a stupid Avite doesn't pay his garbage bill?" asked Yassib. The Canadians looked at him expectantly and he answered, "They don't bring him any more!" The Canadians roared with laughter.

"What's a garbage bill?" asked Niqmaddu.

Just then Aqhat emerged from a tent. "Hey Aqhat, did you hear about the Avite who was so stupid he thought manual labor was the President of Mexico?"

"Yassib, cut it out with the Avite jokes!" Aqhat sputtered. "I've taken enough of your crap!"

"What's Mexico?" asked Niqmaddu. Aqhat ignored him and drained the bottle of vodka.

Rachel approached Ammishtamru's tent. It was zipped up, which was unusual. He usually left it open for her. "Hey Ammy, I'm here," she called out, but just loud enough for him to hear.

She heard movement inside the tent and then Ammishtamru's voice said, "Uh, I'm kind of busy right now, Rachel."

"What's going on? Are you okay?"

"I'm fine. Can you come back later?"

More sounds of movement.

"You're not hurt are you?"

"No, I'm fine," he replied.

"He's anything but hurt," came a female voice.

Rachel's blood froze.

"Ammishtamru, is there someone in there with you?"

"There's *two* someones in here with him," came another feminine giggle.

"Ammishtamru, what the hell is going on?" demanded Rachel. She unzipped the tent and looked inside.

He was naked, positioned between two young, equally naked Toronto girls. One blonde, with a smooth belly and pert little breasts. The other, a sexy brunette, with much larger and very expensive breasts.

"You asked," said the brunette. She reached down and stroked Ammishtamru's little soldier, standing at attention and ready for battle.

"Uh, hi Rachel," said Ammishtamru. "I'll be with you later." He smiled, but tentatively.

"Hey, she could join us," suggested the blonde, and the warrior's eyes lit up.

"She's right, you could!" he said.

Rachel turned and fled.

CHAPTER FOURTEEN

Rachel awoke the next morning with the sun streaming in on her face. She groaned and turned away from the window. She wanted to go back to sleep and never wake up again.

The phone rang. She considered ignoring it but reached over on the third ring and picked it up. "H'lo?"

"Rachel, it's Dave. Dave Gillpatrick."

"Dave, it's—" she paused and squinted at the alarm clock, "eight-thirty in the morning. I like to sleep in on the weekend."

"I'm sorry, but it's an emergency. She's getting closer, Rachel! I was out last night just to pick up a few things at the grocery store for my mother when I saw her. I was in disguise, but she recognized me or something. I was able to give her the slip but Christ, Rachel, she was *three blocks from my home!* If she finds out where I am I'm fucked!"

"And that's absolutely the last thing you want to do," she mumbled. She couldn't deal with this. Not now. "Dave, she can't force you, you know. I don't care how attractive she is, you still have power over your own body. You simply don't have sex with her. Period."

"I don't know what she'll do if I don't."

"You know what she'll do if you *do."*

"Rachel, *please!* You're not trying very hard. It's been three days since I asked for your help. She's closing in on me. *I have to get laid!"*

"Dave," she said, sitting up abruptly, "I'm not your goddamn pimp. If you have so little control over yourself that you don't think you'll be able to run away from her absolutely irresistible vagina, then for God's sake go down to the crappy sections of town and buy yourself a woman! But you don't actually need a hooker, you need to keep your GODDAMN DICK IN YOUR PANTS!"

She slammed down the phone, turned over and began to sob.

Alexis lay in her hospital bed, unable to cry anymore. She'd be released on Monday, they said, after they ran a few more tests, but it looked pretty grim. She was officially infertile. The doctor said it was almost certain she'd never bear children.

She felt like she was being punished for something that wasn't her fault. She'd tried, oh so hard, to find a husband since an age when most young women were more interested in partying and chasing multiple men than in settling down to have children with the man they loved. She'd spent the better part of the last eight years looking, searching, dating, shagging, hoping beyond hope that this one would be The One, and now, after all her hard work, it was over. Pointless. Who would want her now, a ruined woman, useless, worthless, nothing but an empty barren womb?

And now she was trapped in her own head. No job to go back to, no marriage to look forward to, no children to brighten her days or grandchildren to enliven her autumn years. She would die, old and lonely, fruitless.

"It's interesting this woman is said to have a scorpion where her vagina is, Suellen," the blonde, blue-eyed author of *Vulva Underground: Stuff You Never Knew About Your Own Cha-Cha* said to the hostess of *Sunny-Side Toronto*, a Sunday morning news show. "It sounds like a twist on the old myth of the *vagina dentata,* with castrating teeth, the legend that is so common in a wide variety of ancient cultures."

"I've never heard of that before," replied Suellen. Hers was the only show in Canada that ever dared to utter the taboo v-word.

"Many myths around the world speak of it. It represents men's fear of sex and of contact with the vagina."

Suellen allowed a small laugh to escape. "Okay, that's a bit hard to accept," she said. "Most women will tell you that men are forever *trying* to get to their vaginas."

"Certainly, men want sex," the blonde conceded, "but there is a subconscious fear associated with a woman's privates. The French call an orgasm *le petit mort,* the 'little death,' for example. Now for millennia men have revered, honored, even worshiped the penis. Ancient pagan temples and cities were filled with phallic symbols, or phalluses themselves. The Romans, for example, had Priapus, who was depicted with a very large erect penis. On the island of Delos in the Greek Mediterranean, you will find the remnants of statues on pillars that *were* erect penises, although now all you can see is the testicles. Someone knocked the penises off, perhaps the Catholic priests who inhabited the island later."

"Were there any similar symbols or statues for the vagina?" asked Suellen.

"Some, but not nearly as many as for the penis. The phallus represents manhood itself. And the act of having sex is the act of pushing that manhood into a mysterious, dark cavern that devours it. And the act isn't completed until the vagina diminishes it, and it withdraws, once again a wrinkled, shriveled shadow of its former glorious self. For centuries, many cultures believed that sex with a woman drained a man's essence from him - that he contained it in his semen, and that, because she had no life essence of her own, she took it from the man. If he had sex with her enough, it was believed it could destroy him. It's the origin of our expression *femme fatale.*

"So the *vagina dentata,* Suellen, is the expression of man that fears the power of female sexuality. It's the power that diminishes his manhood and of course, the power of a woman's vagina is indisputable.

Men have fought for millennia to control it. It's what's given the world harems, purdah, forced marriage, honor killings, female genital mutilation, and today, hymen restoration. It's the reason why women have traditionally had fewer rights than men - it all comes down to control over the vagina, which men historically regard as ravenous and insatiable."

"Rather like what many women would say about men's appetite for sex," chuckled Suellen, a bit sarcastically.

"There is perhaps an element of psychological projection, yes. The institution of marriage exists not, as many religions would have you believe, because it's a gift from God, but because it ensures the paternity of the children. A man always knows the mother of a child, but he can never be truly certain about its paternity unless that troublesome little vagina has been strictly controlled from birth. And of course, a woman whose vagina he seeks is one who has the power to make him do almost anything. That, perhaps, is what they truly fear - the voluntary loss of their will to *just say no* to a vagina."

"So where does this leave us with this woman Lamashtu?" asked Suellen. "I mean, a *scorpion?"*

"By all accounts she's an incredibly beautiful, sensuous woman, the embodiment of a man's worst nightmare – the loss of his penis. And she appears to steal his mysterious semen power. They feel powerless to say no – or at least that's what they would claim if they survived. Then again, they may be right – the coroner here hasn't been able to state for certain what the cause of death was in any of them – only that it wasn't the sting."

"What do you make of the shrunken, shriveled condition of the bodies found?"

"I'm not sure," said the blonde. Then, with a cryptic smile, she added, "Perhaps the ancients were right all along and we really *can* drain them of their life's essence through their precious penis."

"So what, then," asked Suellen, "is the need she supposedly has for virgins?"

"Ya got me," the blonde shrugged. "That's a new one."

CBC viewers were treated to a most extraordinary live interview.

Dirk Bly, crack CBC reporter (on crack, as his detractors liked to add), was interviewing Rabbi Chofetz, who had quickly become Toronto's reigning expert on Jewish and Canaanite mythology, particularly as it pertained to Lamashtu, who hadn't been seen in days except by a pack of unruly teenagers. She had, however, left her unmistakeable calling card that she was still at loose in the city and every bit as dangerous.

The interview took place at the Canaanite lakefront camp, not too far from Ammishtamru's Tent O' Debauchery. The day was overcast and the area, as usual, was crowded with people - Torontonians who'd befriended the Canaanites, Jewish protest groups who wanted the pagan enemies off their land (Canada, in this case, and they were *not* keen on any 'reclaiming' efforts for Israel either), Christian protest groups who objected to public pagan fertility orgies, police who were trying to keep the peace until someone figured out what to do with the illegal aliens, and one lone and harried representative from Immigration Canada who couldn't figure out how to return illegal aliens to a homeland that no longer existed.

"Just to update our viewers," began Bly, "another dessicated body has turned up in downtown Toronto with the customary sting on the victim's privates. However, there's now a more sinister side to this than the last murders, if you thought it couldn't possibly get worse—" Bly shuddered. "Police believe that someone broke into the man's apartment on Queen Street West and tied him to his bed. He appears to have struggled against his bonds but nevertheless, he was still stung in the same place. Friends who knew him say it was widely believed that he had never been with a woman before. I'm standing here with Rabbi Barrak Chofetz of Beth Hamidrash Synagogue who we've spoken to a few times before. Rabbi, you have emerged in recent days as an expert on the subject of this woman Lamashtu, who is supposedly a demi-goddess from *ancient Mesopotamia.*" He emphasized this last point just in case his viewers were too stupid to grasp just how insanely awe-inspiring these visitors were. "If she's the one who committed this latest murder, how did she manage to force him into a, uh, ready state, if he was struggling to be free and probably knew what awaited him if he, uh, gave her what she wanted?"

"I'm certainly unclear on that myself, Dirk," Rabbi Chofetz began. "I can only speculate that perhaps she force-fed him Viagra, since I can't imagine how she could otherwise force an—ah, aroused state in a man without it."

"Perhaps she knows the secret of the Jade Peacock Mulligan," came a female voice, and the most beautiful woman Toronto had ever seen stepped into the camera's view.

✯ ✯ ✯

A zombie walked the streets of Toronto, poorly dressed, unkempt, staring mindlessly. Many of the people walking past ignored her, guessing she was probably another one of the many homeless who peppered the city sidewalks. She had long, dank dark hair and severe rectangular glasses, and her full pink lips hung open as she ambled aimlessly, staring at nothing.

A woman approached her from the opposite direction. She wore a simple black *abaya* in the Saudi style with the face-covering *niqab* and a pair of large blue-tinted sunglasses purloined from a local drugstore (quite easy to do when you're wearing a garment you all but disappear in). The Muslim woman seemed intent on where she was going, but as she approached the young zombie she stopped, as though she thought she'd forgotten something back home, then slowly turned and walked down the street, following the dark-haired woman.

When the zombie woman stopped and leaned forlornly against a building, the Muslim woman moved in and took her hand. "My sister," she said, and the woman looked up.

"Oh, uh, hello," said Alexis, completely stymied that a Muslim woman in the most conservative garb had approached her. Muslims in Toronto weren't famous for their friendliness, although the less conservative they were, the more likely they were to mix with and be friendly with others.

"Come with me, I wish to speak with you for a moment," said the Muslim woman, and she led Alexis by the hand around the corner and into an alley.

"Who are you?" asked Alexis a bit uncertainly.

"I am a friend. I know and feel your pain," said the woman. "I sensed your anger, and your need for revenge. I am here to give it to you."

She lifted the *niqab* and removed the sunglasses, and Alexis gasped.

☆ ☆ ☆

Dave the Virgin sat on a hard stone bench at Union Station. He clutched his boarding pass in one hand, and a backpack with the other.

A young man sat down next to him. He was probably less than thirty, medium height, very skinny, with long dirty-blonde hair and round wire glasses on a thin face. His clothes hung off his bony frame like it was a rack of clothes hangers. He had the look of a classic geek, and he too carried a boarding pass and a backpack.

"You taking the train to New York?" he asked Dave.

"Uh-huh. You?"

"Yep. Why are *you* leaving?"

"Uh, vacation. I have to get away for awhile."

"Yeah, me too. What's your name?"

"Dave."

The young man laughed. "Hey, I'll bet you're in computers, too, am I right?"

"Yeah, how'd you know?" Dave looked astonished.

"The 'If You Can Read This, You're As Big A Nerd As I Am' t-shirt written in binary," he grinned. "Plus, your name is Dave. Have you ever noticed how many I.T. people there are in Toronto named Dave?"

"I can't say as I've ever noticed. But, I don't have many friends," he said, looking away. "So you're in computers? Does that mean your name is Dave?"

"No, but you can call me Dave if you want. It's better than my real name. It's kind of embarrassing. I don't know *what* my parents were thinking."

"So what is it?"

"Thor."

☆ ☆ ☆

"Wh—who are you?" stammered Dirk Bly, awestruck at the woman's beauty.

"My name is Lilith," answered the woman. "I'm Lamashtu's mother."

Rabbi Chofetz just gaped. Whether it was because he, too, had been rendered dumbstruck by her perfect porcelain skin, sensuously elongated eyes and river of long brown hair spilling down her back, or merely by her name, was unknown.

"You're her *mother?"* Bly asked, with eyes the size of Dundas Square.

She nodded and smiled, displaying beautiful ivories couched by the most perfect lips the world had ever seen. A tight but tasteful white dress hugged her awe-inspiring curves and displayed a bit of leg. She was hotter than her daughter, even though she favored somewhat more modest garb.

"And what was it you mentioned before—the jade *what?"*

"The Jade Peacock Mulligan. It's an ancient secret technique for orally stimulating a man to erection under any circumstances. If you've been trained properly, it's foolproof. You could raise a man from the dead with it. Literally."

Bly wasn't sure whether to be astounded at the idea that such a marvelous talent existed or horrified and sickened at the disturbing mental image.

"I invented it myself," continued Lilith. "I did it for my ex-husband, who really enjoyed a good blowjob. Of course, some idiot Chinese guy during the Zhou dynasty pretended to discover it, which is why he gave it the silly name. I will always regret the time I spent with Confucius." She looked away, annoyed.

"You—you are Lilith?" asked Rabbi Chofetz, finally coming to life.

"Yeah. Oh, hey, Barrak, I'm sorry, I didn't recognize you! It's been awhile. How've you been?"

"You know him?" asked Dirk Bly.

"Know him? Hell, baby, I knew him in the *Biblical* sense. The good rabbi used to be a right stuffy old prude back when he was in the seminary. So I came to him at night and gave him the wettest dreams of his life!"

"She lies!" the rabbi yelled. "Lilith! Bringer of storms, foul temptress, vile witch, destroyer of men, demon of *Sheol!"*

"I see you haven't lightened up much, " Lilith drawled. "Or did you backslide? I guess I didn't shag you long enough. My bad." She looked past Rabbi Chofetz and broke into a large grin. "Reverend Mudge!" she called and waved. "Yoo-hoo! Hi there! It's Lilith! Long time no see! How's the wife and kids?"

She turned back to Bly. "I used to shag him too."

"Did you, uh, say you were Lamashtu's mother?" asked Bly, clearly shaken.

"That's impossible, Lilith is barren," Rabbi Chofetz spat. "She was cursed by God with infertility for her disobedience!"

"Oh, cut it out with this infertility crap, it's my daughter who's barren, not me. That's just something you people made up because you couldn't stand the fact that I'm a hot, sexy woman in full control of my sexuality who wouldn't take any nonsense from that idiot Adam."

"Adam?" asked Bly.

"My ex-husband," she explained.

Bly turned to Rabbi Chofetz. "Do you know who this woman is?" he groaned.

"Yes," he growled. "Christians wouldn't know her. She was Adam's first wife, before Eve."

Bly shook his head several times, like a dog shaking water from his ears.

"Eve? Like, you mean, the world's first woman?"

"The world's *second* woman," Lilith corrected. "The Christians cut me out of Genesis because they were embarrassed. God originally made man and woman together, you know. The story's still there. But then later he does the rib thing with Eve. Why? Because, see, I left Adam because I wouldn't put up with his macho ca-ca. He wanted me to be submissive to him, and he always wanted to be on top during sex. Now hey, I like the missionary position as well as the next woman, but, you know, I also like a little variety too. And let me tell you, Dirk, I *know* how to make a man scream when *I'm* on top."

Bly's eyes widened, the microphone stiff in his hand.

"And no one gets stung on the ol' tallywacker either."

Rabbi Chofetz looked like he'd just swallowed a pork pie.

"That's why the prophets put all that crap in later about how God commanded the woman to be submissive because she hadn't listened to Him and ate of the Tree of Knowledge. Isn't that a typical man, especially a sexually-repressed Jew like Yahweh? It just set the scene for future crusades against the chicks - always keep knowledge from the woman. And what was unclean about us? Our holy monthly blood, with which they banished us to the infamous Red Tent. Can't let her study the Qabbalah because she's unclean. Can't let her study the Torah because she bleeds every month. Keep 'em stupid and uneducated and they'll cater to your every need because they won't have any other choice. So they make it *very clear* in Genesis that what happens to naughty little chickie-boos who disobey the boyos is they're cursed to suffer pain in childbirth and submit unto the man. God says it! They believe it! That settles it."

Rabbi Chofetz turned red. He shook and trembled.

"You know what?" she said, leaning in with her arms crossed, "your God is a real *prick*. So frankly, I said *fuck this* and I took off. I decided I would fight this penis-obsessed patriarchal crap with the thing they feared most, my vagina. You know what the problem is with all these damn conservative religionists? What they all need is a really good lay. These people are *so* repressed, I don't know how they don't explode from it all. Oh wait, they *do* explode. Make war, not love."

She turned and pointed away from the camera. "You see that guy over there, that Reverend Mudge? He's the wanker on TV who's always going on about how we have to fight sex education in the schools and use more corporal punishment. You know what he doesn't know? His teenage daughter gives the best blowjobs in school. Does that shock you? Well don't look at me, *I* didn't teach her anything. His repressive, autocratic style at home has turned her into a teenage hooker."

"You slut!" Rabbi Chofetz cried.

"Slut is such an ugly word," she purred, nonplussed. "I prefer the term *player."*

She turned back to Bly. "This is what I do. I shag uptight religious guys who desperately need it in an attempt to get them to lighten up. It doesn't always work, though. Obviously I didn't have much luck with Osama bin Laden. And if there are any Americans watching—" She turned and faced the camera, "I'm really sorry about the whole Bush Cabinet. I honestly tried, but there are just too many of them and they were particularly resistant. Maybe I could have done it if Lamashtu had followed in my footsteps, instead of being an evil killer-crotch psychopath."

Bly and Rabbi Chofetz looked like they'd just witnessed Chewbacca making the beast with two backs with Jabba the Hutt. "Listen, this is important, Toronto," Lilith said. "I'm looking for my daughter. You all know what she looks like, she's really really beautiful and has long silky dark hair and she usually doesn't wear much. She looks kind of like me, except browner and way nuttier-looking. Although she might be in disguise now. You already know what she can do, and she likes virgins. The male kind. And damn, there are a lot of them here! You can't kill her, and I suggest you don't try. Leave her to me and I will take care of her. Permanently."

Someone called her from behind and she turned around. "Heeeeeeey!" she squealed, and she jerked her perfect body sensuously as she raised her arms in greeting. "Ammishtamru! Aaaahhhhhhmmmmy baaaaaaaby! Long time no squeeze, eh, Long Spear?"

She raced into his arms and passionately soul-kissed him with grinding movements in the background while Dirk Bly, Crack CBC Reporter and Barrak Chofetz, Cracked-Up Rabbi, stood motionless before the camera.

CHAPTER FIFTEEN

"What are you going to do in New York?" Thor asked.

Dave shrugged. "I don't know. Look around, sight-see I guess. I've never been to New York before."

Dave stared at his shoes. Thor watched him for a long time.

"You're trying to escape *her,* aren't you?" he asked.

Dave looked up, slightly annoyed. "What do you mean? What *her?"*

"Lamashtu. The one who likes, you know."

"Oh, the crazy chick on TV? She wouldn't be interested in *me."*

"Yeah, sure. Look, haven't I proven that I already know my own? It's okay, dude, believe me, I won't tell anyone. That's why I'm leaving Toronto. She might come after me too."

Dave's eyes widened.

While Dirk Bly, crack CBC reporter tried to figure out with his cameraman whether they were going to get fired for allowing an interview with someone who'd said *blowjob, shag, fuck,* and *tallywacker* on live TV, and Rabbi Chofetz went back to his office to try to figure out how to get rid of the foul demoness Lilith and her *le grand mort* hellspawn, Lilith had a confab with the Canaanites.

"I need your help, guys," she told the semi-circle of warriors.

Ammishtamru, a red-haired twin under each arm, nodded.

✯ ✯ ✯

"Oh my God, Dave, fancy meeting you here!"

Dave looked up from his quiet conversation with Thor. It was the pretty girl who'd talked to him several weeks ago in Nathan Philips Square. Who was also on the subway with him during the Great Gerbil Fiasco.

"Hi, uh—?"

"Alexis," she said. She sat down beside them with a grave face. "Dave, you're in a lot of trouble."

"What do you mean?" he asked.

"I just had a really—scary encounter with someone," she replied.

"Who?"

"Lamashtu."

His eyes widened, but he tried to play it cool.

Alexis glanced uncertainly at Thor.

"It's okay, you can speak in front of him," said Dave.

"I—is he—I, uh, think maybe we should speak in private," Alexis stammered. "I, uh, know about—your, uh, problem."

"I have the same problem," said Thor. "That's why we're both trying to escape to New York."

"You're going to New York?" Both men nodded.

"You met Lamashtu?" asked Dave.

"Yes. She tried to recruit me."

"Recruit you? For what?"

"To—to be like her."

Thor's eyes widened. "Did she give you her killer coochie?"

"Thor!" Dave looked disgusted with his new friend. "You can't talk to her like that."

"Sorry." Thor looked embarrassed.

"It's no wonder *you're* still a virgin."

"No, no she didn't," Alexis assured them. "But she told me she was looking for this one guy who was supposedly going to restore her to her full powers. She's the one behind all the near-baby deaths in Toronto."

"Yeah, we know, we saw her on the news," said Thor.

"So she thinks if she shags you, Dave, she'll get her full strength back. I didn't know who she was talking about at first, of course. But she described you and said your name was Dave Gillpatrick and even though I didn't know your last name I eventually realized it was you. She's looking for you everywhere."

"How did you know I was here?" said Dave. His mother was the only person he'd told about going to New York. He said he was going to an anime and manga festival.

"I didn't. I just was about to get on the subway to go home when I saw you here. Listen, you don't have to go to New York."

"But people say Lamashtu can't cross the border."

"She doesn't need to. She has, uh, recruits everywhere. She told me about them. You're no safer there than you are here."

"Why'd she try to recruit you?" asked Dave.

Alexis's face fell, and she glanced down at her lap. "I just got some bad news from my doctor," she said. "I can't have children. I'm infertile."

"How does she know that?" asked Dave.

Alexis shrugged. "I don't know. I passed her and I didn't even see her, she was dressed like a Muslim woman in one of those black robe things and sunglasses. She pulled me aside. She wouldn't tell me how she knew I was upset about it."

"She's got some weird power," Dave told Thor. "I never gave her my last name but she always knew where to find me. I think she was stalking me."

"Wow," breathed Thor with respect. "Stalked by a really beautiful woman." His voice trailed off as he contemplated such an unimaginable thing.

"Yeah, a chick with a scorpion in her thingy!" Dave cried.

"So what did you tell her?" asked Thor. "When she tried to recruit you. Did she promise to make you really beautiful?"

"Thor!" Dave cried, exasperated. "Alexis already *is* really beautiful! You can't insult her like that!" He suddenly realized he'd just called a woman really beautiful. In her earshot. He turned to look with horror at Alexis, wondering if she was going to reel back from such unwanted attention from a geek like him.

"It's—I didn't mean—" Thor stammered, but Alexis reached out and took his hand.

"It's okay, I know what you meant. And no, I'm not even close to being as beautiful as she is, but you were kind to say so, Dave," she said, and she bestowed the nicest smile a woman had ever given him. At least a woman who wasn't showing relief that he was about to leave.

"And I told her that becoming an evil hell-slut wasn't on my agenda for today," she told both boys pointedly. "Now listen, I've got an idea. Why don't you guys come back to my place and I'll protect you."

Thor brightened up. "Are you going to shag us?" he said. "Because that would ensure she'd never bother either of us."

"Thor!" Dave yelled. "Don't be such a pig! She's trying to help us."

"I can't think of anything that would help us more right now, can you?" he asked.

"Actually, that was exactly what I had in mind," said Alexis.

Their eyes bugged out.

☆ ☆ ☆

After the three of them got off the subway, Dave's cell phone rang. He flipped it open.

"Hello, Dave?"

"Uh, hi Rachel."

"Look, I'm sorry I yelled at you. I was completely out of line. I had had—uh, something really horrible happen to me the night before, and I was extremely upset and angry when you called. But not at you," she added hastily.

"Oh. Okay. Gee, I felt really bad. I didn't mean to treat you like—uh, you know."

"I can't—I don't think I can get you a woman, but I think I can still help you find a girlfriend. Maybe after this is all over."

"It's okay, my problem's about to be solved."

"It is? How?"

"I'm with a couple of friends. I was at the train station to go to New York and I met this guy Thor who has the same problem I have, but then we ran into this girl named Alexis who I'd met a few weeks ago, and she said she ran into Lamashtu who tried to recruit her. She's taking me and Thor to her apartment because she said Lamashtu has recruits everywhere."

"She's named Alexis? And she was recruited by Lamashtu?"

"Not quite. She told her no. She's going to—" He lowered his voice so strangers couldn't hear. "Shag us."

"She's going to *what?"*

"You heard me. We'll be useless to Lamashtu."

"Oh. Uh, that's great, Dave. A little weird, under the circumstances, but—you said her name was Alexis?"

"Yeah, you know her?"

"I have a client named Alexis. Young, very pretty, slim with long brown hair and glasses."

"Hey, that sounds like her."

"What's her last name?"

"Hey Alexis, what's your last name?" asked Dave.

"Jacquard," she replied.

"That's my client!" said Rachel, who overheard. "She's a nice girl. Wow. She said she'd shag *both of you?* To help you out?"

"Uh-huh."

"Wow. That's—that's really great. I wouldn't have thought it of her, she's kind of conservative. She's—she's a real hero."

"Yeah," said Dave. He grinned as they continued down the street. He was about to get laid, by a really pretty girl, and even if she was only doing it as a favor, she wasn't even acting like she had to lie back and think of Canada.

And then, finally, he'd be free!

☆ ☆ ☆

Rachel hung up the phone and thought for a few minutes. Something was wrong with this picture. She didn't believe for a moment that Alexis intended to shag Dave as a favor, or some friend of his, particularly if he was a stranger. Not even to get pregnant – if she was that desperate she would almost certainly pick a worthier candidate.

She retrieved her phone book from the kitchen cabinet and flipped through the Yellow Pages. She dialed and patiently waded through all the automated attendant instructions.

"You have reached Dr. Barrak Chofetz in Jewish Studies at the University of Toronto." The message cycled through a lengthy list of office hours. "If this is important you can call me on my cell phone." Rachel wrote it down. She hung up and redialed.

"Hello, Rabbi Chofetz? Or should I call you Doctor?"

"Either is fine. Who is this?"

"Oh, sorry. This is Rachel Brinkerhoff. I met you downtown near the Canaanite campground."

"Oh yes, the *shtik goy.* The one who looks like the *shiksa* movie star."

"Yes. And I'm not a *goy."*

"No, you're just not very knowledgeable about Jewish history. A *shtik goy."*

Yeah, well, at least no Underworld sex bomb was trying to shag me *to lighten me up,* Rachel wanted to say, but she had never developed

Brillo-pad New York sarcasm and hadn't called the rabbi to argue with him anyway.

"Listen, you seem to be the expert in Toronto about this Lamashtu chick," she began. "I wonder if you'd be interested in helping me protect a guy she might come after. A friend of mine."

"Who?"

"One of my clients. He's still a virgin and she's after him specifically."

"He is? How old is he?"

"He's—" Rachel began, then realized she was sharing confidential information. "It's—it's not important. Older than most. She came very close to—killing him recently. Before she got famous on the news."

"Is he Jewish?"

"No."

"*Oy,* a *goy.*"

"What, you only help Jews?"

"No, no. What do you mean, he's your client?"

"I'm a matchmaker by profession."

"*Oy Gevalt,* a *shadchen.*"

Rachel didn't know what a *shadchen* was, but she didn't want to ask. "I just talked to my client. He's going to a friend's apartment - in fact, she's another one of my clients - but I think we should go there. To protect him. Apparently they've got another virgin with them but I'm afraid this Lamashtu woman will catch up with them. I saw her mother on TV and she says this woman can smell peoples' emotions and states of mind. That's how she identifies virgins. Among others."

"And why do you think I should go with you? Do I look like I slather steroids on my bagels?"

"You know her better than I do. You can stop her."

"And how? She's partly divine. I wouldn't trust anything her mother says anyway. The woman is a *witch!*"

"Alexis, you'll never know how grateful I am for this," Dave said as they stepped into her apartment. She turned around and gave him a knowing smile. "I know how hard this is for you."

"Why should it be hard?" she asked. "Come on, Dave, you're not half-bad-looking. You just need a little more confidence." She tried not to look at the other one, who she didn't find the least bit attractive.

"Which one of us are you going to do first?" asked Thor eagerly. He hated sloppy seconds.

"You," said Lamashtu as she stepped out from the hallway. "I need an appetizer before the main course."

☆ ☆ ☆

"I don't like what you should be having me doing," warned Rabbi Chofetz. He secured his seat belt as Rachel drove away from the campus building. "I don't know what you expect me to do if this murderous woman shows up. Or why two strong young men can't defend themselves if she does."

Rachel hadn't told him about Alexis' plan. She was afraid the rabbi wouldn't join her if he thought he was walking into a den of iniquity.

"For example, the young man she desires can simply refuse the act."

"It's not that simple anymore, you know that. She tied down the last one and made him do it."

"Oh, yes, she forced him. With what? This Chinese thing her mother mentioned? I don't believe that. There's no such thing."

"How do you know?"

"Rachel, it's silly. You tie a man down and threaten to sting his *schvantz* with a scorpion, I tell you, that man will remain as limp as a plate of overcooked *varnishkes."*

Rachel's cell phone rang. She fumbled for it.

"You want we should both go to meet our Maker this afternoon, young lady? Drive, don't talk!"

Ignoring him, Rachel flipped the phone open. "Hello?"

"Rachel, it's Chao. I hope you are well."

"That's a loaded question. But never mind. What's going on?"

"I spoke to Mahliqa earlier today. She told me what happened with the Canaanite soldier."

"Oh she did, did she? She had no damn right to do that," Rachel remarked, annoyed. She should have known better than to trust the Ghawazee Gossip Girl.

"Please, Rachel, don't be angry with her. She meant well. She and Amita are worried about you. She said you didn't come in to the office today. And that she spoke to you Saturday and you were beside yourself, and wouldn't let them come over and talk to you. I am calling as a friend. I am concerned about you too."

"We barely know each other, Chao, although I appreciate the concern. I'll deal with Mahliqa later. Listen, I've got a question for you. Have you ever heard of the Jade Peacock Mulligan?"

She heard Chao's sudden intake of breath. There was silence. Then he said, "You know the Jade Peacock Mulligan?"

"Er, well—I know *of* it. I don't know how to do it." She laughed nervously. "Whaddaya expect, I'm Jewish." She glanced at the rabbi, who raised his eyes and fingers to heaven as if to ask, *Why me, Lord?*

"Where did you hear of this?"

"It was on the news. Someone mentioned that this Lamashtu can do it."

Chao muttered something in Chinese that sounded like it might mean, *Holy shit!*

"So it does exist?"

"Oh, it does, I assure you."

"Do you know this for a fact, or is this just Chinese legend?"

"I know it to be true, Rachel. Don't ask me how. All I will tell you is if you know the right places to go in Shanghai you can find the Jade Peacock Mulligan." He chuckled a bit.

"Is it everything they say? Can it raise a man, for, uh, battle no matter what the circumstances?"

"It could raise a man being burned alive."

"Thanks. Good to know. I'll talk to you later." She snapped the phone shut and shot the rabbi a victorious smirk.

★ ★ ★

Dave stepped back against the wall. Thor looked around wildly.

"This is the only way in or out, and I live on the twenty-third floor," Alexis told him.

"You said you'd turned her down," Dave cried accusingly.

"I only said I hadn't counted on becoming like her *today,"* Alexis reminded him. "I never said anything about *tomorrow."* She locked the door and stepped in front of it.

"I can't believe you're doing this," Dave said. "You seemed like such a nice woman. Rachel said so too."

"Tomorrow night, she's going to be the—*second* most beautiful woman you've ever seen. Except, oh wait, you won't be around tomorrow night," Lamashtu smirked.

"There's two of us, and they're both chicks," Thor cried. "I'll take Alexis."

Lamashtu's hand shot out and grabbed him by the collar. As though he was little more than a leaf to her, she picked him up and threw him hard against the wall. He fell onto the couch, dazed.

"Yes, those teenage boys who chased me through town really gave me a lot of my strength back," she giggled. "Easy to track them down once I knew what they smelled like. Alexis, you said your bedroom door locks from the outside, didn't you?"

"This is an older building. It certainly does."

"Let's lock up Loverboy here. I want his friend first."

Lamashtu hauled a struggling Dave to the bedroom and threw him onto the bed, shutting the door. A key scraped in the lock.

She walked to the couch and pulled Thor up to a sitting position. "Where can we tie him up?" she asked Alexis.

"Er, I don't know," Alexis replied. "I've, uh, never tied anyone up before." She looked around the apartment.

"God, you Canadians are so uptight. You mean you've never tied a man up for bondage games?"

Alexis slowly shook her head.

"Get the rope. C'mon, your dining room table is big enough."

Thor began to scream.

Lamashtu pulled a leather ball gag out of the pocket of her low-hipped jeans. Expertly, she whipped it around Thor's mouth and secured it in the back. His frantic cries were reduced to muffled noises.

"I love these sex shops you've got in Toronto," she said with a large grin. "If only I'd had these things back when I was terrorizing ancient Troy." Together the two women tied the struggling young man to the table.

Alexis watched as Lamashtu unzipped his jeans. She was just able to shimmy them enough off his hips. "Get me a knife," she commanded.

"You're not going to, uh, cut him, are you?"Alexis asked. Her face was ashen. Her hands trembled a little. She hadn't banked on anything ugly, like sacrifice. Or torture. Just one quick sting and it was over, Lamashtu had said.

"Don't be silly, I'm going to cut his underpants off."

Alexis dutifully retrieved a large knife from the kitchen.

As Thor struggled vainly against his bonds, Lamashtu revealed him. She flicked his limp member and turned back to Alexis. "Stop being such a shrinking violet," she said. "Now watch and learn, young lady."

She bent down and opened her mouth.

CHAPTER SIXTEEN

"Very nice. Perpetuate the stereotype of the uptight Jewish girl who doesn't like marital relations. Perhaps next you would like to be running the World Bank or validating the blood libel?"

Rachel threw a sidelong glance at Rabbi Chofetz. "He says the Jade Peacock Mulligan is real."

"Who does?"

"My friend Chao. He's Chinese. He says it exists."

"He wishes it exists. Sixty-seven years I've been living on this planet, Rachel, and never have I heard of the Jade Peacock Mulligan. And I've heard a lot of sins in my day."

"He says it could raise a man who's being burnt alive."

"Oy, such a nightmare I'm going to have tonight!"

"Dammit, he broke the ropes," Lamashtu said. She climbed down from the table and looked for her pants. "The scrawny little chit was stronger than he looked. Where did you get this cheap crap anyway?"

She stood before Alexis, flushed and fairly pulsing with life. She was naked except for the shorty t-shirt which had hiked up over her breasts. She didn't toss so much as a glance at the motionless figure on the table.

Alexis blinked several times, licked her lips, and tried to quiet her brain. Not to mention her heart. "I bought it at Canadian Tire," she said. "But I needed to tie up some old junk for the Salvation Army, I wasn't thinking about—uh, this."

"This is little better than spider silk," Lamashtu spat. She paused, closing her eyes, and wriggled with pleasure, as though enjoying something deep within herself. "We'll have to get some more. *I'll* go. You keep a watch on Loverboy." She gestured to the bedroom door. "Is there a window in there?" She reached for her pants.

"There is, but it's stuck. I never open it anyway. We have air conditioning here. He'd have to break it open. We'd have heard it. And anyway, I'm so high up he'd die for certain."

"Been known to happen," Lamashtu shrugged. "Make sure he doesn't kill himself. Now give me some money. Where's this Canadian Tire?"

Alexis fetched her purse, happy to do anything except look at the dried-up thing on her dining room table. She handed Lamashtu her wallet.

"What are we going to do about him?" she asked, pointing to Thor.

"We'll leave him here."

"What? You can't be serious!"

"Sure I am. Dave too. You don't need this apartment anymore. You're coming with me. Your training has already started, little girl. When the moon next passes into Scorpio I'll be able to give you the same powers I have. You will become many times more beautiful than you already are, and eternally young."

Alexis gulped nervously.

"Think of it, little girl!" Lamashtu smiled. "I know you're nervous about this. You shouldn't be. It's no big deal. The first kill is always the worst. Just wait until someone lowers himself onto you and you pull him inside, wrapping your arms and legs around him in a lover's crablike grip. His first cry is his last; when the scorpion stings one's throat feels like it has closed up."

Alexis paled and resisted the urge to step back.

"Then you will feel your own incredible power to make a man, any man, do what you want. Your face will be irresistible, your body forever lithe and bouncy. Your breasts will never sag. Your stomach will always stay flat. Your hips will enchant the hardest heart and when you feel a man slip inside you for the first time, *his* first time—"

She stopped and leaned forward. Her voice took on a throaty purr.

"You pull his unchristened member into you, and see the expression on his face when he tries to cry out from the sting but finds his throat paralyzed. Then when his struggles cease, you complete the act, drawing his powerful energy from the carnal connection. "

"D-does it hurt him?" breathed Alexis. "You know, after the initial sting."

Lamashtu shrugged. "Who knows? Who cares? Do they care about the pain they've caused *you,* little girl? These men are just using you, or they think they are, to lose their cherry. Just as others have used you for their own purposes with no intention of marrying you and giving you children. Now it's time to fight back!"

Alexis thought of all the men over the years who made pretty promises, who spoke flowery words of love, then who didn't return her phone calls or emails, or said, vaguely, "I've been really busy with work," or "I haven't had time, it's just been so crazy." They might as well have said, "I just can't be arsed."

"You will know the complete power of making him yours. Forever. You will have the power of life and death over him. It's what they fear most, Alexis, and it's also what they want the most. A man thinks he's a hero, a champion, when he conquers a woman, but little does he realize, *he* is the conquered one. You let him have a few seconds of fun, you let him think that this is the moment he's awaited for so long, now he will be a stud, and then—"

She snapped her index finger forward. Alexis winced.

"You slide down one last time, give him one last moment of glory, then you strike, he jerks once more, and then he is still. And then, of course, you feed." Lamashtu closed her eyes and wriggled again. She opened her eyes. “It feels like a prolonged orgasm.”

Alexis gulped again.

"Oh, don't hurl on me," Lamashtu pulled back, disgusted. "Wait until you feel a man's life pouring from his *lingam* into your *yoni.* Wait until you feel your strength increase, your powers frightening even God. You will join a sisterhood that stretches back to the beginning of time. Men only think they have the power. We rule them with this little cleft they so desire and fear. Remember, for every man you conquer, more babies will die. After I get back and take care of Dave, I'm going to lay waste to this entire city."

She looked up at the ceiling. "Hey Yahweh, are you watching?" she called out. "If you thought the slaughter of Egypt's first-born was something, wait'll you see this!"

★ ★ ★

"Alexis? Are you there? Pick up, dammit!" Rachel stared angrily at her cell phone.

"Maybe she's not even home," Rabbi Chofetz drawled.

"She has to be. Dave said she was bringing him and the other guy back here."

"So, what's with the calling? We'll knock when we get there," he replied as they waited for the elevator.

"I just want to let her know we're coming," Rachel explained. She disconnected and redialed. "I suppose I should have done this sooner. I didn't really think this thing through."

"*Oy,* I imagine there's no plan if the psycho demon and her wicked mother show up."

"Hello?" The voice sounded shaky.

"Alexis? It's Rachel. Are you all right? Are the guys upstairs?"

"What do you mean, 'upstairs'? Where are you?"

"I'm down in your lobby. I've got a friend with me."

"Who? No! Wait! You can't come up. Go away, Rachel, I'm busy."

"I know what you're doing. Dave told me."

"Yes, I know, I was right there. He and Thor are—uh, fine."

"Lamashtu is coming. She'll find them."

"Yes, I know. I won't let her in."

"We're coming up to help you."

The elevator arrived.

"We? Who's the other person?"

"A very nice man named Rabbi Chofetz. He's an expert on Jewish history and mythology. He knows all about Lamashtu and her mother Lilith."

"You can't come up, Rachel! I can't let you in."

"Yes you can. I swear she's not with us. Let me talk to Dave."

"I can't do that."

"Why not?"

"I just can't."

"Alexis, what is going on? He's got his own phone, I can call him."

"Okay. I have to go. Goodbye." Alexis hung up.

"It sounds like she doesn't want company," Rabbi Chofetz commented.

"She needs our help," Rachel insisted. "Something's wrong."

The rabbi let out a long sigh. The elevator let them off.

Rachel led them to Alexis' door and knocked. "Alexis, please let us in."

"I can't, Rachel. I'm very busy."

"Are you still deflowering the guys?"

"Is she WHAT?" howled the rabbi. His eyes bugged out of his head.

"Uh, didn't I tell you about that part?" Rachel asked guiltily.

"No, you didn't mention that part!" he screamed. *"Oy Gevalt!"*

"I can't let you in, Rachel." Alexis's voice sounded high-pitched, like she was on the verge of tears.

"Alexis, please. Don't try to defend yourself on your own. We want to help you."

"You've got a naked *shiksa* in there deflowering a couple of young men? I want nothing to do with this, young lady!"

"Rabbi, we've got to help her."

"She doesn't sound like she needs help. And if there's one thing I don't do it's deflower young men."

"Alexis!" Rachel rapped angrily on the door. "Let me speak to Dave."

"I can't. He's, uh, busy."

"Alexis," she growled, "if you don't let me speak to him right now I'm calling the police!"

There were several seconds of silence.

"Rachel, I can't let you in. It's—uh, bad. Really bad."

"Alexis—" Rachel said quietly. "Has she already been here?"

Alexis' response was a quiet sob.

"Alexis, sweetie, please let us in. Whatever trouble you're in, we'll help you."

"Put your clothes on!" Rabbi Chofetz roared.

The door slowly opened. Alexis' tear-stained face appeared.

"She—killed him," she sobbed. "And I—let her."

"Oh my God," Rachel breathed. She fell back. Her heart leaped to her throat. "Dave's—dead?"

"Not Dave," Alexis sniffled. "His friend. Thor."

"Who's Thor?" asked Rachel.

Alexis held the door open. "He's on the dining room table."

Rachel froze when she saw Thor's body. Rabbi Chofetz gasped and muttered something in Hebrew.

Slowly they approached. Alexis had pulled his pants on again, but Rachel knew what had happened. She could see it in the poor man's terrified face. His body was rigid. And he was wrinkled and shriveled, like a corpse that had lain in the desert.

"Who—did—this—thing?" Rabbi Chofetz growled. He stepped

forward, his eyes ablaze. He turned to Alexis. "Was it you? Or was it—*her?"*

Alexis just stood there with tears running down. Rachel slowly put her arms around her.

"She forced you to watch," she said quietly as the girl collapsed against her.

"No, Rachel," said Alexis. "She didn't force me."

"RACHEL!" came a voice from the bedroom. "Help me! It's Dave Gillpatrick! They're holding me prisoner! You've got to get me the hell out of here, Lamashtu is coming back soon and she's gonna kill me!"

Rachel pulled away from Alexis. "What the hell is going on here?" she demanded. "Are you *working* with Lamashtu?"

"Yes, she is! She's been recruited!" Dave screamed. "Kill her, Rachel! Please! Just get me the hell out of here, or I'm gonna die!"

"Is this true?" Rachel shook Alexis by the shoulders. "Are you in league with that hell-bitch?"

Alexis shook her head. "Not anymore. No. I can't do this. Not—what she did to him." She couldn't look at Thor.

Rabbi Chofetz took her from Rachel. "Listen to me, you crazy woman!" he yelled. "You give me the key right now to that room!"

"I—I—no," Alexis stammered, and she looked toward the bedroom. "She'll kill me."

"I'LL kill you if you don't give me the key!" the rabbi screamed. He shook her hard. "Give it to me!"

Alexis reached into her pockets. Her hands shook. She looked up at the rabbi. "I forgot," she said. "She took it with her. She said she wasn't sure if she could trust me yet."

Rabbi Chofetz shoved her at Rachel. "Search her," he commanded. "Search her pockets, her clothes, her bra. Make sure the little witch isn't lying to us. NOW!" he bellowed.

Rachel searched an unresisting Alexis.

"She doesn't have it."

"That's because I have it," came a voice from the doorway.

Lamashtu leaned against the doorjamb, her bare midriff gloriously serpentine, as she dangled the key from her hand.

"Rachel, get me out of here!" Dave screamed, hysterical.

"Shut up, Loverboy," Lamashtu called. She walked over to Thor's corpse and pulled off the ball gag. "Looks like I'll be needing this again." She turned to Rachel and Rabbi Chofetz. Her eyes narrowed again upon seeing Rachel. They looked her up and down, head to toe.

"I don't know who you are but I can tell you're trying to deflower my virgin."

Rachel wasn't quite sure how to respond to this. Now she was sorry she hadn't tried harder for Dave.

"*And* you're really old-looking," Lamashtu added nastily.

"I'm a baby compared to you," Rachel muttered.

Lamashtu gave Rabbi Chofetz a contemptuous once-over. "I don't know who you are either but I guess I'll just have to kill you."

"You're not doing your—Jade Dragon Gilligan thing on me," Rabbi Chofetz growled.

"Don't be ridiculous, you shriveled-up old fart. You've been married. You're of no interest to me."

She picked him up and flung him against the wall like she had Thor. Except this time, so hard Rachel heard several loud cracks.

"One down, two to go," Lamashtu said and she turned to Rachel.

"The odds are two against one," Rachel said, and she glanced at Alexis. Who looked about as useful as a ceramic hammer at the moment.

"Don't kid yourself, bitch. She won't defy *me*. She'll be just like me tomorrow night."

"I guess I'll just have to call the police then," said Rachel.

"I guess you'll just have to live long enough to do so," said Lamashtu.

Rachel flung open the door and ran. Lamashtu was right on her heels.

☆ ☆ ☆

Alexis closed the door and locked it. She turned around and surveyed the apartment. What should she do? Call the police? Rachel was in trouble. Maybe she should follow her? "Rachel! Get me the hell out of here!" screamed Dave. "PLEASE!"

Should she call the police? No, Lamashtu had cut the phone cords. Taken her cell phone. She wanted to make sure Alexis didn't lose her nerve. And of course they'd taken Dave's cell phone.

Maybe she should run next door and ask to borrow their phone?

"Rachel! Please, get me out of here!"

She'd find him. No matter where he went, she'd find him. And she would be back within minutes. Alexis had no doubt of how long Rachel would last in a fight.

She ran to the kitchen and rummaged through her junk drawer. She found it - the spare key.

She raced back to the bedroom. Fumbling, she dropped it, picked it up, fumbled again. It wouldn't turn. She twisted.

"RACHEL!"

It turned. She threw open the door. Dave waited, terrified, in one corner of the room.

"Get away from me, you bitch!" he screamed.

Alexis slammed the door. She pulled her heavy oak bureau in front of it - how, she didn't know, especially since its feet dragged across the rug - but maybe it was the adrenaline. When it blocked the door, she turned to Dave. "Help me push the bed against this!"

"What do you mean? What the hell do you think you're doing? Get the hell out of my way, bitch, I can take you even if I can't take her!"

She yanked on the bed. It took all her strength, but she managed to drag it close to the bureau. She turned to him.

"Take off your pants."

"WHAT?"

"You heard me. Take off your pants. Come on, we don't have much time!"

"Are you crazy? You think I'm gonna trust *you?"* "What choice do you have? Look, Dave, I can't hurt you. I don't have the scorpion power yet. Now take off your pants and I'll deflower you. NOW."

"Are you out of your mind? I can't get it up now! When that psychotic bitch comes back she's gonna kill me! Just like she killed Thor! I heard it all! I saw it through the keyhole—" his voice cracked.

Alexis pushed him onto the bed. She pulled back her blouse and quickly unhooked her bra. She pulled them both off and climbed onto his legs.

"Shut up. Distract yourself with these for a moment," she ordered.

She *did* have pert pink nipples. Just like he'd imagined.

And he was distracted. But only for a moment.

"I can't. And you can't. She alone knows the—the—peacock stew thing."

"The Jade Peacock Mulligan. And she's not the only person who knows it now."

She stood up before him, pulled open his pants, and yanked them down his hips.

"Now shut up and enjoy."

✯ ✯ ✯

"OH—MY—GOD!"

Lamashtu stormed down the hallway and flew into Alexis' apartment.

"AAAAHHHHH—AAAAAHHHHH!" Dave squealed.

"Alexis!" Lamashtu shouted, and she hurled herself at the bedroom door. "You'd better not be doing what I think you're doing, or so help me, I will flay you alive and turn you inside out!"

"AI-AI-AI-AI-AI!" Dave shrieked. "Oh God, she's coming!"

"I hobe oo mean oor cubbin," said Alexis.

"It's her! She's outside the bedroom door! I can't function under this pressure!—"

"Waib a mimit, lemme try fis—"

"Oh God I'm losing it! Ohhhhh—HUH! HUH! HUH! HUH! No, I'm not! AAAAAAHHHHAAAAAHHHHH!"

"Alexis, you goddamn bitch! Open the door now and let me in! Don't you dare fuck him! I will flay you alive with my fingernails and that's no idle threat, bitch, I mean that literally!" Lamashtu hurled herself at the door again. The bureau moved, and the door jimmied open slightly.

"ALEXIS!" A brown hand clawed the air. "Let me in and don't you dare touch him!"

"OHHHHHHHHHHHHHHHH!"

Lamashtu hurled herself at the door again. It cracked, and it slammed against the bureau, which shoved against the bed.

"Hurry, Alexis, HURRY!"

"No, OO hurby!"

Lamashtu slammed against the door. It split further. She was able to push her head in just enough to see Alexis's head bobbing over Dave's lap.

"OH GOD I'M COMING!" he shrieked.

"Not yet!" cried Alexis, and her head popped up. She looked back, saw Lamashtu's demonic anger and her eyes grew wide.

"DON'T YOU DARE!" screamed Lamashtu. Alexis rose up on the bed. Buck naked.

"I'LL KILL YOU, YOU DIRTY LITTLE MORTAL SLUT!" she screamed. Alexis straddled Dave's rock-hard schlong.

"NOOOOOOOOOOOOOOOOO!"

Alexis dropped. Dave shrieked. Lamashtu screamed the tortures of the damned banshees.

She hurled one last time. The door broke with a terrible crack and she fell into the room, ass-over-heels over the bureau. Alexis was pumping furiously on top of Dave.

"If you've ruined him there will be hell to pay, I promise you! And I should know, because that's where I've been for the last thousand years!"

She picked Alexis up by the hair and neck. Alexis screamed. Lamashtu flung her across the room. She hit the mirror on the wall which cracked and splintered. Alexis fell to the floor, and the mirror shattered and rained down.

Lamashtu turned back to Dave, who screamed and tried to roll away. She pinned his shoulders to the bed. She straddled him, and in a move he didn't think was humanly possible managed to shimmy out of her jeans without removing her hands from his shoulders. His rod stood erect, quivering. He was so close, there was no hope of losing it now.

"It's not over until you *come!"* she hissed, and she spread her legs and centered.

Which he did, right into her left eye.

And judging by her reaction, Alexander Portnoy was dead right.

CHAPTER SEVENTEEN

Rachel moaned and moved her head slightly. Something was cold and gritty beneath her cheek. She opened her eyes and saw acres of gray concrete before her. With a start, she realized she was still in the parking garage beneath the high-rise.

She tried to pull herself up but she cried out in pain. It tore through one of her kidneys and she reached back to grab it. More pain, centered in her shoulder, stopped her. She paused to catch her breath while it all subsided and remembered that Lamashtu had thrown Rabbi Chofetz against a wall too.

She carefully pulled herself to her knees. Her vision wobbled. She remembered running around the cars, chased by Lamashtu, who leaped over the hood of one of them, caught up with Rachel, and with inhuman strength lifted her up and threw her against the wall like a rag doll. She hit her head first, then fell to the ground, and that was all she remembered.

The parking garage was quiet. Was she still there, waiting? Why hadn't she just killed Rachel?

And then she remembered: *Dave.*

She had to get back to Dave. And Rabbi Chofetz. He was probably injured, maybe even dead. And Dave, what had become of him? Was it too late? Had Lamashtu murdered him already? Was she feeding on him even while Rachel kneeled on the cold concrete?

She checked herself quickly for broken bones. There didn't appear to be any, but she'd have to be careful. There might be internal injuries. She rose shakily to her feet, with one hand against the wall. She looked around. Her vision wobbled again. Oh God, her head ached in two places. She touched them gingerly. The first, at the back of her head, was tender to the touch but there didn't seem to be any blood. There was at her temple, where she'd hit the ground, and her neck hurt too.

Still, she was up and walking. Well, standing. She looked around. The lights seemed to flicker like a strobe light, or some early silent movie.

Rabbi Chofetz. She had to find him. It was all her fault this had happened. What if he was dead? What if Dave was dead? What had happened to Alexis? When had she joined Lamashtu?

Rachel reeled and fell to the floor. She caught herself on her hands, and pain shot up both arms, exploding in her injured shoulder.

Call someone. She had to call someone.

Her head reeling, she reached for the cell phone. She was supposed to call someone or something in an emergency, but she couldn't quite remember who. She flipped it open. The screen said *Last call: Incoming Chaoxiang Wan.*

Rachel hit the Dial button.

Dave thought she was going to beat him, but instead Lamashtu, once she could see again, strode over to Alexis, who lay motionless on the floor.

She picked her up by the shoulders and yanked her to her feet.

"Wake up, bitch!" she yelled, and she shook Alexis, who looked dead. Her head lolled about her shoulders.

Lamashtu pulled back with one hand, and still managed to hold

Alexis aloft with the other. "I said, *WAKE UP, BITCH!"* She slapped Alexis's cheek ferociously.

To Dave's relief, Alexis cried out. She wasn't dead.

"LOOK AT ME!" Lamashtu demanded.

Alexis' eyes fluttered. Briefly, her eyes rolled back into her head but Lamashtu slapped her again. Her cheek flushed bright red.

"I WANT YOU AWAKE WHILE I FLAY YOU ALIVE!" Lamashtu screamed. She pulled her hand back again.

"Don't hit her!" Dave screamed, and he leaped up from the bed. He quivered with fear, but he stood before her, naked, his wilted manhood a slap in the face of a different kind.

"You get back there on the bed," Lamashtu growled like something out of the darkest level of hell, "or I will flay you *first!"*

Dave picked up Alexis' hairbrush, which had fallen from the bureau to the floor when Lamashtu forced her way in. It was the kind with stiff wire bristles.

"Or I will flay *you* first!" he growled.

She dropped Alexis to the ground, who cried out as she fell on the glass shards from the mirror. She moaned and writhed a bit, but lay there, whimpering.

"You dare to defy me?" Lamashtu hissed as she slowly advanced on Dave. In a nanosecond he lost his nerve. The strongest woman he'd ever seen was about to—do something horrible to him, maybe flay him, maybe twist his dick off, he wasn't sure, but suddenly, a wire hair brush seemed like the puniest of weapons.

"You were supposed to restore my powers," she hissed, and her eyes flashed so cruelly she looked more like a manga demon than the most beautiful woman he'd ever seen. In fact, she looked—*hairier?!?* "I would have never lost them again. I could have destroyed all the babies in this city by nightfall. I could have made every pregnant woman abort. I wanted to hear the lamentations of the mothers!"

Dave backed up a few steps. The hand holding the hair brush felt like a limp noodle.

Lamashtu held up her fingers like claws. Her fingernails suddenly seemed much longer than he remembered them. Had they grown, or did they seem longer through his fear? Dave dimly remembered something he'd read in a novel about vampires whose fingernails grew long in the grave so they could scratch their way out. He didn't remember anything about them getting hairier. And not only did Lamashtu now sport the beginnings of a five o'clock shadow, but her long, lustrous, beautiful hair had gotten shaggier and more unkempt.

"I'm going to gut you like a deer," she hissed, and then her hands were upon him. He screamed and she lifted him up, holding him by the back of the neck. She brandished dangerous talons. They *were* longer, and she *was* going to gut him like a deer.

"Awwwww, so there's my pwecious wittle lamby-kins," came a voice from the doorway. "And I see you're beginning to show your true colors."

Lamashtu dropped Dave and whirled around. Slipping through what was left of the door and lithely gliding over the bureau was, now, *the* most beautiful woman Dave had ever seen.

Rachel made her way to the elevator. Where did Alexis live? The twenty-third floor. She jabbed a finger at the button in the wall, missed, and jammed again. Missed. *Damn button, hold still!* she thought. It was dancing around the wall like a fairy in a garden. After several more unsuccessful jabs, Rachel put both palms against the wall in the general vicinity of the dancing elevator button. She felt it, beneath the base of one thumb.

"Caught you, you slippery little bastard," she breathed, and she shifted her hand and jabbed.

When the elevator arrived, she pulled herself in and stared at the rows of buttons by the door. Fortunately, they weren't dancing around like the button outside had. She found 23 and jabbed again. The doors closed.

She wondered who the Chinese guy was she'd been talking to.

"Mother!" Lamashtu's faced twisted into an ugly snarl.

Mother? This exquisite creature was her mother? Oh God no, not another homicidal hoo-ha!

Lamashtu's mother turned and looked at Dave. He could see from whom Lamashtu had inherited those beautiful elongated eyes. And those perfect breasts—Mom dressed a little more conservatively, but there was no denying the woman had a figure that could make a grown man cry. Her hair, much longer than her daughter's, was pulled back by a jeweled headband of some sort, so that it rose up from behind like a prom queen's. It spilled down her back and over her shoulders in infinite waves, over her porcelain skin.

"Y—you—you're much paler than your daughter is," breathed Dave, as it was the only thing he could say while he marvelled at her unearthly beauty.

"Yeah, that's because her father was a Sumerian," she replied. "I'm Lilith, by the way. I assume you're one of my daughter's intended victims. Goodonya for surviving her, however that happened. I salute your strength."

"Get the hell out of here, Mother," Lamashtu growled.

Lilith turned to her. Her cool blue eyes raked her largely naked daughter appraisingly. "You're in your natural state, I see," she sneered. "Soon to impress the world in your *original* state. Funny you should mention hell, because that's where you're going very shortly."

"I'd like to see you make me," Lamashtu growled. She still held up her killer-claw hands. They *had* gotten longer. Her nails were claws, like a lion's.

Lilith smiled a slow half-smile that turned Dave's blood to ice. He stood up and fell back on the bed, shaking.

"What's your name?" Lilith asked.

"D-D-D-Dave," he breathed.

"Well, Dave, you need not fear me, Lamashtu didn't inherit her murderous muff from *me*. Now I wonder if you could excuse us for a few moments? I need to have a private word with my daughter."

Dave looked back and forth between the two women. He thought he detected a note of fear in Lamashtu's eyes. Which had, bizarrely, turned a tawny yellow that filled her entire eyes save for their small pupils.

"I—I need to—" he began, and Lilith regarded him quizzically.

"What?" she asked.

He gestured toward Alexis.

"Oh my Goddess." Lilith relaxed for a moment as she gazed with pity on the prone form. She turned to Lamashtu with accusing eyes. "Did you kill her?"

"I hope not. I wish to torture her some more!"

Lilith nodded at Dave. "You take the girl and see that she gets help. I'll keep the brat at bay."

Dave stepped toward Alexis and winced as some of the mirror shards found the soles of his bare feet. Gingerly, carefully, he bent down and lifted her. Dave had never been a strong man but he felt as though there was no room to screw up on a carpet of broken glass. He pulled her up and she cried out. He tried to brush some of the worst of the shards away. She cried out again and he was relieved to see that most of the shards were large and flat and they didn't catch in her skin. Still, some of them were embedded and she would need medical help.

"Move away from the door, daughter," commanded Lilith, and to Dave's surprise, Lamashtu did. There was a frightened glint in her eye.

He carefully pulled Alexis through the tiny passage leading out of the bedroom and took her to the living room where he laid her carefully on the couch.

He tried not to think about the fact that Lamashtu's nose had grown large and dark and that her upper lip had split down the middle.

☆ ☆ ☆

The elevator crept upwards. Where the hell had was everyone, anyone, anyway? Did no one notice the fight that had gone on in Alexis' apartment?

The elevator stopped at 23.

She had to find some guy. She thought he was Jewish, but she couldn't quite remember who he was.

She heard something that sounded like a herd of elephants stampeding down the hallway. Then voices, and yelling.

☆ ☆ ☆

"Guess who's going to lead you to the gate that smells of burning garbage?" Lilith asked calmly. When Lamashtu failed to answer she said, "Adam."

"Adam would never do anything to hurt me," Lamashtu snarled. "He loves me. He told me so. You always hated that he loved me more than he loved you. I could please him in bed the way you never could."

"Adam was an idiot who invented irresponsibility, passing the buck, and male chauvinism. Although doubtless that last was probably a design flaw from his Creator, who made Adam, of course, in His own image. Fortunately, Yahweh's hardly the only game in town. Which He admitted as much to the Hebrews when He drafted His commandments."

"Spare me the Bible lesson," Lamashtu snarled. "I hate you, and as soon as I can figure out a way to kill you I will!"

"You're not killing anyone anymore, young lady. Your terrorist twat days are over. I've had a talk with your father, and since the Egyptian underworld can't hold you, we'll have to send you to a more—permanent fate."

"Sheol?" Lamashtu smirked. "You can't be serious." Large hairy ears poked through the unkempt mane of her hair.

"Oh, but I am, child. You're going to where no one has ever returned. You may be half-Sumerian but you're also half-Jewish. That means you can go to either afterlife. It's like a metaphysical dual citizenship. And I've also had a chat with Yahweh and he agrees that you belong in *Gehenna* now."

"Gehenna. Where the souls of the hopelessly wicked go," Lamashtu said sarcastically.

"And, eternal punishment," Lilith added. "You will be subsumed in the flames of your own wickedness."

"Yeah, and who's gonna make me?" Lamashtu spat. "You and

whose army?"

"My army," came a voice from outside the bedroom, and they turned to see Ammishtamru and the Canaanite Liberation Front.

* * *

The elevator doors opened and Rachel stumbled out. Her vision focused a bit and she looked down the hallway. *Follow the elephants,* she thought.

She staggered, marveling at how all the apartment doors danced like the elevator button in the garage. What was the girl's apartment number again?

Follow the elephants. She could hear them, arguing loudly.

The Chinese guy said he was coming.

Lamashtu's eyes widened.

"Sorry, Daughter Dearest," Lilith said, her eyes hard. "But the choice was yours."

"Oh, like the Baal Brigade is going to stop me. I know what this is all about, darling Mother. You've always hated me," Lamashtu growled. "This is because of Adam."

"No, this is because you chose a life of evil misdeeds, consumed by your anger at male abandonment and being unable to have children. You chose to give pain and death with your power, rather than pleasure like I chose."

"Men deserve what I give them!" Lamashtu cried. "They discriminate against me because I'm barren. They're willing to play with me, but not to love and cherish me because I'm unable to give them sons."

"You didn't look hard enough," replied Lilith. "Even in the patriarchal days of your birth, there were men with good hearts."

"You filled Adam's head with poison about me. You hated that I'm younger and more attractive than you."

"Don't flatter yourself," said Ammishtamru. "Your mom's way hotter."

"Yeah, especially now," came a voice from behind him. "Great Gods, Niqmaddu, I thought you said Lamashtu was a babe!"

Lamashtu turned leonine eyes on Ammishtamru, but he looked bored. He banged the butt of his spear on the ground as though to reinforce the reason why he was there.

"Adam was angry because I wouldn't bear his children. He abandoned you because you *couldn't,"* Lilith said. "Adam is a pale imitation of his Creator - self-obsessed, tyrannical, thinking the whole world revolves around him and his precious penis." Lilith rolled her eyes and reached for the sky. "If you'd given Asherah a chance to invent the Universe before you did, Yahweh, I guarantee You men wouldn't have nearly as much reason to worship their own *schmeckel."*

She turned back to Lamashtu. "Thank Him he mellowed as he got older. His Son wasn't nearly the *schmendrick* he was. I liked Jesus. I left him alone because he wasn't obsessed with his ding-dong. I didn't want to have to do this, Daughter," she said. "I tried to bring you to my side. I tried to persuade you to give up your evil ways. There is no good that can come of your scorpion's death, although I have to hand it to you, that is one devilishly creative little evolutionary advantage you've developed."

"And I will continue using it," Lamashtu snarled. "Men don't show women and their sacred *yoni* nearly enough respect. I will make them pay for their infidelities and their obsession with maleness and all things phallic."

"Not looking like that you won't," Niqmaddu muttered.

"I can't argue with you, Daughter," Lilith conceded, ignoring the Peanut Gallery. "Especially the Catholic Church which can't get around the fact that even Jesus came from between the legs of a woman, but damned if they'll admit Joseph entry. Never mind the fact that Jesus had more brothers and sisters than the Brady Bunch. *Oy!"* She raised her hands to the sky again. "Still, Daughter, there were better ways to seek your revenge. Teach men a good hard lesson—" she stopped to titter for a moment, "like I do, and show them that their precious *lingam* doesn't possess nearly the power they think. Show them how powerless they are before the allure of the *yoni.* But don't destroy them. That legitmates their fear of our power. Our vaginas were created to give life, not to take it."

She turned to Ammishtamru. "Okay, I'm sorry about the feminist rant, but it had to be said. If my daughter is being banished to the darkest, most desolate quadrant in *Sheol,* then she needs to understand why. Because she will not die, only remain imprisoned forever. She will have much to think about."

Ammishtamru scowled, and several of his soldiers banged their spears.

"You'll never take me," Lamashtu snarled. "I'm too strong now."

"Not for long," Lilith reminded her.

"Which is why I'm going for broke," Lamashtu added. "The whole enchilada. With my perfect virgin ruined, there's only one other way for me to get my powers back permanently."

For the first time, Lilith looked frightened. "Don't you dare. Don't even think about it."

Lamashtu smiled slightly, which was all she could do with a face and hair transformed into a lion's. The golden fur ended at her collarbones where it turned into the stiff gray hair of a donkey. Which went well with the ass's ears that sprouted out of her mane.

Lamashtu grabbed Lilith by the arms, who cried out with pain. Lamashtu's sharp talons dug into her skin and bright red splotches of blood appeared. She threw her mother away from the door with herculean strength. Lilith crashed against the wall and fell onto the bed.

"Okay boys," Lamashtu said as she waggled her talons. "Who's next?"

✯ ✯ ✯

The apartment door was open, and inside it sounded noisy. Rachel stumbled in and saw some old guy crumpled behind a widescreen TV, which had fallen to the floor in front of him. "Hey, you!" Rachel exclaimed as she dropped to her knees. "Wake up! Are you alive? We've got to get out of here—"

"He's alive," came a voice from the other side of the room. Rachel looked up. It was Dave. She remembered he was her client. He was sitting on the couch, buck naked, with a very pretty naked girl who looked a bit battered and bloody.

"Hey Dave," Rachel exclaimed as she tried to smile, "did you finally get laid?"

✯ ✯ ✯

The hallway resounded with terrified screams. Rachel looked up to see a frightening battalion of ancient bronzed warriors. They fell back through the hallway, toppling over like dominoes.

There was a horrifying roar. The ancient instincts ingrained in every human being warned Rachel that she was in terrible danger. It sounded like a lion.

Rachel and Alexis screamed. Over the bodies of the fallen warriors leaped a monstrous chimera. It had the form and ears of an ass, and the head of a lion. Its arms were still somewhat human-like although covered with stiff gray hair. They ended in hands with lethal-looking talons. Large pendulous breasts swung from its chest, and its legs were like an ass's, except that instead of hooves it possessed bird's feet.

The thing looked around, poised on the writhing body of Niqmaddu. In a horrible lion-like demonic voice it looked at Alexis and Dave and said, "I'll deal with you two later!"

It barely glanced at Rachel and Rabbi Chofetz, then leaped out the door.

From the bedroom emerged the most beautiful woman Rachel had ever seen. She was rubbing the back of her head and wincing.

"We've got trouble, kids, big trouble," the woman said. She turned and looked at Rachel. "Who are you?"

Rachel could only stare.

"Hey, is that you, Barrak?" The gorgeous creature stooped down and touched his face. Rabbi Chofetz groaned and raised his head. He took one look at Lilith and screamed.

"Oy Gevalt, I've died and gone to *Sheol!"* he screamed.

"Surrounded by demons I am!"

"Oh, don't be such a drama queen. You were screaming something of a different sort when I visited you in the seminary." She helped raise him to a sitting position.

"Rabbi Chofetz," Rachel stated. "I remember you now. You're the guy who always makes me feel like a crappy Jew."

"He has that effect on people. By the way, my name is Lilith." She held out a hand and Rachel shook it.

"Rachel Brinkerhoff. My God, you are gorgeous, if you don't mind my saying so."

"Thank you. So are you. You look like some movie star. I've seen some of her movies, when I'm roaming around the world. What's her name? Oh yeah, Jane Russell!"

Rachel's eyes widened and she glanced down at her considerably less-endowed chest, but Lilith didn't notice.

"How do you feel, Barrak?" she asked.

"Oy, like I've been run over by a tractor-trailer which then dropped a load of bricks on me."

"How many fingers am I holding up?"

"Three."

"Okay, you're going to need a doctor, and conveniently we'll find one where we're going. But we've got to hurry, my hellspawn daughter is on the loose and she's headed for the hospital."

"The hospital?" Rachel asked. She looked at Alexis. *I remember her too,* she thought. *She's my client. And she joined Lamashtu or something. She doesn't look so evil now, though. She looks naked and scared.*

"Don't trust Lilith, she's a witch!" Rabbi Chofetz cried.

"Oh, for the love of God, Barrak, will you get over yourself?" Lilith groaned. "I'm not a witch or a demon. You guys made that up because I booked on your boy Adam."

"If you're not a demon then why are you *immortal?"* he cried with an accusing finger. "You should be dead already, like Adam!"

"Adam and I were both created immortal," explained Lilith. "It was

Adam's and Eve's slip-up eating the forbidden fruit that made them mortal. Because I wasn't there, I wasn't affected. Geez, Barrak, when's the last time you broke open a *Tanakh?"*

"Yeah, now who's a crappy Jew?" Rachel muttered.

Dave rose to his feet, then looked down and turned around, covering his groin with his hands.

"Oh, don't be so shy," Lilith told him. "You've nothing to be ashamed of, young man! Such a nice-looking *schtupper* you have. My ex-husband Adam doesn't have so nice a one."

"Uh, thank you, I think," mumbled Dave. He looked away, embarrassed.

Lilith went into the small bathroom and came back with a towel which she threw at him. "Here, cover up if you can't share your glory with the rest of the world," she said. She looked around at the four of them. "Does anyone know where the biggest collection of babies and children might be in this town?"

Dave thought a moment and then answered, "Uh, probably the Sick Kids Hospital. It's on University Avenue. Why?"

"Because that's where Lamashtu is going. She doesn't have time anymore to look for another really good virgin. The only other way she can get all her powers back is to eat a couple of dozen infants and toddlers."

Rachel gasped and held her hand to her mouth. "You can't be serious!"

"As serious as a plague of emerods, young lady. If you've got a hospital here devoted strictly to children, I guarantee you that's where the little psychopath is headed."

"We've got to stop her!" Dave cried.

"My sentiments entirely," said Lilith. She looked at Rachel and Rabbi Chofetz. "I need to get to the museum. The one with the Crystal. Can anyone get me there?"

"The best thing would be to drive, except I don't think I can right now," Rachel answered. She touched her head. "Lamashtu threw me against a wall in the garage, and I don't think I'm thinking so good right now."

"Oy, me too," echoed Rabbi Chofetz.

"Yeah, she's good at that, isn't she?" Lilith remarked. "How about you, Dave? Can you drive?"

"W-well, I can, but I don't have a car," he replied.

"You can use mine," said Rachel.

"Okay then. Let's go."

"Why do you want we should take you to the Royal Ontario Museum?" asked Rabbi Chofetz. "Did you not just tell us that your hellbeast of a kid is headed to the children's hospital?"

"She is, but the five of us can't stop her. We need to bring in a really big gun."

Rabbi Chofetz groaned and rubbed his head. He tried not to look at the very attractive and naked-as-the-day-she-was-born *shiksa,* not to mention the vile temptress, and he didn't mean the crappy excuse for a Jew. Well, at least Lilith was wearing clothes. Which was more than could be said for her lunatic daughter.

"And where, exactly, do you think you're going to find a gun at the ROM?" asked the rabbi with exaggerated precision.

"No, you fool, not a literal gun. The ROM Crystal is one of several portals in this city to the Underworld. I need to call forth the only true enemy Lamashtu has, and the only creature who has any chance of defeating her before she eats her way to permanent power. I need to bring in Pazuzu."

Rabbi Chofetz's head shot straight up. "PAZUZU?" he screamed. "Woman, are you completely *meshuggina?"*

CHAPTER EIGHTEEN

"You can't do this! This is madness!" screamed Rabbi Chofetz. "You can't seriously expect to unleash an evil like Pazuzu onto the city!"

"Have you got any better ideas, Barrak?" she spat back. "Pazuzu is her sworn enemy. He's the only one who can defeat her long enough for Ammishtamru and the boys to drag her evil ass into Gehenna!"

Rachel started at the name of her ex-lover. Her heart twisted briefly in painful memory.

"Who's Pazuzu?" asked Dave.

"Only an evil so vile I want you should not mention his name, in case he hears!" Rabbi Chofetz yelled. "He is the most horrible of the wind demons, one who brings death and disease and destruction wherever he goes. Who do you think was behind the Plagues of Egypt?"

"God," Rachel replied, proud that she'd gotten one right. Even a lapsed Jew could remember one of the most famous stories in the Old Testament.

"No. Well yes," Rabbi Chofetz said. "Yes, God decided to visit each plague on Egypt. But he got Pazuzu to do most of them. The killing of the firstborn sons, though, he left to Lamashtu."

"Guess he doesn't like to get his hands dirty," commented Rachel.

"Don't be such a smarty-pants," Rabbi Chofetz chastised. "God hears everything you say and you will have to answer to Him one day."

"Yeah, well, I'm gonna ask God why he was such a vengeful bastard," Rachel snapped back. "Let me tell you, Rabbi, this ain't the story I got in Sabbath school."

"Nor did I," conceded the Rabbi. "I had to learn this from the legends—outside our own." He turned to Lilith. "And you, you foul hag, you can't be allowed to do this foolish thing. The cure will be worse than the disease!"

"What can be worse than a demon who EATS BABIES?" Lilith screamed.

"Malaria, SARS, locusts, sandstorms, tornadoes, gnats, pollution from the U.S., as though we don't have enough of our own, just to name a few. Why not shouldn't we call the police instead?"

"Because they can't handle her either. She's too strong, Barrak. She doesn't have her full powers back but she's getting close. This kid she killed—" Lilith gestured toward Thor's forlorn corpse, "—must have been pretty close to Dave's purity for her to be this strong. Or maybe she killed others before she got here."

"I wasn't very pure," Dave the Ex-Virgin grumbled, red in the face. "I had had some contact with women before. Like kissing and boob-touching and stuff." He didn't add that it had all been with Lamashtu.

"We should call this hospital and warn them," Lilith said. "They can lock the doors or put up barricades or something. It won't hold her off forever, but it might buy us enough time until Pazuzu gets here."

“We can bring Alexis,” Dave the Ex-Virgin said. “She needs medical attention and all the hospitals are right there.”

“Shouldn't we just call an ambulance?” Rachel asked.

“We have to go to the ROM first. Pazuzu's the only pers—er, thing—god-thing—that can stop Lamashtu. We can't lose any time,” Lilith said. “Besides, the ambulance likely won't come. They have WAY bigger problems right now than emergency calls.”

"I want nothing to do with this," Rabbi Chofetz exploded. "All right, you do what you want, I'll take care of the—departed. Then I want to get as far away from Toronto as I can if you're going to call *He Of The Stinking Genitals!"*

"Pazuzu's genitals stink?" asked Rachel.

"Oy!" he exclaimed, shaking his head as he held it in his hands. "And wait'll you see the *schmeckel* on him!"

✯ ✯ ✯

Lilith paused in front of the ROM Crystal while Dave the Ex-Virgin idled the car. She stooped down to look through the window.

"Just wait for me here. This should only take a few minutes," she said.

"Do you really think he's gonna help us if he's all that evil?" Rachel asked.

Lilith nodded. "He and my daughter have been enemies for thousands of years. Yeah, Pazuzu's one of the biggest rat-bastards of all the gods and demons in the world, and that's saying something for the ancients. I tell you, Rachel, the world would be much better off run by vaginas than by a bunch of pricks."

Dave looked away, embarrassed and a bit P.O.'ed.

"Now keep in mind that in the old days, when Lamashtu roamed the earth, before we imprisoned her in the Egyptian Underworld—"

"Why the Egyptian Underworld?" interrupted Rachel. "I thought you said she and her father were Sumerian."

"They are, but the Sumerians don't have any Underworld for those who are unworthy to dwell in the better neighborhoods. So we sort of outsourced Lamashtu's banishment to the Egyptians. Unfortunately, their security sucks. She escaped."

Rachel tried to process this latest weird information.

"Anyway, getting back to Pazuzu, people used to protect their infants with an amulet bearing Pazuzu's likeness. He's one vicious shit, but he *did* protect the babies. She'd take one look at that thing hanging around the infant's neck and decide that maybe the uncircumcised Ethiopian kid down the street whose parents didn't know about Lamashtu was a better bargain."

"How are we going to get rid of him?" Rachel asked nervously. "Once he defeats her."

But Lilith turned and disappeared into the Crystal. Dave and Rachel waited for several tense minutes. Then the Crystal began to pulse with a mysterious light that grew and grew. It wasn't nearly as dramatic in the middle of the afternoon as it was in the middle of the night, but still, it was pretty wicked cool. And frightening.

"Oh no, not another damn hot skank!" groaned one woman as she passed by. "Look at that, Loretta! Remember what happened the last time the Crystal glowed like that? If another damn perfect naked chick walks out of there I'm gonna puke."

They could see the faint silhouette of Lilith inside the Crystal. She appeared to stand with arms raised. There were some deep rumblings inside the Museum, then dozens of terrified people came streaming out of the exit, shrieking and scattering down Bloor Avenue.

Lilith came to the door and raised her hand to her mouth. "Hey, I'm sorry about scaring you," she called after them. "But I DID warn you that a big-ass demon was coming!" She waved at Dave and Rachel. "I'll only be another minute!" she hollered.

She disappeared back inside.

A few seconds later, something large and ominous appeared inside the Crystal. The unearthly light began to dim, and Rachel and Dave heard what sounded like a swarm of flies buzzing.

Lilith came running out of the building. She jumped into the car. "Drive to the bank building," she ordered. "The one where all the Canaanites came out. Pazuzu's going to meet us there."

"What's wrong with here?" asked Rachel, confused.

"Oh, I forgot how big he is. He can't fit through the door."

✯ ✯ ✯

Dave the Ex-Virgin pulled up to the Bank of America building and parked across the street. Technically, this was illegal, but he was far more worried about what might come out the door than he was about a parking ticket. He and Rachel watched as Lilith got out of the car, ran across the street, and poked her head through the large glass doors. Alexis didn't watch so much as sit in the back seat and occasionally moan.

Lilith turned back and waved to Rachel and Dave. "Oh, here he comes now!" she shouted across the street. "Just stay in the car. He won't be interested in you. All he wants is Lamashtu."

If there was anything Rachel and Dave were *so* not planning to do, like this was Number One on their List Of Things Not To Do Today, it was getting out of the car at a time when some big-ass evil wind demon was about to emerge.

"Here he comes!" Lilith shouted. Crowds began to gather on the street. Something was clearly coming out of the bank building again, but what was it? More ancient warriors? Another Fountain of Youth? Better yet, another really hot-looking skank, hopefully one with a friendlier *punani* than the scorpion chick?

"You might want to scooch out of the way. This is gonna get ugly," Lilith warned the crowd. The people gave the entrance a wide berth.

The new glass doors blasted off their hinges. They landed on the street and shattered into a thousand pieces. A great rushing wind blew forth from the bank building, bringing with it a horrible miasma of rotting flesh, of weeks-old garbage, of death and decay. Rachel and Dave heard the ominous buzzing sound they'd heard at the ROM.

A large head poked through the doors. Rachel gasped to see it. Dave uttered a small, high-pitched sound that sounded like a cross between a squeak and a moan. The crowd screamed and people began running away.

"May God help us awwwll," Rachel breathed in horrified awe.

Pazuzu had the shrunken head of a dead dog. Not a particularly small head, just a horrible skull, really, with a thin layer of skin stretched tightly over it. He bared his sharp canine teeth at Lilith and tried to force huge scaly shoulders through the doors. Lilith stood back to give him some room.

"Suck it in, Pazuzu!" she called. The buzzing sound was louder.

Pazuzu pushed through but his shoulders jammed the entrance.

"THIS PORTAL ISN'T BIG ENOUGH EITHER!" he growled in a

horrible, unearthly, demonic voice. It sounded like the bellow you'd expect to hear in the ninth level of hell in their otherworldly service station where someone really really has to go to the bathroom badly and realizes the bathroom hasn't been cleaned since Methuselah was alive and on top of that, they've been out of toilet paper since the Bourbon Restoration.

"Oh crap. Push, Pazuzu! We don't have much time!"

"I CAN'T GET THROUGH THE DAMN DOORS, WOMAN!" Pazuzu bellowed. He grunted horrible otherworldly tortures-of-the-damned noises as he jerked and shifted and tried to push his broad shoulders through the entrance.

"I wonder if others can get in there and push you?" Lilith mused, but as she looked around she realized there weren't any volunteers and anyway, no mortals could get into the building, what with it being a portal to the Underworld and all.

"YOU FOOL! YOU IDIOT! YOU VILE STINKING CRUD!" Pazuzu thundered. "HOW DARE YOU SUMMON ME ONLY TO MAKE A FOOL OF ME, WEDGED INTO THIS DAMNED CREATION OF FOUL HUMANS! I WILL FEED YOUR ENTRAILS TO THE FIRES OF GEHENNA FOR THIS!"

"No no no, you're supposed to feed *Lamashtu* to the fires of Gehenna," remarked a completely nonplussed Lilith. "Look, Pazuzu, I'm sorry about this. I'd forgotten how huge you really are. Look, I'm afraid you're going to have to come out the back way."

"THE BACK WAY?" Pazuzu exploded. "ARE YOU OUT OF YOUR FILTHY MIND, CROTCH-ROT?"

"I don't see any other way," answered Lilith. "Look, I know it's a bit out of your way, you'll have to travel to the other end of the ley line to do this, but you've got two sets of wings, you can come back here fast enough."

"THE OTHER END IS IN BLOODY SAN DIEGO!" Pazuzu bellowed, as he began to inch his bad self back into the bank building.

When Rachel, Dave, and Lilith got to the entrance of Sick Kids, it was barred and barricaded by employees inside. Outside, Lamashtu strode back and forth, the talons of her feet clicking against the hard cement as she shook the windows with her terrible roars.

"What's going on, eh?" Dave asked a man who was watching near the street.

"This—this *thing,* this demon, is demanding all the babies in the hospital," he said. "The people inside have kept her out so far but she seems pretty strong. The cops tried shooting her but it didn't seem to hurt her much and she killed one with a swipe of one of those claws. I tell you, man, this city is getting scarier and scarier!"

"BABIES! GIVE ME YOUR BABIES OR MORE WILL DIE!" the horrid demon screamed in a voice not unlike the little girl in *The Exorcist.*

Dave escorted Alexis across the street to Toronto General Hospital.

✯ ✯ ✯

Ten minutes later, the screaming began anew in Toronto. People pointed to the sky and began running into buildings.

A terrible wind swept down University Avenue. It reeked of carrion and festering infection and the contents of outhouses. It was hot and devoid of moisture and felt like something more appropriate to the desert than in often-rainy Toronto.

Something darkened the sky. It was huge and demonic-looking, a flying monster with two sets of wings. As it drew closer it dipped down and buzzed low over the cars stuck in traffic with the area in front of Sick Kids blocked by onlookers and police cars and barricades.

Rachel and Lilith watched from across the street. Rachel desperately wanted to get the hell out of town but she and Dave were Lilith's wheels, and Lilith seemed to be the only person who knew how to handle her wayward daughter.

Following the evil being was that buzzing sound. Pazuzu paused at Sick Kids, hanging in the air, two sets of eagle wings flapping to keep him aloft. The stench of carrion was overwhelming, and Rachel gagged and leaned over to puke. Lilith seemed largely unaffected except for the expression one customarily makes after stepping in dog doo. She waved her hand back and forth in front of her face.

The crowd dispersed quickly to see the most fearsome sight hovering over one of Toronto's most famous edifices. Rachel stared in abject horror.

"Oh my God, look at the size of that—*thingy!"* she cried out, utterly repulsed.

Pazuzu's penis was at least three feet long, and Rachel shuddered to see that it ended in a snake's head. The ominous buzzing sound came from a hideous swarm of flies that fought for access to the horrifying appendage, for it was that that smelled of ripe carrion.

"Okay, it's not like Rabbi Chofetz didn't warn us," Rachel groaned.

"Fingers crossed, girlfriend," said Lilith. "This is our last chance to get rid of Lamashtu. If he fails, this town is completely screwed."

"Why did you call on *him?*" Rachel asked. "Is it because he's bigger, or because he's more evil?"

"Neither. Lamashtu and Pazuzu have a history going waaaaay back. They hate each other, always have."

"Why?"

Lilith shrugged. "Beats me. My daughter and I don't exactly have *tête-à-têtes* over coffee, you know?"

Lamashtu turned around. She looked much smaller, but not particularly frightened.

"Pazuzu," she growled, and her lion's tail twitched. "My ancient enemy. Did you wake up this morning and say, 'Hey, I know, I want to die in Toronto today?'"

"I WILL DESTROY YOU!" Pazuzu growled.

"He's trash-talking," Lilith commented. "They can't destroy each other. They're both immortal."

"Where did he come from?" breathed Rachel.

"Oh, that's a long story," Lilith shrugged. "Yahweh couldn't manage his children back in the day."

"GOD created that—that—thing?" Rachel gasped. "With that—that —*thingy?"*

"God created everything, you dipstick. Except he's not as omnipotent as the book says. You know the story of Lucifer, how he started out as an angel, rebelled against God, and was cast down into Hell? Well some of the badasses, like our boy with with the putrid pud here, joined the Big L. Some of the angels, however, rebelled later, which the Book doesn't mention. They had better reasons than Lucifer, who was simply power-hungry. The angels didn't like the shabby way God treated his own people - favouring the Hebrews over the Canaanites, allowing freaks like Lamashtu and Pazuzu to run roughshod over them, and they were really unfond of the way the Hebrews were always conquering others and taking their stuff with God's blessing. That's what war's really all about, you know - it's never about this god or that god, it's about taking everyone else's stuff."

"You think you can take me, Stinkydick? Have at it, baby!" Lamashtu roared, and she lunged at Pazuzu. He swiped at her with one of his clawed feet as she did the same with one of her hands. They both missed.

"Idiots," Lilith muttered as she shook her head. "Anyway, there was an organized rebellion later by some of the angels who wanted to improve things for the humans with God. It wasn't successful, but they left Heaven and because they were immortal they became gods and goddesses."

“What if he can't subdue her?” asked Rachel nervously.

“Then we're screwed,” remarked Lilith. “The only other thing she's afraid of besides him are those big-ass desert spiders.”

Rachel's eyes widened.

“I think I've got us a Plan B,” she grinned and she pulled out her cell phone.

Twenty minutes later, the battle still raged. Lamashtu crouched down, her tail twitching. Pazuzu dipped up and down in the air, teasing her, taunting her. She leaped. He pulled back, his four wings beating like a dragonfly's. She caught the calf of one leg.

"Oooo, good one," Lilith commented. She turned back to Rachel. "Don't believe all the crap the prophets claimed about Heaven. Okay, it's a great place in many ways - streets paved with gold, benches with luscious fruits and buildings studded with fine gems and all - but it's also a hotbed of political lunacy. If you've ever wondered why the Middle East is so fucked up, well, remember that the three religions were all born there, and they're products of the same dysfunctional Father."

Lamashtu and Pazuzu rolled around on the ground, tails whipping back and forth. Lamashtu dug her mighty fangs into Pazuzu's shoulder who screamed with rage. Pazuzu's dick bit her savagely on the leg.

"Ow, that really hurts!" she roared.

"So—God—*our* God, the one who led us out of captivity in Egypt and into the Promised Land - he's a real—a real—" Rachel stammered.

Lilith turned and placed a comforting hand on her shoulder. "He's actually a really great God," she said. "He changed a lot. He saw the error of his ways. He realized he'd kind of been a really crappy God, especially to those people he made who weren't born *Habiri* and who could hardly be blamed for not jumping on the Hebrew bandwagon just because the prophets knew a few stale magic tricks. So he sent his Son to try and fix things and then God *really* changed after the Crucifixion. He felt terrible about that. He realized people are supposed to be responsible for their own salvation."

"So—uh, are we—uh, you know, us Jews—supposed to believe in Jesus?"

Lilith laughed to see the look on her face. "Only as a teacher. Jesus came here to teach and try to clean up all those idiot religious leaders. Hey, does sticking up for Him make me a Jew for Jesus?" she laughed.

"Rachel!" She looked down the street and sighed with relief. It was her client Dave the Tarantula Guy, hurrying up the sidewalk with a small box, glancing at the ongoing battle fearfully.

"Who's that guy?" asked Lilith.

"This is Dave, one of my clients," Rachel explained as he came up to them. "We may need him." She turned to Dave the T.G. "This is Lilith, this crazy monster's mother, if you can believe that. Show her what's in your box."

Dave the T.G. offered her a peek, and she grinned. Her smile melted his knees.

Lamashtu clung to Pazuzu, ripping at his neck and shoulders. Foul black goo splattered on the pavement and the shrubbery. A terrible wind blew up. It was like a whirlwind, enveloping the two warriors, and the flies and evil smells swirled around them too.

"That wind curse crap isn't going to work with me!" Lamashtu roared. Her clawed hands raked down Pazuzu's back. Rivers of black goo followed.

"Oh shit, here come the gnats!" Lilith cried. "C'mon, into this building!" She took Rachel by the hand and threw open the glass doors.

The three of them ran inside and Lilith pushed the door shut. A cloud of tiny bugs splatted against the glass. People outside screamed and fought the gnats off.

"There's going to be a run on Bactine at the drugstore," Dave the T.G. commented nervously.

Rachel turned to Lilith. "I don't think Rabbi Chofetz would like what you said about God."

She rolled her eyes. "Oh, that old fool needs to lighten up. You know, I'm the reason why he's an Orthodox Jew."

"You are?"

"Yeah, he was born into an ultra-Orthodox family. But I was able to, er, lighten him up a little too much to stay," Lilith grinned sensuously. "Problem was, I was aiming for Conservative."

Pazuzu rose into the air, his wings beating furiously. Lamashtu clung to him, her jaws dug into his neck. His monstrous penis reached around and bit her on one of her buttocks. She roared with pain, releasing his neck, but not Pazuzu himself. She reached around and grabbed the penis. Now it was Pazuzu's turn to roar.

"I will bite this off!" she roared.

"I WILL STRIKE YOU DOWN WITH HEMORRHAGIC FEVER!" Pazuzu roared back.

"That was totally lame," Lamashtu sneered. "You suck at sarcastic repartee."

The serpentine penis wrenched out of her grasp and bit her buttock again. She roared, and lunged forward as best she could, capturing a wing.

"Oh shit!" Lilith cried. "That's not good. If he can't fly—"

Pazuzu's penis reached around and bit Lamashtu on the inside of her thigh.

"OW!" she roared. "Dammit, that REALLY hurt! I'm going to feast on your entrails for that!"

With his wing freed, Pazuzu rose high in the air, taking Lamashtu with him. The gnats followed him, like faithful sheep. Lamashtu struggled violently and for a moment it looked like he might lose his grip. But higher and higher he took her, and then, when he was just a speck in the sky, he paused.

"Holy shit," Lilith cried. "LOOK OUT BELOW!"

Something was dropping. Fast.

"That fly-infested moron!" Lilith groaned. "That's not going to kill her!"

The few onlookers left scattered on the street. Lamashtu hit the ground with a window-shaking thud. Her mighty lion's head bounced off the pavement. The donkey's ears twitched briefly, then lay still.

"Dave, this is your moment for glory," Rachel prodded. Dave the T.G. looked at her nervously and glanced down at the box.

"You gotta do this," Rachel urged. "For all of us."

"Will Pookums get hurt?"

"Not if he wins the battle," she replied.

She pushed Dave the T.G. through the glass doors. He, along with several of the sort of people who usually die in monster movies, hurried across the street to see if Lamashtu was dead.

"NO! Don't!" Lilith cried, but no one listened. They never do.

Dave the T.G. ran ahead of the others, clutching his box. Everyone crowded around Lamashtu's motionless corpse, marvelling at the strange combination of bird, donkey and lion. It was hard to believe she'd been the breathtakingly beautiful creature that had stalked Toronto for weeks, seducing innocent young men with her fatal attraction.

A clawed hand reached up and seized Dave's wrist. He cried out and tried to pull away but she roared and squeezed. Bones crunched and snapped and Dave screamed in agony. The others scattered, glad it wasn't they who found out the hard way Lamashtu wasn't really dead. Dave dropped the box, which landed and fell open on Lamashtu's hairy belly, just beneath her pendulous breasts.

"I will kill and eat you all!" she roared.

Pookums looked over the brim of the box. Her eight eyes registered the crowd, and her sensitive feet and leg hairs quivered, registering the scent of the enemy. The box fell to its side and she crawled down Lamashtu's belly, pausing just over the pubic bone - or what passed for it in a bird-lion-donkey chimera.

"And I will start with YOU!" she hissed at Dave, who had sunk to his knees in agony.

And then she cried out in pain and jerked once, twice—then lay still, and dropped Dave's wrist. He stood up, clutching it protectively to his stomach. "Pookums, where are you?" he asked shakily.

The spider pulled back, waving her pedipalps in the air. Had anyone understood the tarantula victory dance, they would have realized she was saying, *I* so *kicked the skanky scorpion bitch's ass! I rule, I rule, la-la-la-la-la!*

Dave the T.G. leaned over and looked up at Rachel. "Pookums is a heroine," he said. "You were right. This was a great idea."

"Is she dead?" asked one of the crowd members, who didn't know either that Lamashtu was immortal, or that tarantula bites usually weren't fatal.

"No," Dave the T.G. replied, "she's paralyzed. I think Pookums scented the scorpion. This woman—thing—is supposed to have a scorpion in her, right?"

Several faces around the crowd assented.

"Well, tarantulas and scorpions are enemies, and when they fight, the scorpion usually wins because it can just sting the tarantula with its tail. But if I understand correctly, the scorpion is, uh, in her—"

"Cunnikin," replied one man, who taught medieval studies at one of the local universities.

"Er, yes," Dave the T.G. mumbled. "Hence the inability to strike back, I guess."

CHAPTER NINETEEN

Lilith ran into the street. Rachel hung back, then joined her when she saw the gnats and no-seeums had risen up to join their demon master and his sweet-smelling wangdoodle. She followed Lilith and pushed through the crowd to see what had happened to Lamashtu. Dave the Ex-Virgin joined them, having gotten Alexis checked in.

The horrible creature lay unmoving. "What are we going to do with her—it?" asked someone in the crowd.

"Shall we call the police?" asked a woman, cell phone at the ready.

"I've got it taken care of," said Lilith. She turned and looked around. "Hey! Yo! Ammishtamru! Where the hell are you?"

Rachel looked around nervously. The last thing she wanted to see was her slutty ex-lover.

"Where the hell is he?" Lilith spat. "I told him to get his ass over here as soon as possible!"

"It's going to take awhile to walk here from Alexis's," Dave the Ex-Virgin pointed out.

“I told them to take the subway! It's much quicker."

"Do they have money?"

Lilith looked stricken. "Oh, crap. I forgot about that."

And then they heard war cries, from far away. The crowd moved to the street and saw the Canaanite Army, such as it was, hurrying up the street with spears, swords and shields.

Then they stood before Lilith. Bronzed, beautiful, and fierce-looking.

"Wow, how'd you guys get here so fast?" she asked.

"We took the subway."

"Man, you guys are turning into regular Canadians," commented a young woman.

"How'd you do it without money?" Lilith asked.

"They let us on for free. We explained we were coming to save their babies from the monster. The TTC guys opened the gate and let us through," said Aqhat.

"She doesn't look like she'll fight much," commented Ammishtamru, brow furrowed as he regarded the prone form of his enemy.

"No, she's stone cold paralyzed. This gentleman here had a big-ass spider that fought her scorpion and won."

"Oh." Ammishtamru looked a little confused. "She's dead?"

"No, just stunned. She'll come to eventually. So take her back to Sheol. She's going to Gehenna."

"The flaming garbage dump?" Ammishtamru shuddered. "You *Habiri* mean business with your evildoers, don't you."

"That's where God sends the hopelessly evil," Lilith replied, a bit sadly.

"Rachel?" Ammishtamru looked into the crowd. Someone turned away from him.

"Rachel?" He pushed through and turned her around.

"So, how's it goin', Am?" Rachel asked tightly. Her face was inscrutable, her eyes more violet than ever.

"I can't believe how young and beautiful you've become. No, you were beautiful before. Now you are—gorgeous!" His eyes swept her again. He stepped back for a better look. "You went to that fountain again, didn't you. I want to visit too, when I get a moment—"

"Yeah. Well. Nice seein' ya, Am. We've got an ancient evil god guy to get rid of, so I don't have time to chat."

"Wait, Rachel. Don't go," he said. He pulled her into his arms and looked down into her mesmerizing purple pools. His touch electrified her. "I want to be with you."

She pushed him away. "Yeah. I'm shooah. Been there, done that, bored now."

"No, no, Rachel, listen to me. I'm sorry about the other women. It wasn't my fault. It was kind of an accident—"
"You *accidentally* had sex with other women?"

"I'm different now. They're gone." Ammishtamru waved his hand dismissively. "None were so beautiful as you are now. I am in love with you."

Those words that she'd so wanted to hear again some day.

He was so hot and large and desperately sexy—

And all she really wanted was to bury her lips in his again—

He smiled, slowly and sensuously and with eyes that burned into her soul. Just like Austin's once had—

She reveled in his attention and his utter charm. He stood before her, so strong and handsome, with a mischievous smile on his face that promised he would make it up to her in his tent later if they ever got rid of Pazuzu.

Would they get rid of Pazuzu? Who could defeat such an adversary?

She waited for Ammishtamru to move in, take her in his powerful arms and kiss her like no one had ever kissed a woman before. That was what was supposed to happen next, she was sure of it. Instead, Ammishtamru pulled away a bit.

"I have to take care of Lamashtu," he told her. "I will find you later."

Puzzled, Rachel watched him turn away and join his compatriots. Surely there was time for one halacious Elizabeth Taylor-worthy movie kiss before they faced the peril of Pazuzu?

But Ammishtamru was already squatting on the ground, helping to tie the chimera to the long spear.

"Pazuzu!" Niqmaddu cried, pointing.

The horrible demon dropped like a rock.

Pazuzu paused just above the crowd, his four wings beating the air. The gnats and no-seeums swarmed about him, although some swooped down on the crowd, who beat about their faces trying to ward them away.

"I WANT LAMASHTU!" Pazuzu bellowed in his terrible tortures-of-the-damned demon voice.

"Uh, sorry, Paz, but she's going to Gehenna. We want to eliminate her permanently. Yahweh's orders," Lilith told him nervously. Rachel walked back to her and the Daves.

"I DON'T GIVE A DAMN ABOUT YAHWEH!" Pazuzu bellowed. "LAMASHTU IS MY ENEMY! I CAME WHEN YOU BECKONED, HUMAN FILTH! I DEMAND HER AS MY PAYMENT!"

"Uhhhh—no can do, Pazuzu! We never agreed that you can take her away. You can't secure her forever. She will eventually overcome her paralysis. Yahweh and her father are in agreement - she has to go where she can never escape again."

"I WILL DEAL WITH HER MYSELF! I WILL MAKE SURE SHE SUFFERS FOR HER CRIMES!"

"Yeah, and when he gets bored with her he'll just let her go," Lilith whispered as an aside to the Daves and Rachel. "Except after his tender ministrations she'll be ten times more psycho than she is already."

Rachel glanced at Ammishtamru. His bronzed back was hunched over his task. His muscles glistened in the sunlight, corded like a magnificent classical statue. She wanted him more than ever.

Lilith turned back to Pazuzu, who landed on the ground and approached her menacingly. He towered above her. She looked paler than usual, but she gulped and offered what she hoped was her most winning smile as she kept safely out of reach of his poisonous penis.

"Believe me, Paz, we're grateful for what you did," she said. "You stunned her long enough for our friend the spider here to bite and immobilize her. But she's got to go back to Gehenna. Maybe we could offer you—uh—" She paused and looked around. What can one offer an evil demon whose debt you are in and who wants the one thing you simply cannot give him?

"IF I CAN'T HAVE LAMASHTU THEN I DEMAND THE KINGDOM OF TORONTO IN PAYMENT!" Pazuzu bellowed. His penis rose up, cobra-like, and hissed.

"Holy shit," Dave the T.G. breathed. "Look at the size of his—uh —"

"Yeah, it's pretty impressive," Dave the Ex-Virgin replied.

Dave the T.G. gave him A Look.

"In a bad way, dude! Geez, I'm not like gay or anything!"

Rachel grabbed Lilith's arm. "Do something!" she yelled. "We didn't stop this hellbitch kid of yours to have the whole damn city levelled by this—by this—" she lowered her voice, "this *freak!"*

"Yeah. Well. I, uh, had to think quickly to get rid of Lamashtu," Lilith explained in a shaky voice. "I admit I hadn't actually worked out how to deal with *him* later."

"What's he going to do to us?" asked Dave the Ex-Virgin.

"I—uh—don't really know," Lilith stammered, wide-eyed, and Dave the Ex-Virgin had a very bad feeling that she was lying.

"I don't want Pookums going near that thing," Dave the T.G. said. "He looks dangerous!"

"You think?" snarled Dave the Ex-Virgin.

Rachel looked back at Pazuzu. He rose to his full height, his trouser snake hissing like a leaky tire. When she turned back to Lilith, the confused immortal looked more like a timid little girl than the not-necessarily-a-deity-even-if-she'd-shagged-a-lot-of-them/all-powerful sex bomb.

Ammishtamru stood up, turned around, and looked at her.

Rachel smiled nervously.

"Rachel, get away from him! He will kill you!"

"You can't do anything about him, Ammy," Lilith said.

"Get away from him. We will handle him after we return from Sheol."

Rachel glanced at Lilith. She looked utterly terrified, and unimpressed with Ammishtamru's promise.

Shakily, Rachel stepped forward.

"What the hell are you doing?" cried Dave the Ex-Virgin, but Rachel ignored him.

"Rachel! I told you to get away from him!" Ammishtamru bellowed.

She forced herself forward and stood in front of Pazuzu. Far enough from that evil penis.

"Let's make sure you understand exactly who you're dealing with, Ammy," Rachel said under her breath. She gagged on the foul demonic smell and swallowed. She looked up, up. At the hideous dog's skull.

"WHO ARE YOU?"

"Rachel!"

"Hi, uh—Pazuzu, isn't it? Or should I call you Mr. Pazuzu?" Rachel began. She considered a handshake but didn't want to touch him in any way. "My apologies if I don't know, uh, what to call you. This is the first time I've ever spoken to a god. Well, uh, personally."

"I WILL DESTROY YOU!" Pazuzu bellowed.

"Rachel, get the hell away from him!" Dave the Ex-Virgin yelled.

"Yes, well, you can do that, I guess. What were you, uh, planning to do with Toronto once you, uh, seized power?"

"WHAT DOES IT MATTER TO YOU, FOUL STEW OF THE DIARRHETIC CAMEL?"

He may have sucked at sarcastic repartee, but he really was a master of imagery.

"Well, I, uh, kinda wondered if you were planning to destroy it. You know, just curious."

"AND WHAT DO YOU INTEND TO DO ABOUT IT IF I DO?"

"Well, not a lot, obviously. I mean, me against you? As if. I mean, you totally neutralized Lamashtu, and I guess she's all like this powerful demi-goddess and stuff. So, like, I'm curious as to why a great god like you is wasting your time with Toronto when you could, like, be protecting the babies of the world. Isn't that what you do?"

"HOW DO YOU KNOW, AFTERBIRTH OF THE LEVIATHAN?" Pazuzu's scorpion tail twitched like a cat's. It really looked weird.

"Well, y'know, Lilith says people who lived thousands of years ago looked to you to protect their children from Lamashtu. That people hung charms around their childrens' necks or hung them over their cradles to keep Lamashtu away. That the charms were actually your amulet, because, even though you're evil and stuff, you still protected the babies. And Lamashtu couldn't harm them because she was too afraid of your, uh, retribution."

"YOUR FRIEND SPEAKS THE TRUTH," he thundered.

"So do you protect all babies?"

"I PROTECT ALL BABIES! EVERYWHERE!" His dinner plate-sized hands clenched.

"Well now, that's very interesting," said Rachel, with one arm folded across her belly and the other perched on it. Her finger tapped her cheek, rather like a psychiatrist analyzing a patient. "I mean, you're into mass destruction and stuff—"

"I HATE HUMANS! THEY SHOW NO RESPECT TO THE ANCIENT GODS!"

"—But you still protect babies. Y'know, baby humans. So how come, uh, Mr. Pazuzu?"

"WHY DO YOU CARE?"

"Oh, well, you know, I'm just curious. Since we're probably all about to die, I thought I'd just ask. Otherwise this question's gonna bug me for all eternity. At least until my mother joins me, then *she'll* bug me for all eternity. 'So, why does Mr. Pazuzu hate humans but love babies? Why does he protect them?'"

"WELL—" Pazuzu's arms and hands relaxed and he hunched down a little, as though in thought. "YOU KNOW, I NEVER REALLY THOUGHT ABOUT IT BEFORE—"

"Hmmmm," said Rachel, all Freud-like.

Pazuzu's head hung a little and he stared at the sidewalk. "GEE, WHY DO I LIKE BABIES? LET ME THINK ABOUT THAT A MINUTE." The ancient god-demon looked lost in thought.

Rachel glanced over at her friends. Dave the Ex-Virgin looked like he was about to crap his drawers and Lilith was giving her a what-the-bloody-fuck-do-you-think-you're-*doing* look. Except that she also looked massively relieved not to be the one trying to stop Pazuzu.

"I GUESS IT'S BECAUSE THEY'RE SO LITTLE AND CUTE," Pazuzu finally said, and he straightened up. "THEY'RE JUST ALL PINK OR BROWN OR BLACK AS A JERUSALEM CAVE AT MIDNIGHT. THEY LOOK UP AT YOU WITH THOSE BIG BROWN OR BLUE OR GREEN OR BLACK EYES, AND THEY SQUIRM AND GURGLE, AND I JUST GO ALL OOGLY INSIDE—"

Pazuzu smiled, or at least Rachel thought he tried to smile. It looked more like a corpse's rictus grin. She waved away the flies buzzing around her face.

"Well, isn't that nice," Rachel said, a bit heartened by his reaction. He didn't look quite so terrifying now, looking off into the distance and thinking of all the cute little babies he'd saved over the millennia.

"DID YOU KNOW THAT BLACK BABIES COME OUT WHITE AT FIRST?" Pazuzu mused, staring at the Queen's Park Legislative Building a few blocks ahead. "IT'S SO FUCKING FUNNY, IF THE FATHER DOESN'T KNOW THAT FACT HE HAS A COMPLETE CONNIPTION FIT, BECAUSE HE THINKS HIS WIFE HAS BEEN MAKING THE TWO-BACKED BEAST WITH A WHITE MAN—"

"Oh, really? I didn't know that. How interesting," Rachel said. She tried frantically to think of what she'd say next. She hadn't put any thought into this at all. She just knew she had to try and save Toronto and maybe impress Ammishtamru. "You know, I've heard that all kittens are born with blue eyes, and that the eyes change color after a few days."

Lilith and the Daves looked at her like she was stone-cold mad.

"So you know, I'm wondering, Mr. Pazuzu," Rachel said suddenly, with a jerk, "uh, since you love babies so much, how come you're wastin' your time here in Toronto, where we don't have too many babies in distress, at least not with Lamashtu, uh, vanquished, and with the

Sick Kids Hospital taking care of the rest, how come you don't go some place where a lot of babies need your protection?"

"WHAT? WHERE ARE THERE BABIES WHO NEED MY PROTECTION?" asked Pazuzu.

"Well, uh, you know, I was just readin' *Time* magazine last week, I was in a restaurant waitin' for my friend Chao to show up, and he was runnin' late because, you know, the traffic in Toronto is always really really bad, and I was readin' this article about babies in Africa. How so many of them are dying or in trouble because they don't have enough to eat and they've got curable or preventable childhood diseases, or their parents were killed by all the wars and stuff they have there, and a lot of them have AIDS or they don't got any parents because their parents died of AIDS, and they look like they could really use some help—"

"BABIES IN AFRICA DON'T HAVE ANY PARENTS?" Pazuzu said. "HOW SAD!'

"Yeah, it is! Y'know, there are people over there trying to help them and all but it's pretty hard, and these babies need someone to watch out for them and protect them from soldiers and insurgents and stuff."

"REALLY," Pazuzu said, and he sniffled.

"Yeah, and you should see them, they're really cute. Well okay, they would be if they had someone to watch over them and keep them safe and make sure they've got enough food and medicine and stuff—"

"I MIGHT BE ABLE TO HELP OUT A LITTLE," said Pazuzu thoughtfully. Now it was his turn to look like a psychiatrist with his patient. His massive finger tapped his shrunken cheek. "I COULD BRING PESTILENCE AND DESTRUCTION UPON THE ARMIES WHO THREATEN THE LITTLE ONES—"

"Yeah, I'm sure they'd like that," Rachel said. "The babies, I mean, not the armies."

"EBOLA," Pazuzu mused. "I THINK EBOLA IS BIG IN AFRICA. HOW MANY BABIES COULD A CORRUPT DICTATOR OR A VICIOUS ARMY HURT WHEN THEY'RE TURNING INTO A GIGANTIC BOWL OF BARLEY SOUP?"

"Yeah," said Rachel, trying not to grimace at the graphic imagery.

"AND MALARIA. I'M VERY GOOD AT MALARIA," Pazuzu

continued. He began walking back and forth, the ground beneath him shaking with every footfall.

"I'm not sure that'll do much good. They have vaccines for that now, and you don't want to hurt the babies," Rachel noted. "Remember, malaria is spread by mosquitoes."

"LASSA FEVER, THEN," Pazuzu replied. He half-turned away in thought. "YOU HAVE TO COME IN CONTACT WITH MOUSE FECES TO CATCH IT. LOTS OF BLOODY DIARRHEA AND VOMITING. NAUSEA. STOMACHACHE. YOU JUST WANT TO DIE, AND YOU OFTEN DO."

"Well, that sounds like a pretty awful way to die, but I guess you deserve it if you've killed a lot of babies," Rachel said.

"YES, YES. YOU ARE RIGHT, FOUL MUCUS OF THE SINUS-INFECTED ELEPHANT."

"So you'll do it? You'll go to Africa and defend the babies?"

Even Dave the Ex-Virgin and Lilith looked heartened.

"YES, I WILL DO JUST THAT. I MUST PROTECT THE AFRICAN BABIES FROM THE MONSTERS WHO RUN THEIR COUNTRIES!"

"Wow, Mr. Pazuzu, you're a real *mensch* after all, you know that?" cried Rachel with a vastly-relieved look.

"MENSCH?" Pazuzu bellowed, whirling on her. "ARE YOU *JEWISH?"*

☆ ☆ ☆

Chao Wan checked his GPS again.

"Where is she?" asked Mahliqa.

"Still on University Avenue. She hasn't moved much in the last few minutes. I hope she isn't—"

"She isn't!" cried Amita from the back seat. "Rachel is a smart, strong woman! She won't die! She *can't!"*

"No, she can't," Chao said, and he gulped. He kept his eyes stuck resolutely to the road. "We have to find her. We have to get there in time."

"In time for what?" asked Mahliqa.

"I don't know. But something's going on in the city. Look at how hot it suddenly got. And the bugs – these damned insects!" Gnats and flies and tiny no-seeums obscured Chao's view by splattering his windshield. For the fifth time, he pushed the windshield wiper button and blue liquid sprayed across.

"It's a good thing you have that electronic thingamajig or we'd never know where to find her," Amita moaned.

✯ ✯ ✯

Oh shit.

"YOU ARE JEWISH, AREN'T YOU, VILE DONKEY VOMIT!"

"Well, I, uh—"

"I SHOULD HAVE KNOWN IT! YOU LOOK JEWISH!"

"I do not!" Rachel protested. "No one ever accused Elizabeth Taylor of looking Jewish!" Which she hadn't been, although she'd converted when she was an adult.

"WHAT CARE YOU, EJACULATE OF THE BABOON? YOU DON'T LOOK A THING LIKE HER!"

Rachel's eyes narrowed.

"I *so* look like her after I visited the Fountain of Youth—"

"I HATE JEWS! THEY TURNED THEIR BACKS ON US, THEY TURNED INSTEAD TO THAT PATHETIC YAHWEH, WHO WAS A POOR EXCUSE FOR A GOD! NONE OF THE REST OF US TOOK HIM SERIOUSLY, BUT HE MANAGED TO WREST AWAY THE POWER FROM US ANYWAY!"

"I do too look like Elizabeth Taylor!' Rachel fumed. "Everyone says so! Well, except for this one guy who thought I looked like Hedy Lamarr!"

"I WILL DESTROY THE JEWS! I WILL NOT REST UNTIL I'VE KILLED THEM ALL!"

"Yeah, well, take a numbah, Mr. Pazuzu, because people have been tryin' to kill us for thousands of years and we keep comin' back! Even Hitlah couldn't kill us all!"

"AND I WILL START WITH YOU!" Pazuzu bellowed. He pulled back a massive fist and swung.

She never felt herself fly through the air and hit her already-concussed head on the statues of the women cradling little children in front of the Sick Kids Hospital.

"Oh my God!" Lilith cried. She and the Daves ran to Rachel.

"TORONTO BELONGS TO ME NOW!" bellowed Pazuzu, and he beat his wings. The foul hot winds of the desert swirled around the crowd, then began to expand outward across the street, around the Sick Kids Hospital, up toward the town green and down toward the lakefront. The gnats and no-seeums fanned out and descended upon the hapless Torontonians, who tried to brush them off and beat them away from their faces as they began to scatter. Some of them ran to Toronto General or St. Margaret's Hospital across the street.

"Is she all right?" Lilith cried when Dave the Ex-Virgin checked for a pulse.

Pazuzu began to walk down University Avenue, beating his wings and holding up his terrible arms. "I CALL UPON THE POWERS OF THE DESERT! ARISE! WE WILL RULE TORONTO AND BRING SUFFERING AND DESTRUCTION TO ALL!"

"I can't find it! I can't find her pulse!" Dave the Ex-Virgin cried. His voice touched the razor edge of hysteria.

People cried out in pain. Several suddenly broke out in terrible boils. Lilith grabbed the two Daves. "One of you bring Rachel," she instructed. "Stay close to me and none of this will hurt you."

The Canaanites scattered, seeking cover.

Dave the T.G., the bigger of the two men, pulled Rachel to a sitting position and picked her up as gently as he could manage.

"DO something!" Dave the Ex-Virgin screamed. The air swirled and eddied about them, bringing a fouler stench than Pazuzu's family jewels. "People are going to die!"

An ominous buzzing sounded above them. They looked up, and a great dark cloud spread across the Toronto sky.

"Oh no, here come the locusts," Lilith groaned.

The three of them screamed as the plague descended. Lilith and the two Daves, burdened with Rachel's still form, huddled close as the large bugs landed everywhere and began eating anything green.

"POWERS OF THE DESERT!" Pazuzu bellowed. "HEAR ME! JOIN ME! ALL THINGS CREEPING AND CRAWLING, THOSE THAT DWELL IN THE SANDS OF THE ETERNAL, COME FORTH AND RULE THIS LAND!"

"Snakes!" shrieked Dave the Ex-Virgin, and horrible serpents began crawling up from the sewers. He jumped on a nearby bench and the others followed. Dave the Ex-Virgin held Pookums in his box while he and Lilith helped Dave the T.G., with the dead weight of Rachel in his arms, climb up. Cobras, sidewinders, and rattlesnakes slithered around the sidewalks. They came from all the deserts of the world. Great gila monsters, large and beaded, joined them, their forked tongues flickering as they crawled up onto the street.

"I don't remember lizards in the Great Plagues of Egypt!" screamed Dave the T.G. The insects merely flew around the park bench as though it was encased in an invisible cylinder.

"He's just making it up as he goes along," explained Lilith.

"I CALL UPON THE BRINGERS OF MALARIA!" Pazuzu bellowed as he marched down the street. "THE STINGING INSECTS SHALL DESCEND UPON TORONTO AND BRING MISERY AND DEATH TO ALL!"

"Ma'am, I don't know who you are but you seem to be friendly with that guy," Dave the T.G. said as he gestured toward Pazuzu, "but if you could get him to stop this that would be—uh, just great."

"I don't know how," Lilith breathed, and her gorgeous great eyes looked around morosely. She stood straight and tall, looking around at the horrible cloud of insects, the vile reptiles twining around the legs of the park bench, and the Daves knew there was no way she was going to stop him.

"I CALL UPON ALL THE PLAGUES OF THE DESERT!" bellowed Pazuzu. "AVENGE MY WORK IN TORONTO BY DESTROYING EVERY FOUL MORTAL HERE!"

"We're all going to die," Dave the Ex-Virgin mumbled, almost matter-of-factly. He thought of his parents and wondered if they were okay. He watched the locusts devouring all the grass and trees and shrubs, the gnats and no-seeums descending on anything alive that wasn't already standing on a park bench with Lilith, and he choked on the foul stench that enveloped them all.

"What's that?" asked Dave the T.G., and he pointed south down University Avenue.

They turned and looked. From far away, there appeared to be a brown puddle moving toward them from the street. It moved fast.

"It looks like The Blob," Dave the Ex-Virgin commented, who'd seen the movie many times on late-night TV when he was younger.

"I don't remember a plague of blob," breathed Lilith.

"No, it's furry," Dave the T.G. said.

"Oh my God," Lilith breathed in horror. "It's *rats!"*

The brown wave moved toward them. They weren't running so much as leaping, high in the air.

"Not rats," Dave the Ex-Virgin replied. "They're *gerbils! My* gerbils!"

And so they were. Hundreds of gerbils which had had several weeks to breed in the TTC underground. They'd emerged from the Osgoode subway stop and followed the call of the mighty Pazuzu. Like a giant brown wave they leaped and jumped, parting around cars as they moved relentlessly.

"Wow. Now that's a new plague," Lilith commented in wonder.

"What are gerbils gonna do?" asked Dave the T.G. "They're not exactly killer rats, are they."

Except that these were very hungry gerbils. They're mostly herbivorous, living on seeds and the green parts of plants and the occasional fruit. But when a gerbil is very hungry it will occasionally eat flesh. And these gerbils, who had bred mightily since their escape into the bowels of Bloor station, had cleaned out the TTC underground of all its garbage, and had turned all the mice into gerbil chow.

They moved down the street toward Pazuzu. He stopped his march, turned, and waited as the great brown herd approached. His horrible dead dog's mouth pulled back into a horrible leer of a smile, bearing all his canine teeth, as he raised his arms higher and his penis waved back and forth to see the latest plague on Toronto.

"DO YOU SEE THOSE FOUL CREATURES ON THE BENCH?" he bellowed as he pointed at the four of them. "KILL THEM! EAT THEM ALIVE! LEAVE NO FLESH ON THEIR BONES FOR EVEN THE VULTURES TO PECK!"

But the great Plague of Gerbils kept advancing. They swarmed and pooled around Pazuzu's legs and then began to leap onto him.

The huge demon began swatting them away. "LEAVE ME ALONE!" he bellowed. "KILL THEM, OVER THERE! I COMMAND YOU!"

But it was too late. The gerbils had found food and they were too hungry to stop. The ones on the ground bit and tore at Pazuzu's ankles. He roared and tried to shake them off, then to stomp them. The gerbils leaped up and swarmed about him, biting and tearing at his flesh. He bellowed and swung his arms, then brushed at himself in a panic. He tried to run, then fell, and the ground shook as his great body hit the ground. Within moments, he was swarming with gerbils, and he looked like a great furry brown creature struggling and bellowing and kicking.

And then Pazuzu stopped fighting.

EPILOGUE

When Pazuzu was no more, the plagues faded away as quickly as they had come.

The gerbils, stuffed and sated, moved down the street and back into the subway system. The snakes and lizards crawled back into the sewers, fueling urban legends for many decades to come. The gnats and no-seeums and locusts and mosquitoes all arose up in a mass and, clouding the sky, flew away in the general direction of San Diego. The horrible hot winds ceased to blow, and the cooler gentler breezes of Toronto prevailed (at least until the next monsoon).

The good people of Toronto tentatively emerged again from the buildings on University Avenue and made their way to what was left of the ex-demon Pazuzu, declaring what the gerbils had done to him, 'totally gross.'

The Canaanite Liberation Front, with a great long spear which they used to tie up the still-paralyzed Lamashtu, carted her down University Avenue all the way to the lakefront, parading her for all the city to see, so they would know that she would never plague them again with her sinister and fatal charms. Or eat their kids.

★ ★ ★

When Rachel woke up in the hospital, the first thing she saw was a dark figure sitting in a chair reading a book. Her heart sped up and a feeling of incredible love flowed through her.

"Ammishtamru, you're here," she whispered in the dim light.

"Rachel, you're awake!" The figure stood up.

"Chao, what are you doing here? And where am I?" *More importantly, where was Ammishtamru?*

Chao moved beside her bed. "We're at Toronto General. I brought you here. Do you remember anything?"

Rachel thought for a few moments. She reached up to touch her head and found it swathed in bandages. "Oh my God, am I gonna be all right?" she asked.

"The doctors say they think you will be okay, but they want to keep you here for some tests."

"Where's Ammishtamru? Is he all right?"

Chao glanced down at the sheets. "Who's that? The big guy?"

Rachel nodded.

"Oh, uh. Well," he stammered.

"Oh my God." Rachel's heart leaped to her throat. "He's not dead, is he? Please tell me Pazuzu didn't kill him!"

"No, I do not believe he is dead. Uh, at least no more than he was before he came here."

"Do you know what happened to him?"

Chao glanced up, and gently took her hand. "He went home, Rachel."

"Who? Ammishtamru or Pazuzu?"

"The big guy. The ancient one."

"Well—that's both—"

"The man. The warrior. Amish-whatever-his-name-is."

"Is he coming back?"

Chao shrugged. "The last we saw of them, they were carrying the monster thing down the street. Your friend Dave said they were taking it down to—I can't remember the name, he said it was the Jewish hell. With garbage."

"Sheol," Rachel breathed. "Gehenna. What happened to me?"

"The large demon hit you and knocked you out. I arrived, according to the other man named Dave, just seconds after that happened. We weren't sure if you were dead or alive."

"Did Ammishtamru come to help me?"

Chao looked away and shook his head. Once.

"Did he ask about me?"

Chao waited several seconds. "I'm afraid he didn't, Rachel."

She fell silent.

"So he didn't try to help me."

Chao shook his head.

"At all."

He squeezed her hand.

A tear slid out of the corner of her eye. "Y'know, Chao, I've seen this movie before and I know how it ends. I don't frickin' learn, do I? Here I am telling my clients they need to see beyond the superficial, to address a person's values and history and common goals, and what do I do? I fall for another big dumb lunk with great muscles and a bedroom smile. I'm such an *idiot!*"

Chao massaged her palm gently with one thumb. "The heart cannot control what it desires, my friend." He paused thoughtfully. "He was a worthy man in many ways, but I do not believe he was worthy of you."

A choking sob escaped Rachel's throat. "It didn't matter. That trip to the stupid fountain didn't matter! I thought guys weren't interested in me on account of my not bein' beautiful anymore, but it really didn't matter, did it?"

"Rachel, my dear friend," Chao replied, and he pressed her hand to his chest, "I hope I do not speak out of line, because I do consider you my dear friend, but you never stopped being beautiful. No man who is worthy of you would have begrudged you at any age. That fountain is for people whose hearts are small and thin."

The tears came fast. Rachel sobbed, great spasmodic convulsions that racked the bed. "I thought maybe if I looked more like Alexis men would want me again, and I'd have a youngah body that could almost certainly make a baby, so I go down to that *stoopid* fountain and make an idiot of myself, yeah, I'm youngah now and the spittin' image of Elizabeth Taylah, but what difference does it make? I'm followed down the street by the same old horndogs who make every woman's life miserable and who don't know what they want because—" Rachel stopped and clenched her fist, "because *they* think with their crotch just as much as I do. They won't give a second thought to a woman who ain't their idea of drop-dead gawgeous anymore than us gals will give them the time of day if they don't make enough money or drive the right car —"

"Do not shed any more tears over that man, my friend. He did you a huge favor. He is not worthy of you. He did not value you the way you deserve. You are right, he thinks only with his yinyang. And I don't mean the opposing forces of the Tao." Chao pulled his chair beside her. His black eyes looked into hers and for a moment Rachel felt she was looking into the face of Confucius.

"There is a man worthy of you, Rachel, if only you will open your heart to him. There is an ancient Chinese proverb that says, *If I keep a green bough in my heart, the singing bird will come.* It means as long as you keep your sense of optimism and never let your heart grow old and bitter, eventually you will find what you seek."

Now Rachel pulled his hand to her heart as she sobbed.

When she was finished, Chao stood up. She looked up at him through her tear-stained reddened eyes and said, "I didn't save Toronto, did I. Did anyone else?"

"Well, we're still here."

"Did Lilith think of something?"

"No, the big demon died in a massive gerbil attack."

"A what?"

"Don't ask. It's a long story."

Rachel looked at him long and hard. Chao looked away, embarrassed.

"How come you're here? You're not family."

"I talked them into letting me stay. I told them your family was in New York."

"I don't remember anything after Pazuzu hit me."

"I arrived with Miss Mahliqa and Miss Amita just as the big guy died. Your friends, the ones named Dave, and your lady friend, gave you to me. I carried you here to the hospital."

"You did?" Rachel's eyes grew wide.

"Yes. You had such a faint pulse we were afraid you were dead. We checked you in. Amita and Mahliqa were able to supply the information I couldn't."

"Wow Chao. You are such a good friend. You didn't have to do that. Or put up with all my stupid crap about Ammishtamru."

Chao looked away. "I would never desert you, Rachel."

"Just like you wouldn't desert your sister-in-law back in China."

"That's correct." Chao's eyes grew distant. "Even though she squandered my late brother's money after he died, even though she drinks too much wine. She is my family. She always will be. I must watch after her, as much as I can from Canada. I cannot abandon the love of my brother's life."

She stared at the slight Chinese man squirming a bit.

"How did you know where to find me? I called you from Alexis' apartment complex. But then I left. How did you know where I was?"

"I tracked you on your GPS."

"My what?"

"Your Global Positioning System."

"My *huh?* I have a Global Positioning System?"

"Yes, Rachel, in your cell phone. You didn't know what? You have it enabled."

"Oh. Huh. Well I'll be damned. No, I didn't know that. Of course, I haven't messed around with all the features on my cell phone much. I just use it to make and receive phone calls."

"Lucky for you it was working, or I wouldn't have found you."

"Yeah. Thanks again. You're the best, Chao."

She fell silent and pondered why this made her feel really weird.

The truth was, the Canaanite Liberation Front left Toronto, and Canada, and, in fact, this entire plane of existence. Elat, their astrologer, determined by the position of the stars, and a handy tip from Jimmy Hoffa's ghost, that another earthquake was coming and that it would shut the portals from Toronto to the Underworld. After a lot of discussion and a conversation with Immigration Canada, it was pointed out to the ancient warriors that they had been gone for thousands of years and that Israel was already engaged in a continuous battle that they'd be extremely wise not to join because both sides had much better weapons than anything the C.L.F. had. It was also pointed out that taking a leaf from the Native Canadians' playbook and attempting a bunch of non-hostile blockades in Israel was not going to work either as neither the *Habiri* nor the Palestinians were as nice or guilt-ridden as Canadians. And after hearing about warships, battle tanks and suicide bombs, Ammishtamru knew they would be crushed like stupid Avites and that this world of lattes and speed boats and Google wasn't right for them anyway. So they marched victoriously with the trussed-up Lamashtu into the Bank of America building for the last time, and were never seen again. And the portal therein closed up and Torontonians could go back to seeking mortgages and making investments and stuff.

Dirk Bly went down to Nathan Philips Square looking for a good story but he found that the mysterious Fountain of Youth had closed up. Old people were wading back and forth and splashing around in the water but they mostly just got wet and chilled.

What was worse, the folks that *had* bathed in the actual Fountain found that the effects weren't permanent. Apparently one needed to bathe semi-regularly in it if one wanted to stay eternally young. Slowly people began regaining their former looks, and the ones who had learned a lesson stayed with their new partners because they had already glimpsed the beauty within, and the rest broke up and went back to wanking off over computer porn. Others around the world mourned their missed opportunity to visit Toronto and be young again, at least for a little while. Although jealous cosmetic companies peddling epidermal snake oil danced a wicked jig up Madison Avenue in New York.

Unfortunately, very few learned a damn thing from any of it. People still judged each other by what they looked like or how much money they made rather than what they were like on the inside, and a lot of good people went back to loneliness and solitude while shallow, self-obsessed rich men collected catalog models and wannabe actresses, who all wondered why their rich, powerful boyfriends and husbands couldn't keep their dick in their pants, nor did they plan for the future because it never occurred to any of them that he'd ever dump *her* for a new trophy wife when she joined the Middle-Aged Army of Expressionless Plastic-Faced Ex-Hotties.

Hordes of witches, Pagans, Wiccans, ceremonial magicians, New Agers and dead-serious Goddess-worshipping aging feminists descended upon the ROM Crystal and tried to revive its ancient magical powers again, but it remained maddeningly dim at night. Neither it nor the Stealth Sexual Fountain ever again spat forth any more really hot-looking chicks, which is probably for the best anyway.

✯ ✯ ✯

Lilith visited Rachel once before she disappeared. It was about a week after all the madness ended, while Rachel was at home recuperating from her injuries. Chao was out picking up some groceries for her in Chinatown.

"Hey Lilith, didn't think I'd see you again," Rachel smiled as she held the door open. She'd never really believed Michael Moore's claim that Canadians could leave their doors unlocked and not be attacked by marauding bands of criminal gangs, or, more likely lately, ancient Mesopotamian hell-demons.

She shuffled back to the couch in her fuzzy bathrobe and reclined. Lilith took a seat on a packing box.

"I'm sorry I didn't visit while you were in the hospital," Lilith began. "I was kind of, uh, busy. Making sure Lamashtu was secured in Gehenna."

"Oh. Well. I, uh, hope she's going to be okay," Rachel said, for lack of anything better to say.

"She's not. But that was her choice."

"I guess you're right."

"Are you healing okay?"

Rachel reached for the lukewarm ginseng tea on the coffee table. "I'll be okay. The doctors say there should be no lasting damage."

"But how are you *doing?"*

Rachel glanced away. "I told you, I'm gonna be okay. I had a concussion but there's no real damage. Of course, I suffered lasting brain damage the first time I sat down." She smiled lightly.

"You know what I mean, *bubeleh.* How is your *soul* doing?"

"My, uh, soul?" Since when did Jews ever ask about the state of your soul?

"Don't toy with me, young lady. I know what happened with Ammishtamru. I can practically smell him on you. He broke your heart, didn't he."

Rachel shrugged. "I don't want to talk about it."

"You don't have to, if you don't want to. But I don't want you thinking the problem was with yourself. It was never with yourself. Ammy's just not the settling-down kind of guy."

"I know that now."

"He's a good shag, but he's like a rock musician or a movie star. Don't try to make him more than he is. He's not the kind of man you take home to Mamelah."

Rachel chuckled. "Ma would sooner I bring home a *schvartzer!"*

"I know you went down to that silly fountain because you thought you weren't beautiful enough to land a man anymore. Honestly, Rachel, what did you do, watch every last episode of that ridiculous *Sex In The City?"*

"Well, yeah, but it was research!"

"Don't watch it anymore. It's for women who are as false as Ammishtamru's heart."

"I know, you don't have to tell me." Rachel fell back onto the couch with the mug on her stomach. "I told Alexis that rich men aren't all they're cracked up to be, because they think when they have money and power they can do whatevah the hell they want and don't have to be faithful to no one. And there I was chasin' aftah anothah spoiled rich guy, except he was thousands of years old, and his wealth was in sheep and goats. If he'd been born today he'd be some snotty CFO with a trophy wife and eight mistresses. Or maybe Hugh Hefnah."

"Without question. Although he's a way better lay than Hugh Hefner."

Rachel stared at her. "Is there *anyone* you haven't shagged, Lilith?"

"Yeah, Hugh Hefner. Wouldn't touch him with a ten-foot longspear. Speaking of shagging, I visited your friend Dave today."

Dave? Shagging? "Which one?"

"The younger one. The one Alexis de-cherried. The one my evil daughter almost destroyed. I helped him out a little."

"Yeah? What did you do?"

"I shagged the hell out of him."

Rachel choked on what was left of her tea.

"You did *what?"*

"I shagged him. Silly. Figured once with Alexis, under duress, wasn't enough to get him over his hangups. So two hot chicks in one week, what do *you* think?"

Rachel stared at her, agog. "Well, I think he's probably a better shag now than Hugh Hefner!"

Lilith laughed. It was a melodious sound that hinted of a far-flung time when humankind still lived in relative innocence in the Garden of Eden.

"I told him the same thing I'm telling you. Stop looking in the mirror so much. You're a silly fool. You were beautiful before, and you've got lots more to offer than a pretty face. I know, it's hard in this town, which is so sexually repressed the Fountain of Youth picked *here* of all places to make its next grand entrance."

"Where was it before? Florida?"

"No, Sybaris. Ponce de León was an idiot. Anyway, I know Toronto is where women are women and the men run scared, but hopefully the ones who bathed in the Fountain got their young stones back long enough to learn their penis is good for more than just writing their name in the snow."

"Maybe I shoulda moved to Montreal," Rachel muttered.

"Nah, the food would have killed you. Do you know how much fat is in that *poutine* stuff?"

Rachel drained the last of the tea. "So I'm not gonna keep my youth?"

"No, you're not, and good riddance. A woman your age is light-years more experienced than some little chickie-boo half your age. True sex appeal, mortal goddess, is within *yourself,* a lesson very few people, either male or female, ever learn."

Rachel half-snickered. "Yeah, says the gorgeous immortal."

"All right, I'm immortal. And Yahweh was quite kind to me in the looks department. Hell, if you think I'm good-looking you should have seen *Adam!* He was all that and a bag of chips, let me tell you. Adonis had nothing on him."

Lilith stood up. "Look, I have to go, and I mean in a permanent way. I still have a lot of work to do on your mortal coil. I just wanted to tell you that true chemistry has a lot less to do with what you look like than what you're like inside. A woman who is strong and confident exudes a *je ne sais quoi* that men find irresistible. They may need a little more time to recognize it because they *do* think with the ol' tallywacker and they believe the hot lingerie model is the woman of their dreams. But they forget that whoever she is, someone somewhere is getting really sick of her shit."

Rachel nodded. "I've noticed that about hot women. They can be psychos because they can get away with it. And hot-looking men can get away with it too."

"Especially if they've got a really big—credit card limit," Lilith grinned as she walked over to Rachel. She leaned down and kissed her forehead. "Men think with their penis, women think with their purse. You'd all be better off thinking with your brains for a change."

She headed for the door and then turned once more. "And Rachel?"

"Yes?"

"There's a quote from an old Rodgers & Hammerstein musical. 'Do I love you because you're beautiful, or are you beautiful because I love you?"

Reports came out of Lebanon that a certain uber-conservative extremely religious high-level commander in Hezbollah was apparently squealing and crying out in ecstasy in the middle of the night, and had lately been saying that maybe Jews weren't so bad after all and hey, why don't we see if we can organize a picnic in Tel Aviv to get to know some of them better, and let's make sure we invite all the really hot Jewish chicks, okay?

They're still looking for his body in Juniyah. They've found his head, though.

So how did everyone else wind up? Well, I'm glad you asked.

The news is mostly good. With some bittersweet and some sadness thrown in. I mean, there are people who make bad decisions and they, like everyone, have to live with the consequences. Sometimes people pay when it's not their fault, and there's nothing to be done about that. That's life.

Take Thor. I'd like to tell you he somehow came back to life. But there was so no way that was going to happen. Okay, maybe if someone performed the *Greater Resurrection Spell of Finkelstein the Sage-Mage,* but considering that was a ritual that dated back to the thirteenth century and had been lost in the annals of time, and required a really excellent magician of top-notch high-caliber magical talents, there was so no way poor Thor was coming back to complete his young life. Tragically, he stayed dead. His family had to live with that.

Dave the Ex-Virgin was pretty messed up about it. He went back to his parents, fell to pieces, drank heavily, got laid a lot because he really was awesome in bed now, picked up an incurable but fortunately non-fatal social disease, and eventually wound up in therapy. A lot of anguish and liver damage might have been saved if he'd just gone into therapy first, but some people are just really stubborn that way. Anyway, his therapist suggested he go to a motivational seminar which Dave didn't think would do any good, but it did, and after a furious round of self-help courses he became a motivational speaker himself, moved out of his parents' house, and got married. Betcha can't guess to who?

No no no, it wasn't Alexis. Don't be silly. I know, I s'pose you want me to tell you that her heart was turned around to what was really important in life, and that she realized that inside geeky, largely inexperienced Dave there lay a good man with a big heart and a lot of potential that was about to explode. And you know what, she did realize that.

Except that Alexis had far more important things to think about than getting married for the next several years as, overcome by remorse for how she allowed Thor to die, helped even, she turned herself in to the police and did several years' time for being an accessory to murder. She knew she needed to be punished and even though she could never bring Thor back to life, even though she had ripped the heart from the body of his family with her stupid, self-obsessed, momentary turn to the Dark Side, she knew his family needed the closure and that she herself needed to suffer as she had made others suffer.

She learned a lot in prison, as a model inmate who studied hard and learned some manual trades since she knew she would never hold a respectable job again. She got to explore her bisexual side in the sense that she was kind of forced into it and found it largely disgusting. However, Wanda turned out not to be so bad and she even learned a few valuable new skills from her like how to disable car alarms and how to steal credit card numbers from bank machines. And oh yeah, that Jade Peacock Mulligan thing can be altered for the ladies, too.

She did odd jobs for a few years after prison, living hand to mouth until she became a writer of cheap prison novels featuring torrid lesbian love affairs. It made her very popular in the kinkier sections of the Church & Wellesley neighborhood in Toronto, not to mention with a fair amount of straight men.

Dave the Tarantula Guy married a woman his parents met outside a trade show for keepers of exotic pets at the Jacob Javits Center in New York City. Dave's parents immediately knew she was the one for Davey after they took her to dinner and interviewed her extensively, and the lady readily agreed to meet Dave since she was fifty-two and had just about given up on men. Janie was into boa constrictors, and kept no less than five of them, which meant after she and Dave married and they bought a house in Westchester, between the spiders and the snakes, only their bravest friends would come over for dinner parties.

As for Dave the Beowulf Freak, he also learned something from this whole ley-line-search-for-love-during-a-paranormal-shakeup mess. He found himself disillusioned with the pretty young things he could now get, since they were fairly inexperienced and didn't read much or watch anything weightier than *Friends* and *Seinfeld* reruns and they tended to say 'and stuff' a lot. Like, "I went down to the grocery store and stuff and I met my friend Mandy and stuff and we went down to the campus bar and got totally wasted and stuff and like we totally blew our Business Principles exam and stuff—"

His new wife Dolores was actually Dave the T.G.'s reject, who put her off to marry the snake lunatic. Dave the Beowulf Freak asked to meet her, and found she was a very nice woman who wasn't as young and pretty as he would have liked, but she actually knew what Beowulf clusters were and loved to engage in heated debates with him about such things as whether or not Linux should have a binary kernel driver layer. She didn't share any of his other interests but she didn't mind when Dave lost his looks after the Fountain of Youth's effects wore off. She also didn't mind if he went out at night with the guys and she came from a good family who accepted him. Amita and Mahliqa were invited to the wedding and they both cried with happiness over Love Comes Later's first success story.

Oh, who did Dave the Ex-Virgin marry? I forgot to say, didn't I? He married an ex-crackhead from an Oshawa trailer park who'd been clean for eight years who came to one of his seminars and talked to him for several minutes after everyone had left. He invited her to go for coffee, and it was just love at first sight. Everyone told him she was bad news because of her history and the fact that her father was in jail for counterfeiting Canadian Tire dollars, but she had a good heart and the right values except they got divorced a couple of years later because she relapsed into drugs and wasn't interested in going back into rehab. The moral of *that* predictable tale, children, is don't get involved with people who have more problems than Job, especially if their bad judgements led them there in the first place.

As for Rachel?

Wait. Whaddaya mean that's not how Dave the Ex-Virgin was supposed to end up?

All right, all right, I was messin' with ya! Ha ha. He actually *did* marry Alexis, a few years later. They moved to a farm in Sudbury where she took out her wasted maternal talents on the livestock. And yes, I promise, they did live happily ever after. Both were much older and wiser and more experienced and after Alexis taught Dave how to alter the J.P.M. for the ladies, they had wild mad monkey sex that shook the walls and rattled the chandeliers.

Okay. Back to Rachel.

Well, Amita and Mahliqa took her out to lunch shortly after the last earthquake, because she was showing all the classic signs of depression again, and it was affecting her work.

"We have a proposal to make, Rachel," Amita began over the appetizer.

"Oh. I know what this is about." Rachel's head dipped low and her fork dangled over her plate. "You wanna sever our relationship. It's 'cause I'm not gettin' anything done anymoah."

The two friends looked at each other. "Oh no, dear, please don't get that idea," Mahliqa said. "We think you're going to do some wonderful work with us. More and more people are coming for help. They saw the stories in the newspaper. You're just in a slump right now, because of your melancholy."

"I'll be awll right," Rachel mumbled, but she didn't sound so sure.

"Rachel." Amita gently clasped her arm and she looked up. "We want to help you. We think we know what to do. But you have to listen to us with an open heart and an open mind."

"What?" she asked, a bit suspiciously.

The two friends looked at each other again, then Amita took a deep breath and said, "We want to arrange a marriage for you."

Rachel dropped the skewer of beef satay.

"You're kidding me, right?"

"Er, no."

"Look, I can't do that, I'm Jewish!"

"What, like Jews never arranged marriages before?" asked Mahliqa, dumbfounded. "I've seen *Fiddler On The Roof!"*

"Well—er, what I mean is—uh, I can't do that. I'm too old. And you have *no idea* what nightmares my mother would find for me." Rachel shivered.

"Then why don't you let us stand in for her?" asked Amita. She put down her fork and stared bravely at Rachel. "Mahliqa and I have a great guy for you."

"You're kidding me. Who?"

"He's kind and warm—" began Mahliqa.

"Tender and very well-educated," continued Amita.

"We've spoken extensively with him and we had dinner at his family's last week, and we can vouch for the fact that they're all decent, honest, hardworking people—" said Mahliqa.

"He's honest and forthright himself, of course," cut in Amita.

"He's well-travelled too. He's lived in many different parts of the world and is as at home in the heart of Africa as he is in Toronto."

"Don't forget, he has very enlightened opinions about women!" Amita exclaimed. "None of this chest-beating stuff. He never roughed up a little boy for trying to bring home rocks from the beach."

"Is he good-looking?" asked Rachel.

"Well—he's not bad," said Mahliqa. She glanced at Amita. "If I wasn't already married I'd marry him myself."

"Oh, you would not, you fool," said Amita. "He's not a Muslim. Your parents would disown you."

Mahliqa nodded. She understood the importance of preserving one's culture, especially in a foreign country, and the difficulties of family. But she also understood the difficulty of finding the right person —especially when you're older.

"I think I know where this is going," Rachel said with a wry smile.

"Jews trace their bloodline through the mother, don't they?" Amita asked.

Rachel nodded.

"And how many Jews have you met since you've been here?"

"Not many, and a lot of them are, uh, more traditional than I am," Rachel admitted.

"Would it be so terrible if you married a man who is not Jewish?" Mahliqa asked.

"I don't know. I don't suppose Ma would have welcomed Ammishtamru with open arms," she half-smiled.

"Rachel," said Mahliqa, "do you know why I wear the *hijab?"*

"Uh, I don't know, because you're Muslim?"

Mahliqa shook her head.

"Because your husband expects it of you?"

She shook her head again. "I never wore the *hijab* before in my life," she said. "I was born and raised in a liberal family in Pakistan. I dressed conservatively, as I still do now, but I never covered my head until 9/11. After that terrible tragedy many Canadians turned against Muslims. They harassed us, called us names, defaced our mosques, and accused us of being terrorists and lovers of that awful Osama bin Laden. And I got so mad, I was so furious at the way they were treating us, that I decided to rub it in their faces that I was a Muslim and *proud* of it!"

Mahliqa shook with a forgotten rage.

"My family didn't like it. My husband said it made me look old-fashioned, and my children were afraid it would make me a target for extremists. Of the Canadian variety," she added. "But I refused to be ashamed of being a Muslim and I would not let them silence me. I have lived too long in this country to be silent, Rachel. So today I wear the *hijab* so that everyone can see I'm a Muslim and I defy anyone to give me a hard time about it!"

"So that's why you're so friendly," Rachel mumbled. "I always wondered. It's—unusual for a traditionally-dressed Muslim woman to be friendly and open with people. I wondered why your husband let you run your own business."

"You are right, Rachel. Muslim women are often timid and unassimilated. It's the way they were raised. I don't dress like a Middle

Eastern frump, either. Who says Muslimas have to dress like their old aunty?"

"What is that, a Hermès hijab?" Rachel laughed.

"Prada, actually. I made it myself."

"Oh." She wasn't kidding.

"The point is, I was true to myself, Rachel. And now I ask you to open your heart and be true to yourself. I believe you know deep within your soul that what we are about to suggest is right."

Rachel took a bite of satay and winced.

Mahliqa smiled knowingly. "You bit your cheek, didn't you. In my culture, we say good fortune is coming your way, my friend."

✯ ✯ ✯

Two months later, Rachel called her mother in New York.

"Hello, Ma?"

"Who's this?"

"Whaddaya mean who's this? Who do you think?"

"I have no idea. I'm an old woman. I don't have time for guessing games. My caller ID indicates this is a call from Canada but I can't remember if I know anyone there."

"Okay, Ma, be that way. Here I wanted to tell you some very happy news which could involve your fondest wish finally coming true, but since you've forgotten me already I guess I'll just have to hope you remember by the time you get the invitation."

"Invitation? To what?"

"To my wedding. *I'm getting married, Ma!"*

"Gott in Himmel! Surely you wouldn't joke with your old gray-haired mother, would you?"

"It's no joke, Ma. And we're getting married soon so you'd better start looking for a plane ticket to Toronto."

"Oy! You're not *trogedik,* are you?"

"No Ma, I'm not pregnant. But I want to be. We want to start having children as soon as possible!"

"Finally, my daughter has time to make some babies, God willing, if it's not too late, given the age of her ovaries—"

"We're getting married in October. The weather will be real nice then, not too hot, not too cold. You'll love Toronto, Ma."

"Wait! So who's this lucky man already?"

Rachel took a deep breath. Here it comes.

"His name's Chao, Ma," she said. "Chaoxiang Wan."

There was dead silence for several moments.

Finally a heavy sigh. "Is he Jewish?"

"Er, not exactly, Ma."

"I didn't think so."

"He's Chinese."

I don't care how old you are, Chao had told her after one of their many late-night talks. *I think I loved you the first time I saw you. Yes, I admit, you are a very beautiful woman and I am not so much to look at. But I don't care how old you look. I want to kiss your crow's feet when you are eighty. I never visited the Fountain of Youth because I am not a young man and have no desire to be. In my culture, Rachel, we venerate our elders, we don't shove them in a nursing home to die alone. And while we will both grow old and wrinkled, your beauty will never die for me.*

Another heavy sigh. "Rachel. *Rachella.* My only child, ingrate that you are. Have you really thought this thing through?"

"Actually I've talked this thing through, Ma. Chao's a great guy. He's been married once before but his wife died. They didn't have any children. You will love him when you meet him, Ma—"

"Rachel. You know I'm not a prejudiced woman, but—"

"Yes, I know you're not, Ma, which is why I know you'll be perfectly gracious to my bridesmaid Mahliqa. She's from Pakistan. And she's a Muslim. But she's a wonderful lady, and she won't mention Zionism or nothing."

Ma let out the longest sigh so far. When she spoke her voice contained a barely-suppressed nuclear explosion.

"You're marrying a Chinese man and your best friend's a Muslim."

"Well, I don't know if I'd call her my *best* friend, Ma, but—well, she and her partner Amita are my good friends."

"Amita. Is she Muslim too?"

"No, she's Indian."

"Gott in Himmel. Do you know *any* Jews up there in Goynada?*"*

"I've met Chao's family already—"

"Oh good, are *they* Jewish, at least?"

"—They're wonderful people. They're dying to meet you. They want you to come for dinner the night before the wedding. And oh Ma, you are going to EAT! You have no idea. If you think Jews know how to eat, wait until you meet a Chinese family!"

"Rachel," came her mother's weary reply.

"Yes Ma?"

"If my grandchildren are going to be half-Jewish and half-Chinese, what religion will they be?"

"Well. I guess they'll be Jewddhists, Ma!"

✯ ✯ ✯

And later, on the honeymoon in the Bahamas...

"Y'know, Chao, we got a wedding gift from Alexis Jacquard," Rachel said as they climbed into bed the first night.

"From Alexis? The girl who's in jail?" he asked. "How was she able to send us anything?"

"She emailed it to me. They've got limited computer access at the prison."

"What was it? Will we need to send a thank-you note?"

"That's up to you." Rachel pulled back the covers and disappeared beneath them.

"AIEEEAAIIIEEAAEIIIIEEE!!!"

Love comes later, but Chao didn't.

ABOUT NICOLE

Nicole Chardenet, author of Young Republican, Yuppie Princess, lives in her Toronto den o' debauchery with Belladonna, her evil henchkitty. When they're not plotting world domination together, Nicole is a business developer in the glamorous world of workforce management consulting. Sumer Lovin' is her second book, and she can't swear there won't be others forthcoming.

17261743R00146

Made in the USA
Charleston, SC
03 February 2013